Edmond Biré

The Diary of a Citizen of Paris

During 'the Terror': Vol. II

Edmond Biré

The Diary of a Citizen of Paris
During 'the Terror': Vol. II

ISBN/EAN: 9783337044961

Printed in Europe, USA, Canada, Australia, Japan

Cover: Foto ©Andreas Hilbeck / pixelio.de

More available books at **www.hansebooks.com**

JÉRÒME PETION

THE DIARY

OF

A CITIZEN OF PARIS

DURING 'THE TERROR'

BY

EDMOND BIRÉ

TRANSLATED & EDITED BY JOHN DE VILLIERS

WITH TWO PORTRAITS

IN TWO VOLUMES
VOL. II

LONDON : CHATTO & WINDUS
NEW YORK : DODD, MEAD & CO.
1896

CONTENTS OF VOL. II.

THE DIARY OF
A CITIZEN OF PARIS

CHAPTER LXI.

A FORTNIGHTLY REVIEW.

Tuesday, April 2, 1793.

WITH all due deference to Beaumarchais, his 'Figaro' is but a fool after all. There was some good in Comte Almaviva, and I liked him. The reign of the fine gentlemen 'who took the trouble to be born, and nothing more,' was, in my opinion, better than that of the insipid varlets who now govern us.

Not a day passes that does not bring us some fresh cause for humiliation, fear or sorrow—some idiotic decree, villainous law, plot or riot. This is the balance-sheet of the past fortnight

Friday, March 15.—It was to-day decided that the Special Criminal Court should be composed as follows :

JUDGES : Liébault, of the Doubs ; Pesson, a Judge from Vendôme ; Montané, a lawyer from the Haute Garonne ; Desfougères, from the Châtre ; Dufriche des Magdeleines, from Alençon ;[1] Grandsire, from Noyon ; and Étienne Foucault.[2]

PUBLIC PROSECUTOR : Faure.

DEPUTIES : Fouquier-Tinville ;[3] Donzé-Verteuil and Lescot-Fleuriot.[4]

The Girondists received the news of these appointments with

---

[1] Brother of the Girondist Dufriche de Valazé.
[2] Guillotined May 6, 1795.   [3] Guillotined May 7, 1795.
[4] Guillotined July 28, 1794 (10th of Thermidor).

joy that seemed to me rather premature. This is how Girey-
Dupré, the editor-in-chief of Brissot's journal, expresses himself
on the subject:

'The courage of the Convention is well sustained; the assembly
is unwilling to part with the glory of saving the nation's liberty.
This special court, which its inventors hoped to make an instrument of despotism, will serve to consolidate Liberty by
defending it both against the anarchists, who sully it, and
against the aristocrats, who are trying to destroy it. The composition of the court is such that no Patriot need fear the faults
of its organization.'[1]

Saturday, March 16.—Decree closing the seminary of Saint
Louis, at Saint-Cyr-les-Versailles.[2]

Sunday, March 17.—A large concourse of people having assembled in the Place du Carrousel, the Brissotin deputies became
alarmed, and one of them, Izarn-Valady,[3] proceeded to several
guard-houses, in order to call out the soldiers. At the Oratory,
a prisoner was detained, and he wrote to the Convention demanding his liberation. Maribon-Montaut, deputy for the
department of the Gers, spoke in defence of the leaders of the
gathering, declaring that it was formed of the most honest and
inoffensive people in the world—the members of the Jacobin and
the Grey Friars Clubs, who, having met the Defenders of the
Republic and other excellent Patriots, were simply exchanging a
brotherly kiss. 'Since these pretended Defenders of the Republic,'
says Brissot's paper, 'are the same men who smashed the printing-
presses last week, and who together with the Grey Friars and a
portion of the Jacobins had woven the plots of the 9th, 10th
and 11th, it is easy to understand Valady's anxiety.' The President of the Convention was charged to order Marat's liberation.

[1] *Le Patriote Français*, March 16, 1793.
[2] The young lady students of Saint-Cyr were turned out on March 30,
1793, and the following days. In January, 1794, the black marble slab
that covered the tomb of Mme. de Maintenon was broken; the coffin was
opened, and the body, in a perfect state of preservation, was dragged round
the courtyard by the Patriots, who afterwards threw it, stripped of its
clothes, into a hole dug in the middle of the cemetery.
[3] Izarn de Valady, deputy for l'Aveyron, proscribed on July 28, 1793,
was arrested at Périgueux, condemned by the Criminal Court of the
Dordogne, and executed on December 5, 1793.

Monday, March 18.—In the Convention, one of the Secretaries read some despatches from the administrators of the Deux-Sèvres and of the Vendée announcing that the counter-Revolutionaries had assembled in great force, seized the arms and cannon of a number of communes, and taken and set fire to the town of Cholet. Citizen Gallet, one of the administrators of the Directory of the Vendée, marched against them, and put them to flight. The rebels retired to Saint-Fulgent, and, after destroying the bridge, sounded the tocsin. They were led by some refugees wearing the white cap, and shouting : ' *Vive le Roi! We are acting for the Regent of France !'*

Lasource, in the name of the Committee of General Security, gives the movements of the counter-Revolutionaries in the department of Ille-et-Vilaine. The rebels wear the white cockade, and are in possession of more than ten leagues of territory ; at Redon a constitutional curate and three gendarmes have been massacred ; at Bains it is impossible to obtain recruits ; and at Rennes the maintenance of order is threatened. On the proposal of Lasource, the Convention decrees that ' the prisoners charged with being concerned in the plot discovered in *ci-devant* Brittany are to be sent to Paris in safe custody, in order to be tried by the Revolutionary Tribunal.'[1]

In the same sitting a letter was read from Leonard Bourdon, a deputy sent on a mission to the Doubs and the Jura, who pretends to have been the victim of a violent outrage while passing through Orleans on March 16. The following is an extract from his letter :

' Thirty counter-Revolutionaries attacked me in the town-hall, showering blows upon me with bayonets and pistols, and shouting, " Go and join Lepeletier !" My wounds are not dangerous, for my coat being buttoned up, and my hat well

[1] The *Brittany Plot*, better known by the name of the *Conspiration de la Rouarie*, was discovered in the beginning of March, 1793. The plot was never put into execution, its chief, the Marquis Armand Tuffin de la Rouarie, having died in the Château de la Guyomarais, in the forest of La Hunaudaie, on January 30, 1793. Twenty-seven prisoners were charged before the Revolutionary Tribunal on June 4, 1793, with having taken part in the plot. Nine were condemned to death, and guillotined on June 18.

stuck down upon my head, the bayonets were unable to penetrate very far. It is sweet to be a martyr in the cause of Liberty. I am proud of the wounds I have received.'

This pretended outrage reduces itself to a very small matter, after all. I hear that Leonard Bourdon, after a dinner given to him by the Directory of the department and the officers of the National Guard—a rather festive gathering—was returning home, escorted by his friends, when, in passing the town-hall, one of the company attacked the sentinel on duty. A struggle ensued, in which Bourdon was slightly wounded in the arm with a bayonet.

Be this as it may, the Convention, acting on Barère's report, decreed that the Corporation of Orleans should be suspended, that the Minister of Justice should hold an inquiry, and bring the culprits before the Revolutionary Tribunal, and that the Minister of War should send an armed force to Orleans to ensure the carrying out of the Decree. The town is declared to be in a state of rebellion until the citizens shall have given up the offenders.[1]

Duhem, member for the Nord, and Charlier, member for the Marne, succeed in getting the following resolution passed :

'Every citizen is bound to denounce, arrest, or cause to be arrested, any exiles whom he knows to have returned to France. The exiles when arrested shall be taken to the prisons of the district, tried by a military jury, and executed within twenty-four hours.'[2]

Garnier, a member of the Left, thinks this decree spoilt by its moderation. He would have preferred that every citizen might be authorized to run down any exile he met—that is,

---

[1] Nine inhabitants of Orleans, all merchants and National Guards, arraigned before the Revolutionary Tribunal on July 12, 1793, as the authors and accomplices of the outrage committed upon Leonard Bourdon, were condemned to death. They were executed on July 13, all wearing the red shirt. Prudhomme relates that Leonard Bourdon said to the surgeon who was called to dress the slight wound he had received : 'This little cut can only be healed by a far greater. Twenty-five heads shall fall for it, or my name is not Leonard Bourdon !' It did indeed cost him his name, as it happened, for ever since that time he was called *Leopard* Bourdon.

[2] 'Collection du Louvre,' tome xiii., p. 457.

anyone whom he suspected of being an exile. Instead of legal murder, this would mean murder in the open streets!

At the same sitting, the Convention, acting on the report of Barère, unanimously adopts the principle of progressive taxation.

Yet another measure is unanimously adopted. The credit of it is again due to Barère, who proposed it in the following terms : ' In order to thoroughly stamp out all traces of feudalism, one thing still remains to be done. There are throughout the land a large number of castles that belong to exiles, old strongholds of tyranny which will naturally remain unsold. . . . These prisons, which disgrace the soil of Liberty, might well be demolished, and I move that the Directories be requested to give particulars of such castles as are fitted for no better use than that of furnishing materials for the construction of dwellings for agricultural labourers.'

This act of Vandalism was a fitting end to a sitting in which so many decrees of banishment and of death had been passed.

Tuesday, March 19.—A letter from the administrators of the department of Mayenne-et-Loire informs the Convention of the progress made by the rebels of the Vendée, now masters of Saint-Florent, Cholet, Chemillé, and Vilhiers. They wear the white cockade, and demand a King and the recall of their priests.

A few moments later, Cambacérès, Chairman of the Committee of Legislation, gets a law passed enacting that all persons known to have taken part in any of the risings respecting the recruitments, or who have displayed the white cockade or any other sign of rebellion, shall be treated as outlaws, and therefore deprived of the right to be tried by a jury. All such persons are to be given up to the executioner, and put to death within twenty-four hours. The death penalty, with an equally short shrift, is prescribed for those who have borne arms, or taken any part in the rising, although they may have been arrested after laying down their arms.

Wednesday, March 20.—Lepage, member for the Loiret, gives an account in the Convention of the rising that took place on the 14th at Montargis, on the occasion of the recruitment, and in which Manuel, the former Procureur de la Commune, nearly

lost his life. The part played by Manuel during the first years
of the Revolution, and especially during the massacres of
September, has marked his name with an indelible stain. There
are, however, some honest people who do not forget his repentance,
and the courageous attitude he took up during the King's trial.
It was he who, thinking that sentence was about to be pronounced by a majority of one only, went out and brought in
Duchastel to vote against it. On January 19 he handed in his
resignation, declaring that it was impossible for the Convention,
composed as it was, to save the country, and that there was
nothing left for an honest man to do but to wrap himself in his
cloak. He retired to Montargis, his native place, and he might
have lived there in peace, if he had had naught but the crime of
September with which to reproach himself; but having come
round to sentiments of humanity and justice, he attempted to
atone for that crime, and such atonement meets with no pardon,
as the patriots of Montargis plainly let him see. They fell upon
him in the most brutal manner, and the Corporation could only
save his life by giving him a prison as a refuge. There is no
doubt that he has only escaped the dagger to be given up to
the executioner. Take part in a massacre, and you will have
nothing to fear, but do not take it into your head to be an
honest man, for then a prison awaits you, and on leaving it, the
guillotine.[1]

This, too, is what the administrators of the city of Arles have
learnt to their cost. In February, 1792, they defended the
Constitution and the law against the Patriots, and for so doing, the
Girondists in the Legislative Assembly vainly attempted to get
them arrested. After a year had passed, charges were again
preferred against them, and the Convention, on the motion of
Grangeneuve, impeached Dufour, Jobert, and Debourge, formerly
Civil Commissaries of Arles; Loïs, ex-Mayor; Estrangen, formerly
Procureur de la Commune; and Guibert, Procureur-Syndic of
the district.

---

[1] Called as a witness in the Queen's trial, Manuel brought no accusation against her, but praised her courage and lamented her misfortunes.
Tried by the Revolutionary Tribunal, he was condemned to death on the
24th of Brumaire, year II. (November 24, 1793).

Thursday, March 21.—A letter from General Dumouriez, dated from Tirlemont on the 19th, informs the Convention that our Belgian army has been beaten at Nerwinde, a small village about nine leagues from Liège. We have lost 4,000 men. The Austrians were commanded by the Duke of Coburg. On July 28, 1693—just a century ago—Nerwinde was the scene of a bloody battle, in which the Maréchal de Luxembourg defeated the Dutch and English, commanded by William III.

Jean Debry, member for the Aisne, brings up a report from the Diplomatic Committee, in conformity with which the Convention, desirous of aiding the magistrates in every possible way in putting down sedition, decrees the formation in every section and in every commune of a Vigilance Committee composed of twelve citizens.[1] These citizens may not be chosen from amongst the members of the clergy or nobility, and must be elected by ballot.

Friday, March 22.—Quinette and Isnard get a law passed establishing a Committee of Public Safety. Its organization is entrusted to the Committee of General Defence, which is to present its report as speedily as possible.

Saturday, March 23.—All French refugees caught taking part in an armed or unarmed gathering, or such as, being caught on the frontiers of a hostile country, or of a country occupied by French troops, have previously been in the ranks of the enemy, or taken part in a gathering of refugees, are outlawed.[2]

General Marcé, whose troops were defeated on the 29th by

---

[1] 'Vigilance committees, which have since been turned into 40,000 or 50,000 bands of robbers.'—Beaulieu, *Diurnal,* March 22, 1793.

[2] 'Collection du Louvre,' tome xiii., p. 690. The monstrous proceeding called outlawry, which sends its victims to the scaffold without a trial and upon the mere proof of their identity, seemed quite natural to the Girondists, and they unhesitatingly voted its application against priests, refugees, and counter-Revolutionaries. When, a little later, it was turned against themselves, they cried: 'Outlawry! What a horrible sentence of death! From what savage and barbarous nation has the example of such an atrocity been taken? By what civilized people has this bloody law been invented? Nature and humanity shudder at such horrors, and when a whole nation, once so gentle and so humane, gives way to such ferocity and to such cold-blooded murder of its innocent and brave defenders, there is nothing for an honest citizen to do but to cover his head with his cloak, or forestall the assassin's dagger by a more independent and honourable death.'—'Mémoires de Buzot,' Dauban's edition, p. 93.

the rebels of the Vendée at Pont Charron, near Chautonnay, is to be tried by a court-martial at La Rochelle.[1]

Sunday, March 24.—General Miranda, who commanded the left wing of the army at the battle of Nerwinde, has been arrested, together with the Colonel of the 73rd Regiment of Cavalry.[2]

A letter, dated March 19, is read from the members of the Administration of Nantes. It contains the following words : ' Nantes is the only town in the whole of the department that is not in the power of the rebels. Their number is so great that, if we were to tell you that there are 40,000 within a circumference of three miles, we should still be below the mark.'

Monday, March 25.—The organization of the Committee of Public Safety, agreed to in principle at the sitting of the 22nd, has been laid down in a Decree issued to-day. The Committee will be composed of twenty-five members, and its duties will be to prepare and propose all measures necessary for the defence of the Republic at home and abroad. Its sittings will be attended at least twice a week by the Ministers forming the Provisory Executive Council. The Executive Council, and each of its Ministers individually, are to furnish it with all the information it requires, and to lay before it once a week a report of all their proceedings. The Committee will report to the Convention every week upon the state of the Republic, and its members will have the right to speak on each one of these reports.

Tuesday, March 26.—The nominations for the Committee of Public Safety were made to-day, and are as follows : Dubois-Crancé, Petion, Gensonné, Guyton-Morveau, Robespierre the elder, Barbaroux, Rühl, Vergniaud, Fabre d'Églantine, Buzot, Delmas, Guadet, Condorcet, Bréard, Camus, Prieur, Camille Desmoulins, Barère, Quinette, Cambacérès, Jean Debry, Danton,

---

[1] General Marcé was, however, not tried at La Rochelle, but in Paris. The Revolutionary Tribunal sent him to the scaffold on January 28, 1794.

[2] Brought before the Revolutionary Tribunal on May 16, 1793, Miranda was acquitted. ' They had not yet,' says M. Wallon, 'got as far as condemning a General to death for a simple reverse, and were, moreover, disposed to throw the whole blame of the battle and the campaign upon Dumouriez' ('Histoire du Tribunal Révolutionnaire de Paris, tome i., p. 99).

Sieyès, Lasource, and Isnard. The majority of the members are Girondists.

Converting into a general Decree an Order which the section of the Réunion had demanded for itself alone, the Convention unanimously agrees upon the disarming of suspects, priests, all members of the nobility, their agents and servants.

Wednesday, March 27.—After an exceptionally violent speech from Danton, the Convention ' declares its firm intention of making neither a peace nor a truce with the aristocrats or any other enemies of the Revolution, decrees that they are outlawed, that all citizens shall be armed, and that the Revolutionary Tribunal shall enter upon its duties that very day."[1]

The Conseil-Général de la Commune addresses the following letter to the Presidents of the sectional committees :

' CITIZENS,—You will be good enough to convoke a general assembly of your section to-morrow, March 28, before nine o'clock in the morning. If there be any barriers in your district, the Assembly will immediately appoint officers to stop at such barriers any men who may be suspected, or who carry no passports, as well as all horses not used for purposes of trade.

' 1. You will consider as suspects all holding passports for Boulogne or Calais, and all whose certificates of citizenship are less than a month old.

' 2. You will put into execution the Decree passed on the 26th instant relating to the carrying of arms.

' 3. You will pay special heed to all suspects, and arrest those concerning whom your suspicions are well grounded.

' 4. You will appoint a Vigilance Committee, in conformity with the Decrees of the 18th and the 21st instant.'[2]

Thursday, March 28.—The Convention completes and passes the law concerning refugees. On Marat's proposal it is decided that the law shall be immediately promulgated in the provinces.

To get a man condemned to death as a refugee, it is not necessary to prove that he did leave the country ; it is quite sufficient if the accused is unable to prove the contrary ; the *onus* of proof lies with him.

[1] ' Collection du Louvre,' tome xiii., p. 761.
[2] Buchez et Roux, ' Histoire Parlementaire de la Révolution Française,' tome xxv., p. 167.

The Corporation to-day formally installs the Revolutionary Tribunal.

Last night the Committee of Public Safety met to discuss the measures relating to the disarming of suspects. The department, the Mayor and the Corporation, had also been invited to attend. Marat and a large number of the members of the Convention attended the meeting and took part in the discussion.[1]

Early this morning the roll of the drum was heard in every section calling the citizens to general meeting, and in many cases soldiers were sent round to fetch such as were detained at home by their occupations. The city is terror-stricken, and the most strange and disquieting rumours circulate freely. It is said that we are betrayed, and that the deputies who voted for the appeal to the people have deserted their posts, many of them having been stopped at the barriers. It is also announced that the Jacobin Club, escorted by a large number of Patriots and citizens, will hold a meeting in the Champ de Mars.

By mid-day every section is fully armed. Every barrier, every street, every bridge, and every alley, is blockaded. No one is allowed to pass along the public thoroughfares unless he can produce his certificate of citizenship. Many houses have been entered by the authorities, and arrests have been going on all the afternoon.[2]

This deplorable day, in which Liberty has once more been so cruelly outraged, has been celebrated as a day of victory by the *statesmen* of the Girondist party. Brissot's paper speaks of it in the following terms:

'The day just past has been a glorious one for Paris. The city rose as one man, and rose only against the aristocrats. From early morn was heard the sound of the tocsin calling the sections together: the doors of the Treasury and the gates of the prisons were forced open, and strong patrols were set on duty. A house-to-house search for the purpose of disarming suspects was carried out in the most orderly manner. A large number of men not possessing cards of citizenship were arrested, and it is to

---

[1] *Courrier des Départements*, 1793, No. 29.   [2] *Ibid.*

be hoped that amongst them may be found some returned refugees or agitators."[1]

Friday, March 29.—The house-to-house search was resumed at break of day, the barriers being guarded as before.[2]

In order to facilitate arrests, the Convention has given its sanction to the following measure proposed by the Commune :

'Within three days of the passing of this law all landlords and householders, farmers, agents, lodging-house and inn-keepers in any part of the Republican territory, are to post up outside their houses, farms, or habitations, in a convenient place and in legible characters, the names and surnames, age and occupation, of all the persons now residing in the said houses, farms, or habitations.'[3]

This measure had been advocated a few days before in the Jacobin Club by Citizen Dufourny, who had observed 'that in China every householder is obliged to exhibit on the threshold a list of the names of all persons dwelling in his house.'

Lamarque, in the name of the Committee of General Security, complains of the pamphlets which have been so widely distributed since the death of Louis XVI., and which demand the liberation of the Royal Family, the re-establishment of the Monarchy, and the recall of the priests. He says, 'On Monday last, March 25, a seizure was made at Webert's[4] bookshop of at least thirty different works of this kind.' Reminding the Convention that it has disarmed suspected citizens, he adds : 'There are no arms so dangerous as the seditious writings your committee complains of. We must therefore hasten to tear them from the hands of our enemies, and restrain by severe laws those who would henceforth have the criminal audacity to write or to distribute fresh ones.'

After having heard Lamarque, the Convention passed a law prescribing the penalty of death for the offence of writing or printing any matter proposing the re-establishment of the Monarchy in France or the dissolution of the National Convention.

---

[1] *Le Patriote Français*, March 29, 1793.
[2] 'Histoire Parlementaire,' tome xxv., p. 170.
[3] 'Collection du Louvre,' tome xiii., p. 810.
[4] Webert, the bookseller, was guillotined on May 20, 1794. His shop was in the Palais Royal, No. 203.

The men who passed this Decree are those who maintained, with Robespierre, that 'the right of proclaiming one's opinions either in print or in any other way is so evident a consequence of the liberty of man that the necessity for declaring such right supposes either the actual or recent presence of despotism';[1] and, with Condorcet, that 'every man is free to publish his thoughts and his opinions'; that 'the liberty of the press and any other means of publishing one's thoughts cannot be suppressed, suspended, or limited.'[2]

Saturday, March 30.—The Convention summons General Dumouriez to its bar. Five of its members—Camus, Quinette, Lamarque, Bancal, and Beurnonville, Minister of War—are commissioned to proceed to the Army of the North with power to suspend and to arrest all Generals, officers, and men, whoever they may be, and such functionaries or other citizens as they may suspect.

Sunday, March 31.—A deputation from the Conseil-Général de la Commune lays before the Convention a petition read by Chaumette, demanding the impeachment of Dumouriez, and the punishment of this *new Brennus*. The Convention orders this address to be printed and sent to the armies.[3]

Immediately after condemning Dumouriez, the Convention proscribes 'Mérope,' which is like acting a farce after a drama. The Mayor is ordered to take the necessary steps for preventing the performance of Voltaire's masterpiece. 'We cannot,' said Génissieux,[4] 'allow a piece to be played in which a Queen is shown mourning for her husband and praying for the return of her two brothers.'[5]

---

[1] 'Declaration of the Rights of Man,' presented by Robespierre to the Jacobin Club, Article 4; *Journal du Club des Jacobins*, No. 399.

[2] 'Declaration of the Natural, Civil, and Political Rights of Man,' presented to the National Convention on February 16, 1793, by Condorcet, in the name of the Committee of Constitution. This committee was composed of the following nine members, nearly all of whom belonged to the Girondist party: Brissot, Vergniaud, Petion, Condorcet, Gensonné, Thomas Paine, Sieyès, Barère, and Danton.

[3] *Révolutions de Paris*, tome xvi., p. 83.

[4] Génissieux, member for the Isère, was made a Judge in the Tribunal de la Seine under the Consulate, after having been Minister of Justice under the Directory. He died in 1804, leaving a considerable fortune, which he was accused of having accumulated during the Revolutionary disturbances.

[5] *Moniteur*, April 1, 1793.

CHAPTER LXII.

Thursday, April 4, 1793.

'No; this cannot possibly go on. We cannot be longer condemned to behold the triumph of the greatest villains breathing; the Jacobins will not be permitted to inflict upon a nation like the French their shameful rule. Honest men are in the majority, and——'

'You forget, *mon ami*, that when a nation is in revolt, honest men go to the wall and make way for the insolent.'

The conversation took place in the small suite of rooms occupied by François de Pange[1] in the Place de la Nation, where Charles Lacretelle, François Chéron,[2] the two Trudaines,[3] Beaulieu, and two or three others, had met.

I must confess that it was I who had just expressed myself concerning honest men and a speedy return to law and justice

---

[1] Marie François Denis Thomas de Pange—born in Paris on November 9, 1764, died in September, 1796—was an intimate friend of André Chénier, and his colleague on the staff of the *Journal de Paris;* his articles, gracefully written, though correct and always to the point, show proofs of rare courage and superior talents. They have been collected by M. L. Becq de Fouquières—'Œuvres de François de Pange,' one vol., 1872.

[2] François Chéron (1764—1828) was one of the principal editors of the *Journal de Paris.* He wrote, in collaboration with Picard, 'Du Haut Cours, ou le Contrat d'Union,' a comedy in five acts and in prose, performed at the Louvain Theatre on August 6, 1801. His brother, Louis Claude Chéron (1758—1807), a deputy in the Legislative Assembly, is the author of 'Le Tartufe de Mœurs,' a comedy in five acts and in verse, performed at the Théâtre Français on April 4, 1805. See the 'Mémoires' of François Chéron, published in 1882 by M. Hervé Bazin.

[3] The two Trudaines were guillotined on the 8th of Thermidor (July 26, 1794), one day after their friend, André Chénier.

in terms which no doubt did more honour to the feelings that animated me than to the reliability of my opinions.

Beaulieu—for it was he who had called me down from the clouds—added :

'Since you still harbour illusions concerning honest men—since you think them capable of coping with their adversaries and of coming out of the combat victorious—let me remind you of the history of the Société des Feuillants. Never, perhaps, was there seen such a gathering of eminent, enlightened, devoted, and courageous men. You are as well acquainted as I am with the list published by order of the Commune in August last. This list comprised no less than 833 names, and though some of these, such as mine and yours, my dear Lacretelle, and yours, too, my good Chéron, are somewhat obscure, how many others were there that shone with the splendour of birth, wealth, and talent ! Had we not in our ranks Mathieu de Montmorency, La Trémoille, La Rochefoucauld, Regnault de Saint-Jean d'Angély, Joseph de Broglie, Lavoisier, Beugnot, Jaucourt, Lanjuinais, Michaud, Duport, Destutt de Tracy, D'André, the two Lameths, Liancourt, Thouret, Lacépède, Rulhière, Ramond, the eloquent Barnave, and our wonderful André de Chénier ? Led by such chiefs, animated by the love of right, full of most generous ardour, we began to wage war against the Jacobins ; you shall hear the success of our efforts.

'The narrative of our campaign seems to me to point more than one moral ; I shall therefore make it as complete as possible. So many events already separate us from this tale of yesterday that you must allow me to dwell upon some of the details, especially as I myself took a leading part in it all.

' You all know as well as I do how on July 16, 1791, a schism was produced in the "Society of Friends of the Constitution" on the question of the Abdication Petition drafted by Laclos ; how Bouche, who was then president, Salle and Anthoine, the two secretaries, Barnave, Duport, the Lameths, Dubois-Crancé, Goupil de Préfeln, and all the other members of the society who formed part of the Constituent Assembly, with the exception of Robespierre, Petion, Roederer, Coroller, Buzot and Grégoire, left the Jacobins and founded a rival club, which also met in the

Rue Saint-Honoré, opposite the Place de Louis-le-Grand,[1] in what had formerly been the Church of the Feuillants. '[2]

Here François Chéron observed with a smile that amongst the founders of the new club there were several who had taken part in the demolition of the convents, and that it was rather curious to see the different parties who had driven out the religious orders adopt the very names of the monks they had proscribed — the 'Jacobins,' the 'Feuillants,' and the 'Grey Friars.'

'Chéron's remark,' observed Beaulieu, 'is both correct and smart, but in July, 1791, Barnave, Duport, and their friends were doing all they could to stem the torrent of the Revolution. The affair of the Champs de Mars[3] opened the eyes even of the dullest. Names came flowing in ; many who until then had never belonged to any club—I was among the number—became members of the new society. For a moment it enjoyed full confidence, and the dawn of the Feuillants was full of promise. Immediately did the worshippers of the rising sun turn towards the new luminary, and many a one now sitting in the Mountain then thought it prudent to be one of us. Barère attended our sittings most assiduously for some time, and even presided over them occasionally.[4] Louis de Lavalette,[5] who is to-day one of Robespierre's henchmen, made himself quite conspicuous by the ardour of his zeal.

'But these fine days did not last long.

'The Feuillants, like the Jacobins, had adopted the title of "Society of Friends of the Constitution," to which they had a better claim. But the name was not all ; the difficulty was to get hold of the journal of the society[6]—that formidable instrument of propaganda—to draw into the fold all the affiliated

---

[1] Now the Place Vendôme.
[2] The Convent des Feuillants stood on the present site of the Rue de Castiglione.
[3] July 17, 1791.
[4] 'Essais Historiques sur les Causes et les Effets de la Révolution de France,' by Beaulieu, tome iii., p. 48.
[5] Executed on the 10th of Thermidor (July 28, 1794) as an accomplice of Robespierre.
[6] *Journal des Débats de la Société des Amis de la Constitution*, meeting at the Jacobins, in Paris.

clubs throughout the country. We failed in this undertaking, and to some extent by our own fault. Our rules excluded all who were not active citizens, or the sons of active citizens. A very proper and a very reasonable measure, no doubt, but which had the effect of alienating from us almost all provincial Jacobins. Our rivals made a great number of fresh recruits, whilst we were left isolated. The deputies who had deserted the Jacobins soon perceived that they would not find the same advantages at the Feuillants; that restraining the acts and the language of the populace would be neither so easy nor so popular as urging it onwards and giving its passions free rein, and that jeers, instead of applause, would be the reward. Already on August 7, 1791, Anthoine, one of our secretaries, went over to the Jacobins and shamelessly declared that he had only joined the Feuillants in order to counteract the plots of the enemies of the country. Following his example, the Constituent members one after another abandoned our unfortunate club, which soon found itself reduced to infinitesimal numbers. I belonged to the small battalion which saved at least the honour of the flag. For nearly two months, until the meeting of the Legislative Assembly,[1] we succeeded by an immensely active correspondence in making the provinces believe that the great Society of Friends of the Constitution still existed not at the Jacobins, but at the Feuillants; that we were daily growing in numbers, and that we were continually forming fresh ties of affiliation. Do you know how many of us there really were at the moment? Eight, all counted.[2]

'As soon as the Legislative Assembly had met, a few of the Constitutionnels came to the Feuillants; the majority of them, however, taken aback by our small number, thought it preferable to form an entirely fresh club, composed only of deputies. This association met in the mansion of the late Maréchal de Richelieu, but, unable to rival the ever-increasing power of the Jacobins, and divided among themselves on questions of principle and interest, its members did not hold together long. Some resolved to be connected with no club at all, and flattered them-

---

[1] October 1, 1791.   [2] Beaulieu, tome iii., p. 47.

selves on being superior to all party ties ; others went to the Jacobins ; others, again, with Beugnot, Ramond, Jaucourt, and Dumolard, came to us, and we began to hope that our club was to enjoy a recrudescence of its former splendour and importance. Many members of the Constituent Assembly who had not left Paris came back ; amongst them were the Lameths, Barnave, D'André, Thouret, Le Chapelier, Talleyrand de Péri-gord, Beaumetz, and Desmeuniers. It was at this moment that the list of 833 names that I mentioned just now was drawn up. We had with us nearly all the Right of the Legislative Assembly,[1] the departmental Directory, the best men of the National Guard and of the Parisian *bourgeoisie*, and a number of courageous journalists and eloquent orators.

'What a journalist and what an orator was our good friend André de Chénier !' exclaimed Lacretelle. 'You all know his fine articles in the *Journal de Paris* ; his oratorical powers are quite equal to his literary talents. It was at the Feuillants that I saw him for the first time and received an ineffaceable impression of him. His athletic form, his immense head, as large as Mirabeau's, his sunburnt complexion, his flashing eyes —all served to give strength and colour to his words. The ideas he put forth were always marked by intense energy and most eloquently expressed. It was easy to see that his fiery and brilliant language came from an intrepid soul, and that he possessed not only great talents, but a noble nature. His true place was the tribune of the National Assembly ; I am sure that he would have taken the palm of eloquence from Vergniaud him-self.'[2]

---

[1] The Legislative Assembly consisted of 745 members, subdivided as follows : On the benches of the Right sat the Constitutionnels, about 160 in number ; on the Left sat the Jacobins, numbering 330 ; in the centre sat the *Independents* or *Impartials*, nearly 250 in number. One of the most distinguished members of the Assembly, E. H. Hua, thus describes the Independents : 'A phalanx that never supports what is right, and which can only be influenced by fear. It gives the majority, but it always gives it, not to the Right, which it esteems, but to the Left, which it fears' ('Mémoires d'un Avocat au Parlement de Paris, Député à l'Assemblée Législative' (E. A. Hua), published by his grandson, E. M. François Saint-Maur, 1872).

[2] 'Dix Années d'Épreuves pendant la Révolution,' by Ch. Lacretelle, p. 82.

'He was indeed a mighty orator,' said Beaulieu. 'Talent was therefore not lacking in the club of the Feuillants during the first months of the Legislative Assembly, and it seemed as if it would easily regain in November what it had lost in August. The society which could boast of such a combination of intellectual greatness and of social strength was, alas! to be dispersed by a boy of twenty and the sling of a journalist.

'One evening in December we were having a quiet discussion; d'André was in the chair, and the sitting was drawing to a peaceful end, when suddenly our public galleries were invaded by a band of shameless women and some riff-raff that had been picked up at the Jacobins or in the Rue Saint-Honoré; they were led by Girey-Dupré, the collaborator of Brissot.[1] The newcomers soon drowned the words of the speakers with their shouts. It would have been easy enough to drive these ragamuffins out, especially as the National Guard stationed outside our place of meeting was entirely devoted to us, and Dijon, a lieutenant in the battalion of the Filles Saint-Thomas, who was seated beside me, would have enjoyed administering a few blows with the flat of his sword.[2] But instead of that we were obliged to submit unflinchingly to the most brutal insults; such was the decision of the wise men who governed us. They shouted silence with all the strength of their lungs, and gravely invoked the Constitution. It was your brother, my dear Lacretelle, who was the happy inventor of our parrot-like cry: "The Constitution, the whole Constitution, and nothing but the Constitution!"—an admirable formula which delivered us helplessly into our unscrupulous adversaries' hands. The hooting and jeering was at its height when a noise imitating the crowing of a cock came from one of the galleries, and was immediately repeated by the crowd that had made its way into our hall, and by the mob that thronged the entrances. It was a young surgeon named Boi who first uttered the cry; it must be confessed that the idea was a happy one, our president, M. d'André, being the founder of the paper published each

---

[1] 'Histoire de la Révolution de 1789,' by Two Friends of Liberty, tome viii., p. 178.
[2] Révolutions de Paris, tome x., p. 581.

morning under the title *The Crowing of the Cock*. We had faced all the insults, but before this piece of ridicule we could only take refuge in flight. It was raining, and as many of the Jacobins were moving about in the lobby with their umbrellas under their arms and inciting the mob to create further disturbances, a rumour was set afloat in Paris next day that we had been driven out at the point of the umbrella.

'We nevertheless continued to assemble on the following days, but it was only a renewal of the same scenes. We then decided to send a deputation to the Mayor, asking him to guarantee us the free exercise of our rights. I was one of the delegates. Petion, who was one of our enemies, thought it enough to give an order to the chief police-officer of the district, who was " to take such conciliatory measures as would tend to re-establish peace between the members of the club and the strangers who made their way into the club premises." We immediately betook ourselves to this police-officer, who, animated by the same sentiments as the Mayor, faithfully carried out his intentions. He accompanied us to the club, where we found that the sitting had commenced. The tribune was occupied by a young ragamuffin of sixteen or seventeen, who, assisted by a few other intruders of a like age, was teaching our gray-beards a lesson. The police-officer sits down, calls for silence, and with the utmost seriousness pretends to seek some means of reconciling the rights of the members of the club with those held, in his opinion, by the stranger who is in possession of our tribune. Some of us begin to lose patience, and talk of taking the law into our own hands. The officer, fearing that we may put our threats into execution, at last decides to turn out the disturbers. The sitting ends, and we retire overwhelmed with ridicule.

'On the morrow we were not only subjected to a shower of lampoons and songs, but the Jacobin newspapers anathematized this " monarchical, aristocratic, and constitutional " club, which was alone the cause of all the mischief.[1] They demanded the extermination of this turbulent and pestilential society, and their demands were very soon granted.

'On Sunday, December 25, 1791, Merlin - Moustaches, a

---

[1] *Révolutions de Paris*, tome x., p. 584.

member of the Legislative Assembly, entered the club hall, and insulted the members in the grossest fashion. This time our people got quite out of temper; Merlin was severely taken to task, hustled, and thrown out of doors.[1]   On the morrow he complained in the Assembly of the insult offered to the representatives of the nation in his person.   Lacroix and Grangeneuve made the most violent attack upon our unfortunate club, and their words were drowned amidst the applause of the galleries. During the sitting of December 27, the Legislative Assembly, at the instance of Lacroix and upon the recommendation of M. Houssi-Robbecourt, made in the name of the committee of *inspecteurs de la salle*, decreed that no political association should be allowed to establish itself upon the premises formerly occupied by the Feuillants and Capucines.

' Obliged to seek fresh quarters, we first went to the Lucignan Mansion,[2] and then to Richelieu's house, which was the headquarters of the battalion named after the Filles Saint-Thomas. Two cannon guarded the door, and the commanders of the battalion were fully prepared to keep the peace without the intervention of the Mayor or his officers. There was, unfortunately, no room for the outside public in these premises, and we were therefore compelled to betake ourselves elsewhere if we wished to maintain our influence. The club hired the church of the Saint-Honoré cloister, and in arranging it thought as much of the public as of its own members.

' But all our efforts were in vain. The majority of our members were of the higher walks of life and in fairly good circumstances; they had no desire to compromise themselves uselessly, and certainly none to enter into a conflict with the populace. They thought the matter over, and their reflections led them to abandon the whole thing. When we met in the

---

[1] Beaulieu, tome iii., p. 56.

[2] The Mélusine-Lucignan Mansion was situated in the Rue des Bons-Enfants. After having served as the offices of the Chancellerie d'Orléans, and after having been inhabited by Cardinal Dubois, it had become in 1752 the property of the bibliophile Marc René de Paulmy d'Argenson, Marquis de Voyer, a son of the Comte d'Argenson. The magnificent library of the Marquis de Paulmy was purchased in 1785 by Monsieur, the Comte d'Artois (afterwards Charles X.), and now forms the Bibliothèque de l'Arsenal.

Saint-Honoré cloister nearly 800 failed to put in an appearance. We were only forty. This might be sufficient to form an academy, but it was not enough to form a club. We were obliged to be satisfied with sitting as a small committee, and in holding sparsely - attended meetings until the Tenth of August. Thus ended a club which had at one time comprised nearly all the most eminent legislators and lawyers, all the first financiers and literary men of Paris. It was overthrown by the scum of the pavement, and by the most abandoned women of the capital. And now, my dear friend,' added Beaulieu, turning to me, 'you may, if you wish, rely upon the energy of honest people. I, for one, would rather believe in the courage of Robespierre, or in the virtue of Petion.'

CHAPTER LXIII.

Tuesday, April 9, 1793.

THE first week of the present month was one of the most troubled and threatening periods through which we have yet passed. The factions which tug at the very heart-strings of the Republic are more violent than ever: Girondists and Montagnards wage a war so implacable that it can only terminate in the disappearance of one of the two parties. It is evident that the end is approaching, and there is little doubt that it will be a tragic one.

Monday, 1st.—To-day's sitting of the Convention was one of exceptional importance. It terminated by a vote of which the consequences cannot fail to be terrible. At the instance of a Girondist member,[1] the Convention passed the following Decree :

'Whereas the safety of the people is the supreme law, the National Convention decrees that, irrespective of the inviolability of the representatives of the French nation, an impeachment will lie against any of its members who, upon written proofs or verbal information given to the Committee of General Defence, shall be strongly suspected of being in league with the enemies of Liberty, Equality, and the Republican Government.'

This Decree will undoubtedly lead the representatives of the people to the scaffold, and this the Girondists fully intend. Was it not Lasource, one of their principal speakers, who, at the beginning of this very sitting, spoke these words : 'Remember that the people want justice. Long enough have they gazed

---

[1] Birotteau, member for the Pyrénées-Orientales.

upon the Capitol and the throne; they have now a desire to see the Tarpeian rock and the scaffold.'

That the scaffold may not stand idle there comes quite a shower of denunciations, both from the Right and from the Left.

Lasource denounces Danton.

Penières denounces Lacroix.

Birotteau denounces **Fabre** d'Églantine.

Duhem denounces Roland.

Maure denounces Brissot, Barbaroux, and **Guadet.**

Marat denounces **Lasource and Gensonné.**

Danton in turn denounces every member of the Right. He calls upon the people to take up arms and crush the enemy within, ' all the cowards, villains, aristocrats, and moderates.'

The threats of the Girondist party end in smoke, but the threats of the Mountain have immediate results. This very day seals were placed on all Roland's papers by virtue of an order of the Committee of Vigilance.[1]

The Committee of Vigilance also issued warrants for the arrest of a large number of people, amongst whom are MM. d'Espagnac[2] and Malus, formerly Commissioners in the army of Dumouriez; Hébert, formerly secretary to Adrien Duport; Bonne-Carrère, formerly an official in the Foreign Office; Guy d'Arcy;[3] Asseline, an agent for M. de Liancourt; Lalonde of Cambrai; Sainte-Foy of Mont Saint-Martin, near Cambrai; Candeyron, formerly Mayor of Cambrai; Berneron and Ligneville, two highly-placed

---

[1] *Le Patriote Français*, No. 1,328.

[2] The Abbé Sahuguet d'Espagnac, whose father had been a Lieutenant-General, Governor of the Invalides, and a Knight of Saint-Louis, was before the Revolution a Canon of the Church of Paris. After having embarked upon a literary career, and obtained an *accessit* for oratory from the Académie Française for his 'Éloge de Catinat,' he turned his attention to finance, took up the Revolutionary cause with ardour, and became contractor first to the Army of the Alps and afterwards carrying-contractor to that of Dumouriez. He was guillotined on April 5, 1794, together with Danton, Camille Desmoulins, Chabot, Basire, Fabre d'Églantine, and many others.

[3] Guy d'Arcy, formerly a member of the States-General, in which he occupied rather a prominent position, had been appointed a Field-Marshal at the close of the Constituent Assembly. He was guillotined on July 23, 1794.

officers; Devaux, Adjutant-General in the army of Dumouriez;[1] Citoyenne Beauvais, the mistress of Dumouriez; Victor de Broglie;[2] De Boisgelin,[3] formerly Master of the Robes to Louis XVI.; Mme. de Sillery;[4] Lady Fitz-Gerald;[5] General Égalité; Montjoie, an Aide-de-camp; Choderlos-Laclos, an officer; Lemaire, treasurer to M. d'Orléans; General Valence, M. de Sillery's son-in-law; M. d'Orléans' two sons; and M. Sauvan,[6] one of his officers.[7]

Tuesday, April 2.—The *Tribunal Criminel Extraordinaire* held its inaugural sitting to-day. The proceedings consisted entirely of speeches. According to Article 10 of the Law of March 10, the accusations must be drawn up by a Commission of six members of the Convention charged with the examination of all the documents, with the drafting of the indictments, and with the general management of each case. This Commission has not yet sent anyone before the tribunal.

Judges and jurymen would, no doubt, have been very glad to mark their first day by a goodly batch of sentences. They

---

[1] Philippe Devaux, thirty-two years old, was a Colonel and Adjutant-General in the armies of the Republic, and was guillotined on May 23, 1793.

[2] Field-Marshal his Highness Prince Victor de Broglie was guillotined on June 29, 1794.

[3] Comte Louis Bruno de Boisgelin, a brother of the Cardinal of that name, was guillotined on July 7, 1794, together with his wife, a sister of the Chevalier de Boufflers, a maid-of-honour to Mme. Victoire. Another Boisgelin perished on the scaffold, and yet another in the September massacres.

[4] Mdme. de Sillery (1746—1830), better known as Mme. de Genlis, which was the first name of her husband, Comte Bruslart de Genlis, a Colonel in the Grenadiers, and later Marquis de Sillery. M. de Sillery was a member of the Convention, and was guillotined with the Girondists on October 31, 1793.

[5] Lady Edward Fitz-Gerald was the favourite pupil of Mme. de Genlis, who had given her the name of Pamela, under which she enjoyed some celebrity at the beginning of the Revolution. Lord Fitz-Gerald, her husband, attempted to bring about an Irish rising against England in 1798. Arrested on May 19 of that year, he committed suicide in prison on June 4 following. Lady Fitz-Gerald died in Paris in 1831, one year after Mme. de Genlis.

[6] Jean Baptiste Sauvan was inspector 'of the furniture in the castles of the Duc d'Orléans.' His daughter Adèle, who died on September 7, 1809, had on January 24, 1803, married Gabriel Le Gouvé, author of 'Le Mérite des Femmes.' The issue of this marriage was M. Ernest Le Gouvé, a member of the Académie Française.

[7] *Courrier Français*, No. 94; *Le Patriote Français*, No. 1,329.

therefore hastened to present themselves at the bar of the Convention, and to deplore the inaction to which they were condemned by the sloth of the Commission of Six.

Garran-Coulon, the President of that Commission, declares that 'he has not yet been able to draw up any indictment owing to the fact that the evidence laid before him has not warranted such a course.'

Albitte rushes to the tribune. 'If we were about to try a gang of coiners,' he says, 'I would consent to the observance of all these forms; but when we have to try conspirators forms may be dispensed with. I therefore move that the Commission of Six be abolished, and that prosecutions be in future instituted solely by the Public Prosecutor.'

Rabaut Saint-Étienne, the Girondist, who follows Albitte, is careful not to challenge the words of the orator of the Mountain. Himself a member of the Commission of Six, he declares that he is by no means opposed to its suppression, which is thereupon agreed to without further discussion.

Wednesday, April 3.—The Convention is informed during its morning sitting that Dumouriez has ordered the arrest of Camus, Quinette, Bancal, and Lamarque, the Commissioners sent to him, as well as of Beurnonville, the Minister; that he has sent them to a place of safety as hostages, and that he is preparing to march on Paris with his troops.

On receipt of this information, the Assembly declares its sittings permanent. On the motion of Thuriot, it decrees that every Frenchman who recognises Dumouriez as a General shall be looked upon as a traitor to his country, and condemned to die, and that his property shall be confiscated by the Republic.

The Convention then makes Dumouriez an outlaw, authorizes any citizen to run him down, and offers a reward of 300,000 francs to whomsoever shall bring him to Paris dead or alive.

At the evening sitting Robespierre gave voice to a long philippic against the members of the Right, and particularly against Brissot, concluding with a demand for the immediate impeachment of that member. The Convention, however, passed to the Order of the Day, but issued a Decree for the arrest of all persons who do not wear a cockade.

At the Jacobin Club Robespierre reiterated his accusations against Brissot, and indicated the following measures as the only means of saving Paris and the Revolution :

'We must,' he said, 'raise a Revolutionary army ; we must enlist every Patriot, every *sans-culotte;* the inhabitants of the Faubourgs must form the strength and the backbone of our troops. I do not say that we should sharpen our swords to kill the priests ; we can afford to despise them, and we should only be giving the fanatics another pretext for crying out against us. We must have no compunction in driving from our sections all who have shown themselves to be imbued with the spirit of moderation ; we must disarm not only the nobles and the priests, but every plotter, every suspected citizen, everyone who has given proofs of disloyalty. Let the whole of Paris take up arms, let the sections and the people be vigilant, and let the Convention declare itself the voice of the nation.'[1]

Thursday, April 4.—On March 9 last the Convention had armed the Commissioners sent into the provinces with power to arrest all persons whom they might suspect of treason.[2] On April 4 it hit upon an idea not a whit less odious—that of the arrest of the hostages. It was on the motion of Lasource that this Decree was passed. Whenever an iniquitous measure is adopted, we are sure to see in it the hand of a Girondist. The first article runs as follows :

'The parents, wives, and children of all officers above the rank of sub-lieutenant in the army which was commanded by Dumouriez shall be kept under supervision as hostages by the municipality of the district in which they reside until the Minister of War and the Commissioners sent by the National Convention, and now detained by the treachery of Dumouriez, are liberated.'

Another Decree orders the immediate arrest of the wife and children of General Valence, of Citoyenne Montesson[3] and of

---

[1] *Journal des Débats et de la Correspondance de la Société de Jacobins.* No. 388.

[2] Decree of March 9, 1793 ; *Moniteur* of March 11.

[3] Charlotte Jeanne Béraud de la Haye de Riou, Marquise de Montesson, was born in 1737, and married in 1773, with the King's consent, Louis Philippe, fourth Duc d'Orléans, grandson of the Regent and father of Louis Philippe Joseph Égalité. The Marquise de Montesson has written

Citoyenne Égalité; it also provides for the supervision of Citizens Bruslart-Sillery and Égalité, members of the National Convention, who shall have full liberty to go where they please, but in Paris only.

A third **Decree orders General** Miaczinski to be brought to Paris with a strong guard, and to be secretly lodged in **one of** the cells of the Abbaye.[1]

An open vote is then taken for the election of a Minister of War in place of Beurnonville. Citizen **Bouchotte**, holding temporary command at Cambrai, is unanimously elected.[2]

Gonchon, the spokesman of a deputation from the Faubourg Saint-Antoine, asks for the organization of a company of Scevolas, whose chief should be chosen from the Convention.[3]

Marat is elected President of the Jacobin Club.[4]

Friday, April 5.—The most contradictory rumours continue to circulate concerning Dumouriez. Some say that he has fled from the country; others are confident that he is still at the head of his army.[5]

The Convention, which has already suppressed the greater part of the slender guarantees at first accorded anyone accused before the Extraordinary Criminal Tribunal, has now struck out from its decree of March 10 the article which confined the jurisdiction of the court to cases of conspiracy and treason brought to its notice by the Convention. The Public Prosecutor is authorized to arrest and prosecute all who are suspected of the said crimes either upon his own initiative, or upon information received from the constituted authorities, or from private citizens.

A decree of the Convention is required only in cases where the accused is a Minister, a General, or a representative of the people.

It has been decided to form a camp of 40,000 men outside Paris. None of the former nobility will be admitted into this army either as officers or as privates.

---

rather a large number of plays. She died in Paris on February 6, 1806. See 'Souvenirs et Portraits,' by the Duc de Lévis.

[1] General Miaczinski was guillotined on May 17, 1793.
[2] *Moniteur* of April 7, 1793. [3] *Le Républicain Français*, No. 142.
[4] *Patriote Français*, No. 1,333. [5] *Courrier Français*, No. 97.

After the passing of this motion, Danton spoke as follows : ' You are about to form an army of *sans-culottes*, but that is not enough. Whilst you go and fight our enemies abroad, the aristocrats at home must be kept under the pikes of the *sans-culottes*. I ask for the formation of a popular guard, whose salaries shall be paid by the nation. We shall be well defended when our defenders are *sans-culottes*. I have another proposal to make ; the price of bread throughout the country should be in exact proportion to the poor man's wage—whatever excess there may be must be paid by the rich.' Danton's two proposals were adopted amidst the applause of the whole assembly.[1]

At the Jacobin Club the younger Robespierre invites all good citizens to meet in their different sections. ' You must,' he says, ' come to the bar of the Convention, and oblige us to order the arrest of the disloyal deputies.'

Saturday, April 6.—Official information is received from Cochon, Bellegarde, and Lequinio, the Commissioners sent by the Convention to the northern frontier, that Dumouriez, not having been able to get his army to follow him, has gone over to the enemy with Generals Valence and Égalité, a few officers, and nearly all Berchigny's Hussars.

The Committee of General Defence appointed on January 1, 1793, and reorganized on March 25 as the Committee of General Defence or of Public Safety,[2] is, on the proposal of Isnard, a Girondist member, replaced by an executive committee composed of nine members only, to be called the Committee of Public Safety; this Committee will exercise the sovereignty and all other powers.

The members who are to form this select body, and who are appointed for one month, are nearly all of the Mountain. They were elected by open voting in the following order : Barère, Delmas, Bréard, Cambron, Jean Debry, Danton, Guyton-Morveau, Treilhard, and Lacroix. Jean Debry, who excused himself on the grounds of ill-health, was replaced by Robert Lindet.

Marat demands that 100,000 relatives and friends of the refugees be taken as hostages, so that, if the least harm should

---

[1] *Moniteur* of April 9, 1793.　　　　[2] See Chapter LXI.

befall the Commissioners detained by Dumouriez, these unhappy people might pay for it with their lives.[1]

Jealous, no doubt, of the laurels of the Friend of the People, Boyer-Fonfrède, the Girondist, has proposed to arrest all the Bourbons, and to keep them as hostages. 'Citizens,' he cried, 'all Princes are related as far as crime is concerned; let us, therefore, keep these Bourbons as hostages. Should the tyrants to whom Égalité has gone over dare to lay a hand upon the representatives of the French people, then let all these Bourbons be dragged to the scaffold! Let them disappear from this life in the same way as the Monarchy has disappeared from the Republic, and let the soil of Liberty be freed from their execrable presence!' These words are received with acclamation, and the whole assembly rising to its feet, Boyer-Fonfrède's proposal is unanimously adopted.[2]

It is decreed that every member of the Bourbon family shall be arrested and taken to Marseilles. The prisoners in the Temple will remain where they are.

The Tribunal of March 10, which is now generally called the Revolutionary Tribunal,[3] has pronounced its first sentence. The accused was a gentleman of Poitou, named Louis Guyot des Maulans; he was arrested on December 12, 1792, at the Bourg de l'Égalité, and found to be in possession of two passports and a white cockade. He was condemned to death, and guillotined on the same day. Night had already fallen when he was led to the scaffold, and the execution took place by torchlight.[4]

Sunday, April 7.—The Duc d'Orléans — Philippe Joseph Égalité—has been arrested on a warrant signed by Pache, Mayor of Paris.

Santerre informs the Commune that he has received two

---

[1] *Moniteur* of April 9, 1793.   [2] *Ibid.*

[3] The report of its first sitting has the following heading

    'Report of the Sitting of the Revolutionary Criminal Tribunal established in Paris by the Law of March 10, 1793, and by Virtue of the Powers given it by the Law of April 5 of the same Year.'

See Wallon, 'Histoire du Tribunal Révolutiounaire de Paris,' tome i., p. 84.

[4] On September 27, 1793, the nation paid the widow Favier, who had furnished forty-eight torches for this occasion, the sum of ninety-six francs ('Archives Nationales,' AA., 399 ; 'Le Tribunal Révolutionnaire de Paris,' by E. Campardon, tome i., p. 27).

letters from the former Monsieur, brother of the deceased Louis Capet. They are addressed to *Monsieur le Commandant-Général de la Force Armée de Paris.* In these letters the former Monsieur announces that he is Regent of France, and that the reign of Louis XVII. must be recognised as having commenced on January 21, the day on which, as he says, a criminal blow struck off the head of Louis XVI.[1] Santerre has sent these two letters to the Convention.

Monday, April 8.—The Duc d'Orléans, the Duc de Beaujolaix, his third son, aged thirteen, the Duchesse de Bourbon,[2] and the Prince de Conti,[3] have left for Marseilles, escorted by a strong guard. The Duchesse d'Orléans, who is very ill, and has been living at Bezy-lès-Vernon since the commencement of the Revolution, will continue to reside there under the supervision of the municipality.

At its evening sitting, presided over by Garran-Coulon, the Convention admitted to the bar a deputation from the Bon-Conseil section demanding the arrest of Brissot, Guadet, Gensonné, Vergniaud, Barbaroux, Louvet, Buzot, and others. The spokesman of the section concluded his address with the following appeal to the Patriots of the Mountain : ' The country relies upon you to denounce the traitors. It is time that their efforts to crush Liberty were punished. Awake from that sleep which is a danger to your country ; arise and deliver up to justice the men whom public opinion denounces ; make war upon all Moderates, Feuillants, and agents of the former court of the Tuileries. Face them with proofs like ardent Patriots, help to call down the sword of the law upon the heads of the inviolable conspirators, and posterity will bless the day on which you were born.'

On Marat's proposal the petitioners were awarded the honours of the sitting.

* * * * *

[1] Sitting of the Conseil-Général de la Commune of April 7 (' Histoire Parlementaire,' by Buchez and Roux, tome xxv., p. 309).

[2] Louise Thérèse d'Orléans, sister of the Duc d'Orléans, wife of the Duc de Bourbon and mother of the Duc d'Enghien.

[3] The Prince de Conti was the last descendant of Armand, Prince de Conti, a younger brother of the Grand Condé. He died at Barcelona in 1814.

This first week of April has really belonged entirely to Marat. Having been indefatigable since the beginning of the war in denouncing the Generals and smelling out treason, he is now triumphant. Has not everything happened exactly as he foretold it ? Do not his prophetic faculties equal his incorruptibility ? Was he not right to adopt the title of Friend of the People ? No one, not even Robespierre or Danton, would now dare to dispute his claim to that title. It seems, indeed, as if the people had neither eyes nor ears for anyone but him. Marat is quoted in the public places, he is read in the *cafés*, he is acclaimed in the clubs. It is impossible to go a few yards without hearing the cry of ' *Le Journal de Marat !*'[1]

[1] *Courrier Français*, No. 93.

CHAPTER LXIV.

Thursday, April 18, 1793.

THE battle between the Girondists and the Montagnards rages more furiously than ever, but has not changed its scene of action. The Montagnards say to their antagonists: 'You are the accomplices of Dumouriez; you relied upon him as he relied upon you, for he called you "the healthy portion" of the Convention. You still went on defending him in the tribune and in your newspapers, even when he had already commenced to act a traitor's part.'[1] The Girondists in turn say to the Montagnards: 'Dumouriez is a traitor, it is true; but this traitor was used as a tool for carrying out the ambitious plans of D'Orléans and his son. Is it not you who still protect D'Orléans and oppose his expulsion? Is it not clear that you desire to hold him back like a trump card until the day when you will deem it expedient to *turn up the King*, and re-establish the throne for his advantage—and for yours? When the question of banishing D'Orléans was first mooted, was it not Camille Desmoulins who cried, "If this Decree passes France is lost"? Did we not hear the same language in the Grey Friars and in the Commune? Was it not Marat who said, "Égalité must stop"? Did not this same Marat constitute himself his advocate but yesterday, and did he not use in the Convention language that sounded exceeding strange coming from him? These were his words: "I implore the representatives of the people not to

---

[1] *Le Patriote Français* (Brissot's paper) of April 1, 1793.

adopt hasty measures, and especially not to compromise the dignity of the Convention. Up to the present no proofs have been adduced in support of any charge against Égalité, and there is not even ground for harbouring the slightest suspicion."[1]

Were I called upon to decide this suit, which reminds me very forcibly of *Wolf v. Fox*, I should have no hesitation in finding both sides guilty. Whilst awaiting that verdict, which it is very probable that a more formidable tribunal than mine will pronounce—I mean the tribunal which Girondists and Montagnards were unanimous in instituting on March 10—I will confine myself to noting day by day the progress of the trial.

Tuesday, April 9.—The military power is subordinate to the civil power. A report having been laid before the Convention by Bréard in the name of the Committee of Public Safety, it is decreed that there shall always be three representatives of the people with each of the armies of the Republic. These Commissioners, one of whom is to be changed every month, are invested with unlimited power.[2]

A letter from the Commissioners Lequinio, Bellegarde, and Charles Cochon announces that they have arrested General Lescuyer, as well as several citizens of Valenciennes, who were inciting the people to revolt by treasonable speeches in favour of the Monarchy. The Convention decrees that Lescuyer shall be brought before the Revolutionary Tribunal,[3] rules that incitement to re-establish the Monarchy shall be accounted an anti-Revolutionary crime, and orders the criminal tribunal of the département du Nord to proceed without delay to Valenciennes, and to the other towns in the department. All persons charged with attempting to re-establish the Monarchy, or with inciting to anti-Revolutionary risings, shall be tried without the right of appeal, and the sentences against those found guilty shall be such as are prescribed by the Law of March 10 last. Orders are also sent out to all the departments of the Republic to institute

---

[1] Sitting of April 1, 1793; *Moniteur* of April 9.
[2] *Moniteur* of April 11, 1793.
[3] General Lescuyer was guillotined on August 14, 1793.

proceedings against similar offenders in accordance with the provisions of the said law.[1]

Wednesday, April 10.—Petion reads from the tribune an address which the Section of the Corn-market has distributed in Paris, and in which it is said that Roland deserves to be sent to the scaffold; that the majority in the Convention is corrupt, and that on its benches sit the greatest enemies of the people. After having demanded (1) the impeachment of Roland; (2) the arrest of the guilty deputies; (3) the expulsion of those who have not the courage to defend the Republic, and the election of fresh members in their places, the authors of the address conclude with the following appeal:

'Mountain of the Convention, save the Republic! or if you do not feel strong enough to do so, have the courage to admit it frankly; we will then undertake the mission ourselves. The crisis through which we are now passing must be the last; France must be crushed or the Republic triumphant.'[2]

Frenzied applause breaks from the benches of the Mountain and from the galleries. Frightful yells and cries are heard in all parts of the hall, and the tribune is besieged. Danton tries to make his way into it, but Petion refuses to budge. The tumult does not abate, and the President puts on his hat to intimate that the sitting is suspended. 'You are villains!' shouts Danton, addressing the members of the Right, who reply with cries of 'Down with the Dictator!'

Comparative calm is finally restored, and the Convention listens in succession to Petion, Danton, Boyer-Fonfrède, Lahaye, and Guadet—to whom Marat says, 'Shut up, you carrion!'—to Robespierre, who reads an interminable harangue; to Vergniaud, who refutes Robespierre with some splendid arguments. There was not one of these speeches that did not breathe forth hatred, rage, and revenge. They occupied the whole day; the sitting, which commenced at eight o'clock in the morning, did not terminate until eight o'clock at night, the debate being adjourned till the morrow.[3]

---

[1] *Moniteur* of April 12, 1793.
[2] 'Histoire Parlementaire,' tome xxv., p. 320.
[3] *Moniteur* of April 12, 13, and 14, 1793.

Whilst the chiefs of the Gironde and of the Mountain were engaged in mutual recriminations, which may some day be useful to Citizen Fouquier-Tinville, the Public Prosecutor, the Revolutionary Tribunal was trying a poor devil named Nicolas Luttier, formerly a gunner in the 6th Company, stationed at the Sorbonne. He was accused of having, on March 31, addressed the following words to a group of masons at the corner of the Rue de la Huchette: 'Have you a soul? I have one, but it is for my King, who has always paid me well. He is dead, but there is another who will appear very soon.' Before the tribunal Luttier declared that he did not remember uttering the words attributed to him; that on the day in question he was quite drunk, and that it was not until five hours after his arrival at the Abbaye that he really became conscious of the fact that he was in prison. Having been found guilty, and asked by the President whether he had anything to say before sentence was passed upon him, 'he called the gods to witness that he would never pardon those who condemned him, since he was charged with an action committed whilst he was helplessly drunk.'[1]

He was executed in the Place de la Maison Commune.

Thursday, April 11.—The scenes that took place in the Convention to-day were even more violent than those of yesterday. Of all the newspapers, the *Patriote Français* is the one which gives the most faithful account of the sitting. The following is the report it contains:

'"*Excidat illa dies ævo !*" Such is the wish which every Republican must formulate when the representatives of the people forget the dignity that should clothe them, and set a lamentable example by giving free rein to their passions. During this sitting we have seen the gleam of homicidal blades, and instruments of death have threatened the lives of men whom the nation has declared inviolable. We will not dilate upon the facts which have given rise to this sad occurrence; we would even pass over them in silence, were it not that they may serve as a lesson to our fellow-citizens.

'Some of the sections were insisting upon being admitted to the bar, when Buzot observed that it was a matter of more importance

---

[1] *Bulletin du Tribunal Criminel Révolutionnaire,* Nos. 2 and 3.

to the Assembly to proceed to the nomination of the four Commissioners who were to inquire into the D'Orléans conspiracy in the département de l'Orne. Marat threw doubts upon the culpability of D'Orléans, and regarding only young Égalité and the other Bourbons as the guilty parties, he demanded that a price should be set upon their heads. Lecointe-Puyraveau objected that such measures were impolitic and homicidal, since the enemy held our Commissioners as hostages, and would certainly not fail to make reprisals.

'As all that this deputy said was in refutation of Marat, he was not allowed a quiet hearing, but was constantly interrupted by murmurs of dissent, which afterwards turned to outrageous insults. A frightful tumult then ensued, the members on both sides rushing to the centre of the hall. A member of the Mountain drew a revolver, and Deperret, seeing this, drew his sword. The shouts and yells were deafening, and it was with great difficulty that the President succeeded in restoring calm. Deperret was severely censured, but he exculpated himself, and the Convention proceeded to the next business.

'The Commissioners who are to inquire into the D'Orléans conspiracies were appointed; they are Merlin (of Douai), Cambacérès, Charlier, and Lesage.'[1]

The morning sitting had afforded a comic scene as a prelude to the more dramatic ones of the evening. In the drama now being played before us the grotesque and the horrible are constantly interwoven.

The Decree of the Legislative Assembly, which made cockades compulsory, allowed citizens to wear them of any shape and any stuff, provided they were of the three national colours. The municipality of Paris has *abrogated* this law, and has *decreed* that no other cockades shall be worn than of linen, tricolour on both sides, and that whoever shall wear any of another stuff is to be arrested. In accordance with this Decree of the Conseil de la Commune, Taillefer, member for the Dordogne, has been arrested, insulted, ill treated, and dragged to the guard-house because his cockade, though truly *national*, was not *municipal*. Though Taillefer showed his captors his card as a member of the Convention, it gained him no better treatment. On information to this effect being laid before the Convention, a Decree was passed according to which the Commandant-Général is to issue an Order forbidding the arrest of a representative of the people except when actually caught in the perpetration of a crime.[1]

Friday, April 12.—After a sitting of more than twelve hours' duration, the Convention has decreed that Marat shall be arrested and placed in the Abbaye.

At the opening of the sitting a violent altercation took place between the virtuous Petion and the incorruptible Robespierre, the occasion being the presentation of a report by Poultier, a rather obscure Montagnard.

PETION. I ask for a vote of censure against Poultier.

ROBESPIERRE. And I move a vote of censure against those who protect traitors.

PETION. I shall ask that all traitors and conspirators be punished.

ROBESPIERRE. And their accomplices.

PETION. Yes, their accomplices, and you, too. It is time to put a stop to all this infamy. It is time that traitors and calumniators laid their heads upon the scaffold, and I take upon myself the task of hunting them down.

ROBESPIERRE. Come to the facts.

PETION. I will deal with you first.

Now that the inviolability which protected them has been suppressed, our deputies are perhaps wrong to talk so often of death and the scaffold. But it appears that Petion is not of this way of thinking, for he returned to the charge at the same sitting. 'I shall not be satisfied,' he said, 'until I have seen the men who are trying to ruin Liberty and the Republic lay their heads upon the scaffold.' In the midst of the commotion caused by these words, David, the painter, rushed into the centre of the hall, and, baring his breast, cried to the speaker: 'I call upon you to strike me dead where I stand.'[2]

Petion is succeeded by Guadet, who remains in the tribune

---

[1] *Le Patriote Français*, No. 1,339. This incident does not appear either in the *Moniteur* or in the 'Histoire Parlementaire,' by Buchet and Roux.

[2] *Moniteur* of April 14, 1793.

for two hours and a half.[1] Taller than Vergniaud, but thin
and dark, with a bilious complexion, black beard and black
beady eyes, Guadet is endowed with rare powers of eloquence.
Amongst the orators of the Convention he undoubtedly occupies
the third place, coming immediately after Vergniaud and Danton.
In the midst of the most heated discussions he is able to remain
calm and master of himself.[2] This coolness and presence of
mind, qualities usually excluding ardour and enthusiasm, are
in his case associated with extraordinary impetuosity and
vehemence. No one wields the difficult instrument of sarcasm
with more dexterity, nor is anyone more lavish or bold in the
utterance of bitter epigrams. His denunciations are real dagger-
thrusts.[3]

His speech of April 12 is one of the most remarkable he
ever delivered, and produced a great effect. He did not stoop
to make use of those circumlocutions to which Vergniaud is
so much addicted. Instead of accusing Mr. Pitt, as his colleague
does, he denounced Robespierre; instead of railing against the
agents of England, he showed that the hot-bed of conspiracy
was much nearer home—at the Jacobin Club in the Rue Saint-
Honoré—and concluded by reading an address from the Jacobins
of Paris to their provincial friends. This address was signed
by Marat, and contains the following lines:

'Friends, we are betrayed; up and arm yourselves! The base
treachery of our enemies has at last reached its climax, and, as a
crowning stroke, Dumouriez, their accomplice, is marching on Paris.
But, brethren and friends, these are not your only dangers. Your
greatest enemies are in your midst. It is in the Senate that
parricidal hands are aiming a blow at your hearts. Yes, there is
counter-Revolution in the Government and in the National Convention; it is there that criminal deputies hold the meshes of the web
which they have woven with the help of the despots who are
coming to murder us. There is a cabal directed by the English

[1] Le Patriote Français, No. 1,340.
[2] 'Souvenirs de l'Insurrection Normande dite du Fédéralisme en 1793,'
by Frédéric Vaultier, p. 73 ; 'Essai Historique et Critique sur la Révolution Française,' by M. Paganel, a former member of the Convention,
tome ii., p. 128.
[3] 'Histoire de la Révolution de France,' by Two Friends of Liberty,
tome viii., p. 218.

and other Courts. But already your loyalty and courage are aroused by your indignation. Come, Republicans, to arms, I say !'

' IT IS TRUE !' cried Marat, from his place.

At these words three-fourths of the members present leap to their feet ; the Mountain alone remains immovable. The Right shouts with fury: 'To the Abbaye with Marat ! Impeach him !'

The Friend of the People makes his way to the tribune. The galleries break out into frenzied applause, but the indignation of the majority of his fellow-members seems to have intimidated Marat himself. He tries to parry the blow that threatens him, and invents miserable subterfuges. ' I was chairman of the Jacobin Club,' he says, ' for seven or eight minutes. A document was laid before me, bearing the signature of the secretaries ; I signed it without having read it, and without knowing anything whatever of its contents. It was a resolution of the club, to which, according to custom, I appended my signature, merely to prove that it emanated from the club.'[1]

The debate closed after a speech from Danton, in which he moved that the accusations made against Marat might be referred to a committee, and a reply from Boyer-Fonfrède, who demanded nothing short of impeachment. There was first a sharp struggle for priority between the authors of these two resolutions, and Danton's motion was then negatived by a majority of two-thirds. Lacroix next proposes that Marat be immediately sent to the Abbaye, and that the Committee of Legislation be requested to draw up a report on the charges made. The Friend of the People reappears in the tribune pale and trembling ; he asks that he may be taken to the Jacobin Club under the escort of two gendarmes, in order to advocate peace and prevent a rising. ' We have no fear of any rising,' is the cry by which he is answered. ' Paris will be obedient to the law,' adds the President.[2]

The resolution moved by Lacroix is agreed to, and the sitting, which had commenced at eight o'clock in the morning, adjourned at nine p.m.

---

[1] *Moniteur* of April 14, 1793.   [2] *Le Patriote Français*, No. 1,340.

Proud at having voted for the arrest of Marat, the members of the Gironde hastened off to their suppers without troubling themselves to ascertain whether their decree was being executed or not. As they marched off, leaving the Friend of the People in his seat, a number of the *habitués* of the galleries slid down the columns, and, entering the precincts sacred to deputies only, formed a group round Marat and the Montagnards who, to the number of fifty, had remained with him. The leader was then led to one of the exits, but a sentinel barred the way, and objected to his leaving. The officer on duty, being sent for, came hurrying up with the decree that had just been handed him, but on examination it was found that this document had not been signed either by the President or the Secretaries. 'This is only a worthless scrap of paper,' shouted the by-standers, and losing his head, the officer made no further attempt to stop Marat, who passed out followed by a numerous escort, and made his way to a safe place of concealment.[1]

Saturday, April 13.—A fresh resolution concerning capital punishment is passed at the beginning of the sitting on the motion of Robespierre, supported by Danton. It runs as follows :

The Convention decrees sentence of death against anyone who shall propose to enter into negotiations with any hostile Power that has not formally recognised the independence and sovereignty of the French nation, and the indivisibility and unity of the Republic, based on Liberty and Equality.

After a letter from Marat has been read, in which he declares that he has no intention of obeying the decree of the Convention, since he owes his services to the people, the younger Delaunay presents in the name of the Committee of Legislation a report upon all the charges against the Friend of the People. The report commences with a reproduction of the famous circular signed by Marat, which but yesterday furnished grounds for the attacks upon him. Delaunay has scarcely finished reading it, when several members of the Mountain rise and declare their willingness to append their signatures to that document. 'I

---

[1] *Le Publiciste de la République Française*, No. 169.

move,' says David, 'that this address be laid on the table, and that all Patriots be allowed to sign it.' Following on David, Thirion,[1] Dubois-Crancé, and Camille Desmoulins rush to the table, and after them some hundred of their colleagues. It is observed that Danton does not leave his seat. As for Robespierre, he advances with measured step towards the table, but returns to his place without having signed the document.[2] During the whole of this scene the Right and the Centre remain silent and motionless, the galleries, on the contrary, applauding frenetically.

Granet moves that the Address of the Jacobin Club be printed and sent to the provinces and the armies; his motion is supported by Vergniaud and Lacaze. Gensonné, too, gives it his support, and demands the immediate convocation of the primary assemblies. The Mountain, which has its reasons for desiring that the nation shall not be consulted, sees the mistake it has made, and again the majority of its members make their way towards the table, but this time in order to erase their signatures.[3]

The debate on Gensonné's motion having been adjourned until Monday, the 15th, Delaunay resumed the reading of his report, which includes a *résumé* of all the articles in Marat's journal, demanding 250,000 heads, and asking for a dictator, a triumvirate, or a military tribune.[4] Each of these quotations was hailed with applause by the Mountain and the galleries. Delaunay concluded by proposing the impeachment of Marat. Hereupon the galleries became furious, and now commenced a scene of uproar that lasted for quite twelve hours. During all this time a few moments' calm could only be obtained whilst Marat's partisans were speaking; for the remainder of the period nothing could be heard but terrific shouting and sanguinary threats—in fact, it was nothing short of an open revolt of the galleries against national representation.[5]

---

[1] Thirion, member for the Moselle, and not *Thuriot*, as Mortimer-Ternaux erroneously states, tome viii., p. 134.

[2] *Le Patriote Français*, No. 1,341.   [3] *Le Moniteur* of April 17, 1793.

[4] The *Moniteur* did not reproduce Delaunay's report, although the Convention ordered the same to be printed. See the interesting notice on the younger Delaunay by M. Bougler in tome ii. of his 'Biographie des Députés de l'Anjou.'

[5] An unpublished letter of Dufriche-Valazé, dated April 14, 1793. See

It is finally decided that an open vote shall be taken, and that the division lists shall be printed and sent to the departments together with Marat's letter.

Worn out with fatigue, the President calls upon the Vice-President or an ex-President to relieve him. The ex-President Lacroix and the Vice-President Thuriot insolently declare that they cannot preside over deliberations that menace Liberty. The Convention is obliged to ask the Secretary, Garan-Coulon, to take the chair.[1]

The voting begins at ten o'clock in the evening, a large number of members giving the reasons for the manner in which they record their votes. Amongst those who are against the impeachment there are some who see in Marat the saviour and the father of his country; others ask that he be presented with a civic wreath; others, again, suggest that a statue be raised to the Friend of the People. As each vote is recorded the galleries break out into prolonged applause or hooting, according as it coincides with, or is contrary to, their opinion.

The voting was not over until seven in the morning, and the result was as follows: The number of voters was 360; 220 voted for the impeachment, 92 against, and 7 for an adjournment, whilst 41 refused to vote at all.[2]

The impeachment was formally pronounced, and the Convention rose after having sat for twenty-two hours.

Saturday, April 14.—On the morrow of this extraordinary sitting, the Parisians were treated to an entertainment of a different kind—the *Fête* of Hospitality.

Upon the entry of the Austrians into Liège, about a hundred of the inhabitants of that city took refuge in Paris. The Conseil-Général de la Commune having placed at their disposal the Salle de l'Égalité, in the Maison de Ville, in which to hold

---

[1] 'La Démogogie en 1793 à Paris,' a work by Beaulieu, edited by C. A. Dauban. *Le Patriote Français*, No. 1,341.

[1] This incident is not mentioned either in the *Moniteur* or in the 'Histoire Parlementaire,' by Buchez and Roux. *Le Patriote Français*, No. 1,341.

[2] M. de Barante (tome iii., p. 39) is inexact in his figures of this division, giving the number of those who voted against the impeachment as 132 instead of 92. Louis Blanc (tome viii., p. 280) is also wrong in giving the total number of voters as 367. See 'Archives,' 269, W. 16, dossier Marat.

their meetings and to deposit their archives, formal possession was taken of this *locale* on Sunday. Deputations from every constituted body set out from the Place de la Bastille, and went to meet the Liégeois at the Porte Saint-Martin, which had been fixed upon as a rallying-point. The following was the order of the procession :

Hussars of Liberty ; banner : '*Down with Tyrants!*'

Mounted gendarmes ; banner : '*Hospitality.*'

Sappers, gunners, drummers.

The Legions with their standards.

Declaration of the Rights of Man.

Political clubs.

Judges, Magistrates, and Commissioners of Police.

A bust of Brutus.

The Revolutionary Tribunal.

Judicial bodies.

The fasces of each department.

The department of Paris.

The Revolutionary Vigilance Committee of each section.

Bands.

Statue of Liberty.

The Electoral Body.

The Corporation of Paris.

The Corporation of the Tenth of August.

A model of the Bastille made from stones taken from the fortress, and presented by the Patriot Palloy.

The Tribunal of the Nation.

The Executive Council.

The Book of the Law.

The Convention.

Banner bearing the words '*Tyrants shall pass away, but Nations are Eternal.*'

A tablet bearing the names of the killed and wounded on the Tenth of August.

The widows and children of those who died for the defence of Liberty.

Light Cavalry ; banner : '*The French Republic, One and Indivisible.*'[1]

[1] *Chronique de Paris*, No. 105.

When the procession reached the Porte Saint-Martin, where the municipal officers of Liège, wearing their scarves of office, and guarding a chariot laden with the archives of their city, stood in waiting, a salvo of artillery rent the air. The procession then continued on its way to the Maison Commune escorted by an immense crowd. Whenever one or other of the numerous bands ceased playing their patriotic and martial airs, the soldiers and the crowd sang a hymn especially composed for the occasion by Dorat-Cubières, to the air of the *Marseillaise*.[1]

Monday, April 15.—The trial of Rouxel-Blanchelande, formerly Maréchal de Camp and Governor of the French Windward Islands, after lasting for four days, terminated on Monday, the 15th, at seven in the morning. The accused, who was charged with having favoured the counter-Revolutionary party in St. Domingo, was condemned to die, although no absolute proofs could be brought against him, and his innocence had been fully established by Trouson-Ducoudray in a speech of which the *Bulletin du Tribunal Criminel Révolutionnaire* speaks in the following terms: 'Trouson-Ducoudray's defence of his client was as remarkable for its clearness as for its eloquence, and refuted each count in the indictment *seriatim*. We will not dwell further upon the details of this interesting address, lest in dissecting it we might mar its beauty. We will content ourselves with saying that for three whole hours the immense audience (although it was past midnight) listened to the orator with admiration and in deep silence.'[2]

Rouxel-Blanchelande was executed the same day in the Place de la Réunion at three in the afternoon. He was fifty-six years old. The *Révolutions de Paris* contained the following account of his death:

'The people confirmed by their applause the sentence of the Revolutionary Tribunal against Blanchelande, who was guillotined on Monday last in the Place de la Réunion. The stoicism of the counter-Revolutionist made little impression upon the crowd. It is

---

[1] The whole of this hymn is reproduced in the *Révolutions de Paris*, tome xvi., p. 164.

[2] *Bulletin du Tribunal*, No. 10.   Transported as a Royalist after the 10th of Fructidor, Trouson-Ducoudray died at Sinnamari on June 23, 1798.

a blot on humanity that so many apostles and martyrs are to be found in the cause of Royalism.'[1]

The Revolutionary Tribunal need have no fear of being left idle; the Convention will see that it is well provided with work. At the opening of the sitting on the 15th it sent for trial General d'Harville, General Boucher, the Army Commissioner Barneville, and several subaltern officers.[2]

Two days ago it was Marat's turn. Can it be that Brissot and his friends will have their turn to-day? The delegates of the majority of the sections of Paris, with the Mayor at their head, are admitted to the bar of the Assembly. Rousselin,[3] their spokesman, is a young man of about twenty, an out-and-out Jacobin, and one of Danton's satellites. He reads a petition signed by thirty-five out of the forty-eight sections and by the Conseil-Général de la Commune. It aims at the expulsion of the following twenty-two deputies: Brissot, Guadet, Vergniaud, Gensonné, Grangeneuve, Buzot, Barbaroux, Salle, Birotteau, Pontécoulant, Petion, Lanjuinais, Valazé, Hardy,[4] Lehardi,[5] Louvet, Gorsas, Fauchet, Lanthénas, Lasource, Izarn-Valady, and Chambon.[6]

Boyer-Fonfrède made a most admirable remark. 'If modesty,' he cried, 'were not a duty rather than a virtue in a public man, I should consider it an insult that my name has been omitted from the list of honour which has just been laid before you.' 'All! all!' cry three-fourths of the members, and the whole Assembly, with the exception of the ninety-two friends of Marat, Danton, and Robespierre, rise from their seats.

---

[1] *Révolutions de Paris*, tome xvi., p. 166.

[2] *Moniteur* of April 18, 1793.

[3] Alexandre Rousselin-Corbeau, called de Saint-Albin, was born in 1773, and died in Paris on June 15, 1847. He was one of the founders and principal editors of the *Constitutionnel* under the Restoration; he also wrote a life of Lazare Hoche. His son, Hortensius de Saint-Albin (1805—1878), was a deputy for the Sarthe from 1837 to 1849, a conseiller of the Cour d'Appel of Paris, and author of 'Poésies Lyriques' and 'Tablettes d'un Rimeur, Contes, Apologues et Anecdotes.' Another son of Rousselin, Philippe de Saint-Albin (1810—1879), was private librarian to the Empress Eugénie.

[4] Antoine François Hardy, member for the Seine Inférieure.

[5] Pierre Lehardi, member for the Morbihan.

[6] Louis Blanc (tome viii., p. 281) is wrong in bringing the presentation of the petition against the twenty-two members into the sitting of April 14; it was not presented until the 15th.

The debate on the petition presented by the sections of Paris is adjourned till the morrow.

The majority—a considerable majority—still belongs to the Girondists; but what a deal of ground they have lost during the past month! On March 10 only four sections opposed them: neither Pache nor the Conseil-Général de la Commune dared then to take sides with their enemies. On April 15 they have thirty-five sections and the whole of the Commune against them: even Pache—*papa Pache*, as he is called[1]—has no hesitation in signing the denunciatory address before a full sitting of the Convention.[2]

One last feature—and not the least curious one—will complete the picture of the physiognomy of Paris during this first fortnight of April. I borrow it from the *Courrier Français*: 'Peace still reigns in this great city. Everyone is at his usual work. The gaming-houses, the dancing-saloons, the theatres, and all the haunts of pleasure are open and as busily frequented as in the most quiet times. Our capital resembles the smiling, fertile plains that lie at the foot of the volcanoes of Etna and Vesuvius. What is the cause of this feeling of safety? Philosophy stands lost in wonder, but patriotism sheds bitter tears.'[3]

[1] See the study on Pache, by M. Edouard Gibert, 1888.

[2] At its sitting of April 20 the Convention passed the following resolution: 'The National Convention brands as a calumny the petition presented to it on the 15th of this month in the name of thirty-five sections, and which was adopted by the Conseil-Général de la Commune.' Is it not incredible that towards the conclusion of this very sitting a complimentary vote was accorded the municipal officers by 143 against 6? The 'incomprehensible Girondists,' as Beaulieu calls them, had all gone home, leaving the field free to their enemies.

[3] *Courrier Français*, No. 95. 1793.

CHAPTER LXV.

Saturday, April 20, 1793.

BENEATH my windows the news-boys are shouting out the
'*Latest Sentences of the Revolutionary Tribunal!*' It has been
a good day for Fouquier-Tinville. Two trials, and death
sentences in both. In the first case heard, Antoine Jean de
Clinchamp, the former incumbent of Clisson, in Brittany, was
charged with having attempted to publish a pamphlet of
fourteen pages bearing the title 'To the Friends of Truth.'
In the second case, M. Gabriel du Guiny, a naval Lieutenant and
also a native of Brittany, was found guilty of having gone to
Brussels in January, 1792, and thence to Spa to take the
waters. '*Ah, mon Dieu!*' cried the pastor, on hearing the
conclusions of the Public Prosecutor. '*Much obliged!*' said
the naval officer.[1] I try to resume my reading, which has
been interrupted by the shouts of the boys. On my table lies
the last number of the *Mercure Français.* It contains an
article by La Harpe on M. de Florian's 'Fables,'[2] and I really
do not know who astonishes me more—the poet or the critic;
the poet, who in the year of grace 1793 publishes a book of
fables, which, with their inoffensive and playful wit, form

---

[1] *Bulletin du Tribunal Criminel Révolutionnaire*, Nos. 13, 14, 15. 'In
going to the scaffold,' said the *Bulletin*, 'Du Guiny saluted several of his
acquaintances in the Rue Saint-Honoré with a jovial air. He betrayed
not the least agitation during the whole of the journey.'

[2] Florian's 'Fables' appeared in 1793, and not in 1792, as stated by
Sainte-Beuve in his 'Causeries du Lundi,' tome iii., p. 187 See No. 87
of the *Mercure Français* for 1793, and the list of poetical publications of
1793 in the *Almanach des Muses* for 1794.

such a striking contrast to the terrible realities of the present hour; or the critic, who weighs so nicely and with such marvellous *sang-froid* the rhyme and metre of the poet. La Harpe chose April 15, the very day on which the Convention was discussing Marat's impeachment, for publishing his very long and intensely didactic article. I am not sure whether I do not prefer the more brief and pertinent remarks of another Academician, the Abbé Morellet,[1] who, in speaking a few days ago of the 'Fables' of the Chevalier de Florian, thus summed up his impressions: 'Placed before us at the very height of the Terror, on the morrow of the establishment of the Revolutionary Tribunal, this charming book, with its bright and happy verses, its pure and harmless morals, seems to me like a lamb that has strayed from the fold and fallen amongst wolves.'

But pray, my dear Chevalier, do not commit such an error again. Do you think that you are still in the reign of Louis XVI., or that of Numa Pompilius? Fouquier-Tinville, not *Florianet*,[2] holds the public ear to-day.

---

[1] André Morellet (1727—1819) was elected a member of the Académie Française in 1785. He maintained a very brave attitude during the Revolution, and left behind some 'Mémoires' of great interest, which were published in 1821 as 'Mémoires sur le Dix-huitième Siècle et sur la Révolution.'

[2] Florian had received the name of Florianet from Voltaire in 1765, when but ten years old. The most inoffensive of poets found no favour in the eyes of the Revolution. He was arrested on the 27th of Messidor, year II. (July 15, 1794), and taken to the prison of Port-Libre. In the *Journal des Événements arrivés à Port-Libre, ci-devant Port-Royal*, we read: '*27th of Messidor.*—The Chevalier de Florian, the author of "Numa Pompilius," "Estelle," and other works, was brought here this morning. He tells us that Parny, another of our most charming poets, had also been arrested, but he does not know where he has been taken.' In a note on p. 464 of tome ix. of his 'Cours de Littérature,' La Harpe gives the following information concerning Florian's death: 'Though he escaped the scaffold in Thermidor, he only passed from his prison to his death-bed, being carried off in a few days by a fever contracted amidst the horrors of his situation. During his state of delirium his sensitive imagination, that had received an irremediable shock, constantly conjured up all the monsters of the Revolution. He will ever be accounted amongst the number of its victims, for in the eyes of God and man it killed him as surely as if it had sent him to the scaffold.'

CHAPTER LXVI.

THE TRIUMPH OF MARAT.

Thursday, April 25, 1793.

'PEOPLE, to-morrow your incorruptible defender will appear before the Revolutionary Tribunal.'[1] This '*Notice to the Reader*,' published the day before yesterday by Marat's journal, and placarded and hawked all over the capital, produced the desired effect. A large number of *sans-culottes* spent the whole night in the hall where the tribunal sits,[2] and yesterday morning before eight o'clock every nook and corner in the Palais de Justice, as well as all the approaches, was thronged with an immense mob yelling the *Carmagnole* and the *Marseillaise*, and shouting, '*Vive Marat!*' '*Long live the Friend of the People!*' '*Down with the Rolandists!*' '*Death to Brissotins!*'

When Marat entered the hall, accompanied by some of his colleagues in the Convention, and escorted by a colonel of the National Guard, a captain in the navy, and several administrators and municipal officers who had passed the night with him in the Conciergerie,[3] he was hailed with thunders of applause.

The whole court, together with the Public Prosecutor, Citizen Fouquier - Tinville, received him with marks of the greatest deference. Was it not Roussillon, one of the judges, who on Monday evening had spoken as follows in the Grey Friars' Club ?—' Have no fear for his life. They speak of

---

[1] No. 176 of *Le Publiciste de la République Française*, by Marat, the Friend of the People and a member of the Convention.

[2] 'Jean-Paul Marat, l'Ami du Peuple,' by Alfred Bougeart, tome ii., p. 219.

[3] Alfred Bougeart, *op. cit.*

arresting him, but I call upon you to cut down anyone who dares to lay a sacrilegious hand upon the Friend of the People. Let the people bring us also the whole of the Girondist faction, and you will see how many will have their heads on their shoulders on leaving the court.'[1]

Hardly had he entered, when Marat said to his judges : 'Citizens, I who appear before you am no guilty man, but an apostle and martyr of Liberty ; it is but a group of factionists and plotters who have brought an accusation against me.'[2] From these first words of his it was easy to see that this was no prisoner appearing before his judges, but a sovereign at the head of his subjects ; it was evident that we were to be present, not at the trial, but at the triumph of Marat.

The Friend of the People was dressed with a certain amount of care. He had laid aside the long overcoat that he usually wore, and was attired in a smarter-fitting frock-coat that had once been green, and that was adorned with a collar of shabby ermine. In honour of this great day he had also left off the greasy cloth he always wears tied round his head ; his brow was left free for wreaths and flowers.

After the reading of the indictment, the witnesses were called. The chief point in the accusation was based upon an article in the *Patriote Français*, and upon the demand of the Public Prosecutor, the deputy Brissot was invited to appear in court. This decision of the tribunal was hailed with applause, and it was Marat himself who asked the public to remain silent. Since he was really presiding over the whole proceedings, it was only right that he should maintain order. A few more witnesses were heard, but only questioned concerning the article in the *Patriote*, and on points entirely irrelevant to the matter at issue.[3]

---

[1] 'J. P. Brissot to his Constituents,' p. 26.
[2] *Bulletin du Tribunal Criminel Révolutionnaire*, No. 16.
[3] **The** following is the article which appeared in the *Patriote Français* on April 17, 1793 (and not on the 16th, as erroneously stated in the *Bulletin du Tribunal Révolutionnaire*) : ' A sad-event has just shown the Anarchists the fatal fruits of their pernicious doctrines. An Englishman, whose name I shall not disclose, left his country because he hated its Monarchical rule, and came to France in the hope of finding true liberty ; he found, however, only a veil, hiding the hideous features of Anarchy. Heartbroken by this spectacle, he decided to commit suicide, and left behind

The President announced that, in answer to the letter written by him to the President of the Convention asking for the attendance of Brissot, the Convention passed to the next business; he then called upon Marat to speak. The address of the Friend of the People was but one long philippic against his colleagues, and each of his sentences was drowned in applause.

The questions submitted to the jury were in the following form:

1. Do you find that in the journals styled the *Friend of the People* and the *Publiciste* the author incited his readers (*a*) to pillage and murder; (*b*) to attack the sovereignty of the people; (*c*) to degrade and dissolve the National Convention?

2. Is Jean Paul Marat the writer of the articles published in those papers?

3. In writing these articles, did Jean Paul Marat have criminal and counter-Revolutionary intentions?[1]

The jury retired to consider their verdict, and returned after an absence of forty-five minutes.

Citizen Dumont, the foreman, gave his opinion in the following terms:

'I have carefully examined the passages quoted from the papers edited by Marat. In order to enter into their full meaning, I have not lost sight of the well-known temperament of the accused, or of the troubled times during which he wrote. I cannot for a moment entertain the idea that the brave defender of the rights of the people had criminal and counter-Revolutionary intentions. It is difficult to repress our just indignation when we behold our country betrayed on all sides, and I declare that I have found nothing in the writings of Marat which might be construed into the crime with which he is charged.'[2]

The other jurymen were unanimous in declaring that the charges had not been proved.

him the following words, which he had placed on paper before his death: " I had come to France to enjoy liberty, but Marat has killed it. Anarchy is even more cruel than despotism. I cannot endure the sad spectacle of imbecility and cruelty triumphing over talent and virtue." '

[1] *Bulletin*, No. 18. [2] *Ibid.*, No. 17.

After this declaration, Fouquier-Tinville asked that Jean Paul Marat might be acquitted of the charge brought against him, and immediately set at liberty.

Acceding to this demand, the tribunal pronounces his acquittal, and the court immediately re-echoes with frenzied applause, which is taken up by the crowd that throngs the corridors and court-yards of the palace. A wreath of oak-leaves is placed on Marat's brow, and everyone is eager to get near the hero and embrace him. The municipal officers, the National Guards, the gunners, the gendarmes, and the hussars on duty in the court, fearing for his safety amidst this impetuous crowd, form a double square, and place him in the centre.[1] The procession starts, and on reaching the top of the grand staircase makes a halt in order to enable the citizens assembled on the steps and in the courtyard to gaze upon the Friend of the People;[2] but the Friend of the People is a little man, and it is difficult to get a glimpse of him. A judge's arm-chair is passed along over the heads of the crowd, and two strong men, taking up the hero, place him on this improvised throne. Here, surrounded by an applauding multitude that weeps for very joy—here, in the palace of Saint Louis and but a few yards from the Sainte-Chapelle, sits Marat, the filthy bandit, his shiny face wearing a hideous grin, and his greasy head wreathed with flowers!

On its arrival at the Quai de l'Horloge, the procession is met with an immense shout of ' *Vive Marat!* ' *Vive le Peuple!* ' *Vive la République!* As far as the eye can see, both banks of the Seine, the streets, and the bridges are packed with people. The arm-chair in which Marat is still seated advances slowly, borne along upon this human tide. Now and then a hitch occurs, but a way is made, and the hero goes on, proudly triumphant. To the shouts that salute him Marat replies with smiles that make him appear more hideous still. He bows his head all covered with the flowers showered upon him, writhes in his chair like one seized with epilepsy, and obligingly lays bare his breast. He stretches out his arms as if to embrace the people, and places his hand on his heart—the heart of Marat! Here and

[1] *Le Publiciste de la République Française*, No. 181.   [2] *Ibid.*

there deputations from the clubs and the sections stop the procession, delivering speeches, and offering wreaths to the object of their worship. It took more than one hour to get from the Palais de Justice to the Pont Neuf. In the Rue de la Monnaie the women of the Halles literally buried Marat in flowers. The poor man, blinded and suffocated, shook himself like a rat, and from his greasy hair and his dirty ermine collar there fell a shower of lilac and roses.

It was in the Rue Saint-Honoré that the ever-increasing enthusiasm reached its height, the pavements, the roadway, the steps of the churches, and all the windows being filled with an expectant crowd waving ribbons, garlands, and bouquets. The Friend of the People must have received enough flowers to-day to crown the 270,000 heads he asked for in his journal. And whilst the earth gave its flowers, and Spring emptied its basket at the feet of Marat, the sun lent its rays, and added to the brilliancy of this strange *fête*.

When, overcome by heat and fatigue, with throbbing temples, and almost mad with rage, I saw this shameful procession advance towards me, I cursed not only the witless people, but I cursed the pitiless sky that stretched its blue vault over Marat's head like a triumphal canopy. The procession came nearer and nearer, and now almost touched me. I wished to close my eyes, but by some irresistible force I was compelled to keep them open. I again fixed them on the blue vault above me, and from this heaven, which but a few moments ago I had cursed in my anger, there seemed to descend a crowd of priests and prelates, of maidens and men; in them I thought I recognised the martyrs of the Carmes and of Saint-Firmin, of the Abbaye and the Force. With livid faces and extended hands they laid bare their wounds beneath their blood-stained shrouds, and formed an immense cloud that hung over the pomp of this flower-bedecked chair and of this rose-crowned head. Meanwhile, fresh blossoms continued to rain down from the windows, but they no longer reached Marat, upon whose brow there now fell only the blood that dropped from the wounds of his victims. The shouts of ' *Vive Marat!* ' had not ceased, but they seemed lost upon the air, and from the heavens above came the avenging cry of ' *September !* How long this vision lasted I know not, but when I once more became conscious of my surroundings the procession had passed, the sun's rays beat down upon the flower-strewn pavement, and silver clouds were flitting like pale phantoms across the azure sky.

It was five o'clock when the Convention was informed that Marat and his procession were at the door of the Assembly. The Girondist Lasource, who was in the chair, wished to adjourn the sitting, but the Mountain and the galleries protested against this proceeding. The space before the bar was already invaded, and the sapper Rocher, who was the gaoler of Louis XVI.,[1] took upon himself to speak. ' Citizen President, we bring you back our brave Marat, and shall be able to confound all his enemies. I have already defended him at Lyons ; I will defend him here, and whoever takes the life of Marat must take mine first.[2] We ask, Citizen President, for permission to march past the Assembly.'

This permission is granted, and a band of National Guards and municipal officers wearing their sashes, followed by crowds of men, women, and children, rush into the hall amidst cries of ' *Vive la République !* ' *Vive Marat !* ' *Long live the Friend of the People !* A part of the procession even overflows upon the benches reserved for members, and the hall re-echoes with reiterated shouts of joy. Borne aloft on the arms of the National Guards, and his brow adorned with a wreath of laurel, Marat at length enters, and his appearance arouses an enthusiasm that almost reaches delirium. His colleagues of the Mountain receive him with open arms, and he places in their hands the wreaths with which he is laden. He is carried to the tribune, but the plaudits for a long time debar him from speaking. At length he begs for silence. ' Legislators,' he says, ' I have been

---

[1] ' Rocher, the gaoler of the Temple Tower, used to station himself on the threshold of the last door whenever the Royal Family were going down into the garden. He would have a long pipe in his mouth, and as the Princesses passed him, he would blow a cloud of tobacco-smoke in their faces. The soldiers on duty were highly amused at this, and indulged in all kinds of insulting remarks.'—' Mémoires pour servir à l'Histoire de l'Assemblée Constituante et de la Révolution de 1789,' by the Marquis de Ferrières, tome iii., p. 274.

[2] *Le Publiciste de la République Française*, No. 181.

basely accused, but a legal acquittal has established my innocence. I bring you back a pure heart, and I shall continue to
defend the rights of the individual, the citizen, and the people
with all the energy Heaven has given me.'[1]

The applause is renewed and prolonged for several minutes.
From all parts come shouts of ' *Vive Marat!* ' *Vive la
Montagne!* ' The deputies of the Extreme Left wave their hats.
The Patriots who escorted Marat throw their red caps into the
air. The march-past is resumed, and in the cries of the mob,
in the gestures and in the faces of the *sans-culottes* who bring
back in triumph the man they sent for trial, the Girondists may
read their death-warrant.[2]

' Michelet has committed only one serious error in his " Histoire
de la Révolution." ' It is M. Jules Simon who, in a *Notice* upon the
historian, presented Michelet with this certificate of precision.
Only one error! As a matter of fact, the work of the celebrated
historian contains a host of errors, the enumeration of which would
require several volumes. I will quote one—and a not unimportant
one—which I find in the narration of Marat's trial. ' To this
tribunal,' says Michelet (tome v., pp. 484-86), ' composed of
Robespierrists and Maratists, the Girondists had sent Marat.
Robespierre presided over this court in the person of his pliable
friend Herman. Dumas, the Vice-President, was also one of his
subordinates. His fanatical admirer, Topino-Lebrun, the painter,
sat in the tribunal only to carry out his will. . . . His printer
Nicolas was a juryman. . . . Neither must Antonelle Dobsent nor
Souberbielle be forgotten.' Of all the personages quoted here by
Michelet, not a single one sat in judgment upon Marat; in the
month of April, 1793, not a single one sat in the Revolutionary
Tribunal either as a judge or a juryman. According to the official
report, the tribunal was composed as follows on April 24, 1793—
President: Jacques Bernard Marie Montané; judges: Étienne
Foucault and Antoine Roussillon; jurymen: Dumont, Coppins,

----

[1] *Moniteur* of April 26, 1793.

[2] ' And this man is borne in triumph into the heart of that very Convention which he had outraged! He reappears in its midst as a conqueror! It is Danton who calls this *a fine day!* It is Osselin who asks
that this scandalous acquittal be published in the *Bulletin!* And the
Assembly is dumb, closing its eyes to prevarication, to violation of the
law, and to the outrage offered to the national representation!'—'J. P.
Brissot to his Constituents,' p. 26.

Jourdenil, Fallot, Ganney, Leroy, Brochet, Duplain, Saintex, and Chretién.'—'Archives' 269, W. 16, dossier Marat.

Though precision may be a quality in which the historians of the Revolution do not excel, it should at least be found in those writers who have limited their subject, and devoted monographs either to a man or to a particular episode.   But unfortunately it is not so.   Let us take, for example, Alfred Bougeart, who wrote a life of 'Marat, l'Ami du Peuple,' in two volumes (Paris, 1865); he designates as liars and calumniators those who accuse Marat of having asked for 270,000 heads, and declares that this figure is a pure invention, and not to be found in any of Marat's writings or speeches.   We need, however, only turn to the *Moniteur* to find it.   In the report of the sitting of the Convention of October 24, 1792, we read :

'N. I move that note be taken of the information given by those who know Marat.   I know that one member of this Assembly has heard Marat say that before peace is restored 270,000 heads must fall.

'Vermont. I declare that Marat used those words to me.

'Marat. Yes ; that is my opinion, and I repeat it.'—*Moniteur* of 1792, No. 300 ; 'Histoire Parlementaire de la Révolution Française,' by Buchez and Roux, tome xix., p. 379.

CHAPTER LXVII.

THE MARRIAGE OF MME. RÉCAMIER.

Saturday, April 27, 1793.

FATE frequently takes pleasure in bringing about strange contrasts. On Wednesday, April 24, at the very hour when Marat was enjoying his triumph in the streets of Paris, there was celebrated the marriage of Mlle. Juliette Bernard and M. Récamier, one of the principal bankers of the capital. In the evening a few friends met, in response to M. Bernard's invitation, in his mansion in the Rue des Saints-Pères.[1] Having somewhat recovered from my agitation of the afternoon, I made my way thither about ten o'clock. As I entered the *salon*, where I found Tassin, the banker, and his brother,[2] M. Lémontey, an ex-member of the Legislative Assembly,[3] M. de La Harpe, and a few others, the beautiful Juliette came forward to greet me. In the Rue Saint-Honoré I had that day beheld crime in all its ugliness, and now I gazed upon innocence in all its beauty.

Juliette is but fifteen years of age.[4] Chestnut hair falling in natural ringlets, a high and noble brow, a delicately-shaped

---

[1] 'Souvenirs et Correspondance Tirés des Papiers de Mme. Récamier,' by Mme. Charles Lenormant, her niece, tome i.

[2] Louis Daniel Tassin, a banker and a deputy for the Third Estate of the city of Paris in the States-General, was an officer in the battalion of the Filles-Saint-Thomas, of which his brother, Tassin de Lestang, was Commandant. The two brothers Tassin were brought before the Revolutionary Tribunal and guillotined on the same day, May 2, 1794.

[3] Lémontey (1762—1826), a member of the Académie Française, was, like Mme. Récamier, a native of Lyons.

[4] Mme. Récamier (Jeanne Françoise Julie Adélaide Bernard) was born at Lyons on December 3, 1777.

nose, a small mouth with cherry lips, two rows of pearly teeth, a complexion of incomparable brilliancy, a well-poised head, a perfect figure, a graceful bearing, and, above all, a frank, open countenance, rendered irresistibly attractive by the sweetness of its smile—such is the creature now called Mme. Récamier, so fairy-like, so ethereal, so divinely fair, that she awakened within us thoughts of the angel of reconciliation and peace. As she crossed the *salon*, M. Lémontey recalled to my mind what Saint-Simon in his 'Mémoires' says of the Duchesse de Bourgogne: 'The graces spring up beneath her tread and at each of her movements. She walks like a goddess on the clouds.' '" *Et vera incessu patuit dea*,"' said M. Récamier, who loves to quote the lines of Horace and Virgil.[1] M. Lémontey is not the man to be outdone in this kind of thing, and at once took up the ball.

> '" Non Beræ vobis, non hæc Rhœteia . . .
> Est Dorycli conjux ; divini signa decoris,
> Ardentisque notate oculos ; qui spiritus illi,
> Qui voltus vocisve sonus, vel gressus eunti."'

Later in the evening, M. Récamier, who had left the room for a few moments, returned with his hands full of lilies, and, placing them in his young wife's lap, said to us :

> '" Manibus date lilia plenis."'

'No, no,' said Mme. Bernard, in a deep, sad voice ; 'no flowers to-day.' I then noticed for the first time that Mme. Bernard's *salons*, usually covered with flowers,[2] contained not a single one. 'Mme. Bernard is right,' observed M. Récamier. 'All flowers belong to Marat to-day,' he added in an undertone, as if he feared that this hideous name might poison the atmosphere of purity and honour that we were happy to breathe for a few short moments.

M. Lémontey and I left together. 'You see,' he said to me, 'that whatever we do, and however careful we may be, there

---

[1] 'Souvenirs et Correspondance,' etc., tome i.
[2] 'Salons Politiques de Paris après la Terreur,' by Louis Lacour, p. 78.

is no family gathering, no meeting of friends, that the spectre of the Revolution does not disturb. In vain did our worthy friend summon the shade of gentle Virgil, and conjure up his smiling pictures. There must have come into the minds of us all those other lines, in which the poet seems to have given a prophetic description of the monsters whom hell has engendered and Paris has crowned :

> ' " Tristius haud illis monstrum, nec saevior ulla
> Pestis, et ira deum Stygiis sese extulit undis." '

CHAPTER LXVIII.

Tuesday, April 30, 1793.

THE first pardon signed by Louis XVI. was that of Claude Lazowski,[1] who served in a cavalry regiment, and had been condemned to death for having struck one of his officers.[2] He was the son of a Pole who had come to France as a follower of King Stanislas. Whilst his brother, appointed in 1784 to one of the four inspectorships of commerce created by M. de Calonne, did not feel himself absolved by the Revolution from his debt of gratitude, and displayed, after the Tenth of August, intense devotion to his former patron, the Duc de la Rochefoucauld-Liancourt, Claude Lazowski took part in the worst excesses, brawling in the clubs, and being one of the first to wear the livery of *sans-culottism*. By following this line of conduct he soon became Commandant of the gunners of the Finistère section.[3]

It was he who on June 20 had one of the cannon carried into an apartment of the Tuileries—the Salle des Suisses.

---

[1] His name is found in contemporary newspapers under the following forms : Lazouski, Lajouski, Laziouski, Latiouski, Lasouski, Lasosky, etc.

[2] 'Anecdotes relatives à quelques Personnes et à plusieurs Évènements Remarquables de la Révolution,' by the Conventionalist Harmand, p. 90.

[3] Mme. Roland, in her 'Mémoires,' has written some very fine pages on Lazowski. On the whole her remarks are correct, but she has allowed a few errors to creep into them. She has, for example, put under one head matters concerning the two Lazowskis, and has made the *protégé* of the Duc de la Rochefoucauld-Liancourt the hero of the Tenth of August. The younger Lacretelle, in his ' Dix Années d'Épreuves pendant la Révolution' (pp. 67, 110), has exposed this error, which he was fully competent to do, having been honoured in his youth with the friendship of M. de la Rochefoucauld.

On the Tenth of August we find him at the head of the attacking party. On September 2 he was at Orleans with Fournier, the American. He shares with Fournier and Bécart, Commandant of the Popincourt battalion, the honour of leading the expedition which took part in the massacres of Versailles, and in the butchery of the fifty-three prisoners of the Haute-Cour.[1] In the month of March last he was one of the ring-leaders of the plot which aimed at the assassination of the principal members of the Right. He was ordered to be arrested, but the Girondists were weak enough to allow the order to remain unexecuted. Since then we have seen him wandering about the streets with a wild, dissipated, and even murderous look on his face[2]—an object of such intense horror to all honest people, and even to his own accomplices, that one of the demagogical papers could not refrain from inserting the following significant confession amidst the praises it showered upon him :

'In view of the services rendered by Lazowski to the Revolution, it were unavailing to reproach the hero with venality that could perhaps be proved, and with other faults of character too often found in great men. Great excesses necessarily accompany great qualities. Let us deplore human weakness, and let us not be ungrateful towards those of our fellow-citizens who have deserved well of their country on those decisive occasions when the ordinary mortal possessing neither vice nor virtue contents himself with bewailing those national misfortunes which he feels unable to minimise.'[3]

This bandit, this outlaw, died at Issy[4] from the effects of a fever brought on by drink and debauchery.[5] Robespierre

---

[1] On p. 326 of Mme. Roland's 'Mémoires' we read : 'Lazowski's exploits date from September 2, from the day when he became actively engaged in a massacre of the priests of Saint-Firmin, in the Finistère section, which was his own.' There is a double error here. On September 2 Lazowski was not in Paris, but in Orleans. The seminary of Saint-Firmin was in the Sans-Culottes section, and not in that of Finistère ; it was situated in the Rue Saint-Victoire.

[2] 'Mémoires de Mme. Roland,' p. 326.

[3] Révolutions de Paris, tome xvi., p. 265.

[4] Mme. Roland makes him die at Vaugirard, but the Révolutions de Paris, tome xvi., p. 265, says that he died at Issy ; the latter statement is evidently correct, for in the procession of April 28 we find a deputation from the Commune of Issy, but none from that of Vaugirard.

[5] 'Mémoires de Mme. Roland,' p. 326. Le Patriote Français of

declared him to be *un grand homme*, and pronounced his funeral oration at the Jacobin Club. 'For the past two days,' he cried, 'have I wept over Lazowski, and my whole soul is plunged in grief at the immense loss which the Republic has sustained.'[1] On the motion of Chaumette, the municipality resolved to demand the honours of the Pantheon for this hero.[2] A public funeral was accorded him, and David, the painter, who organized the magnificent obsequies of Michel Lepeletier, solicited the honour of being entrusted with the interment of Claude Lazowski.

The ceremony took place on Sunday, April 28. The proceedings opened in the Place de l'Hôtel de Ville. The Mayor, at the head of a deputation from the Conseil, received the body of the *grand homme* upon the threshold of the Maison Commune; it was then carried by members of the Finistère section, to which he belonged,[3] to the centre of the Council Chamber, where it was placed on trestles.

The president of the Finistère section was the first to express his patriotic grief in a speech which concluded with these words: 'Glorying in the possession of Lazowski's remains, the Finistère section would never consent to give them up if, convinced of the esteem in which that zealous Patriot is held not only by the city of Paris, but by the whole of the Republic, it did not recognise the necessity of restoring the father of Liberty to all his children. We hand over to you his body in order that you may pay it the honour it deserves, keeping for ourselves his heart, which no one shall ever take from us.'[4]

Citizen Destournelles, a member of the Commune and Registrar-General,[5] then pronounced the funeral oration of the

April 27 speaks of Lazowski's death in the following terms: 'The Jacobins pretend that he was poisoned. I know not whether this be true, but it is probable that he had no other poison than that of the wine-cup, to which, like many other great men, he was much addicted.'

[1] *Journal des Débats et de la Correspondance de la Société des Jacobins*, No. 401.

[2] *Le Patriote Français*, No. 1,356.

[3] Claude Lasosky, Commandant du Bataillon du Finistère, Rue Mouffetard, No. 138 (*Almanach National de France*, 1793).

[4] Sitting of the Commune of April 28, 1793.

[5] Six weeks later, on June 13, Destournelles was appointed Minister of Public Taxes.

hero of June 20, the Tenth of August, and September 9.[1] His speech was received with loud acclamation. Silence was finally restored, and Fleuriot-Lescot, the deputy of the Public Prosecutor in the Revolutionary Tribunal, began to speak. 'Republicans,' he said, 'should not content themselves with merely giving a public funeral to a citizen who has served his country well. I ask the Commune to adopt Lazowski's daughter.' The Conseil-Général unanimously and immediately passed a resolution acceding to this demand. Anaxagoras Chaumette—a man of sentiment!—hereupon covered the poor child, aged three years and a half, with tears and kisses, and placed a laurel wreath upon her brow.

Another member of the Commune then rose, and declared himself willing to undertake the child's education; it was Citizen Blin, a schoolmaster.[2] 'Noble-hearted citizen!' replied the President; 'the Commune gratefully accepts your offer; it expected no less from your patriotism.'[3]

The procession at last started on its way to the Place de la Réunion,[4] chosen by the Commune as the place for Lazowski's sepulture in memory of the services he rendered on that very spot in the attack upon the Tuileries on the Tenth of August.

The first banner bore the following inscription:

'Sans-culottes,
Lazowski is no more.'

On another were inscribed the words which he uttered on the Tenth of August when leading his fellow-gunners to the attack:

'Let those who love me follow me!
By sunrise
The Tyrant shall be no more!'

[1] The massacre of the prisoners of the Haute-Cour of Orleans took place at Versailles on Sunday, September 9, 1792.

[2] A year later, in the month of April, 1794, Blin was appointed Assistant-Secretary to the Commune in place of Dorat-Cubières.

[3] Michelet alludes to the adoption of Lazowski's daughter by the Commune in tome v. of his 'Histoire de la Révolution,' and gives the real date of the death and funeral of the hero of the Tenth of August (April, 1793). This does not prevent him from making Lazowski die in another work ('Histoire du Dix-neuvième Siècle,' tome i., p. 174) on the eve of the Journée de Prairial (May 20, 1795).

[4] Formerly the Place du Carrousel.

On another: 'He was libelled by conspirators; he is mourned by his colleagues.'

On the last: 'He was always a friend of the poor.'

A little farther on in the procession came two standards—one white and one red. Over the white standard was borne an inscription which ran: ''This he took from the enemies of Liberty;' and over the red one: 'He avenged the Patriots by tearing down this standard.'[1]

Behind the flags came a cannon bearing the following inscription: 'He had this cannon carried into the tyrant's lair on June 20, 1792.' Beside it was the bell which rung the alarm on the night between the 9th and 10th of August.[2]

Then followed the coffin, covered with branches of cypress and laurel wreaths; it was borne by gunners from the regiment which Lazowski had commanded.

Other gunners bore aloft a bed of state arranged in classic style. Upon this couch, which was covered with tricolour drapery, the body of Lazowski was supposed to recline. At the foot of the bed sat the daughter of the hero, and by her side Citizen Blin; at the head stood a gunner 'weeping over his dead comrade.'[3] I saw no tears on this Patriot's face, but, anyhow, they were on David's programme.

The political clubs, the sections, the artillery regiments, the Commune of Issy, the Corporation, and the Conseil-Général of Paris, all took part in the procession, each member of which carried a branch of cypress. The Jacobins were conspicuous by their red caps trimmed with black crape, and their women-folk had donned for the occasion white gowns adorned with black sashes.

A number of bands played the funeral march composed by Citizen Gossec, who was present at the ceremony, and led the choirs.[4]

A salvo of artillery hailed the arrival of the procession upon

---

[1] *Le Républicain, Journal des Hommes Libres*, No. 181. On July 17, 1791, martial law was proclaimed, and the red flag, the emblem of that law, had been planted by Bailly over the entrance to the Hôtel de Ville. A few rioters had been killed in the Champs de Mars; hence the hatred of Lazowski and of the Patriots for the red flag.

[2] *Révolutions de Paris*, tome xvi., p. 266.   [3] *Ibid.*   [4] *Ibid.*

the Place de la Réunion, around which were drawn up several battalions of the National Guards. After the singing of a funeral dirge, followed by a second salvo of artillery, the body was placed in the grave that had been dug for it at the foot of the tree of Fraternity, in the open square, a short distance only from the spot where a few hours before the guillotine had been at work. It was then three o'clock, and there had been no time to hide all traces of the execution which had taken place at noon.[1] The victim had been a poor cab-driver condemned to death on the previous evening for having whilst totally drunk—a fact admitted by all the witnesses—given voice to anti-Revolutionary sentiments.

A grass-grown mound now covers the remains of Lazowski, that lie but a few feet from the scaffold. It will be watered each day by the blood of aristocrats; each day fresh hecatombs will be sacrificed to the shade of the hero of the Tenth of August.[2]

Such were the obsequies of Lazowski, the Patriot. There is no doubt that in celebrating with such pomp the funeral of a man whom the Girondists had looked upon as an outlaw the Jacobins and the members of the Commune intend to impose a fresh check and humiliation upon the Brissotins. At the same time, they wish to show not only the Brissotins, but the whole country, that the Revolutionary party possesses no foolish prejudices, no false delicacy; that it demands only to be served, and that it pardons all to him who serves it well—all, even crime!

The following is an unpublished letter written by Lanjuinais to his friends in Rennes at the time of Lazowski's death:

Paris, April 26, 1793.

'DEAR FELLOW-CITIZENS,

'Marat has just been acquitted by a jury partly composed of his accomplices, for two of them had taken part in the massacre at

---

[1] *Le Patriote Français*, No. 1,356; *Mercure Français*, May 4, 1793.

[2] After the death of Marat, a vaulted cenotaph, on which were placed his bust and his bath, was erected to his memory in the Place de la Réunion. Lazowski's monument, ornamented with a kind of flower-bed, was but a little way from it—the disciple lay buried at the foot of the altar to his master ('Biographie Universelle,' by Michaud, tome lxx., article 'Lazowski').

the Abbaye in September. His partisans crowned him, and bore him in triumph to the Convention. Danton says that it was a grand day, but all good citizens have deplored it.

‘Lazowski is dead; he was the chief of the bandits who intended to massacre the Convention on March 10, and who on that day went with his band of murderers from the Jacobin Club to that of the Grey Friars and to the municipality in order to make the final arrangements for that good work. He was the virtuous friend of the virtuous Robespierre. The latter pronounced a tearful panegyric upon him at a public sitting of the Jacobins. “He was my friend,” he said, “and would have commanded the Revolutionary army.” The Jacobins, the Grey Friars, and the Commune will bury him with public honours; we shall be very lucky if we are not invited to pay a last tribute to our would-be assassin. You must not believe that the citizens of Paris approve of such criminal extravagance. They either sit and weep at home, or go to the theatre. The Convention works and dissembles; that is the best course men with any spirit can pursue in that Assembly. They hasten on the Constitution, whilst factionists postpone it. They expose themselves to the tongue of calumny and the assassin's dagger, and yet these are the men against whom are hurled accusations for which the refugees and Coburg would willingly pay a high price if they could be bought.

‘ LANJUINAIS.’[1]

[1] Archives de Rennes, cote 9. No. 4.

CHAPTER LXIX.

FASHIONS AND THEATRES.

Monday, May 6, 1793.

ANARCHY has reached its climax. The sections and the clubs
re-echo with constant calls to insurrection. The Commune is
openly conspiring against the majority in the Convention, and
the Convention is compassing its own ruin. The Revolutionary
Tribunal sends fresh victims to the scaffold every day. Civil
war is laying waste our western departments. The Austrians
are menacing our northern frontier, and Paris—incorrigible
Paris—goes on amusing itself. Since the return of spring, the
promenades are crowded with people, and the women are conspicuous by their gorgeous and tasteful toilets.[1] I have just
had a peep into the wardrobe of a society woman. It contains
a dress of sea-green taffeta, one of blue satin, another of pearl-
gray silk, yet another costume of gray taffeta, a gown combining
the three national colours, a dress of very fine Indian cashmere
trimmed with bouquets of red, white, and blue flowers, and,
besides all these, dresses *à la Psyché, à la Ménagère, à la Turque,*
and *au lever de Vénus.*[2]

The men have no desire to be left behind in all this display
of elegance,[3] and many, far from imitating Marat and arraying
themselves in Jacobin garb, dress on the contrary with remarkable care—white dimity pantaloons and waistcoat, a white

---

[1] *Révolutions de Paris,* tome xvi., p. 285.

[2] Inventory drawn up at Mme. Danton's after the execution of her
husband (Danton, 'Mémoires sur sa Vie Privée,' by Dr. Robinet).

[3] See an advertisement by Citoyenne Rispal, of No. 4, Galerie de la
Rue de Richelieu, in the Palais Égalité (*Journal de Paris,* 1793, No. 58).
See also 'L'Art pendant la Révolution,' by Spire Blondel, p. 214.

cravat with flowing ends, and a long frock-coat of fine cloth.[1]
We find also sky-blue and puce-coloured coats, and with these
are worn white and blue waistcoats of Indian silk ;[2] trousers are
worn wide with variegated stripes, blue and red alternating
with red and yellow. The coats are cut with enormous lapels
reaching to the sleeves ; the loose cravats are of silk or muslin,
and even the dandies carry in their waistcoat or coat pockets
the ornaments *à la mode*—one or two pistols.

At night all the theatres are crowded.[3] Whilst some go to
enjoy a hearty laugh at the 'Triomphe de Marat,'[4] or to see
'La Papesse Jeanne' at the theatre in the Rue Feydeau, others
go to the Opéra Comique Nationale in the Rue Favart to hear
Cherubini's 'Lodoiska.'

Others, again, go to the Théâtre de la République[5] to applaud
Talma in Marie Joseph Chénier's 'Fénelon, ou la Réligieuse de
Cambrai,' or to admire Julie Candeille in 'Cathérine, ou la
Belle Fermière.'

The Théâtre de la Nation still remains the best play-house
in Paris. It has lost Talma, Dugazon, and Grandménil, Julie
Candeille, Mdlle. Desgarcins, and Mme. Vestris ; but it still
has on its bills Fleury, Vanhove, Saint-Phal, Larochelle, Dazin-
court, Naudet, Mmes. Rancourt, Contat, Joly, Thénard, Suin,
Devienne, Lange, and Mézeray.

The company is composed not only of excellent actors, but
also of true-hearted people, as was proved when in January last
they performed 'L'Ami des Lois' during the trial of Louis XVI.
They are now playing a piece which is having a great success, but

---

[1] Charles Nodier, 'Souvenirs de la Révolution.'
[2] From the inventory of Danton's clothes; 'Mémoires sur sa Vie
Privée,' by Dr. Robinet.
[3] *Révolutions de Paris*, tome xvi., p. 285.   [4] *Ibid.*
[5] Rue de Richelieu. The Théâtre de la République was that which
the Comédie Française still occupies. It had then been recently built from
plans drawn by the architect Moreau. In 1791, when Talma and those
of his colleagues who had eagerly embraced Revolutionary principles had
quitted the Théâtre Français, whose actors were, for the most part,
imbued with aristocratic notions, they had betaken themselves to the
theatre in the Rue de Richelieu, which then bore the name of Théâtre du
Palais Royal, and was managed by Gaillard and Dorfeuille. The new
Théâtre Français opened its doors on April 27, 1791, with Chénier's
'Henri VIII.'

which will not bring down upon the theatre the displeasure of the Commune. 'Les Femmes,' a comedy in three acts and in verse by Citizen Demoustier, is the most inoffensive squib that was ever put upon the stage. There are no wolves in Florian's 'Fables'; there is scarcely a man to speak of in Demoustier's piece.

The first performance took place on Friday, April 19, at four o'clock. Before going to the theatre the audience had an opportunity of witnessing a spectacle of a different kind on the other side of the Rue de Rivoli. At one o'clock a woman was guillotined in the Place de la Réunion — one Cathérine Clère, a poor servant, fifty-six years of age, condemned to death for having, whilst drunk, made use of anti-Revolutionary expressions.[1]

[1] *Bulletin du Tribunal Criminel Révolutionnaire*, No. 11.

CHAPTER LXX.

Saturday, May 11, 1793.

YESTERDAY, Friday, May 10, the National Convention took possession of the Tuileries. The Conseil-Général de la Commune had asked that the inauguration of the new place of meeting might be postponed until Sunday.[1] Can the philosopher, Anaxagoras Chaumette, and his colleagues, perchance fear for our legislators the fatal influence of Friday?

Being acquainted with Citizen Berthollet, one of the ushers of the Convention,[2] I was enabled to get into the hall and inspect it before the sitting.

It is situated on the first-floor, between the central pavilion, now called the Pavillon de l'Unité, and the former Pavillon Marsan, now the Pavillon de la Liberté.[3]

Upon reaching the top of the grand staircase, the stone balustrade of which was ornamented before the Tenth of August with lyres interwoven with serpents and other allegorical ornaments bearing the device of Louis XIV. and the arms of Colbert,[4] I pass through what was formerly the chapel, then

---

[1] Commune de Paris : Conseil-Général : sitting of May 8, 1793.

[2] Berthollet, Rue des Bons-Enfants, No. 24 (*Almanach National de France*, 1793, p. 74). There were ten ushers attached to the National Convention. One of them, Louis François Poiré, an old servant of M. de Talleyrand and Mme. de Polignac, was guillotined on the 9th of Germinal (March 29, 1794).

[3] The Pavillon de Flore, the nearest to the quay, was in 1793 called the Pavillon de l'Égalité. The Pavillon de Mesdames, better known as the Pavillon Marsan, was that looking out upon the Rue de Rivoli.

[4] For full description of the Tuileries, see Vol. I. of the 'Diary of a Citizen of Paris' pp. 65-75.

through an ante-room, through the Salon de la Liberté, adorned with a colossal statue of that goddess, and, crossing a vestibule, finally enter the Hall of the Convention.

This hall was formerly known as the Salle des Machines on account of the ballets which were performed here before Louis XIV. and his Court. After the burning of the opera-house in 1763, the actors took refuge in this *salle*; and from 1770 until 1783, when they took possession of their new building in the Faubourg Saint-Germain, it accommodated the Comédiens Français. It was in the Salle des Machines that Lekain appeared as Vendôme, Tancred, and Orosmane for the last time; and that Mdlle. Clairon, also for the last time, played the part of Medea. Voltaire was crowned there on March 30, 1738. The theatre of the Tuileries had three tiers of boxes, and was capable of seating several thousand spectators.

The necessary alterations for the accommodation of the National Convention have been carried out under the direction of M. Gisors. The hall is now arranged as follows:

The amphitheatre reserved for deputies is on the left on entering, and is composed of ten rows of benches, one higher than the other. In the middle of these benches is an empty space for the accommodation of those persons appearing at the bar of the Assembly.

On the right, facing the deputies, is the Presidential chair, placed in a recess and reached by a few steps; the clerks' tables and the tribune are a little lower.

Between the tribune, or rostrum, and the first row of benches, a space has been railed off for those petitioners who are awarded the honours of the sitting.

Along two sides of the hall double galleries have been constructed, to which spectators are to be admitted by ticket only; at the two ends of the hall are vast bays, in each of which an amphitheatre has been constructed for the general public. Seating accommodation has thus been obtained for about 2,000 spectators.[1]

---

[1] 1,400 according to the *Révolutions de Paris*, 2,000 according to the *Chronique de Paris*, 2,000 to 3,000 according to the *Thermomètre du Jour*.

Reporters have not been so well treated; they have been relegated to pigeon-holes near the roof, from which little can be seen or heard.[1]

The lower portion of the walls is draped with green cloth, ornamented with wreaths of oak-leaves and laurel; in the corners are the fasces, with the axe emerging. Here and there are statues of Brutus, Solon, Lycurgus, Cincinnatus, and Camillus.[2] Before the tribune is a bust of Lepeletier de Saint-Fargeau. To the right and left are a pair of candelabras, twelve feet high, each having four branches.

The general appearance of the hall leaves much to be desired, and I have heard excellent judges express an opinion in which I thoroughly concur. It is to the effect that all the good points now visible already existed in the old hall as constructed by Vigarani, and that the new architect has only spoilt whatever he has touched.[3] He has made the place too long and too narrow, and the construction of the galleries has ruined the acoustics. At the Jacobin Club yesterday evening the subject gave rise to grave complaints and violent recriminations. 'It is impossible to hear anything in that hall,' said Citizen Desfieux. 'The party knew what it was about; it rejected the plans of Boyer, a patriotic architect, who would have built a hall in which everyone might have been able to hear—for, after all, it is for the people that we have built it. I demand,' he continued, 'that the hall be rebuilt at the expense of Roland and his clique. Ask Boyer for what reasons his plans were rejected; we can then have Roland arrested.'[4]

---

[1] Guiraut, the editor of the *Logotachygraphe*, sent a letter to the Convention, in which he pointed out that the Legislative Assembly had had a special gallery constructed for him in which to carry on his work, adding: 'Cooped up, like all the reporters, in the ridiculous seats which have been given us, and which cut us off from all communication with the Assembly; unable to obtain a view of the documents and decrees upon which the debates turn; keenly alive to the reproaches of inaccuracy, for which the arrangement of the hall is solely to blame, I must suspend the publication of my paper until the National Convention has recognised the necessity of providing better accommodation. Patriots, be patient!' (*La Chronique de Paris*).

[2] *Révolutions de Paris*, tome xvi., p. 339.   [3] *Ibid.*

[4] *Journal des Débats et de la Correspondance de la Société des Jacobins*, sitting of May 10, 1793. At the sitting of the Convention of February 23,

The new hall has other disadvantages, the most important of which is that there are absolutely no means of ventilation. Another drawback, though a less serious one, is the inconvenience resulting from the absence of tables or desks; if a member wishes to take notes, he is obliged to place the paper on his knees.

It is but right to add that in one particular the new installation is far preferable to that of the Riding-School. The public galleries are much farther removed from the members' benches, and it will doubtless be more difficult for the spectators to interfere in the debates.[1] Again, the deputies, being now seated almost in a line, will no longer be separated like two armies drawn up in battle array.[2] A few optimists (there are still some left) are sanguine enough to hope for the salvation of the country from this new arrangement of seats. To hear them talk, one would think that this mingling of men of different parties cannot fail to result in the reconciliation of a large number of representatives who, though divided to-day, require only to know each other to arrive at a common understanding.[3] No more Right and no more Left! No more Plain and no more Swamp! No more Gironde and no more Mountain!

Beaulieu, who, in his capacity as journalist, has attended the sittings of our three Assemblies since the commencement of the Revolution, passed in review with me this morning the different places in which they have been successively lodged.

On May 4, 1789, the eve of the day fixed for the opening of the States-General at Versailles, a solemn Mass was celebrated in the church of Notre Dame, which is the parish church of the palace. A richly-decorated daïs had been erected for the King. The deputies of the three Estates had come early, those of the

1794, Danton made the same complaints : 'This hall deadens every sound ; one would require the lungs of a Stentor to make one's self properly heard. The legislators of the French Republic should certainly deliberate in a place where their words can be heard by the human ear. I move that the Committee of Inspecteurs de la Salle be instructed to consult experts upon the means of ameliorating the conditions of which I complain' (*Moniteur*, year II., No. 157).

[1] *Mercure Français*, May 18, 1793. [2] *Ibid.*
[3] *Chronique de Paris* and *Mercure Français*, May, 1793.

Nobility in black coats, with waistcoats and trimmings of cloth of gold, silken mantles, lace cravats, and plumed hats *à la Henri Quatre*; the Clergy in their cassocks, mantles, and square caps; the Bishops in their violet robes; the Third Estate in black silk coats and white muslin cravats.[1] The *Veni Creator* was sung. At the conclusion of that prayer the deputies, each holding a candle in his hand, marched in procession to the church of Saint-Louis between two lines of Gardes Françaises and Suisses.[2]

On reaching Saint-Louis the three orders sat on benches in the aisle, the King and Queen taking their seats under a canopy of violet velvet, studded with golden lilies of France. The Host was then carried to the altar amid the chanting of the hymn ' *O Salutaris Hostia*,' and after Mass had been celebrated a sermon was preached by Monseigneur de la Fare, Bishop of Nancy.

On the morrow, May 5, the session was opened in the Salle des Menus or Salle des Trois-Ordres.

The building in which this was located was erected by Louis XV. in 1750, for the work-shops and store-rooms of the Menus-Plaisirs of the King.[3] It is situated in the fine avenue which leads to the palace. Louis XVI. had built an additional wing between the original edifice and the wall abutting upon the Rue des Chantiers. As this wing was very spacious, and capable of being turned to any use, it was chosen for the Assemblée des Notables on February 22, 1787, and it was there, too, that the States-General held their first sitting. Nothing had been altered, except that galleries had been erected for the accommodation of the public. M. Necker was convinced that nothing could be better than to allow the people to witness the peaceful, imposing, and touching spectacle which the representatives of the nation were about to present to France and Europe.[4] The Salle des Menus had accordingly been arranged like a theatre.

---

[1] 'Mémoires du Marquis de Ferrières,' tome i., p. 18.
[2] 'Histoire de Versailles,' by J. A. Le Roi, tome i., p. 227.
[3] The Menus-Plaisirs of the King contained all the apartments for games and bodily exercises, as well as the concert-hall and theatre.
[4] 'Mémoires de Marmontel,' liv. xiii. ; 'Mémoires de Malouet,' tome i., cb. x.

It is a fine large hall, 120 feet long, and 57 feet wide inside the columns which support the roof. Behind these columns were benches and sloping galleries affording seating accommodation for more than 2,000 spectators.[1]

At one end, under a gold-embroidered canopy, stood the throne, the Queen's arm-chair, and the stools for the Princesses. At the foot of the royal daïs was a bench for the Secretaries of State, who sat at a table covered with a violet velvet cloth. The representatives of the Clergy sat on benches arranged lengthwise along the right side of the hall, the Nobility sitting to the left of, and the Commons opposite, the throne.[2]

At daybreak, on May 6, the following poster appeared on the walls of Versailles:

'BY ORDER OF THE KING.—His Majesty having notified to the representatives of the three Estates his desire that they should meet to-day, May 6, the representatives are hereby informed that the place of meeting will be ready for occupation at 9 a.m.'

At the appointed hour the members of the Third Estate entered the hall in which the sitting had been held on the preceding day, whilst the representatives of the Nobility and the Clergy took their places in other departments prepared for them in the Hôtel des Menus-Plaisirs. On the occasion of the convocation of the Assembly of Notables, a suite of apartments had been fitted up in that building for the use of the King. It consisted of a Salle des Pages, of a Salle des Cent-Suisses, of a Salle des Gardes, of a Salle des Nobles, and of the King's Cabinet, which communicated by a small passage with the Salle des Menus. For the meeting of the States-General a part of the King's apartments had been appropriated; the Salle des Cent-Suisses had been arranged for the accommodation of the representatives of the Clergy, and the Salle des Gardes for those of the Nobility.[3] In these two small halls, that could scarce seat the members of the two privileged Orders, there was no

---

[1] 'Tableau de la Salle preparée pour les États-Généraux' (*Moniteur* for 1789); 'Mémoires du Marquis de Clermont-Gallerande,' tome i., p. 55.

[2] Grimm, *Correspondance*, Part III.

[3] 'Histoire de Versailles,' by J. A. Le Roi, tome ii., p. 423.

room for the public. In the Salle des Menus the galleries could accommodate, as I have already said, a large number of spectators; in this the Third Estate therefore enjoyed an immense advantage.

From Paris, from Versailles, and from the surrounding country, there daily came crowds of men of all sorts and conditions eager to hear the orators, and to embrace the principles that were expounded before them. The people soon became accustomed to look upon the hall in which the Commons assembled—the only one into which they were admitted—as the centre of national representation, and to regard the deputies that filled it as the only ones meriting their confidence.[1] At first the hall was continually full of visitors, who made their way into every corner, and even sat on the benches reserved for deputies; the latter, being still strangers themselves, made no attempt to guard against this, and the whole appearance of the place was more like that of a club than of a political body.[2]

With rare *aplomb* the members of the Third Estate pretended to see in the hall they occupied, not a hall specially reserved for the meetings of their Order, but the seat of the States-General itself. They were careful to occupy only the benches which had been assigned to them on the opening day, and, leaving those of the Clergy and Nobility vacant, invited the members of those Orders to come and take possession of them—an invitation which was refused.[3]

At the sitting of June 17, the deputy Guillotin,[4] who probably had no idea at that time of the notoriety that was in store for him, pointed out to his colleagues in the Commons that the arrangement of the seats was contrary to the rules of health; that the members were too closely packed, and that they could hardly breathe. 'See,' he added, 'how uncomfortable these seats are for sittings of twelve to fourteen hours like that of to-day. They ought at least to be provided with backs.'[5]

---

[1] 'Mémoires d'un Témoin Oculaire de la Révolution,' by S. Bailly, tome i., p. 226; 'Mémoires de Ferrières,' tome i., p. 27.

[2] 'Souvenirs sur Mirabeau,' by Étienne Dumont, p. 44.

[3] 'Mémoires de Clermont-Gallerande,' tome i., p. 59.

[4] A physician and a member of the Third Estate of the city of Paris.

[5] 'Archives Parlementaires' from 1787 to 1860, edited by Mavidal, Laurent, and Clavel, tome viii., p. 129.

The Assembly agreed with Dr. Guillotin, and entrusted him with the task of having the necessary alterations carried out.

Before Dr. Guillotin had had time to execute the mandate of the Assembly, and have backs put to the seats, the following proclamation was published in the streets of Versailles on Saturday, June 20:

'BY ORDER OF THE KING.—The King having resolved to attend a sitting of the States-General on June 22, the preparations in the three halls in which the Orders hold their assemblies render a suspension of these assemblies necessary until after the aforesaid sitting has been held. His Majesty will make known by fresh proclamation the hour at which the States-General will meet on Monday.'

M. Bailly, the President of the Commons, and the two Secretaries, MM. Camus and Pison du Galland, junior, presented themselves at the entrance of their usual place of meeting at nine o'clock. They found it closed, and guarded by a detachment of Gardes Françaises. The Avenue de Paris, in which the principal entrance to the hall was situated, soon became filled with members.[1] They were all of opinion that a sitting should be held, and that a suitable place should at once be found. On the suggestion of Dr. Guillotin, they proceeded to the Rue Saint-François, where the keeper of the Salle du Jeu de Paume (tennis-hall) consented to house them. Two deputies were stationed at the door to prevent strangers from entering. Soon, however, an immense crowd that filled the galleries, sat on the window-sills, and blocked all the approaches, rent the air with shouts whilst the members of the Third Estate deliberated within the bare and sombre walls of this vast hall, all the furniture in which consisted of five or six benches and a writing-table.[2]

On rising, the Commons adjourned until Monday, the 22nd, the day on which the royal sitting was to be held; but on Sunday night, M. de Brézé informed Bailly in writing that the sitting in question would not be held until ten o'clock on Tuesday

---

[1] 'Mémoires de Bailly,' tome i., p. 187.
[2] 'Mémoires de Ferrières,' tome i., p. 56; 'Mémoires de Bailly,' tome i., p. 188.

morning, and that the hall would be closed until then. The Commons persisted in their determination to continue their meetings, but not being able to again obtain possession of the tennis-hall, which the Duc d'Artois had bespoken,[1] looked out for another place of assembly. They proceeded first to the church of the Récollets, but the monks would not take in the Assembly,[2] which then made its way to the parish church of Saint-Louis. The incumbent, Jacob, although attached to the Court, dared not refuse the deputies admission.

They sat in the aisle, a table being placed before the President, who was supported by the Secretaries. On his right some chairs were drawn up to represent the seats for the Clergy, while on his left were chairs to denote the places of the Nobility. It having been decided that the public should be admitted, the church was filled in an instant.[3]

Meanwhile, those of the Clergy who were in favour of the sittings of the three Estates being held in common gathered in the choir, which soon contained 134 vicars, 6 canons, 2 *grands vicaires*, 1 *abbé commendataire*, and 5 prelates.[4] They then took their seats in the nave to the right of the President, whilst the Archbishop of Vienne[5] sat immediately next to that dignitary.[6]

The royal sitting of Tuesday, June 23, was held, like that of May 5, in the Hall of the Three Estates. After the King's departure all the representatives of the Nobility and some of those of the Clergy withdrew; the Commons remained in their places, and in the presence of forty or fifty witnesses who were on the platform declared that they persisted in maintaining the validity of the resolutions which they had been compelled to pass elsewhere.[7]

On the morrow and the following days the members of the Third Estate continued to sit in the same hall, where the

---

[1] 'Mémoires de Ferrières,' tome i., p. 56.
[2] 'Beaulieu, ' Essais Historiques,' tome i., p. 24.
[3] 'Mémoires de Bailly,' tome i., p. 198.
[4] The Archbishops of Vienne and Bordeaux, the Bishops of Chartres, Rodez, and Coutances.
[5] Jean Georges le Franc de Pompignan.
[6] 'Mémoires de Bailly,' tome i., p. 200.   [7] *Ibid.*, p. 214.

majority of the Clergy and a small number of representatives of the Nobility joined them. In the interior things had resumed their former appearance, but a great change had taken place outside. The hall and its approaches were surrounded by sentries of the Gardes Françaises, and the principal entrance, with its courtyard leading into the Avenue de Paris, was closed. The members of the Third Estate were consequently obliged to enter by the Rue des Chantiers. Finally, on June 27, by express order of the King, those members of the Nobility and Clergy who had until then strenuously opposed sittings in common appeared in the common hall of the States-General ; they entered in silence, with grief and consternation written in their faces, and headed by Cardinal de la Rochefoucauld and the Duc de Luxembourg.[1] The Revolution had commenced.

The members of the Nobility held three sittings more in their own hall—on July 3, with 138 present ; on the 10th, with 93 present ; and on the 11th, when the number dwindled down to 80.[2]

On October 9, 1789, a letter was read in the National Assembly, informing that body that the King had taken up his abode in Paris, and inviting the Assembly not to separate itself from him. A resolution was thereupon passed that the sittings should be held in Paris as soon as the Commissioners of the Assembly had chosen and arranged suitable premises.

Already on the next day the Commissioners—M. Guillotin, the Duc d'Aiguillon, the Marquis de Gouy d'Arcy, the Bishop of Rodez, M. la Poule, and M. Lepeletier de Saint-Fargeau—announced that they had visited all the largest halls in the capital, and that none seemed more convenient than the Riding-School of the Tuileries. The same benches as they had in Versailles could be transported there, and the public galleries would hold about five or six hundred people. The offices would be installed in the Feuillants, and the committees would sit in the Chancellerie in the Place Vendôme. The choice of the Riding-School was approved by the Assembly.

[1] 'Mémoires de Clermont-Gallerande,' tome i., p. 101.
[2] 'Mémoires de Bailly,' tome i., p. 317

On October 12 the Commissioners presented a further report. They found that the necessary alterations in the Riding-School could not possibly be completed in less than three weeks. Meanwhile, the deputies could be accommodated in the archiepiscopal palace, the prelate, Monseigneur de Juigné, having declared his willingness to do all that lay in his power for the comfort of his colleagues in the National Assembly.

It was consequently decided that the Assembly should continue to sit at Versailles until Thursday, October 15, and that on Monday, the 19th, it should resume its sittings in Paris.[1]

On October 19 all the avenues leading to the Archbishop's palace had barriers thrown across them, and were guarded by artillery and numerous detachments of the National Militia, whilst a troop of 500 horsemen was drawn up in the Parvis Notre Dame.[2] This extraordinary military display had been arranged by the Commune in order to prove to the Assembly that it had nought to fear in Paris; it produced, however, an entirely opposite effect, for it showed to what perils the Assembly was exposed in a city where such precautions were thought necessary. The people regarded these warlike preparations with disfavour, and their attitude towards the newly-arrived deputies was decidedly threatening.[3]

The National Assembly sat in the large hall of the Officialité, where a few months before the electoral proceedings had been carried on. Galleries had been put up for the accommodation of the public, but the work had been too hastily done; the supporting beams had not been carried far enough into the wall, and at the very first sitting one of the galleries fell. The occupants, men and women, were precipitated into the hall, and several deputies who were seated under the gallery were severely injured.[4]

Two days later, on October 21, a horrible deed was perpetrated in close proximity to the Assembly, and almost under the eyes of the members. A baker named François, whose shop

<hr />

[1] *Moniteur* of 1789, No. 73.
[2] 'Mémoires sur la Révolution Française,' by the Comte de Montlosier, tome 1., p. 319 ; 'Mémoires de Ferrières,' tome i., p. 340.
[3] 'Mémoires de Ferrières,' tome i., p. 340.
[4] 'Mémoires de Montlosier,' tome i., p. 319.

was quite close to the archiepiscopal palace, was accused by an old woman of hiding a large quantity of bread, and being arrested by the people, was dragged across the Place de Grève to the Hôtel de Ville. There he was hanged upon the first lamp-post, and his head cut off with a table-knife ;[1] the head was then weighed on a pair of scales, stuck upon a pike, and carried through the streets. The victim's young wife, hearing grave rumours concerning her husband's safety, came running to his defence, and met the procession on the bridge of Notre Dame. She was made to kiss the bleeding trophy and fell into a swoon, her face bathed in gore.[2]

It was amidst such scenes that the debate on church property, which had been opened at Versailles on October 10, was resumed on October 23. It came to an end on November 2. During the sittings of October 30 and 31, the mob had surrounded the archiepiscopal palace, and uttered the most violent threats against the aristocrats. On November 2 the palace was besieged before daybreak by a crowd of ruffians, who, on the appearance of the deputies, saluted the members of the Right with yells of execration, and actually used violence against the clerical deputies. They gained their end, for that day the Assembly decreed that 'all ecclesiastical property was at the disposal of the nation.' By a singular irony of fate the decree which despoiled the clergy of their property was passed on All Souls' Day on the motion of a Bishop—Talleyrand-Périgord, Bishop of Autun—with M. Camus, the solicitor for the clergy, in the chair, and in the archiepiscopal palace !

It was also in the hall of the Officialité that, in spite of Mirabeau's efforts, the Decree debarring deputies from holding any Government office was passed on November 7.

On Monday, November 9, the National Assembly held its first sitting in the Riding-School. This building, which was about 150 feet long, could be reached from two sides—from the courtyard of the school, a long narrow passage running parallel

---

[1] 'Mémoires de Ferrières.'
[2] 'Histoire des Montagnards,' by Alphonse Esquiros, tome i., p. 183.

with the Terrasse des Feuillants,[1] and from the Porte des
Feuillants, which is in the Rue Saint-Honoré. In the courtyard the architect who had been entrusted by the King with
carrying out the necessary alterations had put up one of the
large wooden constructions that formed part of the Hôtel des
Menus Plaisirs in Versailles ; this was to serve as a kind of
vestibule.[2]

Though much smaller than the Salle des Menus, the Riding-
School presented still greater disadvantages with regard to
sound.[3] As at Versailles, there were galleries for the public,
some of them being partitioned off like theatre-boxes. Behind
the President's chair was the reporters' box ; it was twelve
feet wide and six feet high. The Constituent Assembly had
reserved it for representatives of the *Journal Logographique*,
sometimes called the *logotachygraphes*, but more commonly
the *logographes*. When Louis XVI. appeared in the Assembly
on September 14, 1791, to sign the Constitution, he was hailed
on all sides with shouts of ' *Vive le Roi !*' Just as he was about
to begin his speech, the curtains before the reporters' box were
drawn back, and the spectators beheld the Queen holding the
Prince Royal by the hand. The enthusiasm then knew no
bounds, and the plaudits that were showered upon the King
during his speech and during the President's reply were to a
great extent occasioned by the presence of the Queen and her
son.[4] Less than a year later the Queen and her son reappeared
in that same reporters' box, but how sadly changed were all her
surroundings !

The interior decorations of the hall were infinitely more
simple than those of the Tuileries : a few flags, amongst which
was the standard of the Federation of July 14, 1790 ;[5] the

---

[1] ' The courtyard of the Riding-School now forms that portion of the
Rue de Rivoli that lies between the Palace of the Tuileries and the Rue
Castiglione. It was shut off from the Terrasse de Feuillants by a wall
which is now replaced by iron railings' (*Chronique de Cinquante Jours*,
from June 20 to August 10, 1792, by P. L. Roederer, p. 34).

[2] ' Decision of the King concerning the Installation of the National
Assembly in the Riding-School of the Tuileries,' article 2.

[3] *Les Contemporains* of 1789 and of 1790.

[4] ' Histoire de la Révolutions de France,' by ' Two Friends of Liberty,'
tome vii., p. 333.

[5] Assemblée Constituante, sitting of July 15, 1790.

statue of Jean Jacques Rousseau;[1] busts of the King and Bailly. A bust of Mirabeau also adorned this hall, which had so often re-echoed with the accents of his eloquent voice; and a stone from the Bastille, engraved with the effigy of the mighty orator, had been affixed to the balustrade of the rostrum.

After the Tenth of August, the King's bust was replaced by that of Brutus. By a Decree of December 5, 1792, the bust and portrait of Mirabeau were veiled.[2] It is unnecessary to point out that in the new hall of the Convention the busts of Mirabeau and Bailly would be as much out of place as that of Louis XVI. himself. Nor do we find in the Tuileries the monumental stove which for the past few months has been such an ornament to the Riding-School, and which is a model of the Bastille, with its eight towers, its battlements, and its gates. On the fortress stands a cannon, its base adorned with emblems of vanquished Tyranny and with the attributes of Liberty. This stove is of china, beautifully coloured in imitation of different minerals; it came from the workshops of Ollivier, the potter of the Rue de la Roquette, who presented it to the Convention towards the end of last year. Being a somewhat unwieldy object, it has not been removed.[3] The Riding-School contained two other stoves, which M. Guillotin had placed there when it first became the seat of the Legislature; the hall was nevertheless always cold and damp. The Abbé Royou has given us the following graphic description of a sitting of the Legislative Assembly on a winter's night:

'Imagine a hundred deputies arriving one after another, covered with snow, benumbed with cold, shivering, and rubbing their hands, dressed in all manner of garments, some wrapped in old cloaks, some in dressing-gowns, and nearly all wearing their hats. . . . In the paying galleries are two or three dozen of their friends or relatives. In the free seats are some poor *sans-culottes*, who are addressed as 'citizens' by a wretched-looking female, who sells them sour apples and cider more

---

[1] Decree of December, 1790.
[2] *Courrier de l'Égalité*, December 7, 1792.
[3] Ollivier's stove is now in the Musée de Sèvres.

muddy than Brissot's patriotism. Such was on Saturday evening (February 18, 1792), the appearance of the first Assembly in the world, and such was its audience.'[1]

Cabanis, Mirabeau's physician and friend, wrote in the following terms of the unsanitary state of the Riding-School in his ' Journal de la Maladie et de la Mort de H. G. Riqueti Mirabeau ' :

' The most robust members of the Assembly could not fail to be affected by the sudden change from a large and well-ventilated hall (the Salle des Menus) to this narrow, damp building, where the cold compelled them to keep large stoves constantly lit, and to carefully close all the doors and windows. It would be difficult to create a more unwholesome atmosphere ; its chief effect was upon the stomach and the eyes—in fact, ophthalmia became an epidemic, not only among the deputies, but among those spectators who were regular in their attendance at the sittings.'

The Constituent Assembly sat in the Riding-School from November 9, 1789, to September 30, 1791. The Legislative Assembly held all its sittings there from October 1, 1791, to September 21, 1792.

The National Convention held its first sitting in the Tuileries on September 20, 1792, when it proceeded to the election of its officers.[2] On Friday, September 21, it again met in the Tuileries, and proceeded thence to the Riding-School, where it sat uninterruptedly until the 9th of the present month. Since yesterday it has been installed in the Salle des Machines. It would seem—Fate sometimes indulges in such terrible ironies—as if all the places marked out by Royalty for their pleasures were destined to serve as scenes for the principal events of the Revolution.

It was in the Salle des Menus that on June 17, 1789, the Commons constituted themselves into a Constituent Assembly.

It was in the Tennis Hall that the deputies of the Third Estate took an oath not to dissolve until they had established a Constitution.

[1] L'Ami du Roi, February 21, 1792.
[2] For full particulars of this meeting, see Vol. I., Chapter I.

It was in the Riding-School that, on the Tenth of August, 1792, the Legislative Assembly dethroned Louis XVI., and that, on September 21, the Convention decided upon the abolition of the Monarchy.

It is in the theatre of the Tuileries that the National Convention sits to-day, and it is easy enough to foresee what tragedies will be played on that stage set up by Louis XVI.

From the windows of their new palace the members of the Convention will be able to enjoy the sight of an execution daily. By a delicate attention the Revolutionary Tribunal managed to arrange a double execution on Friday morning at eleven o'clock, just as our deputies were meeting at the Tuileries; the victims were Rivier de Mauny, formerly a Captain in the Dragoons, and Beaulieu, a merchant—both condemned to death for having sent money to their relatives abroad.[1]   Formerly, when a great event took place, it was the custom to discharge salvoes of artillery.   To-day, when the occupation of the Tuileries by the National Convention is to be celebrated, the scaffold is erected, and heads are struck off as a sign of joy.

[1] 'The execution took place in the Place de la Réunion at eleven o'clock on Friday, May 10' (*Bulletin du Tribunal Criminel Révolutionnaire*, No. 30).

CHAPTER LXXI.

Tuesday, May 14, 1793.

I STILL come across Marie Joseph Chénier occasionally, but at rare intervals. This morning I met him in the Tuileries; he was in the company of a young man of about twenty-five years of age, with whose face and general bearing I was much struck. He was formerly a private in the Gardes Françaises, and is now a captain and aide-de-camp to General Leveneur, who has just taken command of the camp at Maulde. The young man is of tall, commanding presence and of robust appearance; a sword-cut which he received in a duel, and which has left a deep scar across the right side of his forehead, lends his features a martial air that harmonizes well with the rest of his appearance.[1] 'We shall make a General of this young man,' said Chénier to me, and it is quite probable that the prediction will be realized. Either I am very much mistaken, or this young Hoche possesses both intelligence and courage to a high degree. His brief but smart replies and his well-chosen language prove him to be a man of superior parts.

When Citizen Hoche left us, Chénier had a great deal to say about him—his ardour for work, his passion for a soldier's life, and the talents of which he has already given proofs, were all lauded to the skies. It appears that he has been sent to Paris by his General to enlighten the Executive Council concerning the true state of the army. Before presenting himself to the Council, he thought it best to see a few of the deputies of the

---

[1] 'Vie de Lazare Hoche,' by Alexander Rousselin, tome i., pp. 44, 45.

department of Seine-et-Oise; hence his daily intercourse with Chénier.[1]

Thursday, May 16.

Much impressed by my encounter of Tuesday, I spoke to several of my friends concerning General Leveneur's aide-de-camp. I said to them : 'Remember this name of Hoche well ; you will hear a good deal about it some day.' I was so terribly in earnest that I got almost angry with Beaulieu, who smiled at my enthusiasm. This morning he called on me, and, assuming his most serious air, said : 'I have come to apologize ; you are a better prophet than you thought you were. The week is not yet out, and already the name of your hero is in everybody's mouth. Read this,' he added, handing me the *Publiciste de la République Française.* 'Ah ! ah !' I cried. 'So this filthy rag has libelled my hero, as you call him. I am glad of it for his sake.' 'It's not exactly that,' replied Beaulieu ; 'you had better read it.' I took Marat's paper, which was of to-day's date, and contained a long letter addressed to the Friend of the People. The writer calls Marat '*My dear Friend of the People. . . . Incorruptible Defender of the sacred rights of the people !*' He boasts of having served for two years in the National Parisian Guards, and with having led the vanguard ' when those gallant soldiers went to fetch Capet from Versailles.' He asks for a post as Adjutant-General, coolly enumerates his claims to promotion, and in order to add to the list he denounces to right and left of him. He denounces Marolle and Brancas, who have just been appointed Adjutants-General ; he denounces Colonel Virion and Brigadiers-General Noirod and Marnan ; he denounces even General Ferrand.

And beneath all these denunciations I read : 'Adieu ; I embrace you fraternally. HOCHE, Rue du Cherche-Midi, No. 294.'

I cast the infamous paper from me in a fit of disgust. 'Come, come,' said Beaulieu ; 'you must not pass from one extreme to the other in this fashion. I have it on good authority that

---

[1] Lazare Hoche was born at Montreuil, near Versailles, on June 24, 1768. Marie Joseph Chénier was a member for Seine-et-Oise.

since his return to Paris Citizen Hoche has been in close touch with Marat.[1] But what is there surprising in that ? Since this excellent young man feels it his duty to denounce, is he not quite right in addressing himself to the man whom Camille Desmoulins already in 1791 called the *dénonciateur par excellence ?*[2] If he wishes to obtain promotion, is he not wise in paying his court to the Friend of the People ? Does the latter not hold in his hands the destinies of the Convention, and is it not he who to-morrow will make and unmake our Generals ? It is therefore my opinion that Citizen Hoche is no fool, and that he will succeed.' 'You are at liberty to joke as much as you like about it,' I replied ; 'I, for my part, feel disgusted at such conduct. It is possible that Citizen Hoche may succeed, as you say, and that he may command our armies and cover himself with glory ; but for me it is sufficient to know that his hand has grasped that of Marat—a score of victories cannot efface that stain.'

[1] Rousselin, *op. cit.*, tome i., p. 54.
[2] ' Histoire Politique et Littéraire de la Presse en France,' by Eugène Hatin, tome vi., p. 98.

CHAPTER LXXII.

AN OBSERVER OF PUBLIC FEELING.

Monday, May 20, 1793.

CITIZEN DUTARD is a man whom I frequently meet at the Café de Chartres, and with whom I first became acquainted some years ago. He was at one time a barrister in Bordeaux,[1] has a slender knowledge of literature and philosophy, is very vain and garrulous, but is at bottom an honest sort of fellow. Being fully convinced that his talents fitted him to play an important part in politics, he left the provinces for Paris, where he arrived in 1790. It was about that time that I first met him. Being a friend of the younger Garat, whom he had known in Bordeaux, he was a regular attendant at the history classes which the latter held at the Lycée,[2] and which I also frequented most assiduously. I was then living in the Rue Traversière Saint-Honoré, and after the lecture he would often come to my lodgings, where, before the open window, we would indulge in endless argument and conversation. Although he has warmly embraced the principles of the Revolution, Dutard has remained in obscurity and penury, whilst so many others who are far inferior to him have become personages of note. This is no

---

[1] Adolphe Schmidt, ' Tableaux de la Révolution Française, publiés sur les Papiers inédits du Département et de la Police Secrète de Paris,' tome i., p. 140.

[2] The Lycée, which counted among its professors La Harpe, Garat, Fourcroy, Chaptal, and others, was situated in the Rue de Valois, where it occupied the old Musée de Pilatre. A few men of letters, with MM. de Montmorian and de Montesquiou at their head, had set up the new establishment, which was inaugurated at the beginning of 1786, and enjoyed an immense success until 1789 (' Lycée, ou Cours de Littérature Ancienne et Moderne,' by J F. La Harpe).

doubt due to the fact that his watch, instead of being fast, has always been an hour slow ; he has set it by the Assembly clock instead of by that on the Hôtel de Ville. About two months ago, having come to the end of his resources, and without a shoe to his foot or a rag to his back,[1] he considered it a great piece of good luck to receive from Garat, who is now Minister of the Interior, the post of *local observer of the department of Paris.*[2]

' Be careful, my dear friend,' said Dutard to me but the other evening—' be careful not to confound my duties with those of a common detective.' And as the expression on my face was not probably such as to convince him that he had cleared up all doubts in my mind on that point, he explained to me at great length what the *observers of public feeling* really are.

On entering the Ministry, Garat found that he had not a single agent at his disposal for secret service.[3] Roland had, indeed, established a *bureau d'esprit public* for the purpose of propagating matter for the formation of sound public opinion. But though this was a means of influencing the public, it was not a means of seeing, hearing, and knowing all. Roland's *bureau* had, moreover, been suppressed by the Convention at its sitting of January 21, 1793, on the motion of Thuriot.

If the police, this powerful and indispensable weapon, was no longer in the hands of the Government and under the orders of the Executive Council, to whom had it been given up? Since the Tenth of August it had become entirely subordinate to the municipality ; there was no other police department than that which had its headquarters in the Hôtel de Ville.

In addition to this body of municipal police, unscrupulous and uncontrolled, indulgent to malefactors, formidable to honest folk, instigating and abetting the disorders which it is its duty to prevent or repress, which numbers among its members commissioners of the forty-eight sections, and even some of the most active spirits of the sections and the clubs—in addition to this body, and probably merely for his personal satisfaction, Garat

---

[1] Adolphe Schmidt, tome i., p. 182.   [2] *Ibid.*, p. 140.
[3] 'Mémoires sur la Révolution, ou Exposé de ma Conduite,' by D. J. Garat, p. 97.

has organized a small secret police force composed of a dozen of his own private friends, whose mission it is to promenade the streets of Paris, to watch closely all that goes on, and to submit to him daily, either verbally or in writing, the results of their observations.[1]

It is the Minister himself who presides over this information *bureau ;* the sub-director is Champagneux, chief of the first division of the Interior.[2]

Amongst the observers by whom Garat is surrounded, the most active and intelligent are, according to Dutard, Citizens Perrière, Julian de Carentan, Baumier, and Latour-Lamontagne.[3] Dutard finds fault with them for confining themselves to making reports of what they have seen and heard, and for neglecting to draw from the facts the conclusions and philosophy they contain.

On hearing such words as these I was unable to repress a smile, and Dutard continued with some warmth : ' Yes, sir, the philosophy they contain ! Manuel, in his work on the police of Paris, was quite right in saying, " The police force will never be properly managed until we have philosophers at its head."[4] These words are my guide, and I should like to use them as a heading for each of my reports. A statement of facts is, of course, quite indispensable. *Minima circumstantia facti inducit ad maximam differentiam juris.* This principle of jurisprudence has also its application in matters of police. But when the facts have been stated, I have only fulfilled half my duty, and what remains to be done is the more important part. I must draw conclusions from my facts, and report what I feel rather than what I have heard—in a word, what I have observed rather than what I have seen.

---

[1] ' Mémoires de Garat,' p. 90, etc.

[2] Adolphe Schmidt, tome i., p. 138. L. A. Champagneux was the friend of Roland, who had placed him in charge of the ' Bureau of Public Feeling.' His son married Roland's daughter, Eudora. In the year VIII. Champagneux published the ' Works of J. M. P Roland, Wife of the ex-Minister of the Interior, containing her Memoirs, written in Prison in 1793,' in three vols., with a portrait and the following epigraph ' Fortis, et infelix et plus quam femina !'

[3] Adolphe Schmidt, tome i.. p. 140.

[4] ' La Police de Paris dévoilée,' by P. Manuel, 1791 tome ii., p. 297.

'I will give you an example of what I mean. One day towards the end of April, a quarrel arose between two men in the Palais de l'Égalité. The younger of the two, who appeared to me to be a Brissotin, had a dog; the other, who was a Jacobin, trod on the tail of that dog. This led to recriminations, threats, and shouts, and a good deal of laughter from the by-standers. If I had simply related the facts as they happened, would I have fulfilled my duty as an observer? You surely do not think so. As far as I can recollect, this is how I worded my report on that day; it was, I think, April 29: "I reached the Palais de l'Égalité at three o'clock this afternoon. Three hundred Brissotins and aristocrats were seated in different parts of the garden, and in the *cafés*. There were very few Jacobins. Some of the aristocrats were talking politics, and I heard one make a suggestion that the landlords should impose their will upon the sections, and get fresh administrative laws passed. There were a good many country people about, some in uniform, some dressed as civilians. Everyone seemed to be eyeing his neighbour. Suddenly a Jacobin treads on a dog's tail. The dog howls, and his master, who seemed to me to be a Brissotin, gets angry. A crowd immediately gathers. The Jacobin, who is wearing a long sword, makes a show of drawing it. The Brissotin, though very brave at first, turns pale, and begs his adversary's pardon. A dozen Jacobins thus inspired two or three hundred Rolandists with fear. Why? Because the former have a place of meeting, and the others have not; because in Revolutionary times the bold man is victorious; because the Moderates feel the necessity of being supported by the Government, not only when they attack, but even when they defend themselves. Failing this support, they are powerless, however numerous they may be!" [1]

Dutard stopped. I had listened to him with great interest; was there then, after all, a philosopher hidden in this observer? He appeared flattered by the attention I had paid to his words. 'Well,' he said, 'are you beginning to believe that my duties are something different from those of a common spy or a

---

[1] 'Lettre de Dutard à Garat,' April 30, 1793: Schmidt, tome i., p. 161.

wretched informer?' My only reply was to shake him by the hand. 'What do I do, after all?' he added. 'I study the Revolution. And since you also study the same subject, but in a different way, I shall be glad of your company some day, and I can promise you that you will consider your time well spent.'

I made an appointment to meet him at eight o'clock next Sunday morning in front of the church of Saint-Eustache.

CHAPTER LXXIII.

Wednesday, May 22, 1793.

It was Mirabeau who said, 'If you wish to drive Royalism out of France, you must first get rid of Christianity.' I doubt very much whether this is possible, so deeply rooted is the Catholic religion in the soul of France. The Fête-Dieu[1] is approaching, and I shall be greatly surprised if the people of Paris do not on that occasion repress their Revolutionary ardour in order to celebrate this most popular festival, and to follow through the streets the canopy under which the priest bears aloft the Host.

The almighty Commune was unable to prevent the observance of Christmas; I feel sure that it will meet with a similar defeat in the campaign which it will not fail to undertake against the celebration of the Fête-Dieu.

Already last year, on the motion of Manuel, who was the Procureur de la Commune, the municipality issued a proclamation exempting citizens from decorating the exterior of their houses, and the National Guards from attending the service of any cult whatever.[2] This proclamation, sent to the forty-eight sections, was accompanied by a circular, in which the Procureur de la Commune said: 'The time is near at hand when all religious sects will be compelled to restrict the exercise of their rites and ceremonies to the interior of their places of worship, and when they will no longer be allowed to obstruct the public thoroughfares, which belong to all, and which no particular body has a right to monopolize.'

[1] The festival of Corpus Christi.
[2] *Révolutions de Paris*, tome xii., p. 453.

The proclamation of the municipality and Manuel's circular were expected to be favourably received by the working classes, so well canvassed just then—it was the eve of June 20—by the worst kind of demagogues. We know, however, what happened. Petion was stoned by the *sans-culottes* in the Arcis section for having publicly announced that on the day of the Fête-Dieu people would be at liberty to work or not, as they chose.[1] As for Manuel, he was almost torn to pieces.[2]

The Legislative Assembly, though ever hostile to religious ideas and ceremonies, dared not run counter to the feelings of the people of Paris. On Tuesday, June 5, 1792—the Fête-Dieu fell on Thursday, June 7—a letter was read from the Vicar and churchwardens of Saint-Germain l'Auxerrois, inviting the Assembly to take part in the procession; whereupon it decided to hold no sitting on Thursday morning, in order to give members an opportunity of accepting the invitation.

On the Thursday morning there were processions in most of the parishes. All the shops were closed; the houses were decorated more tastefully than before the Revolution,[3] and on the minor *fête*-day, a week later, the same thing occurred. The procession in each parish was headed by a military band. The National Guards formed an escort, and their officers walked sword in hand before the canopy. The processions of Saint-Eustache and Saint-Roche were particularly conspicuous for the large number of soldiers that took part in them.[4] The canopy of Saint-Sulpice was borne by grenadiers.[5] That of Notre Dame was accompanied by the judges of every court of Paris dressed in gala costume and adorned with the tricolour cockade.[6] All along the line of route the spectators reverently uncovered their heads, and those who obstinately refused to do so were roughly handled

---

[1] 'Rapport de Police de l'Observateur Dutard': 'Tableaux de la Révolution Française,' by Adolphe Schmidt, tome i., p. 302.

[2] *Ibid.*

[3] 'In spite of the inclemency of the weather, the clergy of Paris would not give up their processions, and trudged through the mud. They had the sweet satisfaction of seeing the houses decorated with perhaps greater care than usual, so loth is the ordinary *bourgeois* to give up his old customs. There is still more faith in Israel than the priests themselves dare to believe' (*Révolutions de Paris*, tome xii., p. 457).

[4] *Révolutions de Paris*, p. 494.   [5] *Ibid.*, p. 458.   [6] *Ibid.*

by the crowd; some were even arrested.[1] In the Rue de la Harpe a provision-dealer who had not decorated his shop-front had his windows smashed.[2] The patriot Legendre, who lives in the Rue des Boucheries Saint-Germain, having attempted to disturb the procession of Saint-Germain-des-Prés on the evening of June 7, the people took the law into their own hands, and the notorious butcher was carried to the section amidst the jeers and shouts of the crowd.[3]

Since these events took place Paris has sunk deeper and deeper into the slough of the Revolution—deeper into blood and mire—and yet there are many symptoms which prove that faith is not dead, and that, in spite of the Héberts and the Marats, of the Brissots and the Condorcets,[4] Paris and France have not yet 'got rid of Christianity.'

In the month of November last, did we not see the Commune —the Commune itself—obliged to take part in a *Te Deum*, sung at Notre Dame as a thanksgiving for the victories of the Republic?[5]

On January 11 of this year delegates from forty communes of the departments of the Eure, the Orne, and Eure-et-Loir were admitted to the bar of the National Convention, where they made use of the following language: 'We have been sent to ask you to maintain the free exercise and the purity of the Catholic religion, and to provide for the continued support of our ministers. You were not sent here by atheists, and there-fore you cannot refuse to grant our petition.'[6]

Citizen Perrière, one of Dutard's colleagues, a philosopher and an ardent partisan of the Revolution—one who, in spite of his anti-religious passions, has remained a clear-sighted and judicious observer—spoke as follows but a few days ago to Dutard and myself: 'The fire of superstition that still burns so

---

[1] *Révolutions de Paris*, p. 494; *La Feuilles Villageoise*, No. 39 (June 21, 1792).

[2] *Révolutions de Paris*, tome xii., p. 494.   [3] *Ibid.*, p. 458.

[4] The newspapers of the Girondist party vied with those of the Mountain in showing their disrespect for religion. In this Brissot and Marat went hand-in-hand. See 'Légende des Girondins,' by Edmond Biré, p. 209, etc.

[5] 'Histoire Parlementaire de la Révolution,' by Buchez and Roux, tome xxi., p. 51.   [6] *Op. cit.*, tome xxiii., p. 62.

brightly in the Vendée, in Brittany, in the Lozère, and in most of the southern provinces, still smoulders in places where it is believed to be extinguished for ever. I know a good deal about Auvergne; I lived there for a long time, and I was there but a short time ago. The Revolution, it is true, has no partisans more stanch and true than the Auvergnats; but though they detested their tyrants, they loved, and they still love, their priests. These simple folks are at present divided into two classes. The one accepts the priests who have taken the oath; the other, and this is unfortunately the more numerous class, is still obstinately attached to its refractory priests. I can assure you,' added Perrière, 'that the aristocrat, the Spaniard, and the Austrian had no more dangerous enemies than these hardy and industrious tillers of the soil; but France will lose men who are so doubly precious to her if she persists in demanding the sacrifice of their priests.'[1]

But I come back to Paris, where the survival of Catholic ideas and sentiments—of superstition, to use Citizen Perrière's expression—is still more remarkable, and, in fact, really extraordinary.

On February 9 last the Section of the Butte des Moulins lodged information with the Conseil-Général de la Commune of the holding of parochial assemblies in the church of Saint-Roch on January 25 and February 2 and 3 for the purpose of continuing Divine worship in the same fashion as formerly. 'It is the opinion of the section,' said the Patriots of the Butte des Moulins, 'that the attempted innovation may lead to a schism, not only between the priests who are paid by the nation and those who would be supported by the proposed new administration, but also between the citizens whose principal concern is the common weal and the zealous Catholics of Saint-Roch.' It also gave information concerning an office where voluntary subscriptions are received for the carrying on of Divine worship.[2]

Some refractory priests, heedless of the dangers to which they

---

[1] Schmidt, 'Tableaux de la Révolution Française,' tome ii., p. 8: 'Rapport de Perrière à Garat,' Minister of the Interior.
[2] *Chronique de Paris*, February 12, 1793.

are exposed, continue to hold services in the hall of the Missions Etrangères, in the Rue du Bac. These services are held two or three times a week; admission is only by ticket.[1]

I myself witnessed the following incident quite recently in the neighbourhood of the Halles. As I was going through the Rue de la Poterie, I met a priest carrying the last Sacrament to a dying man. Six armed men, all of the lowest class—real *sans-culottes*—escorted the canopy as far as the house, and waiting at the door until the priest made his reappearance, accompanied him back to his church. Men and women, both young and old, prostrated themselves in the streets and in the doorways as the host was carried by.[2] I knelt down with all the rest. This is a sight which may be witnessed every day, especially in the poorer quarters. The vicars and their curates continue to parade the streets in their cassocks and surplices whenever their duties require it. Funerals are always conducted with great solemnity.

Passing through the Rue Sainte-Avoye, I met two priests, who were returning from an interment. The sacristan happened to touch a drunken porter with his silver cross, causing the man to pour forth a volley of abuse. 'Hush!' said one of his mates; 'it is the good God.' 'Get out with your good God! there is no good God.' Such was evidently not the opinion of the passers-by, for they all uncovered, and nearly all made the sign of the cross and muttered a prayer.[3]

Last Sunday was Whit-Sunday. At one time it was a general, and a very pleasant, holiday. It then lasted for three days, and during that time all business was suspended; there were friendly gatherings, and whole families would meet together to celebrate the festival in truly Christian and Gallic fashion.

In spite of the sorrows that overwhelm us, and the threats of evils still to come, in spite of the fierce struggle of parties, in spite of the clubs, the revolts, and the cries of hatred and death that re-echo on all sides, Paris has not allowed Whitsuntide to

---

[1] Extracts from the police reports of May 24 and 25, 1793; C. A. Dauban, 'La Démagogie en 1793 à Paris,' p. 199.
[2] Schmidt, tome ii., p. 63: 'Rapport de Dutard à Garat.'
[3] Schmidt, tome ii., p. 41: 'Rapport de Perrière à Garat.'

pass without indulging in a momentary truce, without recalling, if but for an instant, that life of yore, filled, perhaps, with pain and misery, but full also of consolation, of simple mirth, and of pure joy.

During these three days—Sunday, Monday, and Tuesday[1]—all the shops were closed. I did not hear a hammer used anywhere.[2]

In the Halles the sellers of second-hand clothes, who are nearly all Grey Friars and Jacobins, took a holiday for the whole of the three days.[3]

Round the cemetery of the Innocents, the hucksters who sell meat and vegetables under their huge umbrellas also indulged in a holiday, and yet these men are the most fanatical supporters of the Grey Friar and Jacobin party.[4]

Yesterday, Tuesday, wishing to speak to my binder, who lives in the Rue de la Montagne Sainte-Geneviève, I knocked at his door, but received no reply. A woman living next door put her head out of the window, and told me that they had all gone visiting. I found the streets full of people dressed in their Sunday clothes, and all bent on enjoying themselves.[5]

To-day the truce is over. Paris has once more become a hot-bed of passion. The religious festivals are past, and it is again the turn of the Revolution to provide us with amusement. We have not been kept waiting long. At eleven o'clock this morning, General Miaczinski was guillotined in the Place de la Révolution.[6] The executioner showed his head to the people from each of the four sides of the scaffold.[7]

---

[1] May 19, 20, 21, 1793.

[2] Schmidt, tome i., p. 265 : ' Rapport de Dutard à Garat. '

[3] Schmidt, *loc. cit.*   [4] *Ibid.*   [5] *Ibid.*

[6] In preceding chapters we have seen that the executions took place in the Place de la Réunion (du Carrousel). On its removal to the Tuileries, the Convention, not wishing to have the scaffold under its windows, decreed that the sentences of the Revolutionary Tribunal should no longer be executed in the Place de la Réunion, and requested the Provisional Executive Council to find another site. The spot chosen was the Place de la Révolution, formerly Place Louis XV., where the scaffold had been erected for the execution of Louis XVI.. The guillotine was put up between the Garde-Meuble and the pedestal of Louis XVI.'s statue, almost on the spot where the fountain now stands, on the north side.

[7] *Bulletin du Tribunal Révolutionnaire*, No. 40, p. 100.

Sentence was passed upon the Adjutant-General Devaux to-day; he will be executed to-morrow.[1]

Twenty-seven prisoners are now waiting to be tried before the Revolutionary Tribunal on a charge of having taken part in the plot concocted by the Marquis de la Rouairie. After them, there will be more unhappy wretches dragged from the prison to the tribunal, and from the tribunal to the Place de la Révolution. For a good many weeks, perhaps months, the executioner will be able to hold up fresh trophies to the gaping mob.

There is this to be said for the *fêtes* of the Republic—they last for more than three days.

---

[1] '"It is impossible," said Dr. Brooks, an English physician, "for a man to proceed to his execution without experiencing some kind of fear that makes him turn pale and gives his face an agitated appearance." Philippe Devaux proved by his demeanour that Dr. Brooks was mistaken, for his face never betrayed the slightest emotion during the whole of the journey from the Conciergerie to the scaffold. He had asked to be allowed to go on foot, but this was refused him' ('Le Glaive Vengeur,' p. 77). The following is a translation of the full title of the interesting work from which the above quotation has been taken (its author was named Du Lac): 'The Avenging Blade of the French Republic, or Revolutionary Gallery; containing the full names, place of birth, rank, age, crimes, and last words, of all the great conspirators and traitors whose heads fell under the national blade by order of the Revolutionary Tribunal established in Paris . . . by a Friend of the Revolution, of morality, and of justice.'

CHAPTER LXXIV

Sunday, May 26, 1793.

I was very punctual in keeping my appointment with Dutard. Eight o'clock had not yet struck from the steeple of Saint-Eustache when I reached the great church doors; Dutard, however, was there before me. Our first visit was paid to a friend of his, a grocer living near the Halles. We found him standing in his doorway, and he told us that supplies were daily getting scarcer—that, in fact, there would soon be none at all. ' I am going to give up selling brandy,' he added; ' it is now more than double the price that it was six months ago.[1] In a letter which I received from a merchant in Orleans yesterday, he tells me that sugar (exclusive of freight and commission) is selling at 3 francs 6 sous per lb.; coffee at 2 francs 14 sous; rice at 15 sous; and oil at 2 francs 5 sous per pint.[2] It is daily becoming more difficult to procure these commodities, and it is the same with manufactured articles.' The worthy man gave us a good deal of other information of great interest. He told us that the paper-money bearing the imprint of the Republic is not regarded with much confidence, and that everyone prefers to receive the *corsets*[3] and the notes for 50 and 100 francs marked with the late King's effigy.[4] When the merchants of Paris send

---

[1] Schmidt, tome i., p. 287. [2] *Ibid.*, p. 329.

[3] The *corset* was a five-franc note. The word is not to be found in Littré's Dictionary; there are about a thousand other words, all created during the period of the Revolution, which are absent from that monumental work. A dictionary of the French language during the Revolution is sorely needed.

[4] Schmidt, tome ii., p. 61.

to the provinces for fresh supplies, they are obliged to remit the amount either in *corsets* or in notes bearing the King's head. No others will be accepted.[1]

Before leaving the grocer, Dutard pointed to the women standing in groups outside the Halles, and asked : ' What do they think of the present state of business ?' ' Why,' was the reply, ' these women are nearly all aristocrats ; the new, the old, or any other *régime*, is all one to them ; they can sell nothing now, and whoever promises them a return to abundance will have their support.'[2]

Passing through the Rue des Lombards and the Rue des Arcis, we reached the Quai Pelletier. Here everything was in a great state of uproar. The street was packed, and from all the windows of the houses people were wildly shouting and gesticulating. Drawn up in military fashion, and with a standard flying at their head, a number of women were just about to start for the Pont Neuf, and were inviting the passers-by to take part in the liberation of good, honest Père Duchêne from the Abbaye.[3] These excellent *patriotes* were no others than the *citoyennes* of the Société Fraternelle, hideous hags whom one is sure of meeting wherever mischief is to be done, or a disgusting sight is to be seen—at the Revolutionary Tribunal, round the scaffold, in the galleries of the Convention, or in the streets when rioting is going on. Some were armed with pikes, others with swords and long knives ; many of them had bottles in their arms, and all were yelling : ' *Down with the Twelve !* ' *Long live the Mountain !* ' *Death to the Brissotins !* ' *Long live Marat !* ' *Long live Père Duchêne !* And this band was allowed to roam through the streets of Paris, no authority attempting to place the least obstacle in its way.[4]

[1] Schmidt, tome ii. p. 61.   [2] *Ibid.*, tome i., p. 272.
[3] Beaulieu, ' Le Diurnal de la Révolution,' May 26, 1793.
[4] On May 20 the Convention had appointed a Commission of twelve members to examine the orders and proclamations issued by the Commune of Paris during the past month. Seven of the twelve belonged to the Girondist party. They were Boyer-Fonfrede, Rabaut Saint-Étienne, Kervélegan, Boilleau, Mollevant, Bergoeing, and Henry-Larivière. The politics of four others—Gomaire, Saint-Martin Valogne, Bertrand (of the Orne), and Gardien—were of a less pronounced type. Viger, the last, had only been in the Convention since April 27. On May 24 the Com-

On reaching the Pont Neuf, we left the *citoyennes* of the Société Fraternelle to continue their way to the Abbaye, whilst we betook ourselves to the Tuileries, where we found another large assemblage of females. They had gathered on the principal terrace of the palace, where an indescribable tumult reigned. The women had sworn to prevent the execution of the new Decree of the Convention, according to the terms of which 400 gallery tickets are to be distributed daily amongst the provincial constituencies. Crowding round the sentry, whose duty it is to examine the tickets, they tore them out of his hands and destroyed them, whilst the people in whose possession they had been were turned away amidst much jeering, and sometimes roughly handled.[1] It is unnecessary to add that the other sentries, who are changed every day, showed no great amount of energy, and took not the slightest notice of what was going on under their very eyes. A member whom Dutard did not know attempted to interfere. 'What are you doing here?' he said to the women who were standing round the sentry. 'By what right are you here?' 'By the rights of equality,' replied one of them. 'Are we not all equal? And if we are all equal, I have as much right here as those who have tickets.' In reply to the deputy's threats that he would have them expelled, they shouted : 'Get out, you Brissotin ! your place is inside. We shall stay here as long as we like, and upset your little game.' It was ten o'clock, and the sitting was about to begin ; the representative returned to the Assembly amidst the shouts and laughter of the mob.

In the garden a cut-throat—one of the *massacreurs* of September—was kind enough to exchange a few remarks with us, and to inform us that he had *worked* at the Abbaye and the Force. According to what he told us, it seems that this worthy man only undertakes big jobs, and that he hopes to be at work

mission of Twelve had issued warrants for the arrest of Michel and Marino, two Administrators of Police, and had sent Hébert, the Deputy-Procureur de la Commune, to the Abbaye for the publication of an article in the *Père Duchêne*, accusing the Girondists of attempting to kindle a civil war and to arm provincial citizens against the Parisians.

[1] Letter from J. P. Brissot to his constituents; Schmidt, tome i., p. 377.

again soon.[1] After we had got rid of this wretch, Dutard confessed that he really thought we were approaching a fresh crisis, and that there would perhaps be more massacres. He has heard that some very suggestive language has been used by Hanriot, the notorious Commandant of the battalion of the Sans-Culottes section. Addressing a workman of the Port Saint-Bernard in his gruff voice, Hanriot said to him : 'Good-day, comrade ; we shall soon require your help again. This time, however, we shall not work upon the aristocrats with pikes, but with iron bars.' Turning to another workman seated on his hand-cart, he asked him : 'Have you any work, my friend ?' 'A bit.' 'I will give you plenty in a few days' time ; you will have a load of corpses in your cart instead of wood !' 'All right,' replied the man ; 'we shall do as we did on September 2. It will put a few pence in our pockets.'[2]

As the Tuileries clock struck eleven, Dutard asked me whether I knew M. Saule. 'No ? Well, let us go into his *café* for a moment ; I have known him for a long time. I will introduce you.'

M. Saule, whose *café* is situated just outside the palace garden, near the entrance to the old Riding-School, is a fat little old man, who potters about amongst his customers, talking, shouting, and laughing all the time. He boasts of having known every member of our three legislative assemblies, as well as all the reporters. He possesses an inexhaustible stock of reminiscences and anecdotes concerning Mirabeau and the Abbé Maury, Robespierre and Barnave, Cazalès and Danton, Petion and Brissot, Camille Desmoulins and Hébert. He told us a few of them whilst we did honour to a cup of his excellent chocolate.

As we left the *café*, and directed our steps towards the Rue Saint-Honoré, Dutard told me something about this curious old man. 'The life of M. Saule,' he said, 'is by no means uninstructive. He was first an upholsterer, then a hawker or charlatan, selling twopenny boxes of hanged men's fat as a cure for lumbago. He sank lower and lower, and at last, in 1790,

---

[1] Schmidt, tome ii., p. 5 : 'Rapport de Dutard.'
[2] Schmidt, tome i., p. 335 : 'Rapport de Perrière à Garat.'

found his way into the galleries of the National Assembly, where his sonorous voice and his well-moistened throat gained him some reputation, and, it seems, some profit. At that time I was also a gallery *habitué*, and I was soon one of M. Saule's numerous friends. Alas! one fine morning we heard that he had been charged with some piece of roguery, the particulars of which I do not quite remember, and that we should see him no more. But those who said this could not have known him. It was quite true that he had been obliged to shoulder his box of ointments, and to resume his travels; but before two months were over, he reappeared in the galleries as fresh as a daisy, and again rendered the cause of the people—without, of course, forgetting himself—the most signal service.

'For nearly three years he directed the expression of public feeling in the gallery entrusted to his care. Having obtained a site for a *café* at the very door of the Assembly, he became a man of still greater importance. Before entering the Riding-School every spectator would call at the *café* to learn from him which way the wind blew, and to receive their instructions for applauding or hooting the speakers. The National Assembly rewarded him for his valuable services, and the Legislative Assembly granted him, besides the sum of 600 francs, a set of rooms in the Maison des Feuillants. He is now a rich man, and has probably forgotten his twopenny boxes of hanged men's fat.'[1]

It did not escape me that there was a certain amount of bitterness in the words of the unfortunate Dutard, who possesses both talent and honesty, and who is, however, as poor as a church-mouse. 'It is only meet,' I observed, 'that M. Saule should have made his fortune by the Revolution. It is the Assemblies who brought about the Revolution, but it is the galleries which have forced the votes upon the Assemblies, and it is such men as M. Saule who have influenced the opinion of the galleries!'

After dining at Venua's, opposite the Jacobin Club, we strolled into the Palais de l'Égalité, where we found a good deal of excitement reigning. In the centre of one of the numerous groups a National Guard was inveighing against the Commission of Twelve. 'These half-measures,' he said, 'have always been

---

[1] 'Rapport de Dutard à Garat': Schmidt, tome i., p. 215.

fatal to the people; we have been too sparing of blood all along. The work of the Tenth of August is not yet complete. All we have done is to change our tyrants. Despotism still reigns in the palace of the Tuileries. We have fresh kings who are surrounded by Swiss Guards of another kind, and there are still too many warrants about; all this must come to an end, and the new tyrants and their satellites must fall under the blade of the people. Half Paris must die to save the other half and to preserve the Republic.' He then went on to say that in his mind there was no doubt that the end of the month would be the end of the world for a great many people.[1] A woman warmly echoed his words, declaring that the citizens of the Butte des Moulins were nothing but Swiss Guards, who would, however, share the fate of their prototypes.

Everything, in fact, seems to indicate that we are to have another Tenth of August, and that the scene of action will again be laid in the Tuileries. Instead of the attack being directed against Louis XVI. and the Swiss Guard, it will be directed against the Girondists; against Brissot, who declared that 'the Revolution of the Tenth of August would for ever remain the greatest day in the history of France'[2]; against Vergniaud, who on that day presided over the Legislative Assembly, and persuaded it to vote for the convocation of a National Convention.

Anxious to hear what had taken place in the Convention, we returned to the Tuileries about three o'clock. The women whom we had seen about the entrance in the morning were still there. They are most probably paid for their attendance. I heard one of them say to a Jacobin who went about from group to group, and seemed to be dealing out instructions, 'You still owe me twenty sous;' and the Jacobin handed her the money.

We were fortunate enough to find seats in one of the galleries, from which we could watch the second part of the proceedings. Isnard was in the chair. The Brissotins are still in a majority, and, in spite of the Mountain, they have just suppressed the Revolutionary Committee of the Unité section and issued an

---

[1] 'Rapport de Latour de Montagne' : Schmidt, tome i., p. 336.
[2] 'À Tous les Républicains de France,' by J. P. Brissot, October, 1792.

order for the liberation of Antoine le Tellier, Professor in the
Collège des Quatre Nations, whom the Committee had placed
under arrest. Le Tellier's crime consisted of having composed
Latin verses against Robespierre and Marat and of having
Cicero's orations against Catilina and Sallust's 'Conjuratio Cati-
linæ' translated in his class. Salle sarcastically moved the impeachment of Sallust, and asked that a warrant might be issued
against Cicero. Some of the members of the Left seemed to
miss the point, and the story was told in the *cafés* to-night that
one of them said to his neighbour, 'Does this Sallust live in
Paris?' 'No,' replied the other, 'in Rome.'

Bourdon, Bentabolle and some others of the Mountain, asked
that Le Tellier's Latin verses might be read; it was, however,
pointed out that this would be useless unless they were translated, and that was a matter of some difficulty.[1] The Girondist
party had saved one of its friends, and the action had no doubt
cost it a great effort. A few moments later it joined the
Mountain in sending before the Revolutionary Tribunal Jacques
Leclerc, editor of the *Chronique Nationale*, Michel-Aumont, a
lawyer, and twenty-one other inhabitants of Rouen, all accused
of having on January 11 and 12 last trampled upon the national
cockade and of having burnt the tree of Liberty.[2]

Just as we were leaving the hall, a deputation from sixteen
sections of Paris presented itself at the bar to demand Hébert's
liberation and the suppression of the Commission of Twelve.

As soon as we had reached the street, Dutard said to me:
'Hébert's arrest will act like a spark falling into a barrel of
gunpowder. The insurrection which has now been in the air
for some weeks cannot fail to burst forth upon the slightest
provocation. The Girondist party will perish, and the triumph
of the Commune is assured. The wealthy and the middle classes

---

[1] *Le Patriote Français*, No. 1,383. *Le Moniteur* bardly mentions this
incident, which had, however, a tragic *dénouement*. Liberated on May 26,
1793, Le Tellier was again arrested, and guillotined on the 6th of Messidor,
year II. (June 24, 1794).

[2] *Le Patriote Français*, No. 1,383. The rioters of Rouen appeared
before the Revolutionary Tribunal in September, 1793. Leclerc, Aumont,
and six of their confederates, among whom there was one woman, were
condemned to death. See 'Histoire du Tribunal Révolutionnaire,' by
H. Wallon, tome i., p. 252, etc.

are threatened with a most terrible form of tyranny; yet do
you think that they are taking any action amongst themselves
to avert the danger, or that they are even troubling their heads
about it? Not a bit of it—they have something better to do.
You may be sure that at this very moment they are all enjoying themselves at the theatre. It is five o'clock, and we cannot
do better than finish our day in the same manner.'

The Théâtre de la Nation, where we took two balcony seats,
was well filled. The play was 'Les Châteaux en Espagne'
(Castles in the Air), by Collin d'Harleville. I had been present at the first performance of the piece in February, 1789,
when we were all building castles in the air.

So great is the contrast between the brilliant illusions which
then filled everyone's mind, and the sombre realities of the
present day, that Collin d'Harleville's simple and harmless play
seemed to me this evening a bitter, stinging satire. Such,
however, did not appear to be the general impression. Nothing
is more remarkable, and, I must add, nothing is more sad, than
the nonchalance with which our middle classes continue to take
their usual pleasures amidst the dangers and the degradation of
their country. Dutard was quite right in saying: 'Let them
continue to have their amusements, let them be free to move
about in the interior of the city, and let them be exempt from
going to war; even if subjected to the heaviest taxation under
these conditions, they will make no attempt to rise, nor will
they give signs of their existence. The most important question for them will always be, "Do we get as much amusement
under a Republican Government as we did under the old
régime?"'[1]

At nine o'clock Dutard left me to go and write his report for
Garat. The post of 'local observer of the department of Paris'
is certainly no sinecure.

---

[1] Schmidt, tome i., p. 378.

CHAPTER LXXV.

Thursday, May 30, 1793.

To-day was the Fête Dieu. Its celebration naturally suffered somewhat from the political situation and from the storm-clouds which are gathering over Paris, and which may break at any moment.

Under these circumstances the vicars of several parishes deemed it prudent to conduct their processions *intra muros.*[1] At Saint-Germain l'Auxerrois, as in many other churches, the procession did not leave the building, but at the Madeleine the old custom was kept up, and rather a large number of National Guards followed the priests through the streets.[2]

The district of the Halles is my principal centre of observation. It is there, in the old streets of Saint-Denis, Saint-Martin, and Saint-Eustache, that we must go if we wish to gauge the feelings of the people, for there lies the heart of Paris. About eight o'clock this morning I was in the Rue Saint-Martin, near the church of Saint-Merri, when I heard the roll of a drum. I saw some banners waving in the distance, and from the passers-by I learnt that it was the procession of Saint-Leu. It was headed by an imposing-looking Suisse, who was followed by a dozen priests, one of whom carried the Host. The canopy was borne aloft by soldiers, and followed by a large crowd. The shops were not closed, neither were the houses decorated; but if there was not the usual pomp, there was at

[1] Schmidt, 'Tableaux de la Révolution Française,' tome i., p. 350 : ' Rapport de Dutard à Garat.'
[2] *Ibid.,* tome i., p. 354.

least sincere respect and true devotion. All the spectators knelt, and there was not a man but uncovered. As the procession passed the guard-house of the Bon-Conseil section, all the men turned out and presented arms.[1]

A few moments later I was again in the Halles. There was general regret that no preparations had been made to receive the procession in a fitting manner, and the loud-tongued *citoyennes* were lamenting that they had credited the rumours which had caused these to be neglected. After some time the procession returned, and some of the stall-keepers, to show their joy, discharged their pistols in the air ; more than a hundred shots were fired.[2] After the priests had passed, there was again a loud chorus of lamentations concerning the absence of any display and the injury thus done to trade. 'Every year,' said a flower-seller to me, 'I used to employ thirty women to make up bouquets for the Fête Dieu, and we always had a very good week ; in every other business you will hear them say the same.'[3] I had no desire to contradict the worthy woman, who added, as she placed her arms akimbo, 'that it was all very well to dethrone a tyrant, but that if the Patriots touched "the good God" it would bring bad luck to the Republic.'

---

[1] Schmidt, *loc. cit.*   [2] *Ibid.*   [3] *Ibid.*, tome ii., p. 6.

CHAPTER LXXVI.

Friday, May 31, 1793.

To-day, May 31, the Central Committee of Insurrection entered upon its career by boldly assuming the direction of public affairs; its authority is recognised by the sections, the Jacobin and the Grey Friars Clubs, and even by the Commune, which abdicates its powers in favour of the new rulers. In a few hours' time the Committee will perhaps have driven the Girondist deputies from the Tuileries, and added one Revolution more to our already long list of such events. It may be as well to define here what this Committee really is, how and when it was formed, and how it has managed to impose its will upon the Commune of Paris as a preliminary to laying its dictates upon the Convention and upon France. The history of the Central Committee will form a sequel to the history of the Société des Feuillants, and unless I am mistaken, it will teach very much the same moral.

On March 30 last, the Rights of Man section, one of the most Revolutionary sections of Paris, invited the forty-seven others to send delegates to a meeting to be held in the Episcopal Palace on the morrow, for the purpose of deliberating upon the means of saving the country.[1] The place of meeting was well

---

[1] The Archiepiscopal Palace had become merely episcopal since the archiepiscopal sees had been suppressed in the civil constitution of the clergy. Jean Baptiste Joseph Gobel, formerly Bishop of Lydda, had been installed as Bishop of Paris on March 27, 1791. He was guillotined on the 24th of Germinal, year II. (April 13, 1794), together with Chaumette, Lucile Desmoulins, and Hébert's widow.

chosen. The Episcopal Palace is situated close to Notre Dame in the section of the City—a section well known for the ardour of its politics, and led by Dobsent, the friend of Hébert.

In the meeting held on March 31,[1] some of the delegates declared that their powers did not warrant them to do more than take note of such measures of public safety as would be proposed, and to lay them before the general assembly of their section — unseasonable scruples, which did not prevent the majority of the delegates from forming themselves into a *Central Committee of Public Safety.*[2] Already on April 1 the Central Committee sent a deputation to the Conseil-Général de la Commune, to inform the latter of its establishment, and to ask that suitable premises might be provided for its accommodation. The Conseil-Général, after listening to a speech from Chaumette, passed a resolution complying with this demand.

I must do the Convention the justice of mentioning that it appeared to understand the danger of this self-styled *Committee of Public Safety*, and that it tried to avert it.

Amongst the sections whose delegates had refused to take part in the vote of March 31 was the section Du Mail, one of the few sections in which the Moderates have still the upper hand.[3] It declared, ' in general meeting assembled, that it approved of the conduct of its delegates in keeping within the limits of the powers granted them ; that it disapproved most strongly of the resolution passed by the delegates who had met in the Episcopal Palace, and that it would submit only to properly constituted authorities and to the laws emanating from the Convention.' It further decided that this resolution should be sent to the Convention, where it was read on April 2.

On Barère's motion, the Convention replied by passing the following Decree :

' Article 1.—The National Convention declares that the section Du Mail has deserved well of the country.

---

[1] The meeting called by the Rights of Man section was held at the Episcopal Palace on March 31, and not on April 1, as stated by Adolphe Schmidt in his ' Tableaux de la Révolution,' tome i., p. 151.

[2] *Moniteur* of April 4, 1793.

[3] The section Du Mail, formerly the section Place Louis Quatorze, held its meetings in the church of the Petits Pères.

'Article 2.—It summons the Mayor of Paris to appear at its bar to give an account of the meeting of delegates from the sections held at the Episcopal Palace on March 31.

'Article 3.—The delegates of the sections who passed the resolution on March 31 are also summoned to the bar to give an account of the motives that actuated them in passing the said resolution.

'Article 4.—The National Convention would have it known to all citizens of the Republic that the firmness shown by it in condemning the Tyrant will not fail to be put forward in crushing the new form of tyranny which threatens to usurp and annihilate national representation.'[1]

These were fine phrases. Unfortunately the firmness which the majority of the Convention boasted of having shown in condemning the Tyrant had been nothing more than cowardly submission to the wishes and passions of the mob. The task now before the Assembly was to resist this self-same mob, and the Convention was perhaps going a little too far in pledging itself so irrevocably.

In its struggle with the Central Committee of Public Safety it was, however, to have some powerful auxiliaries, and at their head the Commune itself, which soon perceived the mistake it had made in stamping the meeting at the Episcopal Palace with its authority.

On April 2, the very day on which the delegates from the section Du Mail appeared at the bar of the Convention, a deputation from the electoral body waited upon the Commune, and expressed 'their indignation at seeing an assembly of individuals who refused to recognise the sovereignty of the people audaciously assume the title of *Central Committee of Public Safety* without the sanction of the majority of the sections.' It was also said that four sections had withdrawn the powers they had given their delegates to be members of this Central Committee, and that the Committee had therefore lost the support of the majority of the sections. The Conseil-Général de la Commune consequently decided to postpone the execution of the decree it had passed on the preceding day.

The Jacobin Club too, had regarded with some jealousy the

[1] *Moniteur*, April 4.

creation of this Central Committee, which, by placing itself in communication with the provinces, was poaching upon the preserves of that society. Should it suffer these insolent rivals to erect an altar in juxtaposition to its own? It was holding a sitting on March 31, when one of the delegates, who had helped to establish the Central Committee at the Episcopal Palace, entered and informed the Club of what had just taken place. The members immediately rose in a body and expressed their disapproval in the strongest possible terms.[1] At the sitting of April 3, one of the members of the Club pointed out that the Central Committee of Public Safety had held a meeting at the Episcopal Palace after the authorities had already declared it dissolved. Another member declared that as nearly all the sections had passed disapprobatory resolutions respecting this Committee, it was now quite harmless and moribund. A third proposed that all Jacobin members who allowed their names to remain on the list of the Central Committee should be expelled from the Club. The motion was carried.

In its earliest stages, the Central Committee was therefore opposed by the Jacobin Club, the Conseil-Général de la Commune and the majority in the Convention. It paid but little heed to this opposition, and ignored the decree of April 2, which summoned to the bar the authors of the resolution passed in the Episcopal Palace on March 31. The Convention suffered this contempt for its authority to pass unnoticed, and on April 10 Vergniaud, in his reply to Robespierre, could only refer to the 'incredible weakness' of his friends in the following terms:

'The formation of this Central Committee has shown the existence of a fresh plot, having ramifications throughout the country. The plot was upset through the patriotism of the section Du Mail, and you summoned to your bar the members of that Central Committee. Have they obeyed your decree? Have they come? No. Who are you, then? Have you ceased to be the representatives of the people? Where are the new men whom it has invested with its omnipotence? Thus are your

[1] Speech by Barère in the Convention, April 2, 1793 (*Moniteur*, April 4).

decrees insulted; thus are you shamefully tossed about at the mercy of plotters.'[1]

The indulgence of the Convention was not calculated to discourage the organizers of the Central Committee of Public Safety, who nevertheless deemed it prudent to throw over their proceedings a veil of some kind—so transparent, however, that it hid nothing from view. For some time past the electors illegally appointed on the Tenth of August had met at the Episcopal Palace, and their meetings bore the name of the Electoral Club.[2] All of them were naturally demagogues, and several of the delegates who sat on the Central Committee had been chosen from amongst them. Nothing was therefore easier for the members of that Committee than to meet at the Episcopal Palace, on the pretence of attending the assemblies of the Electoral Club. In the early days of May we find them preparing a new Revolutionary blow.

On May 12 about eighty of them attended a sitting at which the means of purging the Convention were discussed.[3] They decided that the time had come to disarm and arrest all suspected persons, and that the revolutionary committees of the forty-eight sections should be entrusted with the execution of this measure. The administrators of police, who are all ardent Maratists, and some of whom no doubt were present at the meeting in the Episcopal Palace, undertook to get this resolution passed by the Commune. Already, on May 13, we find the police authorities laying before the Conseil-Général de la Commune a report upon the condition of Paris, which concludes with the following sentence: 'We consider that it is absolutely indispensable to disarm and arrest all the suspects who abound in Paris, and who have frequently endeavoured to plunge us into civil war.'[4] The Conseil was of the same opinion; it decreed that the Mayor and the police were to disarm and arrest all suspected persons, and

[1] *Moniteur*, April 4, 1793.

[2] Lanjuinais' speech in the Convention on May 30, 1793 (*Moniteur*, June 1).

[3] 'Rapport de Terrasson à Garat,' May 13, 1793; 'Rapport de Dutard,' May 14: Adolphe Schmidt, tome i., pp. 217, 225; Barère's speech in the Convention on May 18 (*Moniteur*, May 20, 1793).

[4] *Chronique de Paris*, May, 1793.

that the manner of executing this decree was to be discussed with closed doors.

Without losing any time, the police authorities, in a letter dated May 14 and signed by Léchenard and Soulès,[1] invited the revolutionary committees of the sections to assemble in the Hôtel de Ville, in order to deliberate upon measures concerning the public safety, and more particularly to draw up a list of suspected persons.

From that moment there were thus two perfectly distinct hot-beds of agitation—the Central Committee of Public Safety, composed of sectional delegates, meeting at the Episcopal Palace, and the assembly of delegates of the revolutionary committees, meeting at the Hôtel de Ville.

At first the delegates deliberated with closed doors, according to the commands laid upon them. Something, however, of their two first meetings leaked out, and Barère, in his speech in the Convention on May 18, gave utterance to some of the rumours that were being circulated. After having spoken of the meetings held in one of the apartments in the Episcopal Palace, he added: ' There is another fact concerning which the Ministers of Foreign Affairs and of the Interior may have something to say. A band of men have met in a certain place (the Hôtel de Ville) to deliberate upon the best means of carrying off twenty-two members of the Convention. A petition was to be presented to the Convention, begging it to return to its old quarters, and as we passed through the midst of the crowd, France was to be rid of these twenty-two citizens.'[2]

The third meeting of the Central Committee was held on Sunday, May 19—on the day after Barère's speech and the appointment of the Commission of Twelve : like the first two, it was held at the Hôtel de Ville. Delegates from thirty-six sections were present, and amongst the administrators of police were Marino and Michel. An administrator of police was in the chair, and no member was allowed to leave the room before

---

[1] Soulès resigned his post on May 20, ' because he was unwilling to take part in a plot that was being formed to murder a large number of the citizens of Paris ' (' Pièces Officielles,' ' Mémoires de Meillan,' p. 189).

[2] *Moniteur*, May 20, 1793.

the conclusion of the meeting, which had been called for a triple object: (1) A list of suspects was to be drawn up. (2) A number of members of the Convention were to be proscribed. (3) The measures to be taken against the aristocracy left in the sections were to be decided upon. A proposal was made to seize the principal members of the Right,[1] and to massacre them. After the perpetration of the deed, messengers were to be sent to the provinces to spread the report that the murdered men had left the country. Seven or eight members of the assembly, and amongst them two administrators of police, supported this motion. The delegate of the Fraternité section, who was observed taking notes, was expelled as a suspect. The President of the 1792 section was also expelled for having declared that the proposed measure was contrary to law, and that, if these members were guilty, they should be brought before the proper courts.

On Monday, May 20, another meeting was held, the chair this time being taken by Pache, the Mayor, who opened the proceedings with these words: 'You have met in order to draw up the list of suspects.' A member then rose, and said: 'A proposal was made yesterday to arrest some of the members of the National Convention, to send them to a place of safety, to kill them afterwards, and to pretend that they had emigrated. I move that we discuss that subject.' The Mayor's reply to this motion was as follows: 'There is no question before us of arresting or executing any representative of the people; we have met to decide who are the suspects of this city. I suggest that we proceed to that business.' He thereupon proposed that each one present should hand in the names of those whom he considered suspects, and then, taking advantage of the fact that he had already been twice sent for to preside over the Conseil-Général, he adjourned the meeting.[2]

On May 21 only thirteen delegates attended, and no meeting was held.[3] The agitators had evidently committed a great mistake in imprudently laying bare their designs, and in publicly

---

[1] In the 'Pièces Officielles,' published in the 'Mémoires de Meillan,' twenty-two, thirty-two, and even thirty-three, members are mentioned.
[2] 'Mémoires de Meillan': 'Pièces Officielles.' pp. 181, 185, 186.
[3] Ibid., pp. 177, 178.

implicating the Mayor in their plots. There is not the slightest doubt that Pache is favourable to the proscription of the deputies. Did he not on April 15 sign the petition of the thirty-five sections read before the Convention by Rousselin, and asking it to give up twenty-two of its members? His well-known prudence will not allow him to go farther than that. It was clearly impossible for him to preside over a discussion respecting the best means of cutting the throats of twenty or thirty representatives of the people, and he decided to prevent the delegates of the Revolutionary Committees from meeting at the Hôtel de Ville again. Since May 21 the Episcopal Palace has therefore become more than ever a centre of conspiracy. The most advanced members of the sections have continued to attend the meetings held there. They are presided over by Desfieux ; Varlet, the man who a few days ago was expelled from the Jacobin Club for the excess of his patriotic zeal ;[1] Dobsent, the President of the Cité section ; Maillard, Vice-President of the same section ; Hassenfratz, the chemist ; Du-fourny, a provincial deputy ; and the following foreigners, who are now first-class patriots—Pereyra, a Belgian ; Guzman, a Spaniard ; and the Germans Proly and Frey

On May 27 Pache told the Convention that Paris had never been in a state of greater tranquillity, and the Minister Garat, who was either the Mayor's accomplice or a fool, also assured the Assembly that it had nothing to fear, concluding his report with the following incredible words : ' I again assure the Convention that it is in no danger, and that you will all return to your homes in peace. I am fully aware that by speaking to you as I do I am assuming the responsibility of any attempt that might be made upon you. Well, I accept that responsibility, and that is all I have to say.'[2] Yet on that very day the conspirators in the Episcopal Palace were completing their arrangements. They decided to appoint a very small committee, which was to meet in secret, and notices were sent to the political clubs that at five o'clock on May 28 a public

[1] 'Rapport de Dutard à Garat,' May 18, 1793 : Schmidt, tome i., p. 243.
[2] *Moniteur*, May 29.

meeting, composed of electors and patriots, would be held at the Episcopal Palace, when important resolutions would be passed.[1]

On the evening of the 28th the meeting at the Episcopal Palace appointed a Commission of Six to undertake the measures agreed upon for the public safety. Citizen Boissel reported this fact to the Jacobin Club on May 29 in the following terms : ' The club that meets at the Episcopal Palace has appointed a Commission, which is entrusted with the execution of all the measures agreed upon for the public safety. If the citizen in the tribune[2] has any measures to propose, he had better lay them before that committee.' The Commission of Six was hardly appointed before it entered into negotiations with Dobsent, whose arrest by order of the Commission of Twelve, and whose liberation by order of the National Convention,[3] have gained him a popularity almost equal to that enjoyed by Hébert and Marat. Dobsent and the Six agreed that an executive committee was urgently needed, the members of which were not to be appointed in public assembly as were those of the Commission of Six, but at a meeting composed exclusively of delegates elected for that purpose by the forty-eight sections, and invested with unlimited powers. The Cité section consequently issued an Order inviting each of the other sections to send to the Episcopal Palace, on the evening of the 29th, two delegates to deliberate upon the means of saving the Republic.[4] Thirty-three sections complied with this demand, and on the evening of the 29th two entirely distinct meetings were held at the Episcopal Palace. The more numerously attended of the two, and the only one of which the Convention took note, was in reality the less dangerous ; it may even be that it was held with the object of distracting the attention of the authorities (if we have any authorities), and of acting as a foil to the other.

On Wednesday evening, then, after the first meeting had

---

[1] *Le Républicain Français*, Nos. 116 and 118.

[2] Citizen Grots de Luzenne had stated that he was in possession of information relating to an important plot.

[3] At its sitting of May 27.

[4] ' Histoire Parlementaire,' by Buchez and Roux, tome xxvii., p. 299.

already dispersed,[1] about 600 persons, 100 of whom were women, met at the Electoral Club held at the Episcopal Palace. Admission could only be gained by presenting the card of an elector, or of a member of a political club. There were 500 people on the floor of the hall, and 100 in the galleries. Dufourny, in the name of the Commission of Six, proposed that six delegates should be sent to the municipality to demand the provisional appointment of a Commandant of the Parisian National Guard, a measure absolutely indispensable to any united action. This motion was adopted, as well as the two following, also put forward by the Commission of Six. It was agreed that unlimited confidence would be placed in that Commission, and that all its decisions would be blindly executed. It was further agreed that the sections should be invited to send a petition to the National Convention asking it to punish Isnard for his attack upon Paris,[2] 'so that by arousing a common impulse in all Parisians they might be led to one common aim.' It was Dufourny who thus expressed himself; it was he, too, who led the whole of the discussion, exciting men's minds and preparing them for a speedy rising, but also imposing silence upon all who wished to go into the question of ways and means. To one speaker who touched upon this point he replied: 'I fear that if you take so long deliberating you will arrive a day after the fair.' The meeting finally adjourned until nine o'clock next morning.

Meanwhile, the delegates of the thirty-three sections who had accepted Dobsent's invitation met in secret in another department of the Episcopal Palace, and appointed a Commission of Nine[3]—a real Executive Committee of the insurrection.

---

[1] Notes laid before the Commission of Twelve concerning what took place at the Episcopal Palace on May 29 ('Mémoires de Meillan,' p. 194).

[2] At the sitting of the Convention on May 25, Isnard, the President, replied as follows to a deputation from the Conseil-Général de la Commune, which had come to protest against Hébert's arrest: 'France has made Paris the centre of its national representation. . . . If ever that representation should be attacked, I declare to you, in the name of the whole of France, that Paris would be destroyed' (*Moniteur*, May 27, 1793).

[3] Adolphe Schmidt, tome i., p. 343; 'Souvenirs de Dulaure, Membre de la Convention, sur les Journées des 31 Mai et 2 Juin, 1793'; 'Mémoires de Garat,' p. 131.

Of whom is this committee composed? No one has yet been able to give me information on this point. It is, however, certain that Dobsent, Hassenfratz, Varlet and Fournereau, must be amongst its members. The movement seems therefore to be directed, not by the friends of Robespierre and Danton, but by the creatures of Marat and Hébert.

Yesterday, Thursday,[1] the Episcopal Palace was, as on the day before, the scene of two meetings—that of the Electoral Club, and that of the delegates of the sections. The proceedings of the former commenced at nine o'clock, and admission was again by card or ticket only. The courageous Lanjuinais, who certainly ran the risk of being killed had he been recognised, did not fear to make his way into the hall, and last night gave the Convention an account of the meeting. He reported the following words spoken by Hassenfratz: 'Citizens, remember the Tenth of August! Before that day opinions were divided concerning a Republic, but no sooner had you struck the decisive blow than all were unanimous. The moment for striking fresh blows has come. Have no fear of the provinces—I have been through them, and I know them all; by frightening them a little, we shall bring them all over to our way of thinking. They always follow the lead that the capital gives them. Of the departments immediately round Paris many are devoted to us; that of Versailles, for instance, is quite ready to render us assistance. At the first sound of the cannon it will send us a formidable army, and we shall fall upon the egoists—that is to say, upon the rich. Yes, the insurrection has now become a duty against the corrupt majority in the Convention!' Lanjuinais then spoke of the words used by Chabot, a representative of the people, and by Varlet, both of whom had said: 'We must not immediately kill all the deputies we are about to arrest, but it will be easy to have them tried and found guilty by the departments; we shall do with them as we did with Louis XVI.'

The delegates of the sections, as well as the Electoral Club, remained sitting during the whole of the day, but their

---

[1] May 30, 1793. 'Fragment par M. le Comte Lanjuinais, Pair de France, Ancien Conventionnel, sur les 31 Mai, 1er et 2 Juin, 1793.'

deliberations not being public, nothing was known until some account of their proceedings leaked out during the evening at the Club in the Rue Saint Honoré. When the sitting at the Jacobins commenced, it was announced that thirty sections had met at the Episcopal Palace ; a little later a member imparted the information that the first care of 'the assembled sections had been to pass a resolution by which all property is placed under the protection of the *sans-culottes*.'[1]

Meanwhile what steps were being taken by the Conseil-Général de la Commune? The Conseil was taking no steps at all—it was waiting. Being informed by Chaumette of the rumours afloat respecting a dangerous assembly which meets in the Episcopal Palace, and which might give citizens some cause for anxiety, the Conseil-Général yesterday evening resolved that, in order to stop the tongues of all ill-disposed persons, a deputation be immediately sent to attend the sittings of the said Assembly, and to take note of its proceedings. The Mayor himself headed the deputation, and set out accompanied by six members of the Conseil. On his return he announced that the citizens assembled in the Episcopal Palace had declared themselves in a state of insurrection, and were making arrangements for the closing of the barriers. The Mayor added that he had advised them to postpone the execution of the extreme measures they had adopted until after the conference to be held at the Jacobin Club to-day, the 31st. His representations and those of his colleagues had, however, proved useless.

A few moments only after Pache had concluded his report a deputation from the 'citizens assembled at the Episcopal Palace' entered the Council Chamber. It came to bring to the cognizance of the Commune the text of a resolution passed by the meeting at the conclusion of a speech from Marat. The Friend of the People had spent a part of the night at the

---

[1] 'Procès-verbal de la Société des Amis de la Liberté et de l'Égalité, du jeudi 30 Mai, l'An IIe de la République Française.' This sitting of the Jacobins is not reported in the copy of the journal of the Club preserved in the Bibliothèque Nationale. The original manuscript of the minutes of May 30 was found by Adolphe Schmidt in the Archives of the Conseil-Général de la Seine, and published by him in his 'Tableaux de la Révolution Française,' tome i., p. 358, etc.

palace, preaching insurrection and uttering threats of death, behaving at times like a wild animal, and at others shouting for joy.[1]

The following is the text of the resolution passed by the delegates of the united sections :

'The General Revolutionary Assembly of the city of Paris meeting in the Episcopal Palace, having verified the unlimited and united powers of the majority of the sections, resolves that Paris shall rise against the aristocratic faction which oppresses Liberty : that the barriers shall be immediately closed, and that the men of the Fourteenth of July and of the Tenth of August shall hold themselves in readiness to execute this and other measures. The Assembly will sit permanently in the Episcopal Palace to determine the said other measures.'[2]

Instead of protesting against this act of insurrection, the Mayor remained silent, and the Conseil-Général proceeded with the next business.

At three o'clock in the morning the tocsin was rung from Notre Dame by order of the General Revolutionary Assembly.

At half-past four the Commune, either because it then disapproved of an insurrection which had been initiated by a rival assembly, or because it wished to propitiate the majority in the Convention, decided to issue the following proclamation addressed to the forty-eight sections :

'Be on your guard, for great dangers surround you. Some of our fellow-citizens, led astray, demand that the barriers be closed, and that the tocsin be rung, thus aiming at yet another insurrection. Compare recent events, and you will see who the villains are who thus mislead our citizens and advise this rising. The Conseil-Général has declared its sitting permanent ; do the same ; keep up your relations with it, and restrain the enemies in your midst by observing the strictest vigilance.'[3]

It is half-past six when the ' delegates of the majority of the sections,' headed by Dobsent, proceed from the Episcopal Palace

---

[1] Alphonse Esquiros, ' Histoire des Montagnards,' tome ii., p. 350. The author took his information from notes supplied by Marat's sister.

[2] ' Inventaire des Autographes et des Documents Historiques composant la Collection de M. Benjamin Fillon,' séries iii. et iv., No. 546.

[3] Op. cit., No. 547.

to the Hôtel de Ville. They enter the Council Chamber, and
Dobsent is the first to speak. He announces that 'the people
of Paris have taken measures indispensable for the preservation
of their liberties, and that the powers of all the constituted
authorities are annulled.'

Citizen Destournelles, the Vice-President of the Conseil-
Général, assumes a heroic attitude. (This farcical scene had no
doubt been rehearsed by the principal actors.) He declares that
he and his colleagues are resolved to die, if necessary, on their
benches, and cries: 'Citizens, you may illegally assume an
authority which does not belong to you, but you shall never
deprive us of our powers. Threats of violence are in vain; you
may drag us from our seats, but you shall never make us abdicate
our authority. I read in the eyes and in the hearts of all my
colleagues that there is not one amongst them who is not resolved
to die, if necessary, at his post.' An admirable peroration, but
falling rather flat after an exordium in which the speaker had
said: 'If the people have the right to create, they have also the
right to abolish. If, therefore, citizens, you can prove to us that
you represent the majority of the sections, we will place our
powers in your hands at once. The desire to retain them under
such circumstances would be neither brave nor virtuous, but rash
and criminal.'

Chaumette demands that the powers of the delegates be read
and verified, whereupon the clerks report that thirty-three
sections have given the delegates unlimited powers to save the
Republic. Dobsent then declares that the authority of the
municipality is annulled and takes possession of the presidential
chair. Whereupon Destournelles speaks as follows: 'Citizen
President, and you, members of the Revolutionary Commission
acting in the name of the people—your powers have been examined, and found to be legal. We are therefore enabled to
honourably hand over our functions to you. We simply ask
you to declare that we have not deserved ill of our fellow-
citizens, and that declaration will amply reward us for all that
we have done.'

Followed by his colleagues, he withdraws to another apartment—and waits. It is not long before the door opens, and a

deputation once more makes its appearance. This time it is to invite the Mayor, the Procureur de la Commune, and the members of the Conseil, to return to the hall in which they made such a splendid resistance but a few moments ago. All eagerly respond to this invitation, and Dobsent, the President, then announces, in the name of the sovereign people, that they are reinstated in their functions. They thereupon resume their seats, take a fresh civic oath, adopt the title of Conseil-Général Révolutionnaire, and, as a mark of their obedience to the delegates of the people, they appoint Hanriot, Commandant of the Sans-Culottes section, to the command of the armed forces of Paris.

Meanwhile a similar scene was taking place at the head-quarters of the department. One Wendhin, a delegate of the Revolutionary Committee of Nine, informs the members of the Directoire and of the Conseil-Général du Département de Paris that they are suspended. Directoire and Conseil bow to these commands, and Wendhin then takes from his pocket a second Decree thus worded :

'In the name of the sovereign people the members composing the Directoire and the Conseil-Général du Département de Paris are provisionally reinstated in their functions ; they will take an oath to faithfully fulfil the duties with which they are entrusted, and to communicate only with the Revolutionary Committee of Nine, which holds its sittings at the Episcopal Palace.'

In order to be able to follow the course of events more closely, the Revolutionary Committee of Nine installed itself in the Hôtel de Ville this morning. From thence it transmits its orders to the municipality, the department and the sections. The hour has come for the Vergniauds, the Guadets, and the Gensonnés, to see their eloquence expire in impotence at the feet of a Dobsent and a Varlet speaking in the name of the sovereign people.

The historians of the Revolution have not attached to the meetings in the Episcopal Palace an importance proportionate to the immense influence they exercised upon the events of May 31 and June 2. Thiers, Louis Blanc, De Barante and Mortimer-Ternaux have confined themselves to mentioning the public meeting, which was held on May 29, composed of five or six hundred people, and have merely reproduced the details furnished by the 'Pièces Officielles' given in Meillan's 'Mémoires.' Not one of them has spoken of the Central Committee of Public Safety, organized at the Episcopal Palace on March 31, and not one has drawn attention to the distinction to be made between that Committee, composed of delegates from the sections, and the assembly of delegates from the Revolutionary Committees sitting at the Hôtel de Ville. All have confounded the public meetings of the Electoral Club with the secret meetings of the sectional delegates, and all have omitted to indicate the origin of the Revolutionary Committee of Nine. They do not even appear to have heard of its existence, and yet it is that Committee which directed the rising, and suspended and reinstated the Commune, the Directoire and the Conseil-Général du Département de Paris. Mortimer-Ternaux alone quotes a document in one of his notes in which the Committee of Nine is mentioned, but nothing is said of that body in the text of his work. Schmidt's 'Tableaux de la Révolution Française' contain some valuable documents concerning the different assemblies that met at the Episcopal Palace in April and May, 1793; but the work of the learned Professor of the University of Jena, although written in French, savours somewhat of its Germanic origin, and is not always clear. One of our young scholars should overhaul the subject anew, and give us a work written in French—by a Frenchman.

CHAPTER LXXVII.

THE THIRTY-FIRST OF MAY.

Saturday, June 1, 1793.

THE Parisians have become so accustomed to Revolutions that they look upon them as perfectly natural proceedings ; they stand in their doorways to see the riotous demonstrations pass, and in the evening they dance for joy and illuminate their houses. You must be careful not to shake your head, or express a fear that such joys are not without their dangers, and that they might have troublesome results. Your Parisian does not like a mar-joy, and he might adopt an unpleasant way of proving to you that all is for the best in this best of possible Republics.

Yesterday evening the houses were brilliantly illuminated, and immense crowds filled the streets. A torch-light procession which started from the Terrasse des Feuillants ended its march at the Place du Carrousel, where groups of citizens embraced each other at the foot of the tree of Liberty, and sang the *Marseillaise*.[1]

The following is an account of what had taken place.

Yesterday morning, before daybreak, Paris was awakened by the ringing of the tocsin from all the steeples of the city.[2] At

---

[1] 'Mémoires de Mme. Roland,' p. 195 ; 'Récit Rapide des Événements qui ont eu lieu à Paris, dans les Journées des 30 et 31 Mai, 1er et 2 Juin, 1793,' by A. J. Gorsas, a member of the National Convention, and one of the thirty-four proscribed. 'Guzman, the Spaniard, frequently told me that the insurrection of which he was one of the ringleaders was directed against the whole national representation' ('Le Nouveau Paris,' by Sébastien Mercier, tome ii., p. 267).

[2] 'Souvenirs de Dulaure sur les Journées des 31 Mai et 2 Juin, 1793, et sur la Proscription des Girondins.'

five o'clock drums were heard in the streets, and there was a general call to arms. The citizens, mostly carrying swords and pistols, rushed out of their houses, and asked each other what was the matter, and what they were to do. In the hope of getting some news, some made their way to the Hôtel de Ville, and others to the Tuileries. Others, again—and these were by far in the majority—rallied round the sectional flags which hung over the door of every captain.[1]

The most alarming rumours were everywhere afloat. Some said that the town of Valenciennes was taken ; some that the Twenty-two[2] had quitted Paris, or that they had intentions of doing so.[3] We were told at the same time that measures had been taken to render such flight impossible ; that the military guard had everywhere been doubled, and additional sentries set to watch the post-houses.[4] The barriers were closed, and all external communications cut off ; even the posts were stopped by order of the Insurrectionary Committee sitting at the Hôtel de Ville, and all suspected letters seized. Warrants were also issued for the arrest of Lebrun, Minister of Foreign Affairs, and Clavière, Minister of Finance.

At half-past six a hundred deputies assembled in the hall of the Convention.[5] Amongst them were some of the members who were reported to have fled—Barbaroux, Guadet, Louvet, Bergoeing, and Rabaut Saint-Étienne. On their way to the Tuileries they had had to pass through some groups of *sans-culottes*, who, having recognised them, made a show of attacking them, and only desisted on seeing that the deputies were well armed. The crowd that surrounded the Tuileries at eight o'clock could not have numbered less than ten or twelve thousand men.

At nine o'clock a meeting, convened by the Conseil-Général du Département, was held at the Jacobin Club, to consider what measures should be taken for the public safety, or, rather, by

---

[1] 'Récit,' etc., by A. J. Gorsas.
[2] For the names of the Twenty-two, see Chapter LXIV.
[3] 'Souvenirs de Dulaure.'   [4] *Ibid*.
[5] 'Procès-verbal de la Séance du 31 Mai, 1793.' The minutes of the sittings of May 31 and June 2 were not printed. They were found in the Archives by Charles Vatel, and published by him in his work upon Vergniaud, p. 388, etc.

what means the leading members of the Convention could be dragged from their seats. The assembly consisted of delegates appointed by all the constituted authorities of the department, and by the sections of Paris. There were representatives from the Conseil-Général of the department of Paris, from the Conseils-Généraux of the districts of Saint-Denis and of the Bourg de l'Égalité, from the Conseils-Généraux of the communes of those two districts, from the Conseil-Général of the Commune of Paris, and from the forty-eight sections of the capital. The meeting appointed a Committee of eleven members to take such measures for the public safety as it should think proper, and to put them into immediate execution, the municipalities of the two rural districts and the Revolutionary Committees of the forty-eight sections holding themselves in readiness to aid it in so doing. The meeting also decided to support all the acts of the Conseil-Général, and of the delegates of the sections, and arranged that the Committee of Eleven should hold its sittings at the Hôtel de Ville, and should work in unison with the Conseil-Général Révolutionnaire for the public safety and the maintenance of liberty and equality.

At one o'clock an alarm gun was fired.

Since, in spite of the tocsin and the call to arms, the closing of the barriers and the firing of alarm guns, there had been absolutely no fighting or bloodshed, people began to laugh at their fears of the morning. Laying aside their anxiety, and taking advantage of the fine weather, the citizens closed their shops, and promenaded the principal streets, laughing and joking with the *citoyennes* who sat in their doorways waiting ' to see the rioters pass.'[1]

In the evening, however, things began to look more serious. Some agitators wearing the municipal sash had paraded the Faubourgs Saint-Antoine and Saint-Marcel, and spread the rumour that six sections[2] had raised the standard of insurrection in the Palais Égalité, and were all wearing the white cockade. Meanwhile, other agitators, in league, no doubt, with the first,

---

[1] *Chronique de Paris*, No. 153.
[2] Butte des Moulins, 1792, Mail, Champs Élysées, Molière and La Fontaine.

spread the news in the Section de la Butte des Moulins and the surrounding district, that a raid was to be made upon the neighbourhood.[1] Acting upon this false news the Section de la Butte des Moulins took possession of the Jardin de l'Égalité, and aided by some of the forces of the Section du Mail, held itself in readiness to repel any attack. The gates were closed, and cannon were drawn up round the principal entrances. These precautions turned out to be not unnecessary, for the Palais was soon surrounded by a mob of eight to ten thousand armed men,[2] who stationed their artillery opposite that of their adversaries.

The attitude of the crowd that surrounded the Convention had meanwhile grown more threatening. At nightfall there could have been no less than forty thousand persons present.[3] The majority was no doubt composed of onlookers, but there was, nevertheless, a goodly number of rioters uttering angry and defiant speeches, and accusing the deputies of the Right with raising the price of food. 'They are all thieves,' they cried, 'and must be driven out. We must ask the Convention to deliver up to the people the members of the Commission of Twelve!'

Hisses, applause and shouts of vengeance and death broke from the maddened crowd according as the reports that were brought from the interior of the building by the sans-culottes who filled the galleries were favourable or unfavourable.

The passions which raged in the interior of the Convention itself were not less violent.

Rabaut Saint-Étienne, chairman of the Commission of Twelve, tried to gain a hearing. Three times did the President call upon him to speak,[4] but what cared the noisy minority, what cared the rioters in the galleries for that ? After a struggle that lasted quite three hours,[5] the majority of the members, who wished to give him a hearing, were obliged to yield, and Rabaut Saint-Étienne resumed his seat.

---

1 'Souvenirs de Dulaure'; *Chronique de Paris, loc. cit.*
2 'Souvenirs de Dulaure.'
3 Basire's speech on May 31, *Moniteur* of June 3, 1793.
4 *Le Patriote Français.*
5 'Histoire Parlementaire,' by Buchez and Roux, tome xxvii., p. 338.

The other speakers of the Right were not more successful. The galleries interrupted Guadet with shouts of 'Sit down! Sit down!' and would not even hear the President himself, who on this occasion was Mallarmé, a member of the Mountain. Camboulas was allowed to speak. 'There has been a manifest violation of the law,' he said; 'the barriers have been closed, the tocsin rung, and the alarm guns fired. I move that the Executive Council be instructed to seek out the perpetrators of these crimes.' At this point he was stopped by shouts from the galleries, and the uproar recommenced. For the rest, the sitting, which commenced at six in the morning, and did not adjourn until half-past nine at night, was almost entirely taken up with listening to deputations. There were deputations from the Commune, and deputations from the Département de Paris; deputations from the forty-eight sections, and deputations from the Gardes Françaises; deputations from the Men of the Fourteenth of July, and deputations from the Men of the Tenth of August.

'Legislators,' cried one spokesman, 'a great plot against liberty and equality has been laid bare; the delegates of the forty-eight sections have discovered the ringleaders. You must give them up to the sword of justice.'

'The Committee of Public Safety,' replied the Convention, 'acting in consort with the constituted authorities, will inquire into the plots of which information has been given at the Bar.'

Another spokesman cried: 'We demand a repeal of the Decree which was passed by villainous means in order to crush our freedom.' And the Convention, repealing the 'villainous' Decree of May 28, ordered the suppression of the Commission of Twelve and the confiscation of its papers.

'We demand,' cried yet another spokesman, 'the organization of a central Revolutionary army of *sans-culottes*, who shall receive a wage of forty sous per day.' And the Convention obediently confirmed the order of the Commune, giving all workmen who should remain under arms until the re-establishment of public tranquillity two francs per day.

But were these votes really passed by the majority of the Convention? Whilst the discussion was going on, the

Assembly, as a matter of fact, was again and again invaded by strangers. At the conclusion of a speech made by the *procureur-syndic* Lullier in the name of the Département de Paris, the constituted authorities of the Commune and the delegates of the sections, Grégoire, who had taken Mallarmé's place in the presidential chair, had invited the deputation to the honours of the sitting; but with the petitioners a crowd of citizens had made their way into the hall.[1] In vain did the members of the Right protest, declaring that the Convention was no longer free, and that fair debate was impossible. Their protests only raised a terrible storm; unable to allay this, the majority decided to leave the Assembly. On Lavasseur's suggestion, all the members of the Mountain took possession of the benches of the Right, whilst the petitioners and their followers sat on the Left.[2]

Shortly before the end of the sitting a deputation from the *Sans-culottes* section appeared at the bar and demanded that monopolizers might be brought to justice, and that all commodities of prime necessity be taxed throughout the Republic.

On this deputation, too, being admitted to the honours of the sitting, a fresh band of *sans-culottes* made its way into the space reserved for members. News was now brought that the outlying sections, before making an attack upon the Section of the Butte des Moulins, had sent a deputation into the Garden of the Palais de l'Égalité in order to see whether some understanding could not be come to; that the deputation had found all the supposed insurrectionaries wearing the tricolour cockade, and that a reconciliation had immediately taken place. Upon hearing this the deputies at once adjourned the sitting, which had lasted for more than sixteen hours, and a large number of them proceeded to the Jardin Égalité, to fraternize with the sections.[3]

A most extraordinary day truly! At daybreak the sound of the tocsin and a general call to arms. In the early hours of

---

[1] *Moniteur*, June 3, 1793.
[2] A despatch written from the Convention by the delegates of the Commune and signed HENRY, CAVAIGNAC, and BORRELLE (Mortimer-Ternaux, tome vii., p. 350).
[3] *Moniteur*, June 3, 1793.

the morning the municipality, the Conseil-Général de la Commune, the Directory and the Conseil-Général of the Department of Paris were dissolved by an Insurrectionary Committee
which afterwards reinstated them, and issued warrants against
Lebrun and Clavière, two members of the Executive Council.
The barriers were closed, the posts stopped, and the letters
seized. Ten thousand men marched from the suburbs to attack
the sections entrenched in the Palais Égalité, and a bloody
conflict was only accidentally averted. Forty thousand men besieged the approaches to the Convention, and the Legislative
Chamber itself was invaded. Under cover of the disorder that
reigned measures were passed which will inevitably result in the
speedy decimation of the Assembly, and the final triumph of
the mob over national representation.

And this was the day which terminated with shouts of joy,
songs and illuminations. This is the kind of day which is held
up as an example by those worthy people who go about saying
that more moderate ideas are gaining ground, and that they
alone are dangerous and guilty who take a pleasure in pro-
phesying troubles and misfortunes that are henceforth impossible.

Strange as the proceedings of that day may appear, its most
extraordinary feature is the behaviour of the Girondist deputies,
and that of Vergniaud in particular.

But yesterday the Girondists governed the Assembly. On
Tuesday they voted to the number of 279 for the repeal of the
Decree abolishing the Commission of Twelve, whilst their
adversaries numbered only 239.[1] They had, therefore, on their
side, not only a majority in the Convention, but also the Commission of Twelve—a body armed with very extensive powers—
and all the Ministers except Bouchotte. Under such circumstances they might, at least, have defended themselves in that
Assembly over which they were still masters. Guadet, Dufriche-
Valazé and Doulcet de Pontécoulant displayed great energy, it
is true, and held out stoutly against the enemy. But what of
the others? To begin with, most of them had deemed it
prudent to stay away.[2] Neither Brissot nor Buzot said or did

_____
[1] *Moniteur*, May 30, 1793.   [2] ' Mémoires de Mme. Roland,' p. 194.

anything. I am told that they were not present, and I am inclined to believe it, for how else can we explain their silence ?[1] Condorcet was present in the hall, but he showed no desire to defend his friends. His name was, therefore, not placed on the proscribed list with the Twenty-two, and this was a benefit which he was in no hurry to jeopardize. Did he not vote openly on May 28 against the Commission of Twelve ?

At yesterday's sitting Rabaut Saint-Étienne acted in a fashion not less cowardly. Himself a member of the Commission of Twelve, and actually elected to be its chairman, he mounted the tribune to defend that body. Intimidated, however, by the shouts and the threats of the galleries, he lost his head, and demanded the suppression of the Commission. 'I am willing,' he said, 'to set aside the Commission of Twelve, because I desire but one centre. I therefore move that the Committee of Public Safety undertake all the investigations, and that it be favoured with your entire confidence.'

Vergniaud did better still. When the delegates of the majority of the sections organized the insurrection and loudly demanded the proscription of the principal members of the National Convention, he drafted the following Decree, and got it passed by that Assembly :

'The Convention unanimously decrees that the sections of Paris have deserved well of the country for the zeal they displayed in maintaining order, in defending persons and property, and in ensuring the liberty and dignity of the National Convention during the late troubles.

'The Convention requests the sections not to abate their vigilance until the constituted authorities shall have reported that peace and public order are entirely re-established.'

The delegates of the Commune who were present at the sitting could scarcely believe their own ears, and immediately informed the ringleaders at the Hôtel de Ville of what had taken place in the following terms : 'You will be astonished to

[1] 'After May 23 Buzot does not speak in the Convention. His silence during the stormy sittings which preceded the fall of the Girondist party is most extraordinary On May 31 he does not enter the tribune ; on June 2 he is absent from the sitting' ('Charlotte Corday et les Girondins,' by Charles Vatel, tome ii., p. 333).

hear that on the motion of Vergniaud himself, the National Convention has just decreed that the sections have deserved well of the country for the measures they took to save the Republic.'[1]

A few moments later a deputation of the 'men of the Four- teenth of July, of the Tenth of August, and of May 31' demanded the organization of a Revolutionary army formed of *sans-culottes;* the repeal of the Decree re-establishing the Com- mission of Twelve, the arrest of the members of that Commission as well as of the ministers, Lebrun and Clavière, and the im- peachment of the Twenty-two.

It was on the motion, not of Robespierre, but of Vergniaud, that this petition, aimed at the deputies of the Gironde, was printed and sent to all the departments.[2]

As he bent his steps towards the Tuileries yesterday morning Rabaut Saint-Étienne repeatedly exclaimed : *Illa suprema dies !*[3] On leaving the Convention yesterday evening Guadet, who had fought most bravely, might have quoted to Rabaut, Vergniaud, and the other weak-kneed members of the party, the words of another poet : *Relicta non bene parmula.*[4]

[1] Despatch written from the Convention, and signed by Maudin, Garelle, Cavaignac, and Henry.

[2] *Moniteur,* June 3, 1793.   [3] 'Mémoires de Louvet,' p. 89.

[4] Concerning the events of May 31 and Vergniaud's incomprehensible behaviour in particular, see ' La Légende des Girondins,' ch. x.

CHAPTER LXXVIII.

THE SECOND OF JUNE.

Tuesday, June 4, 1793.

SATURDAY was a comparatively quiet day. The shops were all open, and everyone had resumed work. The storm seemed to have subsided.[1] In the Convention the draft of an address to the nation, submitted by Barère in the name of the Committee of Public Safety, and relating to the events of May 31, was adopted almost unanimously. The optimists triumph once more. 'You see,' they cried, 'your fears were exaggerated; nothing will happen, and everything will come right.' But these simple-minded folk reckoned without their hosts in the Maison Commune, the members of the Conseil-Général, and of the Revolutionary Committee,[2] who were hard at work whilst the Convention was wasting its time in choosing new names for communes, and who were doing everything in their power to turn the partial success of May 31 into a complete victory.

During the night between May 31 and June 1, the Revolutionary Committee ordered the arrest 'of all suspects concealed in the sections of Paris.' It determined to raise a Revolutionary army of 20,000 men, which is to be kept up by a tax imposed upon the rich, and especially upon those who are notorious for their want of patriotism. It also issued an order to each of the forty-eight sections to draw up a list of the *sans-culotte* work-

---

[1] *Chronique de Paris,* No. 154; *Le Patriote Français,* June 2, 1793; Adolphe Schmidt, tome i., p. 374.

[2] 'The Conseil-Général decrees that the Revolutionary Committee now established in the Maison Commune shall be called " Revolutionary Committee elected by the people of the Department of Paris "' ('Minutes of the Commune,' sitting of the Conseil-Général Révolutionnaire June 1).

men in the district, and to send the same to the Commune, who would pay each of these workmen six francs as compensation for the interruption of their work. By another resolution an armed force was told off to accompany the municipal officers who were to go about persuading the people to preserve the rights they had reconquered, and to resume their arms whenever they were again attacked. Twenty-four Commissioners were appointed to promulgate these ideas. Like practical men who know that the most beautifully worded proclamations in the world must be supported by more substantial arguments, the members of the Conseil-Général Révolutionnaire suggested that the sections should send out with each party a few waggons laden with provisions for the relief of those who were found to be in want.

All the arrangements were therefore admirably calculated to bring the *sans-culottes* under the banner of insurrection, and to keep them there until the object aimed at by the ringleaders was attained.

Rightly considering that success was now assured, the Conseil-Général and the Revolutionary Committee determined to strike the decisive blow at once by presenting to the Convention a demand for the impeachment of twenty-seven of its members. This petition was to be presented by eighteen Commissioners, twelve of whom were chosen from amongst the members of the Conseil-Général, and six from those of the Revolutionary Committee.

This decision had not been arrived at until seven p.m. on June 1, and it was then found that the Convention had adjourned. A few moments later Pache, accompanied by Marat, entered the hall of the Conseil-Général, and announced that the Convention would reassemble at nine o'clock. The Friend of the People spoke in the following strain : 'Rise, sovereign people; present yourselves before the Convention. Read your address, and do not budge from the bar until you have received a definite reply. Whatever may be the terms of that reply, you, sovereign people, will act in a manner conducive to the preservation of your rights and the defence of your interests. That is the best advice I can give you.'

This inflammatory harangue was received with acclamation, and Marat left the Maison Commune amidst shouts of applause. His words seemed to have acted as a signal, for almost immediately afterwards the tocsin was rung, and in every section the drums beat the call to arms.[1]

The course of events ran precisely contrary of that of the previous day. May 31 had commenced with alarms, and ended in a patriotic festival. Ushered in with shouts of joy and illuminations, June 1 ended with the ringing of the tocsin and the roll of the drum.

When the Convention resumed its sitting at nine o'clock, the Tuileries was surrounded by an armed force well provided with artillery; the gardens, the quays, the Pont National, and all the adjacent streets, were filled with the sectional battalions.[2] The deputation from the Commune and the Revolutionary Committee duly appeared at the bar, and Hassenfratz, its spokesman, read a petition couched in more violent language than Lullier's of the preceding day. 'Representatives of the people,' it ran, 'the forty-eight sections of Paris, and the constituted authorities of the department, have come to demand the impeachment of the Commission of Twelve, the men who are in league with Dumouriez, the men who are inciting the inhabitants of the provinces to march upon Paris. The people are up in arms.' After enumerating the members whom they desired to be sent before the Revolutionary Tribunal, the petitioners added: 'Legislators, this counter-Revolution must come to an end; all the conspirators, without exception, must fall under the blade of the law. You, Patriots, who have frequently saved the country, must cope with these traitors. You must tell us whether you can ensure us our freedom; if not, we are all ready to defend it. Every conspirator shall bite the dust.'[3]

There was not a single member of the Gironde to protest against this abominable language. Not one of them rose to defend himself, or to defend those of his friends who were attacked. Old Dusaulx, it is true, ascended the tribune, but it was only to stammer forth a few excuses. Where were Vergniaud,

[1] 'Mémoires de Jérôme Petion,' p. 5.   [2] Chronique de Paris, No. 154.
[3] Moniteur, June 4.

Buzot, Guadet, Brissot, Gensonné and Petion? They were
absent from their posts in the hour of danger, and only a few
of their lieutenants and of the rank and file of the party were
present. Five out of the six secretaries at the table were
Girondists—Lasource, Lidon, Fonfrède, Lanthenas, and Rabaut
Saint-Étienne. Not one of them attempted to speak; all
remained silent under the threats of Hassenfratz, and the conspirators of the Hôtel de Ville were admitted to the honours of
the sitting.

The petition was referred to the Committee of Public Safety,
which was ordered to report within three days upon the accusation of treason brought against certain members of the Convention by the constituted authorities of Paris. On the petition
being thus dealt with, one of the delegates wearing a tricolour
ribbon was heard to say to his colleagues, 'Things will not go
off so easily to-morrow.'

The sitting was adjourned at midnight.

During the night between Saturday and Sunday the sectional
battalions remained under arms, their spirits sustained by the
wine and food so thoughtfully placed at their disposal by the
Revolutionary Committee. At half-past three in the morning
Commandant General Hanriot, on being summoned to the
Commune, declared that the people were up in arms, and that
they would not be satisfied until the traitors were arrested.[1]

At four o'clock the tocsin was again rung.[2]

When the Convention assembled at ten o'clock the Tuileries
were surrounded by an army consisting of not less than 80,000
men.[3] Hanriot had been careful to station in the garden and
the courtyards of the palace about 5,000 men upon whom he
could rely. This chosen troop, the body-guard of the insurrection, was separated from the battalions in whom the Com-
mandant-General had less confidence by the displacement of the
Pont Tournant on one side, and on the other by the hoarding
between the Place du Carrousel and the courtyard of the

---

[1] Minutes of the Commune.   [2] *Ibid.*
[3] 'Mémoires de Meillan,' member for the Basses-Pyrénées. Lanjuinais
in his 'Fragment sur les 31 Mai, 1er et 2 Juin, 1793,' computes the number
of armed men that surrounded the Convention at 101,000.

palace.[1]   The rest of Hanriot's army, consisting of infantry, cavalry, and artillery, occupied the Place du Carrousel, the Champs Élysées and the adjacent quays.   It was a strange gathering, composed of divers elements, and one in which the German soldiers of Rosenthal's legion, who do not understand a word of French, were placed next to the federates from Marseilles—the scum of Provence;[2] in which the Vendean contingents[3] were placed side by side with the detachments of the National Guards coming from Courbevoie, from Saint-Germain-en-Laye, from Melun and from Versailles.   There were 163 pieces of artillery served by nearly 3,000 gunners; iron brasiers for heating the shot were placed in the Champs Élysées.   A large body of reserves with fourteen guns was stationed in the Bois de Boulogne.[4]

The password was ' *Insurrection and Vigour.*'[5]

Such a formidable military display was really not required to coerce the majority in the Convention.   Since the day when it met for the first time in this very palace, has not each of its sittings been marked by some weak concession or other?   On the evening of June 2 it complied with the demand of the Commune and the Revolutionary Committee, and ordered the arrest of twenty-nine of its members, and two Ministers.   The two Ministers are Clavière and Lebrun.   The twenty-nine deputies are: Gensonné, Guadet, Brissot, Gorsas, Petion, Vergniaud, Salle, Barbaroux, Chambon, Buzot, Birotteau, Lidon, Rabaut Saint-Étienne, Lasource, Lanjuinais, Grangeneuve, Lehardi, Lesage, Louvet, Valazé, Kervelégan, Gardien, Boilleau, Bertrand, Viger, Mollevant, Henry - Larivière, Gomaire, and Bergoeing.

As the Tenth of August ended with the fall of Louis XVI., so ended with the fall of the Girondist party the rising which is already called the Revolution of May 31.

In default of a complete picture, which it is impossible to draw on the morrow of such a great event, I will try to repro-

[1] 'Mémoires de Meillan.'   [2] Gorsas, ' Récit Rapide.'
[3] Beaulieu, 'Diurnal,' June 2, 1793.
[4] Gorsas, ' Récit Rapide.'   [5] *Ibid.*

duce the leading features of the scenes that took place in the
Convention during that memorable sitting on June 2.

Thanks to young Berthollet, the usher, I was able to get
inside the palace. In one of the vestibules on the ground-floor
I found an uproarious crowd. There was quite a large number
of women, and some of them were loudly boasting that this
was not their first visit to the Tuileries, but that they had
already been there on June 20 and on the Tenth of August.
A man standing on the staircase intimated by signs that he
wished to address the crowd. Silence was at last obtained, and
the speaker, after a few wild phrases, invited his hearers to take
an oath not to allow anyone to leave the hall until the decree
against the traitors of the Right had been passed. All hands
were immediately lifted; the oath was taken enthusiastically,
and by the women in particular with an extraordinary show of
passion. It was then half-past two.[1] From that moment the
Convention was really in a state of siege. When, on Barère's
suggestion, the members left the hall ' to prove that they were
free,' their promenade through the courts and gardens of the
Tuileries only served to demonstrate in what a humiliating
position they were placed. Every door, every gate, and every
opening was guarded by the rioters, and no deputy was allowed
to move about the building on any pretence whatever without
the escort of two or three armed men, who were careful to take
him back to the Legislative Chamber, now turned into a prison.[2]

The greater the degradation of the Convention, the more
praiseworthy was the courage shown by Lanjuinais. Since
1789 we have had many days of Revolution, and the month of
June has had a fairly large share.

On June 20, 1789, the oath was taken in the Tennis Hall.

On June 25, 1791, the Royal Family was brought back from
Varennes.

On June 20, 1792, the Tuileries were invaded by the mob.

On June 2, 1793, the Girondist party was overthrown.

No doubt other insurrections will follow those which we have
been privileged to witness, and the day will come when the
Revolution of June 2 will have disappeared beneath a whole

[1] ' Compte Rendu et Déclaration,' by J. B. M. Saladin.   [2] *Ibid.*

heap of successive Revolutions; but as long as France exists, and as long as the meaning of Liberty and Honour is understood, the memory of Lanjuinais's heroism will live. In the midst of an assembly besieged by 80,000 men, expecting no support either from the almost deserted benches of the Right or from any other part of the hall, he faces the threats of the Mountain and the curses of the galleries, and exposes the plots of the Commune and of the Revolutionary Committee. Again and again is he shouted down and his voice drowned by yells. He conquers the tumult, and continues denouncing the petitions 'dragged through the mud in the streets of Paris.' Legendre, the butcher, swinging his arms as if they held a pole-axe, shouts, 'Get down, or I will fell you!' Lanjuinais coolly replies, 'Pass a law to declare me an ox, and you may do so.'[1]

The Mountain now rises up in arms. Legendre, Chabot, Turreau, Drouet, young Robespierre, Julien, and others, armed with revolvers, climb into the tribune and try to drag Lanjuinais out. Legendre even holds his pistol to his breast to oblige him to get down. Some members of the Right, Defermon, Birotteau, Leclerc (of Loir-et-Cher), Penières and Pilastre, also armed with pistols, come to the help of the brave deputy. Whilst a violent struggle ensues at the foot and on the steps of the tribune, and the whole assembly is one shouting, fighting mass, Lanjuinais remains impassive. He clings to the tribune with all his might, and when the storm has spent itself, and comparative calm is restored, he resumes his speech, which concludes with the following words:

'I move that all the Revolutionary authorities of Paris, but more especially the assembly that met in the Episcopal Palace, and the Central or Executive Committee of that assembly, be suppressed, that all their acts be set aside, and that the Committee of Public Safety report the day after to-morrow that your decree in this matter has been carried out. I move also that all who would assume an authority contrary to the law be declared outlaws, and that all citizens be permitted to run them down.'[2]

---

[1] Lanjuinais, 'Fragment sur les 31 May, 1er et 2 Juin, 1793.'
[2] *Moniteur*, June 4.

Towards the end of the sitting, when Barère had already given the signal for the defection of the *Plain*, when all was lost, and when the members of the Gironde had agreed to their own suspension, Lanjuinais again rose. 'Expect from me neither suspension nor resignation!' he cried. Overcoming the interruptions, he continued: 'In barbarous countries human victims have often been led to the stake after having been crowned with flowers, but never have I heard that the sacrificing priests were allowed to insult them.'[1]

Mirabeau never had a more sublime inspiration, and his famous apostrophe to M. de Brézé pales by the side of these splendid words hurled at a mob of triumphant rioters.

The end of Lanjuinais's second speech was fully in keeping with its opening words, and was almost a prophecy:

'Suppress immediately every authority which the laws do not recognise; forbid the people to obey them; enforce the national will, and you will see the agitators abandoned by the good citizens whom they lead astray. If you have not the courage to do this, Liberty is lost. I see civil war, which is already kindled, extending its ravages on all sides; I see the horrible monster of dictatorship and tyranny stalking over heaps of ruins and corpses, and finally overthrowing the Republic itself.'

It must be borne in mind that Lanjuinais was no Girondist, and I wish to draw attention to that fact before describing the part played by the leaders of that faction in the proceedings of June 2. In the morning, before the Convention assembled, they all met at Meillan's house in the Rue des Moulins. The majority of them had spent the night there on chairs.[2] Amongst the company were Brissot, Vergniaud, Gensonné, Guadet, Buzot, Petion, Salle, Grangeneuve and Barbaroux.[3] They decided that, instead of going to the Convention, they would await events where they were, thus again deserting the battle-field at a decisive moment, as they had already done on March 10 and May 31. Barbaroux alone seemed to understand

---

[1] *Le Républicain Français*, No. 202, June 5, 1793.
[2] 'Mémoires de Petion,' p. 5.
[3] 'Mémoires de Meillan,' p. 52; 'Mémoires de Petion,' p. 6; 'Récit Rapide,' by A. J. Gorsas.

how shameful such conduct was. In spite of the efforts made to keep him back, he went to his post to do his duty.[1] Meillan decided to follow his example, promising his colleagues to send them news from the Assembly hourly. Vergniaud accompanied him, but, unlike Barbaroux, who remained to the end, he soon left the hall, without having made any attempt to save his friends. After his departure—which might have been about one o'clock[2]—his adversaries did not even do him the honour of remarking upon his disappearance.

Thus abandoned by their leaders, it was a difficult task for the Girondist deputies to ward off the attack made upon them. About a third of the party only was present at the sitting,[3] and nearly all of these members were safe on account of their obscurity. A few, however, fought bravely in defence of Lanjuinais, as I have already mentioned. It was about three o'clock when Barère, in the name of the Committee of Public Safety, read the draft of a Decree inviting the deputies denounced by the department of Paris to voluntarily abstain from discharging their functions for a stated time. Only six of the deputies to whom this appeal was addressed were present— Isnard, Fauchet, Lanthenas, Dusaulx, Barbaroux and Lanjuinais. Birotteau had left the hall. Whilst Lanjuinais and Barbaroux refused to resign their rights, Isnard, Fauchet, Lanthenas and Dusaulx expressed their willingness to fall in with the suggestion. By so doing, the two last drew upon themselves the shame of Marat's protection ; he had their names erased from the list. The same form of punishment was in store for Isnard and Fauchet. The Decree which proscribed their colleagues contained a clause providing 'that Isnard and Fauchet, who, for the sake of peace and public tranquillity, consented to their suspension, shall not be arrested, but allowed their liberty in Paris only on *parole*.'

Incredible as it may seem, Brissot, Petion, Gensonné, Buzot, Grangeneuve and Vergniaud were at that moment engaged in

---

[1] 'Mémoires de Meillan.'

[2] 'I left the Assembly between one and two o'clock' (letter from Vergniaud to the President of the Convention, dated June 2, 1793) ; *Le Républicain Français*, June 5, 1793.

[3] 'Récit Rapide,' by A. J. Gorsas.

drawing up a manifesto to the French nation in reply to the attacks of the Mountain and the Commune. The men whom the Friend of the People honours with the title of *statesmen* seek to stave off the consequences of a successful revolt with a sheet of paper! Before they had had time to round their sentences Rabaut-Pommier, Rabaut Saint - Étienne's brother, rushed into the room shouting wildly: 'The Convention is broken up! The mob has burst into the hall, and has seized the deputies! *Sauve qui peut!* *Sauve qui peut!* And each one makes off as fast as he can.[1]

With the exception of Barbaroux, not one of the leaders of e Girondist party did his duty on June 2.

In conjunction with the non-appearance of the principal Girondists in the Convention on that day, it is worthy of remark that the leaders of the Mountain took almost no part in the proceedings. Danton's scant phrases concerned quite a secondary question. As for Robespierre, he did not even ascend the tribune, and uttered but a very few words. As these have not been given by any of the papers, it is as well to note them here, since they were thoroughly characteristic of the speaker. When the President pronounced the impeachment of the twenty-nine members, Robespierre, standing at the foot of the tribune, cried out in a state of great agitation : 'What are you doing? You will spoil the whole thing! You must lay down a principle!'[2] Lay down a principle at the very moment when they were all being violated! That was just like Robespierre, who fully understood that when proclaiming the sovereignty of the people nothing would seem absurd in the mouth of the man who spoke in its name!

[1] 'Mémoires de Petion,' p. 6 : 'There was no time to say a word ; we all ran off as fast as we could to reach some place of safety.'
[2] 'Supplément aux Crimes des Anciens Comités,' by Dulaure.

CHAPTER LXXIX.

ANOTHER TENTH OF AUGUST.

Wednesday, June 5, 1793.

THE Second of June was for the Girondist party what the Tenth of August was to Louis XVI.

The endless succession of insurrections, proscriptions and massacres we have now witnessed for the past four years, with crime triumphant and power made the reward of insolence and villainy, is undoubtedly well calculated to plunge real Patriots into grief and despair. Sometimes, however, a gleam of consolation, almost akin to joy, steals in upon their sorrow when they see the men who have brought about all the mischief caught in their own trap—when they see them overthrown by the rising which they themselves advocated, and persecuted by the mob whose praises they sang when that mob was subservient to their will. In this almost dramatic retribution, I cannot help recognising the intervention of Providence ; in the presence of events like those of May 31 and June 2, I feel impelled to cry out : 'It is the will of God !'

Was that will ever more manifest ? Does it not seem as if the Providence so derided[1] by the Girondists had taken pleasure

---

[1] On March 26, 1792, at the Jacobin Club, Robespierre read a manifesto which he had drawn up on the occasion of the death of Leopold II., Emperor of Germany, and brother of Marie Antoinette, and in which he used the name of Providence. The Girondist Guadet turned Robespierre's manifesto to ridicule. 'You speak again and again,' he said, 'of Providence ; I think you say that Providence has saved us in spite of ourselves. I confess that I see no sense in the idea, and I should never have thought that a man who has worked so hard for three years to drag the people out of the slavery of despotism would help to drag them back to the slavery of superstition.' Durand de Maillane, a member of

in making them traverse the same painful path along which they dragged Louis XVI.; to reproduce in the incidents which accompanied their fall each of those which marked the fall of the Monarchy?

This is not only a striking coincidence; it also teaches a deeply moral lesson, and that is why I think it my duty to dwell upon it.

The prologue to the drama of the Tenth of August was the Twentieth of June.

The organizers of June 20 had aimed at the overthrow of Louis XVI. They had been unable to carry out their designs in their entirety on that day, but by skilful plotting they swept all before them ere two months had elapsed.

The prologue to June 2 was played on March 10.[1] On this occasion it was not a question of dethroning a King, but of overthrowing the Girondists—a party that had applauded the events of June 20, 1792. It was now a question of compassing the fall of Vergniaud and Guadet—men who had on the former occasion demanded that the rioters might be permitted to march through the Legislative Chamber; of Petion, who had then allowed the rising to foment under his eyes, and who, by refusing to sign certain orders, had tied the hands of the Commandant of the National Guard; of Brissot and Gorsas, who had spoken enthusiastically of the rioters, and loudly praised their patriotism and dignified behaviour;[2] of Roland, or rather (for the poor man scarcely counts) of Mme. Roland, who, on hearing the details of the raid upon the palace, and to what shame and anguish the Queen had been subjected, uttered this cry of joy and regret: 'How I wish I had seen her humiliation!'[3]

The rioters of March 10, who, like those of June 20, were abetted by the Mayor of Paris—that dignitary being no longer

the Convention, says, in his 'Mémoires': 'The Girondist party was even more anti-religious than the Mountain.' See 'La Légende des Girondins,' p. 62, etc.

[1] See Vol. I., Chapter LXVIII.

[2] Le Patriote Français, June 21, 1792; Le Courrier des Départements, June 21.

[3] It is Lamartine, one of Mme. Roland's most ardent panegyrists, who is responsible for the above.

Petion, but Pache—were in possession of the approaches to the Riding-School at daybreak. The former Mayor was hounded down on the Terrasse des Feuillants with cries of 'Death to Petion! death to Brissot!' and in the evening a large crowd besieged the doors of the Convention. Vergniaud, Guadet and their friends, knowing that their lives were threatened, did not attend the sitting, and the rioters were finally dispersed by the rain that fell in torrents. The plot had failed as it had failed on June 20, but in the same way as the organizers of June 20 had returned to the attack and struck a decisive blow only a few weeks later, so did the organizers of March 10 reappear before three months had elapsed to provide a sequel to the Revolution of the Tenth of August.

In the interval between the Twentieth of June and the Tenth of August, Petion, the Mayor of Paris, appeared at the bar of the Legislative Assembly and read an address from the sections demanding the abdication of Louis XVI.[1]

In the interval between March 10 and May 31, Pache, the Mayor of Paris, appeared at the bar of the National Convention and presented an address from the sections demanding the impeachment of twenty-two deputies of the Gironde party.[2] Louvet's name occurred in both of these addresses. In the first he figured as a signatory, in the second as one of the proscribed.

From the Twentieth of June to the Tenth of August an endless succession of petitioners against Louis XVI. appeared at the bar amidst the applause of the Brissotins. From March 10 to May 31 the deputations reappeared, and consisted almost entirely of the same Patriots; this time, however, Brissot and his colleagues did not applaud—their turn of persecution had come.

Soon after June 20, Menjaud and Fayel, the Justices of the Peace, issued warrants against Petion and against Manuel, the Procureur de la Commune. A deputation from the Municipal Body protested against this at the bar of the Convention. The

---

[1] Sitting of August 3, 1792.   [2] Sitting of April 15, 1793.

Brissot party admitted the petitioners to the honours of the sitting, and denounced the measures taken by Menjaud and Fayel as a violation of the law, and an attack upon the Constitution. The withdrawal of the warrants was insisted upon.[1]

Soon after March 10 the Commission of Twelve ordered Hébert, the Deputy-Procureur de la Commune, to be arrested, whereupon a deputation from the Municipal Body demanded *his* liberation.

'The Conseil-Général,' said the spokesman from the Commune, 'will defend the innocent with its last breath. It asks the Convention to restore to his duties a magistrate who is as well known for his patriotism as for his learning. An arbitrary arrest is in reality an honour when the accused is an honest man.'[2] A few days later came fresh deputations from the Commune and the sections ; they were admitted to the honours of the sitting, and the Assembly passed a decree liberating Hébert, and suppressing the Commission of Twelve.

On May 29, 1792, the Brissotin party passed a vote disbanding the King's Constitutional Guard. The staff officers of the National Guard and a few companies of nobles having remained loyal to the King, the self-same party, acting in unison with Petion and the Commune, passed a decree a few days before the Tenth of August for the reorganization of the staff, the punishment of any officers giving other orders than those emanating from the civil authorities, the distribution of the artillery of the sixty battalions amongst the forty-eight sections, and the suppression of all the companies of nobles. Whilst depriving the King of his defenders, they decided upon assembling under the walls of Paris an army of 20,000 men, composed of the federates from the provinces, and on July 11 they decreed that each of these federates was to receive thirty sous per day.

On March 10 the federates from Finistère and the Loire Inférieure saved the Girondist deputies. Buzot and his friends, after having vainly proposed the creation of a body of departmental Guards that would have been for them what the Constitutional Guard was for Louis XVI., tried to keep the

---

[1] Sitting of July 11, 1792.   [2] Sitting of May 25, 1793.

provincial volunteers in Paris. The Mountain, however, demanded that these volunteers should be sent to the frontiers within seventy-two hours. This demand was not granted, but the Convention decreed that the armed bodies sent to Paris by the maritime departments should return to their posts, and that the volunteers composing them should be held liable to serve like all other citizens whenever called upon.[1] Before the Tenth of August the Girondists invited the volunteers from Marseilles and Provence to come to Paris. Before June 2 Hanriot recalled to the capital the Parisian volunteers who were on their way to the Vendée. And since it seemed necessary that every event which preceded the fall of the Monarchy should have its exact counterpart in the events preceding that of the Girondists, the Convention, following the example of the Legislative Assembly, which had voted the formation of a camp of 20,000 men outside Paris, decreed that a camp of 40,000 men should be immediately formed.[2] It also determined that besides this army of *sans-culottes* a popular guard should be organized, and be paid by the nation.[3]

To these comparisons a host of others could be added. Never had the *lex talionis*, never had the old adage *Patere legem quam fecisti* received a fuller or more striking application.

On the eve of the Tenth of August several members of the Right—Froudière, Lacretelle the elder, Soret, Calvet, Quatremère, Deuzy, Desbois, Mezières, Regnault - Beaucarron, Dumolard, Jollivet, and Stanislas de Girardin—complained in the Assembly of the outrages committed upon them : volunteers wearing the red cap had flung mud and stones at them, and had threatened to lynch them. Their complaints were answered by sarcastic remarks from the benches of the Gironde.

On the eve of May 31 it was the turn of the scoffers to complain of being insulted and threatened by the ruffians who daily thronged the approaches of the Convention. The Mountain replied with smiles of unconcern. 'For the past two years,'

---

[1] Sitting of March 5, 1793 ; *Moniteur*, March 6.
[2] Sitting of April 5, 1793.   [3] *Ibid.*

cried Marat, ' we have heard your complaints, and you have not a scratch to show your constituents !'[1]

At the sitting of August 9, 1792, the voice of brave Vaublanc was repeatedly drowned by the shouts of the galleries. The President insisted upon having silence, but his orders were disregarded. 'I constantly hear the authority of the Assembly invoked in vain against the spectators,' said Vaublanc. 'Is it not ridiculous to hear the President calling the galleries to order a score of times, and to hear his voice drowned by their shouts? It were best that we betook ourselves elsewhere to deliberate.' The Right applauded Vaublanc's words, and desired that Petion should be called to the bar to declare whether or not he would be responsible for the safety of the representatives of the nation. Isnard and Guadet vehemently opposed this demand, and caused it to be rejected. Since the galleries were on their side, the Girondists looked upon their interference in the debates of the Assembly as legitimate and salutary.

We now turn to May, 1793, when there was not a single sitting at which Vergniaud and his friends, who had then become the Right, did not have to struggle as Vaublanc and his colleagues had done against the shouts of the galleries. 'How,' cried Vergniaud, 'how can you expect to save the Republic if you cannot succeed in stilling the shameful disturbances which interrupt your debates and degrade your Assembly in the eyes of the world?' His words were useless; his complaints were ridiculed as he himself once ridiculed those of Vaublanc.

At the opening of the sitting on May 28, Guadet demanded the repeal of the decree which but the day before had suppressed the Commission of Twelve. He maintained that the decree was invalid, since the legislators, imprisoned in their place of meeting after the dispersion of their guard, had deliberated amidst outrages, insults and threats; whilst several representatives of the nation—Petion and Lasource amongst others—had found it impossible to make their way into the building through the riotous crowd. Guadet's words were

[1] Sitting of May 20, 1793.

eloquent indeed, but how much more eloquent was the speech of Jean-Bon Saint-André, in which he refuted the Girondists with the very principles they upheld on the eve of the Tenth of August. 'It might astonish anyone who has but a limited knowledge of the human heart that principles so boldly put forward at one time could be so disregarded at another. But the interests are no longer the same. When we discussed the suspension of the Tyrant's powers in the Legislative Assembly, Ramond and his party opposed that suspension on the same grounds as those just brought forward. They then said that they had been unable to make their way into the Assembly ; they said that they had been unable to vote upon this great question, and they wished to invalidate the decrees of the Assembly because they had taken no part in them.'

Petion more than once boasted of the important part he had played in the Revolution of the Tenth of August.[1] When Mayor of Paris, and entrusted with the maintenance of public order, he aided the conspirators in their plots, and betrayed Louis XVI. Pache has done no more than copy Petion. When Mayor of Paris, Pache, like Petion, played into the hands of the rioters, and sacrificed the Girondist deputies. At this point the analogy becomes more striking ; a few examples, however, must suffice.

On the eve of August 9 Petion was admitted to the bar of the Legislative Assembly. 'For the whole of the past week,' he said, 'the municipality of Paris has been busily occupied in maintaining peace and order. The Mayor and municipal officers have done all in their power to calm the feeling of unrest. The Corporation has ordered a company of reserves, composed in the same manner as the King's Guards, to be stationed in the Place du Carrousel, and another in the Place Louis XV. . . . I am ready to assume all the responsibility that the law imposes upon me, and I can assure the Assembly that whatever salutary measures are suggested to the Corporation will be immediately adopted.'

[1] See 'Pièces Intéressantes pour l'Histoire, Year II., Récit du 10 Août,' by J. Petion.

In order to reassure the Girondist deputies on the eve of May 31, Pache had only to repeat the language of his predecessor. On May 24 he wrote to the Convention : ' Everything tends to prove that there is no conspiracy at all. I may add that since I have held office I have been very uneasy about many things, but that I have never experienced any anxiety concerning the personal safety of the members of the Convention, and that whatever rumours reach me seem to come from those who are either easily intimidated, or who have an interest in spreading such rumours. I appeal to facts. In the midst of alarms which would lead one to expect the most sanguinary events, amidst the most bellicose preparations on all sides, there is not more real trouble in Paris now than at any other time. There is no town in which the Convention is more respected, and in which the persons of the deputies are more safe than in the capital.'[1]

On the morrow there came another letter from Pache confirming that of the day before, and declaring that he had examined and provided for everything, and that there was nothing to fear.[2]

When these two letters were read, the 'worthy ' Pache appeared at the bar of the Convention in the same way as the ' virtuous ' Petion had appeared at the bar of the Legislative Assembly on August 9, and renewed his affirmation that the plot about which so much noise was being made was an imaginary one.

All was ready for the insurrection of the Tenth of August, and the success of the conspiracy was ensured. It was this moment that Petion chose to speak of peace, order and tranquillity, and to issue the following proclamation :

' CITIZENS,—Attempts have frequently been made to ruin your cause by damping your ardour ; an attempt is now being made to ruin it by urging you along a false path. The Assembly is at this moment deliberating upon matters of the greatest importance ; let no disturbing influences surround it !'[3]

---

[1] Pache's letter is dated May 24, year II. It was read at the sitting of the Convention of May 27
[2] This second letter was also read at the same sitting.
[3] Buchez and Roux, ' Histoire Parlementaire,' tome xvi., p. 402.

In reading this proclamation it is impossible to avoid comparing it with that issued by Pache on May 31 :

'CITIZENS,—Open your eyes, for you are surrounded by great dangers. Those among us who have been led astray demand the closing of the barriers and the ringing of the tocsin ; they ask for another insurrection. Compare recent events, and you will recognise the villains who have led these citizens along false paths, and who advise such proceedings.'

At midnight on August 9 the alarm rang out from all the churches in the sections of Gravilliers, Mauconseil, and the Lombards. Neither the Legislative Assembly nor the special Commission of Twenty-one, composed of Vergniaud and his friends, cared to inquire who were the men who had thus given the signal for the revolt.

On the night preceding May 31 the alarm bells were also heard, but this time they justified their name in the effect they produced upon Vergniaud and his friends. 'We must know,' said Vergniaud, 'who gave the order for ringing the tocsin, and I demand that the Commandant-Général be summoned to the bar.' Lasource read the draft of a manifesto which he proposed issuing, and in which he said: 'Conspirators, disguised as Patriots in order to lead the people astray and ruin the cause of Liberty, have had alarm guns fired and the tocsin rung.' The only reply he got to this was one from Barère, evoking those recollections of the Tenth of August which confront the Girondists at every turn. 'Of what, after all,' cried the orator, 'does Vergniaud complain? Of a few private acts for which we should not blame the successful rising which has just taken place. Did you inquire on the Tenth of August who the individuals were who had rung the tocsin?' Couthon, too, who, on June 2, gave the finishing stroke to the Girondist party, was careful not to miss the opportunity of pointing out the astonishing similarity existing between the Tenth of August and May 31. 'Call to mind, citizens,' he said, 'how the Monarchy, always seeking some fresh means of stifling liberty, established a Central Committee of Justices of the Peace ; in the same way did the Girondists establish a Commission. The Committee of

Justices had Hébert arrested ; so did the Commission of Twelve.
The Justices did not stop there—they issued warrants against
three members of the Assembly, and when they saw that public
opinion was deserting them, they had recourse to armed forces.
Is not all this exactly what the Commission of Twelve did ?
The resemblance is striking, but it is real.'[1]

One of the first acts of the delegates of the sections on the
Tenth of August was to appoint a fresh Commandant-Général
of the National Guards. Santerre, ex-Commandant of the
battalion of the Enfants-trouvés, was unanimously elected and
called Commandant-Général Provisoire.

The first act of the delegates of the majority of the sections
on May 31 was to confer upon Citizen Hanriot, Commandant
of the *Sans-culottes* section, the title of Commandant-Général
Provisoire of the armed forces of Paris.

With Santerre for their leader, the insurgents prepare to
march upon the Tuileries. The supreme moment approaches.
The wildest confusion reigns in the palace. The King alone is
calm and impassive. He is told that his presence will electrify
the armed citizens stationed in the courts and gardens. Accompanied by a few officers, he leaves the palace and inspects the
companies drawn up in the royal courtyard. He then traverses
all the courts next to the Place du Carrousel, and on reaching
the gardens proceeds towards the quay and the Pont Tournant.
The cries of ' *Long live the King!* so numerous in the royal
courtyard, had gradually ceased, whilst those of ' *Long live the
Nation!* had gone on increasing, until finally the unhappy
Monarch had been compelled to hear : ' *Long live the sans-
culottes!* ' *Down with the Veto!* ' *Down with the King!*
When Louis re-entered the royal apartments, the Queen said to
Madame Campan in a low voice : ' All is lost ! The inspec-
tion has done more harm than good.'[2]

On June 2 it was the turn of the Girondists to issue forth
from the palace, to traverse the courts and gardens, to hear the

---

[1] Sitting of May 31, 1793.
[2] 'Mémoires de Mme. Campan,' tome ii., p. 244.

same insults and the same threats, and to return to the Tuileries to be overthrown.

The members of the Convention, with Hérault-Séchelles, the President, at their head, descend the grand staircase, traverse the vestibule, and on reaching the royal courtyard make their way towards the gate opening on to the Place du Carrousel. Hanriot, who is guarding this gate with his artillery, refuses to let the deputies pass, and shouts, 'Stand by your guns, my men!' The President then turns to the left, and proceeds towards the exit on the north side of the courtyard, but here he is met by the same resistance. The members return to the palace, and, again passing through the vestibule, make their way into the gardens. Like Louis XVI., they proceed towards the gate near the river, where the President addresses the officers, who refuse to allow him to pass. The members of the Convention finally return to the palace amidst shouts of ' *Long live Marat!* ' *Long live the Mountain!* ' *Down with Brissot, Guadet and Vergniaud!* ' *Purge the Convention!* ' Humiliated and conquered, the Assembly returns to the scene of its labours, and no doubt more than one of the Girondist members exclaimed, like Marie Antoinette, ' All is lost!'

The promenade of the Convention imprisoned in the Tuileries bore such a striking resemblance to that of the captive King that it was immediately remarked upon by all. When news reached the Hôtel de Ville that the Assembly was traversing the ranks of the armed forces, Hébert, rushing to the tribune, compared ' the conduct of the Convention with that of the Tyrant as, on the morning of the Tenth of August, he inspected the troops upon which he relied.'[1]

In the vanguard of the troops that surrounded the Convention on June 2 were the famous Marseillais who had taken part in the attack upon the Tuileries on the Tenth of August. On the latter date they had obeyed the orders of Barbaroux, but on June 2 they were shouting for his head. Both on June 2 and the Tenth of August was heard the hymn of the Marseillais, and the song of *Ça ira!* It was of the latter that Petion in a letter to the Legislative Assembly once said, ' The famous air

---

[1] ' Compte Rendu et Déclaration,' by J. B. M. Saladin.

which rejoices the hearts of Patriots and makes those of their enemies tremble.'[1] He wrote these words on May 30, 1792. Did the *Ça ira* have the same charms for him a year later ?[2]

One more striking coincidence and I shall have done.

The fall of the Monarchy brought about the imprisonment of the Queen, of that brave and noble woman of whom Mirabeau said : ' The King has only one man about him, and that is his wife.'[3]

Though the Girondists possessed neither the virtue nor the humanity of Louis XVI., they showed the same indecision and the same weakness, and it would be equally true to say : ' The Girondist party had only one man—Mme. Roland.' And the Queen of the Gironde was imprisoned after May 31 as the Queen of France had been after the Tenth of August. She was arrested at seven o'clock on the morning of June 1 at her house in the Rue de la Harpe and taken to the Abbaye.[4] Neither her courage nor her misfortunes can make us forget that from October, 1789, until the Tenth of August, 1792—three years which were for Marie Antoinette one long martyrdom heroically borne—Mme. Roland did not cease to persecute her with her hatred, rejoicing at all the insults which the Revolution heaped upon the daughter of Maria Theresa. Neither on June 25, 1791, when the Queen was brought back from Varennes a

---

[1] *Moniteur* of 1792, p. 632.

[2] 'Mémoires de J. Petion,' p. 8, June 2, 1793 : ' We caught sight of a field of standing barley, and immediately rushed into it, where we lay flat upon the ground. We were in this frightful position for seven hours by the clock without meat or drink, not daring to speak a word, and hardly daring to breathe. We could hear the incessant roll of the drum and the shouts of joy that maddened us. For two hours the warlike strains of the hymn of the Marseillais, once so sweet in our ears, made us shed bitter tears.'

[3] 'Correspondance de M. de Lamark et de Mirabeau ': 'Mémoires de Mirabeau,' tome vii., p. 342.

[4] 'Mémoires de Mme. Roland,' p. 195. On the evening of May 31, Mme. Roland, who throughout the crisis gave proofs of a courage which it is but just to acknowledge, stood talking in the courtyard of the palace with a group of *sans-culotte* gunners, after having vainly attempted to get into the Legislative Chamber. ' To ascertain the will of the departments,' she said, ' recourse should have been had to primary assemblies.' To this an old *sans-culotte* replied ' Was that necessary on the Tenth of August ?'

humble captive[1] to the Tuileries, nor on June 20, 1792, when the mob hurled its insults and curses at Mme. *Veto*, did Mme. Roland hide her joy.[2]   More ardent and passionate than her friends, she reproached them with being too weak and too cowardly to try Louis XVI. and his wife together.[3]

Roland is outlawed, and his wife is now awaiting her trial in one of the cells of the Abbaye.   I stop here; but have I not the right to end this page of comparisons with the words I wrote in beginning it ?

'It is the will of God !'

---

[1] 'Between thirty and forty thousand National Guards surround our *grand outlaws* (Louis XVI. and Marie Antoinette). . . .   I can scarcely contain myself ; I must go out and see my friends to animate them to great deeds' (letter from Mme. Roland, dated June 23, 1792).

[2] See above, p. 147.

[3] 'It seems to me that we ought to brush the royal puppet aside, and put his wife on her trial' ('Lettres de Mme. Roland'').   On June 25, 1791, she wrote to Bancal des Issarts : 'We can only be regenerated by blood.'

CHAPTER LXXX.

Friday, June 14, 1793.

THERE was a time when the posters on the walls related to nothing more exciting than the sale of some piece of land, the disposal of the library or cellar of a deceased nobleman, or the departure of some vessel for the Indies.[1] But those days of obscurity and ignorance are long past. The poster has become a power in the land, and a power greater, perhaps, than all the rest. The tribune and the newspaper hold the ear for a few hours only; the poster attracts attention for several days. A newspaper costs two sous; it costs nothing to read a poster. The editors are so fully alive to the superiority of this form of publicity that, when they wish to deal a decisive blow, they transform their sheets into posters, and have them stuck up on the walls. Marat never fails to do this on great occasions, and it is quite amusing to see the gaping crowds gathered before the green, blue, red or yellow placards.[2] They are printed in all the colours of the rainbow, and the opinions they propagate are as startling and conflicting as their hues; daily do the walls of Paris preach revolt, murder, and pillage—sometimes, *mirabile dictu!* moderation and peace.

The following are a few fresh posters I noticed this morning in the Palais Égalité, the Rue Saint-Honoré, and the Place des Piques.

A proclamation from the Jacobin Club of Arcis-sur-Aube applauding 'the vigorous measures' adopted by the Commune against 'the traitors' in the Convention, and expressing a hope

---

[1] Mercier, 'Le Nouveau Paris,' ii. 284.   [2] *Ibid.*

of speedily seeing the Twenty-two and the Twelve, as well as
Clavière, Lebrun and Roland, pay for their attacks upon
Liberty with their lives.[1]

A poster signed by Pache, the Mayor of Paris. It inveighs
against Fonfrède, a member for the Gironde, who reproached
the Convention with permitting the imprisonment of 10,000
persons, and against Thibault, the constitutional Bishop of
Saint-Flour, and member for the Cantal, who dared to suggest
that bankrupts and swindlers sat upon the Central Revolutionary
Committee.[2]

A manifesto from Jérôme Petion to the people of Paris. The
former Mayor appeals to his old electors, who, to judge by
what I hear around me, are by no means disposed to give him
back his popularity.

A proclamation from the Corporation and citizens of the
town of Chartres applauding the measures taken on May 31
and the following days.[3] Poor Petion receives no mercy at
their hands, though they had elected him to the Constituent
Assembly and to the Convention.

A notice announcing that the orange-trees and shrubs of the
Castle of Chantilly, will be sold on Saturday, June 15.[4]

A manifesto from Boursault senior, secretary to the Revolutionary Committee of Paris, celebrating the late triumph of
the Commune. 'Let them,' he says, 'talk as they will about
the infraction and violation of the laws ; there are times when a
nation must do what it thinks best for its own welfare.'[5]

Another from Prudhomme, the editor of the *Révolutions de
Paris*. Incarcerated for forty-eight hours, he lays the blame of
his arrest upon Lacroix, President of the Revolutionary Committee of the Unité Section, a man whose turpitude he claims
to have laid bare. This, however, does not prevent him from
concluding as follows : 'I am convinced that the outrage committed upon me is the result of a counter-Revolutionary movement.'[6]

[1] 'Tableaux de la Révolution Française, publiés sur les Papiers inédits
du Département et de la Police Secrète de Paris,' by Adolphe Schmidt,
tome ii., p. 16.
[2] *Ibid.*, p. 23.   [3] *Ibid.*, p. 35.   [4] *Moniteur* of June 12, 1793.
[5] Schmidt, tome ii., p. 40.   [6] *Révolutions de Paris*, tome xvi., p. 470.

A manifesto from Hanriot, Commandant of the National Guard, in which he declares that he is not surprised at seeing so many calumnies heaped upon him. Hanriot's address does not find much more favour than Petion's. In some groups he is spoken of in not unfriendly terms, but in others it does not seem to be forgotten that before being Commandant he had been ordered out of Paris. It is told that he was a beggar at the commencement of the Revolution, and that he has just bought some property for 60,000 francs; that he is on the point of making other purchases; that he had played the part of Brutus in his section by denouncing his mother as an out-and-out aristocrat, but that it was rather in order to get rid of her than from motives of patriotism. The bystanders listened to these remarks with every sign of approval. I must say, however, that when I passed the Palais Égalité an hour later Hanriot's placards were intact, whilst those of Petion and Barbaroux had been torn down.

A large yellow poster that made its appearance on May 13 last, by order of the Commune, and of which there have been several later issues, still attracts many readers. It is headed : ' *The Gorsas of September and the Gorsas of To-day.*' ' *The Brissot of September and the Brissot of To-day.*' Below this are two columns in which are reproduced the conflicting opinions concerning the September massacres put forth by Gorsas in the *Courrier des Departements*, and by Brissot in the *Patriote Français.* Last month these two worthies, threatened in their turn by the cut-throats of the Carmes and the Abbaye, saw fit to brand these men as brigands and assassins, whereupon the latter very pertinently reminded them that at the time when the massacres were taking place both had given them their approval—Brissot writing that the people had only struck down the guilty, and Gorsas declaring that it was undoubtedly a terrible but a necessary act of justice.[1]

It is said that Brissot has just been arrested at Moulins.[2]

[1] Conseil-Général de la Commune, May 13, 1793 ; *Journal de Paris National*, No. 137, May, 1793. Buchez and Roux have not mentioned this sitting of the Commune in their ' Histoire Parlementaire.'

[2] Brissot, having concealed himself at Moulins, was arrested there on June 10, 1793. Brought to Paris, he was imprisoned first in the Abbaye,

Gorsas, Buzot, Petion, and a few other members of the Girondist party, have been fortunate enough to escape to Caen, where they are making an attempt to bring about a rising in Brittany and Normandy against Paris and the Mountain. May they avoid falling into the hands of their enemies, and escape the fate already marked out for them![1] But should it turn out otherwise, we should be compelled to admit that, after having for four years incited the mob to fresh revolts, murder and massacre, neither they nor Brissot have a claim upon the pity of honest men.

'Non lex est justior ulla
Quam necis artifices arte perire sua.'

Tuesday, June 18, 1793.

The police authorities have just published a list of the deputies who were formally arrested on June 2, and since then confined to their homes; and also a list of those members who were found to have fled. The double list is as follows:

I.—Members of the National Convention absent from their homes: Brissot, Buzot, Chambon, Gorsas, Grangeneuve, Henry-Larivière, Lasource, Lesage, Lidon, Louvet, Rabaut Saint-Étienne, Salle and Viger.

II.—Members placed under arrest in their own homes: Barbaroux, Bergoeing, Bertrand de l'Hodiesnière, Birotteau, Boilleau, Gardien, Gensonné, Gomaire, Guadet, Lanjuinais, Lehardy, Kervélégan, Mollevaut, Petion, Valazé and Vergniaud.

The two first members on this second list made off after their arrest—Bergoeing during the night of June 6, Barbaroux on the night of the 10th.[2]

The Decree of June 2, ordering the arrest and confinement in their own homes of certain members of the National Convention,

and afterwards in the Luxembourg, and was guillotined October 31, 1793.

[1] Gorsas, having been imprudent enough to return to Paris, was discovered on October 6, 1793, and brought before the Revolutionary Tribunal. He was guillotined on October 7. 'This wretch,' says the 'Glaive Vengeur,' p. 114, 'had the impudence to shout on the scaffold, "I am innocent, and my blood will be avenged." He inspired only disgust and contempt.'

[2] *Révolutions de Paris*, tome xvi., p. 560.

contains thirty-two names, but since that of Rabaut Saint-Étienne occurs twice, and the list also includes that of Clavière, the Minister of Taxes, and Lebrun, the Minister for Foreign Affairs—neither of whom formed part of the Convention—the number of members really impeached was only twenty-nine.

Out of these twenty-nine fifteen were guillotined : Barbaroux, Birotteau, Boilleau, Brissot, Gardien, Gensonné, Gorsas, Grangeneuve, Guadet, Lasource, Lehardy, Rabaut Saint-Étienne, Salle, Vergniaud and Viger.

Four committed suicide in order to escape the scaffold : Buzot, Lidon, Petion and Valazé.

Chambon was killed at Lubersac, his native home, by the Patriots charged with his arrest.

Nine succeeded in baffling their pursuers : Bergoeing, Bertrand de l'Hodiesnière, Gomaire, Henry-Larivière, Kervélégan, Lanjuinais, Lesage, Louvet and Mollevaut.

The Minister Lebrun was guillotined ; his colleague Clavière committed suicide in the Conciergerie.

CHAPTER LXXXI.

THE CONSTITUTION OF '93.

Wednesday, June 26, 1793.

FOR the past two days we have been under the rule of a fresh Constitution.

The National Assembly was engaged for more than two years in preparing and discussing the Constitution of 1791 ; the Convention, however, has taken just a fortnight to prepare and deliberate upon that of 1793. It was a stroke of policy to get the matter through quickly. Was it not the best proof in the world that the Convention had until then been prevented from doing the work for which it was really elected owing to the obstructive tactics of such traitors and plotters as Brissot and the Girondist members ?

On May 29 the Convention had decreed that the Committee of Public Safety should be increased by five members before it proceeded to frame a fresh Constitution. On the morrow the Committee informed the Assembly that it had elected Hérault-Séchelles, Ramel, Couthon, Saint-Just and Mathieu.[1] In reality, the five newly-appointed members were the only ones who prepared and drew up the Acte Constitutionnel. For on May 31 and the following days their colleagues on the Committee of Public Safety had, as we have seen, other matters to engage their attention.[2] Even Hérault-Séchelles and his four collaborators do not appear to have started work seriously until June 7.

---

[1] *Moniteur*, May 31, 1793.

[2] The members of the Committee of Public Safety were Cambon, Barère, Danton, Guyton-Morveau, Treilhard, Lacroix, Bréard, Delmas, and Robert Lindet. The latter was absent on a mission, and Delmas was ill.

On that day the following letter was written by Séchelles to Citizen Desaunays, Keeper of the Printed Books and Manuscripts in the Bibliothèque Nationale :

'CITIZEN,

'Having with four of my colleagues to prepare by Monday next a draft of a fresh Constitution, I beg you in their name and mine to procure us immediately the Laws of Minos, which are probably to be found in a collection of Greek laws. We have urgent need of them.'[1]

Two days later, on the evening of Sunday, the 9th, Hérault-Séchelles and his four colleagues submitted to the Committee of Public Safety the draft prepared by them,[2] and this, after a few slight alterations, was adopted by the Committee on the following morning. It was read to the Convention by Hérault-Séchelles the same day, and on Robespierre's motion it was decided that the debate upon it should commence on the morrow.

It came up for discussion on eleven separate occasions, but very few sittings were devoted exclusively to the subject. The greater number of the articles—and there were 159—were passed without comment. Men's minds were really occupied with other matters, and the authors of the Act were the last to take this farcical Constitution seriously. Never had the people been deceived with greater effrontery.

In the Acte Constitutionnel we find an article which runs : 'No deputy shall at any time be prosecuted, accused, or tried for opinions to which he has given vent in the Legislative Body.' And on the very day — June 15 — on which this article was passed, Duchastel, a member of the Convention, was impeached.[3] Two days later, on June 17, Ramel, one of the authors of the Constitution, moved 'That the authorities of the

---

[1] M. Challamel ('Histoire Musée de la République Française') has given a facsimile of Hérault-Séchelles' letter (Taine, 'La Révolution,' tome iii., p. 8).

[2] Register of the proceedings and of the orders issued by the Committee of Public Safety ('Archives,' 434, AA. 71).

[3] *Moniteur*, June 17, 1793.

department of the Allier be ordered to send to Paris without delay, and under safe escort, J. P. Brissot, a member of the National Convention, arrested in the town of Moulins.'[1] The motion was carried. On June 17, too, Barbaroux, another deputy, was impeached.[2] On June 23 new and rigorous measures were passed against the arrested members. On Chabot's motion it was decided that they were to be kept in closer confinement under the continual supervision of two gendarmes, and no communication with anyone whatever was to be permitted.[3] Finally, on the 24th, on the day when the Constitution was completed, and no doubt to celebrate that event, the Convention passed a decree ordering the deputies, until then confined to their homes, ' to be transferred to the *National houses* other than public prisons, there to be kept in isolation and under strict supervision.'[4]

The new Constitution also says that ' Government is instituted to guarantee to man the enjoyment of his natural and impre-scriptible rights. These rights are liberty and safety.'[5] And farther : ' The law must protect public and individual liberty against the oppression of the Government.'[6] And one of its last articles runs : ' The Constitution guarantees to all French-men, equality, liberty, and safety.'[7] With touching unanimity, and in all seriousness, do the members of the Convention pass these articles establishing individual liberty, and seem to feel no embarrassment when their deliberations are interrupted by the arrival of a communication of this kind :

' The police authorities of the Commune of Paris lay before the Convention the following return of persons confined in the prisons and houses of detention of Paris on June 19.

' Conciergérie, 325 ; Grande-Force, 331 ; Petite-Force, 108 ; Sainte-Pélagie, 131 ; Madelonnettes, 80 ; Abbaye, 69 ; Bicêtre, 214 ; Salpétrière, 45 ; Chambre d'arrêt à la Mairie, 39. Total, 1,342.'[8]

---

[1] *Moniteur*, June 19, 1793. Brissot had been arrested on the 10th.
[2] *Ibid.*, June 20, 1793.   [3] *Ibid.*, June 25.
[4] *Journal des Débats et Décrets*, No. 280, sitting of June 24.
[5] Déclaration des Droits de l'Homme et du Citoyen, Articles 1 and 2.
[6] *Ibid.*, Article 9.
[7] Acte Constitutionnel, Article 122.
[8] Submitted to the Convention June 21 ; *Moniteur*, June 23, 1793.

There seems scarcely any need for me to dwell upon this so-called Constitution—an empty rhetorical document made only to be posted on the walls and to be read in the political clubs. Its execution is utterly impossible. A Constitution, be it good or bad, presupposes some government or authority, but the Constitution of June 24 suppresses all permanent forms of both. It leaves the reins of power entirely in the hands of the Legislative Body. Now, the Legislative Body consists of one Chamber elected for one year only.[1] There is, it is true, to be an Executive composed of twenty-four members; they are, however, merely administrative agents—clerks, in fact, appointed by the Legislative Body. 'These agents shall not form a Council, but are to be separated and to hold no communication with each other. They are to exercise no personal authority,'[2] and 'half their number are to be re-elected annually.'[3]

This instability and perpetual change is the chief characteristic of the Constitution. Municipalities, district and departmental authorities—all are to re-elect half their members every year.[4]

Justices of the Peace are to be elected annually by the primary assemblies.[5] Arbitrators in Civil Law—replacing the former Judges—are to be appointed annually by the electoral assemblies. Criminal Judges are to be elected in the same way.[6]

The people will thus have the right at the end of each year to retain or change the whole of the political and judicial staff of the country. Their powers do not stop there. They are to deliberate upon the laws;[7] they are to vote *aye* or *no* upon the proposals of the Legislative Body, which shall be printed and sent to all the communes of the Republic with the following heading: '*Proposed Law.*'[8] If at the end of forty days a tenth of the primary assemblies in more than half the departments shall have returned a negative reply, the law shall not pass, and the Legislative Body shall then convoke all the primary assemblies,[9] whose decision shall be final. Upon the demand of a tenth of the primary assemblies in more than half the departments, the

---

[1] Articles 39 and 40.   [2] Article 68.   [3] Article 64.
[4] Article 8.   [5] Article 95.   [6] Article 97.
[7] Article 10.   [8] Articles 19 and 58.   [9] Article 59.

Legislative Body shall also be obliged to convoke all the primary assemblies in the Republic, in order to determine the necessity for a revision of the Act of Constitution, or for the election of a fresh Convention.[1]

Briefly, the people have supreme control of all things at all times. As I have said before, the new Constitution is a showy piece of work, and a farce as far as its execution is concerned ; but, then, is not Hérault-Séchelles, its chief author, one of the best actors in the company now performing in the Salle des Machines, once the Tuileries theatre? A nephew of the Marshal de Contades, he was presumably not too much of a Republican when he was appointed Advocate-General by the King, and received from the hands of the Queen a sash that she had embroidered herself. He is a man of talent, I admit, but one who in private life indulges in obscenity and profanity as a relaxation from his arduous duties.[2] He is always very careful about his appearance, and on the day that he read his report on the Act of Constitution before the Convention, this strange *sans-culotte* wore a long frock-coat, of fashionable cut, lined with blue taffeta.[3] Whilst Marat is the Diogenes, he is the Alcibiades of this Republic. As he read his report with the most correct intonation, and in a style that did credit to the art of his teacher, Mdlle. Clairon,[4] all eyes were turned towards *la belle Suzanne*, whom he had brought to the sitting and placed in a prominent seat in the public galleries—Suzanne Giroust Quillet, who has taken advantage of the abolition of titles of nobility to change her *bourgeois* name for the more aristocratic one of Mme. de Morency. This lady should take more care of her love-letters. One of my friends, who is a collector of trifles of this kind, has just presented me with a note addressed to La Morency by Hérault-Séchelles at the end of November last, just as he was about to start for Mont Blanc.[5] Here it is :

[1] Article 59.
[2] According to the testimony of Bellart (' Œuvres de Bellart,' tome vi., p. 124).
[3] Concerning Hérault-Séchelles, see ' Illyrine ; or, The Ills of Inexperience ' (Paris, year VI.), a historical novel by Mme. de G. (Giroust de Morency, a pseudonym of Mme. Quillet).
[4] ' Réflexions sur la Déclamation,' by Hérault-Séchelles.
[5] *Moniteur*, November 30, 1792 ; sitting of the Convention of Novem-

' DEAREST ONE,

'The horses are being put to the carriage as I write you these few words. I am starting at once for Mont Blanc on a secret and important mission. I shall be gone for at least three months. This seems a long separation, charming Suzanne, but I carry your portrait with me in my pocket-book.

'You tell me that you have a jealous nature. There cannot be anyone more afflicted with that terrible malady than myself, and that is why I have never been able to keep a mistress. Sainte-Amaranthe, whom you consider so beautiful, is the most perfidious of women ; she is so well known for that quality that she is called " the fickle Amaranthe."[1] She it was, however, who, in spite of my faults, managed to keep me longest.

'But my pen is running away with me. Good-bye, Suzanne. Go to the Assembly sometimes in memory of me. Good-bye. The horses are chafing, and my travelling companions think me detained by National business, while I am writing words of love to my dear Suzanne.

' SÉCHELLES.'[2]

I shall pin this letter to my copy of the Constitution of 1793.

---

ber 29. The Commissioners sent to the department of Mont Blanc were Hérault-Séchelles, Simon, Grégoire, and Jagot.

[1] Concerning Mme. de Sainte-Amaranthe, see, in Jules Claretie's ' Camille Desmoulins ' (p. 437, etc.), extracts from a very rare pamphlet, ' La Famille Sainte-Amaranthe,' by Mme. A. R. ; Paris, 1864. For a more romantic and pleasing account of her life and deeds, see Paul Gaulot's ' Red Shirts ' (translated by J. de Villiers ; Chatto and Windus, London, 1894).

[2] See ' Illyrine,' tome iii., pp. 252, 257, 258, 280 ; Vatel, ' Charlotte de Corday et les Girondins,' tome iii., 27, etc. ; Claretie, ' Camille Desmoulins,' pp. 217-235 ; Berryer père, ' Souvenirs,' tome i., pp. 177-187 ; Charles Monselet, ' Les Originaux du Siècle Dernier,' ch. x. : ' La Morency.'

CHAPTER LXXXII.

A CIVIC LENT.

OBJECTS of prime necessity are daily increasing in price. Cloth, which three years ago cost 36 francs per yard, now costs 60, and for the coat that then cost me 90 francs I now pay 180.[1] The price of a pair of shoes has risen from 6 francs to 12.[2]

In February we had a riot on account of the price of soap,[3] and in April the fear of a scarcity of bread caused grave disturbances. On Thursday, April 11, a rumour was set afloat in Paris[4] that the supply of flour had run out, and, as corn was very dear, the rumour soon gained credit. Early on the following morning an agitated mob besieged the doors of the bakers' shops, and their proceedings became so riotous that several women were wounded.[5] On the Saturday the situation became still more serious. That day is one of the principal market-days, and formerly the bakers of Gonesse and other villages near the capital used to come and sell their bread in Paris. They have given up coming now, for a four-pound loaf of bread will not fetch more than twelve sous here, whilst in the villages it is sold for sixteen or eighteen sous. But though the bakers of the villages around Paris no longer supply our markets, the country people frequent them in ever-increasing numbers, and on Saturday, April 13, they came in immense crowds. Having heard that flour was scarce in Paris, and fearing that

---

[1] Speech by Ducos in the Convention, April 30, 1793 (*Moniteur*, May 3).
[2] *Ibid.*   [3] See Vol. I., Chapter liv.
[4] *Révolutions de Paris*, tome xvi., p. 158.
[5] Buchez and Roux, tome xxvi., p. 39.

it would soon be the same with them—a reasonable fear, since many country bakers had already closed their shops—they bought large quantities of bread in town. On Saturday evening every coach and boat that left the capital carried at least a hundredweight of bread.[1]

Soon after this a letter from the Corporation of Dijon, addressed to the Municipality of Paris and the Jacobin Club, helped to increase the panic. The letter stated that twenty waggons laden with corn, coming from Paris and having no fixed destination, had been stopped at Dijon; they were to be followed, it was added, by a score of others.[2] Rightly or wrongly, people persuaded themselves that this was a criminal speculation on the part of the bakers of Paris; the latter were accused of buying a sack of flour in the Halles for fifty-five francs—a price beyond which flour did not rise, thanks to the indemnity paid by the Commune—and of selling it outside the town at the rate of seventy francs. Hébert and Chaumette, who never neglect an opportunity of pouring oil upon the fire, did not fail on this occasion to proclaim at the sitting of the Conseil-Général that the guilt of the bakers was fully proved, and that they were in league with Coburg and the counter-Revolutionists.[3] We must do the population of Paris the justice to say that, in spite of such incitement, it did not hang the unhappy men who were thus held up to its indignation and marked out for revenge; the people contented themselves with rising earlier, and with waiting longer hours at the doors of the bakers' shops.

The merit of the Parisians is somewhat diminished, it is true, by the fact that, in spite of their fears, the supply of bread has never absolutely failed, and that they have never paid more than three sous for a pound. In the beginning of February, when a pound of bread could not be obtained elsewhere for less than seven sous, an attempt was made here to raise the price from three sous to three sous and three deniers.[4] In the

---

[1] *Révolutions de Paris*, tome xvi., p. 159.   [2] *Ibid.*
[3] *Le Patriote Français*, No. 1,343.
[4] Lanjuinais' speech in the Convention, February 7, 1793 (*Moniteur*, February 10).

face, however, of the protests that came from the sections, the Commune hastened to give up the attempt. The system adopted by the Commune for the bread supply of the capital is that the Committee of Food Supply purchases all the flour that comes to the market here, and sells it to the bakers at a lower price. At the beginning of February the difference already amounted to 8 francs per sack, and constituted a daily loss of 12,000 francs.[1] Since then this discrepancy has greatly increased. In April the difference was as much as 15 francs, and the daily loss was therefore nearly 24,000 francs. To-day it would be more than 100,000 francs if the law of maximum had not stood in the way.[2] During the discussion which took place in the Convention on May 2, we learnt that in the Beauce district, where corn is most abundant, the price of a sack rose to nearly 200 francs.

Nothing is more natural than that the Commune should take measures to provide Paris with bread at a moderate price; but what is less reasonable than that the expense should be borne by the State instead of the city? In theory, it is true, the Commune accepts this burden, but not in practice. To meet the deficit, additional taxes have been laid upon the towns-people; but as these taxes have not yet been collected, the Commune has obtained the permission of the Convention to draw upon the Treasury for the sums immediately required for the payment of the indemnity. Now, everyone knows how the Commune of Paris repays the advances made to it, and the lax manner in which it keeps its accounts. It is therefore clear that the Parisians pay for their bread with provincial money, and meanwhile the price of bread in the provinces is enormous. In April a four-pound loaf cost thirty-two sous in Clermont, thirty-six in Toulouse, and forty in Grenoble;[3] since then the prices have been doubled. Most of the country people have given up eating bread altogether. On the 21st of this month the Municipality of Vertamon wrote that 'all the inhabitants of

[1] Mortimer-Ternaux, 'Histoire de la Terreur,' tome vi., p. 40.
[2] Law of May 4, 1793 (*Moniteur*, May 6).
[3] *Révolutions de Paris*, tome xvi., p. 259. In August, 1793, a pound of bread cost fifteen to sixteen sous in many departments (*Moniteur*, August 21).

this district were without bread, that the majority lived upon bran and oats, and that starvation was staring them in the face.'

Though the Commune provides the Parisians with cheap bread, it has not been able to do the same for them with respect to meat, which both in Paris and in the provinces is extremely scarce and dear. At the beginning of the month a proclamation signed by the Commissioners of the Food Supply, indicating the causes of this scarcity, was posted on the walls of the capital. 'Considerable purchases,' it ran, 'have been made for the supply of the Army and Navy. The contractors can only make such purchases in France and in those districts where the dealers who attend the markets of Sceaux and Passy usually buy. Large portions of these districts have now been laid waste and devastated by outlaws and fanatics, and but a very short time ago the rebels in the Vendée seized a herd of about 500 oxen. Communications between Paris and some of the districts which used to provide that city with meat are quite suspended, whilst the town of Cholet, which used to send us six or seven hundred oxen every market-day, now sends only sixty or eighty.'[1]

The Commissioners of the Food Supply pointed out where the evil lay, but suggested no remedy; this was left for Vergniaud to do in a sitting of the Convention on April 17. 'Another measure,' he said, 'which I have to lay before you may appear ridiculous at first sight, but I must ask you to examine it carefully. Having regard to the disturbances in the provinces and to the consumption of the Army and Navy, it is to be feared that next year the supply of oxen may not meet the demand. Would it not be wise to proscribe for a time the consumption of veal? (Applause.) Religion imposed abstention from meat to honour the Divinity. Why should not the safety of the country authorize a similar measure?'

Vergniaud's proposal was referred to the Committee of Agriculture.[2]

On June 9, the Convention being again occupied with the question of the Food Supply, Thuriot (of the Mountain) gave

[1] Buchez and Roux, tome xxvi., p. 226.   [2] Moniteur, April 20.

voice to Vergniaud's idea in the following words : 'For the past six months the price of meat has gone up to such an extent that a poor man can no longer buy it. I move (1) that each departmental administration be authorized to determine the price at which meat is to be sold in its own district ; (2) that the citizens of the Republic observe a civic Lent during the month of August.' Thuriot's motion was supported by Gussuin, and referred to the Committees of Agriculture and Commerce.[1]

On the day after Thuriot had brought forward this proposal, I happened to be in the Tuileries. The people in the lobbies were inveighing against the butchers, and especially against Legendre. 'Look at Legendre,' said one of the crowd ; 'he calls himself a patriot. But does he forget his class for his country ? He is a member for Paris, but the interests of his shop in the Rue des Boucheries-Saint-Germain are more to him than those of the nation. Ought he not to set his fellow-butchers an example of selling meat at its real price ? He finds it more profitable to fall in with their thievish ways, and to starve the people. All these patriots are alike, their only object is to get rich ; they give us fine words, and in exchange we have to give them our money.'[2]

Sunday, June 30, 1793.

The question of food supply has become more serious during the past fortnight. The following is a *résumé* of my daily notes on the subject :

June 13.—Both yesterday and to-day people have experienced great difficulty in procuring bread. There have been immense crowds outside the bakers' shops. On all sides were heard grave insinuations against the authorities entrusted with the food supply of Paris ; no one defended them.[3]

June 14.—Crowds still continue to assemble outside the bake-houses, and the public exasperation is increasing. The bakers reply that there is no more flour to be had in the market.[4]

[1] *Moniteur,* June 11, 1793.
[2] 'Rapports de Perrière à Garat,' June 11 and 12 : Schmidt, tome ii., pp. 23, 28.
[3] 'Rapports de Julian de Carentan à Garat,' June 13 : Schmidt, tome ii., p. 33.
[4] 'Rapports de Dutard à Garat,' June 15 : Schmidt, tome ii., p. 54.

June 15.—Visit to Neuilly. The whole district, including the Bois de Boulogne, looks like a desert. I met only two cattle-dealers, who came from Étampes. 'Well, my friends,' I said, 'you are soon going to fight the refugees, for they are marching on your district.' 'Let them come,' replied one of the dealers, 'and let who will fight them; it's no business of ours.'[1] At Neuilly and at Courbevoie I learnt that the bakers had come back from Paris without bringing any flour, and that bread had in consequence risen to four sous per pound.[2]

June 16.—Bought a pound of sugar, for which I had to pay four francs ten sous.[3]

The Mayor has just informed the sections that some evil-disposed persons tried to rob Paris of its bread-supply yesterday, and that, to attain their counter-Revolutionary object, they engaged women to make a raid upon the bakers' shops.[4] This letter only served to increase the popular anxiety, and the bake-houses are besieged more closely than ever; it is said on all sides that before a fortnight is out there will be a famine in Paris.[5]

The butter-merchants who pass through the town of Caen on their way to Paris have been prevented by the inhabitants from continuing their route.

June 17.—The price of food rises hourly, and confidence in paper-money diminishes; famine seems inevitable. Several communes near the capital — amongst others those of Saint-Germain and Saint-Cloud—have come to ask for flour. Soon there will be more demands.[6] Will Paris refuse to open its stores?

June 18.—There is still great difficulty in procuring bread. The first batches are carried off at daybreak, and the later ones are awaited with feverish impatience. Two-pound loaves are still procurable, and cost seven sous each; but it is very difficult to get hold of a four-pound loaf, for which only twelve sous

[1] 'Rapports de Perrière à Garat,' June 15 : Schmidt, tome ii., p. 51.
[2] *Ibid.*   [3] *Ibid.*
[4] 'Rapports de Dutard à Garat,' June 16 : Schmidt, tome ii., p. 57.
[5] Letter from Latour-Lamontagne to Garat, June 16 : Schmidt, tome ii., p. 59.
[6] 'Rapports de Dutard à Garat,' June 17 : Schmidt, tome ii., p. 60.

may be charged. The four-pound loaf is the only one bought
by the poor and by the country people who come to Paris for
their bread.[1] It is therefore not astonishing that the supply
does not meet the demand. The bakers being authorized to
sell a two-pound loaf at a price proportionately higher than one
of four pounds, naturally make only those which bring them the
larger profit.

June 19.—I spent a couple of hours in the Palais Égalité.
The sole question that agitated the promenaders was the price
of meat and the roguery of the butchers.[2]

Since the sitting of the Convention of June 9, the idea put
forth by Vergniaud on April 17 last has continued to find
favour with the multitude. It is almost the only spar from the
wreck of the Girondist party which has been picked up by the
sans-culottes. The Section de l'Homme-Armé has informed the
Conseil-Général Révolutionnaire of the Commune that it has
passed a resolution imposing a civic Lent of six weeks upon all
its members in consideration of the excessive price of meat. At
its sitting on the 22nd the Conseil-Général received a similar
communication from the Montmartre section, accompanied, however, by a request that measures might be taken to prevent any
increase in the price of vegetables.[3]

These good resolutions received the approbation of the
Révolutions de Paris, which speak of them almost pathetically.
' Several sections,' says Prudhomme's sheet, ' have determined to
observe a civic Lent in their respective districts as long as the
excessive prices to which the prime necessities of life have now
risen continue to reign. This resolution is certainly edifying,
and worthy of a Republican people capable of all privations.
To abstain from certain forms of food, or even to limit their
consumption in order that there may be some for everyone, and
that even the poorer classes may have their share, is deserving,
not only of the greatest praise, but of imitation.'[4]

---

[1] ' Rapports de Perrière à Garat,' June 17 : Schmidt, tome ii., pp. 64, 65.
[2] *Ibid.*, June 18 : Schmidt, tome ii., p. 74.
[3] *Mercure Français*, June 29, 1793.
[4] *Révolutions de Paris*, tome xvi., p. 594.

What would Voltaire have said of a civic Lent—he who was so caustic on the subject of that instituted by religion ? The following was one of his questions on the subject : ' Was the loss of appetite in time of sadness the real origin of the fast-days prescribed by sad religions?' His question suggests another : ' Is not the religion of the Republic perchance the saddest of all ?'

CHAPTER LXXXIII.

THIRD FORTNIGHTLY REVIEW.

Saturday, June 29.—On the proposal of Citizen Momoro, one of its members, the Directory of the department decrees that the owners and occupants of houses shall be invited in the name of Patriotism and Liberty to have the following words painted on the façades of their dwellings in large characters :

UNITY AND INDIVISIBILITY OF THE REPUBLIC.

LIBERTY, EQUALITY, FRATERNITY, OR DEATH.

It was further decreed that a tricolour flag, surmounted with a cap of Liberty, should be planted on all public buildings, and all householders invited to place similar ones upon their houses in the course of the next month.[1]

Whilst the departmental Directory is amusing itself with trifles of this kind, the Convention, on the motion of Legendre, declares that the crime of promulgating in the provinces any other Constitution than that adopted by the Convention shall be punishable by death.

Sunday, June 30.—A deputation from the *Society of Young Followers of Brutus*, which meets in the Rue des Deux-Écus, was admitted to a sitting of the Conseil-Général de la Commune, and read the following address :

' CITIZENS,—Our souls are aflame with patriotism ; born, as it were, with the Revolution, we have sworn to uphold it, and

[1] *Journal de Paris National*, No. 182.

our sole ambition is to die in defending it. It is the political clubs, so often calumniated, that have saved the Republic, and that may still prove extremely useful. Filled with a desire to benefit our country, we have deemed it expedient to organize yet another such institution, and have chosen the title of *Society of Young Followers of Brutus.* Should circumstances similar to those which immortalized that great man arise, we have sworn that he would find an imitator in every one of us.'[1]

Each of the young followers of Brutus was honoured with a fraternal kiss from the President.[2]

Monday, July 1.—Hérault-Séchelles, the principal author of the Constitution of June 24, does not brook any interference with his work, and calls down the highest penalty of the law upon whomsoever shall lay a sacrilegious hand upon the sacred ark.   On his motion the Convention passes the following decree :

' Whoever shall print, sell, or distribute one or more altered or falsified copies of the Declaration of the Rights of Man, and of the Act of Constitution drawn up on June 24, 1793, and afterwards submitted by the National Convention to the approval of the French people, shall be punished with death.'[3]

The Committee of Public Safety decrees that young Louis, the son of Capet, shall be separated from his mother and placed in a room by himself—the safest that can be found in the Temple.[4]

Tuesday, July 2.—Emissaries from the Commune proceeded to all the sections in the evening to get the Constitution accepted. It did not meet with the slightest opposition anywhere.

Wednesday, July 3.—Citizens Eudes, Gagnant, Arnaud, Véron, Cellier and Devèze, the Commissioners on duty in the

[1] *Moniteur*, July 1, 1793.
[2] *Journal de Paris National,* July 12, 1793.
[3] *Moniteur*, July 2, 1793.
[4] This decree is signed by Cambon, L. B. Guyton, Jean-Bon Saint-André, G. Couthon, B. Barère, and Danton (' Archives Nationales,' Armoire de Fer, carton 13).

Temple Tower, entered the Queen's room and acquainted her
with the decree of the Committee of Public Safety. It was half-
past nine at night,[1] and the young Prince was asleep; his mother
and his aunt were sewing, whilst his sister was reading her
breviary. It appears that the Queen refused to give up her son,
and stoutly defended the bed on which he was lying. The
municipal officers thereupon threatened to employ force, and to
call the sentries to their assistance. 'Then kill me first!' cried
the Queen. This scene lasted for about an hour. It was not
until the officers pointed out that it would only harm the boy
if the Queen did not give him up, that she yielded to their
demands. Mme. Elisabeth and Mme. Royale then dressed the
unfortunate child, the Queen being too weak and agitated to
help them. When he was dressed she took him and handed
him over to the officers.[2]

Thursday, July 4.—The *Chronique de Paris* publishes the
text of the decree passed by the Commune to-day, containing
the programme for the fête of July 14.

'The Conseil-Général decrees that on Sunday, July 14, its members shall proceed to the National Convention to lay before that
body the wishes of the people of Paris concerning the Constitution,
and that the forty-eight sections shall be invited to send delegates
to assist in handing over the reports containing those wishes. The
Conseil is desirous of discharging this important function with all
due pomp; but taking into consideration the fact that the legislators
have entrusted the Constitution to the virtue of the citizens, and that
virtue should impose itself upon men by conviction, and not by the
force of arms, it has omitted all military display from the procession,
employing only some armed forces to open and close the same. The
procession will be made up as follows:

'A detachment of cavalry; drummers; a detachment of infantry;
the statue of Liberty, draped with the national colours, and borne
aloft by men clad in Greek costume. Every section will appear in
the procession in the numerical order laid down by the municipality,
and will be represented by delegates elected in the General
Assemblies. In front of the group formed by each section will be

---

[1] A report based upon the registers of the Council of the Temple.
See 'Louis XVII.,' by A. de Beauchesne, tome ii., p. 63.
[2] 'Récit des Événements arrivés au Temple,' by Mme. Royale, pp. 220,
221, from the *Journal de Cléry*.

borne a banner inscribed with the name and number of the section. Behind the twenty-fourth section will be carried a bundle of pikes, bound together with red, white, and blue bands, bearing the words "City of Paris," and from which there will depend forty-eight tricolour ribbons, each inscribed with the name of a section. The other twenty-four sections will then follow in the same order as the first. Next will come a group of women chosen from all the sections ; they will be clad in white, and wear tricolour sashes. This group will be preceded by a banner with the words, "Citoyennes, be fruitful, for the happiness of your children is assured." The Act of Constitution will be placed in the arms of a statue of Minerva, a symbol of all the virtues which have presided over its production and acceptance ; the statue will be draped with the national colours, and borne by men dressed in the latest national costume ; it will be followed by old men holding children by the hand.

'Among the latter will be Lazowski's daughter, the child of the Commune, and young Gilbert, the child of the Republic. Over these groups will float a banner with the inscription : "Happy children, enjoy the benefits of the Constitution ; we have long sighed for them."

'Bands of music ; a group of people showing their joy by dancing ; the Conseil-Général. In the midst of the members there will be borne aloft on a stand, draped with the national colours, the minutes of the forty-eight sections recording their votes concerning the Constitution ; the stand will be borne by citizens dressed in a costume proposed by David, and preceded by a banner suitably inscribed. The procession will be closed by a detachment of cavalry, and will proceed at nine in the morning to the Maison Commune ; at ten it will leave the Place des Grêves, and pass along the quays, and so through the Rues du Roule, Saint-Nicaise, and Saint-Honoré to the Place de la Fraternité.'[1]

Friday, July 5.—The march past the Convention of those sections of Paris which have accepted the Act of Constitution commenced on the 3rd. The section of Bondy headed the line ; then followed the Arsenal and Réunion sections, preceded by a corps of blind musicians playing the hymn of the Marseillais.[2]

These patriotic demonstrations continued on the 4th. On that day nineteen sections were admitted to the Legislative Chamber—the section of the Luxembourg, that of the Place

---

[1] *Chronique de Paris*, No. 187.   [2] *Moniteur*, July 5, 1793.

des Fédérés, which is authorized to change its name to that of
Indivisibility; those of Gravilliers, the Muséum, Fraternité,
Unité, Panthéon, République, Beaurepaire, L'Homme-Armé,
Faubourg Montmartre and Lombards; the three sections of the
Faubourg Saint-Antoine; those of the Observatoire, the Corn-
market, Arcis and Bonne-Nouvelle.

To-day all the remaining sections were admitted. I was present
in one of the galleries, and in spite of the dramatic character of
the scene, and the unworthiness of those who took part in it,
I cannot help admitting that it had a certain grandeur of
its own. The entry of each section was announced by a flourish
of trumpets. The spokesman of the deputation then read the
report of the meeting at which the Act of Constitution had been
accepted, and the citizens accompanying him swore to defend that
Act with their lives. Groups of maidens and children, laden
with baskets of roses, strewed the hall with the sweet-smelling
flowers. Others wearing the red cap presented the President of
the Convention—who on that day happened to be Thuriot—
with bouquets and crowns of oak-leaves, and adorned his desk
with flowers and tricolour ribbons; whilst others, again, made
him patriotic speeches. All these citoyennes received a paternal
kiss from the President. Groups of men bearing the Book of
the Law and the bust of Lepeletier took an oath to live free
or die. These patriotic scenes were accompanied by cries of
' *Vive la République! Vive la Constitution!* ' and terminated with
the *Ça ira* and the hymn of the Marseillais.

Three members of the section of '92 (formerly Filles Saint-
Thomas)—Citizens Chénard and Narbonne, of the Académie
Nationale de Musique, and Vallière, of the theatre in the Rue
Feydeau—sang several verses of the latter hymn. The brilliant
manner in which they acquitted themselves aroused indescribable
enthusiasm. At the line

'Amour sacré de la patrie,'

all the deputies rose from their seats and listened bare-headed
to the rest of the hymn, in which a verse had been interpolated in
honour of the Mountain.

Saturday, July 6.—According to a resolution passed by the
Committee of Public Safety on the 1st of this month, young

Capet is to be placed in the hands of a tutor to be chosen by the Conseil-Général de la Commune. The choice of the Conseil-Général has fallen upon Citizen Simon, and at to-day's sitting his emoluments were fixed at 500 francs per month. A payment of 3,000 francs per year is also allotted to Simon's wife.

Citizen Simon is a cobbler, living in the Rue des Cordeliers, a few yards from Marat's house; it is no doubt on the recommendation of the latter that he has been chosen to fill the post of tutor—that is to say, gaoler—to the son of Louis XVI.

Sunday, July 7.—A rumour has been circulated that Capet's son had been carried off from the Tower and borne in triumph to Saint-Cloud. The news caused great commotion, and the Committee of General Security sent four of its members—Chabot, Dumont, Maure and Drouet—to the Temple to assure themselves of the safety of the prisoners. The choice of Drouet, the man to whom the King's arrest at Varennes is due, was a particularly happy one; it was he who had the honour of reporting to the Convention the results of the mission. 'We proceeded to the Temple,' he said, 'and in the first room we found Capet quietly playing at draughts with his Mentor. We then went to the women's apartments, and found Marie Antoinette, as well as her daughter and her sister, enjoying perfect health.'[1]

Monday, July 8.—Barère proposes to turn the Palace of Versailles into a great public school. 'It will be a fine thing,' he says, 'to see citizens brought up in the hatred of tyranny in the palace of tyrants. We will teach drawing in the Salons de Lebrun, horsemanship in the Riding-School, and swimming in the ornamental waters; everything in this colossal pile can be put to educational uses. The Committee of Public Safety further suggests that all the furniture of the former royal palaces be sold.' The Convention thereupon passes resolutions in conformity with the recommendations of the Committee.[2]

At the same sitting Saint-Just reads the report of the Committee of Public Safety upon the thirty-two members placed under arrest by the decree of June 2. This report concludes with the following recommendations :

[1] *Moniteur,* July 9, 1793 ; sitting of July 7.   [2] *Ibid.,* July 10, 1793.

' That the National Convention declare Buzot, Barbaroux, Gorsas, Lanjuinais, Salle, Louvet, Bergoeing, Birotteau and Petion traitors to their country, in that they did flee before the resolution passed against them on June 2 last, and did place themselves in open rebellion in order to bring about the overthrow of the Republic, and the re-establishment of the Monarchy.

' That Gensonné, Guadet, Vergniaud, Mollevant and Gardien be declared guilty of the crime of aiding and abetting the rebels who have fled.

' That Bertrand, a member of the Commission of Twelve, but one who bravely opposed all its more violent measures, be re-instated in all the rights and privileges of a deputy, and that the National Convention extend the like clemency to all the other prisoners.'[1]

On Legendre's motion, the Convention orders the report and all the documents to be printed. On Fonfrède's proposal it is decided that the debate on the report shall be opened three days after the documents are placed in the members' hands.[2]

Chabot, in the name of the Committee of General Security, draws the attention of the Assembly to a pamphlet by Condorcet, entitled : ' To French Citizens, concerning the new Constitution.' Another member charges Devérité, deputy for the Somme, with having distributed this pamphlet in his constituency. The Convention thereupon decrees that warrants be issued for the arrest of Condorcet and Devérité.[3]

---

[1] Saint-Just's report is published *in extenso* in the *Moniteur* of July 18 and 19, 1793.

[2] *Moniteur*, July 10, 1793.

[3] *Ibid.* Devérité had not voted for the King's death. Impeached July 8, 1793, outlawed October 3, he succeeded in escaping from his persecutors. Under the Consulate he was appointed a Judge in the Civil Court of Abbeville. Condorcet, arrested at an inn at Clamart on March 27, 1794, and taken to the prison of Bourg-Égalité, was found dead the next morning, having committed suicide by taking some poison that he always carried with him, and which had been given him by his friend Cabanis (' Déclaration du Comité de Surveillance de la Commune de Clamart, 1794, 27 Mars ;' ' Procès-verbal de l'Arrestation de Condorcet ;' ' Musée des Archives Nationales,' No. 1,399). Concerning the Marquis de Condorcet, see Sainte-Beuve, ' Causeries du Lundi,' tome iii. ; Edmond Biré, ' La Légende des Girondins,' ch. ii. and vii. ; André Chénier, ' Œuvres en Prose,' pp. 308, 309, édition de L. Becq de Fouquières.

Tuesday, July 9.—Garat, Minister of the Interior, announces that the number of departments, districts, and municipalities that have received and accepted the Act of Constitution with transports of joy is already so great that its acceptance by a very large majority may be looked upon as certain. The enthusiasm is universal. ' At Lille,' he says, ' the Act of Constitution was received by the administrative officers as if it were not a mere draft, but an actual bond destined to bring about the happiness of the French nation ; they danced round the packet, and carried it with a flourish of trumpets to the place where the General Assemblies are held. The citizens crowded round the messenger who had brought it, and eagerly embraced both him and his horse.'[1]

In concluding his report, Garat suggested that the Assembly, taking into consideration the feelings so widely and spontaneously shown, should prolong the term of three days which has been accorded to all dissentient public functionaries for consideration. This appeal for further indulgence called forth the indignation of Robespierre, who rushed to the tribune and shouted :

' Away with such weakness at a moment when Liberty is triumphant, and the Republic feels its strength ! It is of little importance whether our officials, urged by public indignation, resume their duties now or at a later time, but it is of great importance that the majesty of the people be avenged ; we cannot uphold that majesty if we allow the greatest traitors to remain unpunished, and when we are betrayed by so many faithless public servants, we must ensure the tranquillity of the nation by making an example of a few villains.

' Far from sharing the sentiments of the Minister, I think that the sword of the law should fall on all the functionaries who have raised the standard of revolt, and I move that the suggestion of the Minister of the Interior be not adopted.'[2]

The Assembly agreed with Robespierre, and Garat's suggestion was negatived.

Wednesday, July 10.—The Convention decides that the Committee of Public Safety shall in future be composed of nine

[1] *Moniteur*, July 11, 1793.   [2] *Ibid.*

members only, instead of fourteen as at present. The following members were accordingly elected this evening : Jean-Bon Saint-André, Barère, Gasparin, Couthon, Saint-Just, Hérault-Séchelles, Robert Lindet, Thuriot and Prieur (of the Marne) ; the two last only are fresh members, the other seven being already on the committee. The seven members who were not re-elected are Danton, Berlier, Lacroix, Delmas, Guyton-Morveau, Cambon and Ramel.[1]

Thursday, July 11.—In the name of the former Committee of Public Safety, Cambon gives an account of its operations, and lays before the Convention the details of a conspiracy led by General Dillon for the re-establishment of the Monarchy. These are as follows :

' A few days ago the officials of one of the Parisian sections informed the Committee of Public Safety that a plot was in existence for carrying off the son of Capet on July 15 and proclaiming him King ; that, in order to make the affair a success, General Dillon, together with twelve other officers, was to command the army of conspirators ; that there were five ring-leaders of the plot, all of whom had conferred with Dillon ; that each of these five ringleaders had five subaltern conspirators attached to him ; that they had visited all the sections and talked the people over on the pretence of opposing the Anarchists and re-establishing order ; that they were already sure of sixty individuals in each section ; that the first proceeding of the conspirators would be to carry off the cannon from each guard-house ; that they would then assemble in the Place de la Révolution, pretending that they were recruits for the Vendée ; that there they would divide into two columns, one of which would march along the Boulevards and carry off young Capet, whilst the other would make its way into the Convention and oblige the members to proclaim him King ; that Marie Antoinette was to be proclaimed Regent during the boy's minority ; that those who had brought about this Revolution were to form her special guard'; that they would be given

---

[1] Register of the proceedings of the Committee of Public Safety (' Archives,' 434, AA. 71).

medals depending from ribbons of white moire, and bearing an eagle, with the words " *Down with Anarchy! Vive Louis XVII.!*"[1]

Cambon also announced that the Committee of Public Safety, having got wind of General Miranda's intention to proceed to Bordeaux, the cradle of another conspiracy, had requested the municipality of Paris to prevent the General's departure, and that the Mayor had thereupon had that officer placed under supervision.

The Convention ordered Cambon's report to be printed, and passed the following resolution :

'The National Convention, having heard the report of its Committee of Public Safety, approves of the measures taken by that Committee respecting the separation of young Capet from his mother, and the arrest of General Arthur Dillon, Esprit Boniface Castellane, Ernest Bucher, Edmé Rameau and Louis Levasseur, upon information received of a plot for the re-establishment of the Monarchy.

'It also approves of the measures taken with regard to General Miranda upon the receipt of information giving ground for suspicion.'[2]

Apartments are being prepared in the Luxembourg for the deputies arrested by virtue of the decree of June 2.   The windows of these apartments are being partly walled up, and all communication between one room and another is to be rendered impossible.[3]

Friday, July 12.—The trial of the citizens of Orleans, who

[1] *Moniteur,* July 13, 1793.

[2] *Moniteur,* July 13, 1793. Dillon, Bucher, and Rameau were guillotined April 13, 1794 (24th of Germinal, year II.), together with Chaumette, the Deputy Simond, the ex-Bishop Gobel, Grammont-Roselly, the actor, Adjutant-General of the Revolutionary Army, the widow of Camille Desmoulins, the widow of Hébert, and nine other victims. General Miranda, acquitted by the Revolutionary Tribunal May 16, 1793, again imprisoned and released in July, and finally condemned to exile at the end of 1795, escaped from the gendarmes who were taking him out of the country, and, coming back to Paris, was included in the order of banishment of the 18th of Fructidor (September 4, 1797). He then took refuge in England, but returned in 1803, to plot this time against Bonaparte, who had him arrested and banished a second time. In 1806 he proceeded to South America, where, in 1811, he led a successful rising against the authority of the King of Spain, and attempted to establish a Consular form of government in Caracas. He was taken prisoner and brought to Cadiz, where he died in 1816 ('Biographie Moderne,' 1816, tome ii.).

[3] *Mercure Français,* July 13, 1793.

were charged with committing an outrage upon the person of Leonard Bourdon, a representative of the people, concluded to-day. I have already shown how slight this pretended outrage really was. On March 16 last, Bourdon, after attending a patriotic dinner, had paraded the streets of Orleans at the head of a small band of roysterers. They insulted the sentinel on duty at the Hôtel de Ville, who called out the guard, and the latter treated the disturbers of the public peace rather roughly. In the affray Bourdon received two or three scratches.[1] Twenty-six persons were summoned before the Revolutionary Tribunal, and charged with having assassinated a representative of the people! Thirteen appeared in court; the others had fled. The trial commenced on June 28, and sentence was not pronounced until July 12. Nine of the accused were condemned to death: Benoît Louet, a money-changer; Buissot and Gellet-Duvivier, merchants; Jacquet and Poussot, men of independent means; Quesnel, a musician; Nonneville, Commandant de Bataillon in the National Guard; Tassin-Montcourt, a house-holder; and Broue de la Salle, also a Commandant in the National Guard.

When the verdict of the jury was announced, it created a tremendous sensation in court. Intense grief was manifested by the crowd, and the prisoners, falling on their knees, and lifting their hands to heaven, swore most solemnly that they did not know Leonard Bourdon, and that they had never seen him. When the Judges pronounced sentence of death, the whole of the audience burst into tears.[2]

Saturday, July 13.—As soon as the sitting of the Convention was opened, Jean-Bon Saint-André, who was in the presidential chair, informed his colleagues that ' the relatives of the nine citizens of Orleans condemned to death by the Revolutionary Tribunal, as the perpetrators and instigators of the outrage on Leonard Bourdon, wished to present a petition.'

---

[1] In his letter to the Convention, dated March 16, Bourdon himself says : ' My wounds are not dangerous ;' an overcoat that I was wearing deadened the blows.'

[2] 'Procès de Fouquier-Tinville,' No. 21, p. 4. Evidence of Montané, who presided over the Revolutionary Tribunal during the trial of the twenty-six citizens of Orleans. See Henri Wallon, 'Le Tribunal Révolutionnaire de Paris,' tome i., p. 184.

A small band of weeping women were accordingly admitted; they were accompanied by one man only, and their petition ran as follows:

'Citizens,—We have come to appeal in the name of humanity and justice. Our fathers, our brothers, and our children, are being dragged to the scaffold. One of the condemned is the father of nineteen children, four of whom are in the army fighting for their country.[1] Leonard Bourdon himself will not oppose our prayers; we believe that he is generous enough to help us to obtain a respite which will afford our unhappy relatives the means of proving their innocence.'

Leonard Bourdon remained silent, and several deputies demanded that the Assembly should proceed to business.

Sobs and lamentations broke from the petitioners, many of whom were on their knees before the Assembly. The shrieks of two women in particular were most heartrending.[2] Leonard Bourdon remained impassive,[3] but one member rose and said: 'Although our hearts may be torn with pity, we must nevertheless do our duty. As men we weep, but as legislators our compassion must spread itself over the whole nation, incessantly exposed as it is to the danger of these internal plots. We must not forget what we owe to justice and to national honour, outraged in the person of one of your colleagues discharging important functions in the people's name. I move that we proceed to business.'

The President thereupon ordered the petitioners to be removed, and the Convention proceeded with the business of the nation.[4] The same afternoon the nine condemned men, all wearing the red shirts of assassins, were executed in the Place de la Révolution.

---

[1] Another was a widower and the father of five young children (Émile Campardon, 'Le Tribunal Révolutionnaire de Paris,' tome i., p. 55).

[2] Harmand, deputy for the Meuse in the National Convention, relates the following in his 'Anecdotes Relatives . . . à la Révolution.' 'Saint-Just,' he says, 'turns to me, and, looking in my face, says: "Do you weep, coward?" "Well," I reply, "it is impossible to witness such grief without sharing it; I cannot help it." "I am happy to say," remarks Saint-Just, "that I do not think I have ever shed tears in my life."'

[3] Roussel, 'Histoire Secrète du Tribunal Révolutionnaire,' ch. v., p. 151.

[4] *Moniteur*, July 15, 1793.

CHAPTER LXXXIV.

THE DEATH OF MARAT.

Sunday, July 14, 1793.

YESTERDAY nine innocent men were murdered in the Place de la Révolution. Though their wives and children had begged the Convention to grant them a respite, the deputies had mercilessly put the petitioners aside and gone on with their business, not a single one having been brave enough to raise his voice in their behalf. To strike a member of the Convention, even unwittingly, is a crime punishable with death. The person of a deputy is sacred !

The reply was not long in coming. At eight o'clock yesterday evening—whilst the blood of the citizens of Orleans was still running through the gutters of the square—a member of the Convention was struck down by what was this time a death-blow. Marat was killed, not like Lepeletier, by one of the King's body-guard, but by a girl !

It may well be imagined that since the perpetration of the deed the talk has been of nothing else, and people are now in full possession of all the details of this tragic event, which took place at No. 30 in the Rue des Cordeliers.[1]

At mid-day on Thursday the Normandy coach set down in the Rue Notre-Dame-des-Victoires Nationales one Citoyenne Marie Charlotte Corday, coming from Caen. She hired a commissionaire to take her to a hotel, the address of which she held in her hand—the Hôtel de la Providence, Rue des Vieux

---

[1] The Rue des Cordeliers was afterwards called the Rue de l'École de Médecine, and Marat's house became No. 18. Like the hotel at which Charlotte Corday put up, it has now disappeared.

Augustins. Whilst a waiter was putting her room in order, she entered into conversation with him, and spoke of the rising in Calvados, mentioning at the same time that 60,000 men were marching on the capital. Shortly afterwards she inquired what the Parisians thought of little Marat. 'The Patriots think very highly of him,' replied the man, ' but the aristocrats do not like him ; he has been ill for some time now, and seldom appears in the Convention.'[1]

The traveller then asked her way to the Palais de l'Égalité and the Rue Saint-Thomas du Louvre, the abode of the deputy Lauze Duperret, for whom she had a parcel of books and a letter. Not having found him in, she went back in the evening and asked him to accompany her on the morrow to the Minister of the Interior, in order to obtain certain documents belonging to one of her friends.

At ten o'clock on Friday morning Duperret called upon her at the Hôtel de la Providence, and escorted her to the offices of the Minister. They were not admitted, but told to return in the evening between eight and ten. Meanwhile seals had been placed upon Duperret's papers, he having been denounced by Chabot as one of Dillon's accomplices ; he immediately came and informed Mlle. Corday of this, and pointed out that his influence would now be rather detrimental than otherwise. Left alone, the traveller wrote *An Address to the French*, in which she explained the motives that led her to commit the act she was contemplating.

She went out early yesterday morning and proceeded to the Palais de l'Égalité, where she read the sentence passed upon the nine citizens of Orleans, and where for forty sous she bought a sharp knife with an ebony handle, like those used for carving. At half-past eleven the cab which she had engaged in the Place des Victoires put her down in the Rue des Cordeliers at the door of the People's Friend. She was dressed in brown, and wore a high-crowned hat with a black cockade and a triple black cord. On reaching the first-floor she asked to see Citizen Marat. Simonne Evrard — the woman who is now called

[1] Evidence given by Pierre François Feuillard, a waiter in the Hôtel de la Providence.

Marat's widow—replied that the Friend of the People was ill, and could see no one. Hereupon Mlle. Corday said that she had something of the greatest importance to tell him. But Simonne was immovable. 'When must I come back, then?' asked Charlotte. 'I can give you no definite reply,' said the other; 'how can I tell when Marat will be better?'

Mlle. Corday at length decided to return to her hotel, which she reached about mid-day, and whence she wrote to Marat as follows :

'CITIZEN,

'I have just come from Caen; your love for the Republic causes me to believe that it will give you pleasure to hear what is taking place in that part of the country. I shall call upon you at about one o'clock; be good enough to receive me, and to grant me a moment's interview; I can give you an opportunity of rendering a great service to France.'[1]

She also wrote another note which she intended to send to Marat in case she was again refused admittance. Expecting that before nightfall she would either be killed or imprisoned, she pinned her *Address to the French* inside the long white gown which she was then wearing. At half-past seven she again took a cab, and once more drove to Marat's house. This time she was stopped by Citoyenne Aubin, the concierge of the house, and one of the folders of *L'Ami du Peuple*; this person summoned Simonne Evrard, who persisted in her refusal of the morning. An altercation ensued, and Marat, hearing the noise, thought it must have something to do with the letter he had just received, and accordingly ordered the visitor to be admitted.

Marat was in his bath, over which a sheet had been thrown, leaving his arms and shoulders exposed to view. A plank placed across the bath itself served as a writing-desk. Simonne Evrard having left the room, he remained alone with his visitor. 'How do matters stand in Caen?' he asked. 'Eighteen deputies, acting in accord with the departmental authorities, are

---

[1] Letter produced at the trial.

organizing a rising. Everyone is enlisting in the cause ; four
members of the department are marching with a party of
volunteers upon Evreux.' 'What are their names?' As Mlle.
Corday enumerated them, Marat wrote them down. 'I shall
have them all guillotined in Paris.' The words have scarcely
escaped him, when his visitor plunges her knife into his side.
' Help, love—help!' he cries. At these words Simonne Evrard
rushes into the room, and, hastening towards the bath, shrieks :
' Oh, my God ! he is murdered !' She then turns to Mlle.
Corday, who is standing against one of the curtains, and, seizing
the girl by the head, she calls for aid.[1] Her sister Catherine,
Citoyenne Aubin, the concierge, Jeannette Maréchal, the cook,
and a man named Laurent Bas, another folder of the newspaper,
come hurrying up in response to her cries. Laurent Bas seizes
a chair, and, hurling it at the head of Mlle. Corday, brings her
to the ground. Meanwhile Simonne Evrard returns to Marat,
and attempts to stanch the blood that streams from the wound.
Citizen Antoine de Lafondée, a surgeon who lives in the house,
is immediately summoned ; he makes a compress to stop the
blood, and at the same time sends for further help to the
Surgical Schools. The pulse of the wounded man is now
becoming almost imperceptible ; he is taken from his bath and
carried to his bed in the room looking out upon the Rue des
Cordeliers. On the arrival of Citizen Pelletan, consulting
surgeon to the armies of the Republic, and a member of the
Committee of Health, Marat was already lifeless.

In an instant an immense crowd had gathered in the street ;
the mob struggled to get up the staircase, and a few people had
already made their way into the bathroom itself, when Guellard,
the Commissary of Police of the section, appeared on the scene
with Marino and Louvet, two police officers attached to the
municipality, and the men on duty at the Théâtre Français.
It was then a quarter to eight, and there was still daylight
outside, but in the ante-room and the bathroom it was almost
dark, and candles had to be lit. The scene was a terrible one.
Blood everywhere. It had spurted all over the floor, where it
lay in a thick pool, and the bath itself looked like one immense

---

[1] Evidence of Citoyenne Evrard before the Revolutionary Tribunal.

red stain in the deepening twilight. The ante-room was filled with a compact mass of humanity—neighbours, employés of the paper, printers, folders, and all sorts of people—shouting and yelling in impotent rage. In the midst of these men with their convulsed features, of these women mad with fury and hideous in their grimy, unkempt state, a young and beautiful girl, with a sweet, resigned expression upon her pale and noble face, was tranquilly seated on a chair, and looking, with her long hair falling down upon her shoulders and upon her elegant white robe, like a fairy fallen into a witches' lair, like an angel surrounded by demons. It was the assassin.

After having received the report of the Surgeon Pelletan and examined the body, the police authorities took their prisoner into the parlour, which looks out upon the Rue des Cordeliers, and there subjected her to a long interrogatory.

She described herself as Marie Anne Charlotte Corday d'Armont, a native of the parish of Saint-Saturnin-des-Ligneries, aged twenty-five years, and living at Caen.[1] She admitted that her act was a premeditated one, and that she had come from Caen for the express purpose of committing it. Her courage and presence of mind did not leave her for a single moment ; a quiet sarcasm could even be detected occasionally in her replies. Maure, Legendre, Chabot and Drouet, sent by the Committee of General Security, arrived towards the end of her examination, and when Legendre tried to make out that she had come to his office in the morning, no doubt with the intention of murdering him, she replied : ' I do not think you have sufficient talent to be the tyrant of your country ; besides, sir, I did not wish to punish everyone.'[2] To Chabot, who held out his hand for the gold watch found upon her, she said : ' Don't you know that the Capucines take an oath of poverty ?'[3]

It was past midnight when she was placed in a coach and taken to the prison of the Abbaye. She was accompanied by Drouet and the two police officers, Louvet and Marino. The

---

[1] ' Procès-verbal,' drawn up by Jacques Fillibert Guellard.

[2] Letter from Charlotte Corday to Barbaroux, commenced in the Abbaye and finished in the Conciergerie. It is exhibited in the Musée des Archives, case 213, Nos. 1,367 and 1,368.

[3] ' Charlotte Corday,' by Couet-Gironville.

streets were filled with an enormous crowd, and the public
agitation was so great, the threats of death so constant and
violent, that for a moment Mlle. Corday almost fainted away.[1]
On recovering, she seemed surprised to find herself still alive.
Her astonishing coolness soon returned to her, and she repeated
again and again : ‘I have fulfilled my task ; others will do the
rest.’[2]   She was imprisoned in the Abbaye, in the cell formerly
occupied by Brissot.[3]

[1] Drouet's report to the National Convention, July 14, 1793.
[2] *Moniteur*, July 17, 1793 ; *Républicain Français*, July 16.
[3] Her letter written in the Abbaye is thus headed : ‘At the Abbaye
Prison, in the cell ouce occupied by Brissot, on the second day of my
preparations for peace.’

CHAPTER LXXXV.

MARAT'S FUNERAL.

Friday, July 19, 1793.

On the afternoon of July 14, Citizen Deschamps, head-surgeon of the Hôpital de la Charité, made a post-mortem examination of Marat's body. 'It appears,' he says in his report of this operation, 'that the instrument with which the deed was done entered the breast between the first and second rib, and then, passing through the upper portion of the right lung, made its way into the heart itself.'[1] The body of the People's Friend was immediately embalmed, all except the face and the breast, 'which,' said Deschamps, 'must be exposed to the gaze of his fellow-citizens.'[2] This process was attended with great difficulty, the decomposition of the body being so rapid that it would scarcely bear handling, and the funeral had in consequence to take place a day earlier than was originally intended.[3]

The honour of organizing the obsequies naturally fell to David, the most eminent member of the Mountain. At Monday's sitting of the Convention the painter spoke as follows :

'On the day before Marat's death the Jacobin Club deputed Maure and myself to go and see him. We found him in an attitude that impressed me deeply. Before him lay a wooden

---

[1] Reports of the examination and embalming of Marat's body, signed by Deschamps, Head Surgeon of the Hôpital de la Charité ; Bernard, vice-President of the Conseil de la Commune ; and Dorat-Cubières, Secretary of the same, July 14 and 17, 1793 ('Inventaire des Autographes et Documents Historiques,' forming the collection of Benjamin Fillon, 1877.

[2] The process of embalming was completed on July 16 in the garden of the Grey Friars Club.

[3] 'Marat, l'Ami du Peuple,' by Alfred Bougeart, tome ii., p. 280.

plank, on which was placed the paper destined to receive his last thoughts for the safety of the people. The surgeon who embalmed his body has sent to inquire in what position we would like to exhibit him to the gaze of the people in the church of the Grey Friars.

'There are certain parts of his body which cannot be uncovered, for, as you know, he was afflicted with leprosy; I therefore think it will be most interesting to place him in the attitude in which I found him—writing for the happiness of the people.'

Having been appointed a Commissioner to assist in the exhibition of Marat's body, David presented a report on the matter at the sitting of the 16th.

'In conformity with the decree passed yesterday, I proceeded with my colleagues, Maure and Bentabole, to the Section of the Théâtre Français. After having imparted to this section my ideas concerning Marat's funeral, I was forced to admit that they were impracticable. It was then decided that his body should be exhibited covered with a wet cloth, representing his bath, and which, if moistened from time to time, would stop the course of putrefaction. He will be interred at five o'clock to-day under the trees where it was his wont to sit and talk with his fellow-citizens. His sepulture will be conducted with the simplicity befitting an incorruptible Republican who died in honourable poverty. I have not lived with Cato, Aristides, Socrates, Timoleon, Fabricius or Phocion, whose glorious lives we all admire; but I have known and admired Marat—posterity will do him justice.'[1]

Whilst David was uttering these fine phrases, Marat's body was lying in the Church of the Grey Friars under a canopy forty feet high, adorned with tricolour hangings. On the right was the bath in which he received the fatal blow, on the left his shirt all stained with blood. The body, lying on a bed of state—the same which had done duty at Lazowski's funeral[2]— was uncovered as far as the waist, in order that the wound might be fully exposed; it had a greenish hue, like the corpse of a drowned man.[3]

---

[1] *Moniteur*, July 18, 1793.   [2] *Mercure Français*, July 20, 1793.
[3] 'Souvenirs de la Terreur,' by G. Duval, tome iii., p. 361.

The head was crowned with a laurel wreath. By the side of the bed stood two men constantly besprinkling the body, and the sheet which partly covered it, with aromatic vinegar, whilst throughout the church perfumes were continually kept burning. In spite of these precautions, the odour was insupportable, and Marat's devotees themselves were obliged to make their visits as short as possible.

The body was to be interred in the garden of the Grey Friars Club, a few yards only from the church ; it had been decided that the procession should make a long circuit, for it was intended to give the people a second edition of the funeral of Michel Lepeletier.

On Chabot's proposal,[1] the Convention had determined to attend Marat's funeral in a body, and here I must not forget to note a circumstance which has the double advantage of graphically describing Robespierre's real character, and of relieving somewhat the lugubrious scenes now before us. Poor Robespierre is as jealous of Marat assassinated as he was of Marat alive. He feels hurt by the honours which are being paid to the dead hero, and he would rather have seen him buried without pomp or ceremony. When Bentabole brought forward a motion at the Jacobin Club on Sunday, that the honours of the Pantheon should be accorded to the Friend of the People, it was most enthusiastically agreed to. Robespierre thereupon ascended the tribune. ' I would not have taken upon myself to speak at this moment,' he said, ' if I did not foresee that I too shall be honoured with a dagger-thrust, that priority has only been a matter of chance, and that my fall is rapidly nearing.'

What Robespierre meant to say was, that, though it was Marat that had been killed, it might just as well have been the speaker himself, who therefore claimed the honour and advantage of a blow which he had not received. ' You ask,' he continued, ' that Marat shall be admitted to the honours of the Pantheon ! What are those honours? Who are they that lie buried there ? With the exception of Lepeletier, I do not see

---

[1] And not on David's, as Louis Blanc says, following on Buchez and Roux ; ' Histoire de la Révolution,' tome ix., p. 93 ; ' Histoire Parlementaire,' tome xxviii., p. 343. See the *Moniteur*, July 17, 1793.

a virtuous man there. Is it by the side of Mirabeau that you would place him, by the side of a man who is notorious for his villainy only? Are these the honours that you solicit for the People's Friend?' 'Yes,' cried Bentabole, 'and which he will obtain, in spite of those who are jealous of him!' Robespierre continued as follows: 'It is not at such a time as this that we should dazzle the people with a great display, but when the Republic is once firmly established, and we are at liberty to honour its defenders, the whole of France will demand, and you will ungrudgingly grant, the honours which Marat's virtue deserves. Are you not aware what impression the sight of great funeral ceremonies creates upon the human heart? It makes the people believe that the friends of Liberty are thus rewarded for all that they have done, and that there is no longer any need to avenge them; satisfied with having honoured a virtuous man, the nation's desire for vengeance is appeased, indifference succeeds enthusiasm, and the dead hero runs the risk of being forgotten. The municipality must therefore post-pone for a time the sad rites which we may desire to see per-formed with all our heart, but the effects of which, as I have proved, may be quite contrary to what we intend.'[1]

Robespierre is certainly an excellent man and a valuable friend! He is so afraid that Marat may be too quickly for-gotten, that he thinks it best for him to be forgotten at once. In order that he may be honoured later, he desires that no honour at all may be paid him now.

But all Robespierre's eloquent efforts, born of his jealousy, were in vain, and on Tuesday evening he was compelled to join his colleagues in the Convention. It was a great gathering that met in the Church of the Grey Friars a little before six o'clock. The Girondists—that is to say, those who are not yet in prison—vied with the Montagnards in showing honour to the dead.[2]

---

[1] *Journal des Débats et de la Correspondance de la Société des Jacobins,* No. 449; *Le Républicain Français,* No. 245.

[2] Champagneux, the friend of Mme. Roland, and the editor of her 'Mémoires,' went to see her in prison on the day of Marat's funeral. 'I set out on foot,' he says, 'to visit Citoyenne Roland at Sainte-Pélagie. I met the procession on the way, and I noticed that very few members

It was about seven o'clock when the convoy left the church.[1]

The bier was borne by twelve men, some of whom had, perhaps, carried the triumphant hero on their shoulders on April 24. It was escorted by girls dressed in white, and by a group of lads carrying cypress branches and swinging burning censers. Next came the bath and the plank spoken of by David.

Behind these objects marched the members of the Convention, headed by their President, Jean-Bon Saint-André;[2] then the Corporation and the Conseil-Général of Paris, the Judges and other public officials, the jurymen of the Revolutionary Tribunal, the Grey Friars Club in a body, a numerous deputation from the Jacobin Club, the Revolutionary Committees, and finally the people under the different sectional banners.

The procession first passed through the Rue des Cordeliers, Marat's house, situated in that street, being covered with inscriptions both in prose and verse.

On leaving the Rue des Cordeliers, the convoy proceeded along the Rue des Fossés-Saint-Germain, the Rue de Thionville, the Pont-Neuf, the Quai de la Mégisserie, the Pont au Change, the Pont Saint-Michel, the Place Saint-Michel, and that of the Théâtre Français.[3] The women, who seemed to be in a majority on that day,[4] as they had been on April 24, uttered perfect yells of grief, mingled with cries of revenge, which must have rejoiced the shade of the People's Friend.

Night had fallen ere the procession had completed half its course, and the few torches that were carried here and there only served to make the darkness more visible. The fantastic

were missing. Some, it is true, seemed ashamed of being present at the funeral of a man who had instigated so much crime, but their presence, nevertheless, made a great impression upon the people.   . It would be difficult to describe Mme. Roland's fury when I told her what honour was being paid to Marat, and spoke of the cowardice of those representatives whose honesty had until then inspired her with some hope. Her anger soon gave way to intense despair. "I shall only leave here," she said, " to go to the scaffold."[1]

[1] *Mercure Français*, July 20.

[2] And not Thuriot, as erroneously stated by Louis Blanc, who, in this, continues to copy Buchez and Roux.

[3] Now Place de la Réunion.

[4] *Révolutions de Paris*, tome xvi., p. 683.

shadows thrown upon the tall dark houses, the disorderly crowd rushing through the narrow tortuous streets, the sudden silence that frequently succeeded the shouts and the singing, and the thunder rumbling in the distance, all helped to make up a lugubrious and terrible whole.

The hour of midnight was striking when the head of the procession reached the garden of the Grey Friars Club,[1] the gate of which was draped with the national colours, and illuminated with the following words in letters of fire : ' *Temple of Liberty*.'[2] Under the trees in the garden a mound had been prepared which was to serve as a tomb for the People's Friend. This mound was composed of great blocks of stone, and in the centre a space had been left which formed a kind of cave closed by an iron gate. Over the entry stood a funeral urn containing Marat's heart, and the summit of the tomb was adorned by a triangular pyramid bearing this epitaph : ' *Here lies Marat, the People's Friend, assassinated by the People's enemies, July* 13, 1793.'

The crowd stood in silence round the tomb, and the President of the Convention was the first to speak. He declared that the time would soon come when Marat's death would be avenged. After his speech, and those of the principal authorities, the march past commenced. As each section, headed by its banner, stopped for a few moments before the tomb, its president delivered a short speech, and the procession then went on its way. 'Oh, Marat !' cried Citizen Léchard, 'illustrious and cherished shade ! Your deeds will always live in our memory ! Can it be that Marat has gone for ever into the realms of death ? No, such a man must be immortal ; his memory must adorn posterity, and be a standing glory to his country. If he is not in the Pantheon, it is because he has a place in the heart of every Frenchman.' 'May the blood of Marat,' said the spokesman of the République section—' may the blood of Marat be the seed of fearless Republicans ! We will imitate his manly courage, we will strike down traitors with the blade of the law, we will avenge his death in hating our country's enemies and in cultivating Republican virtues. We swear it on his blood-

[1] *Journal de la Montagne*, No. 48.   [2] *Mercure Français*, July 20, 1793.

stained body, on the knife that pierced his heart!"[1]   And the
march past continued.

During the whole of the night men armed with pikes, and
women holding their children by the hand, crowded round the
tomb and its ugly contents—the bath, the plank, and the
blood-stained shirt.   Many of them took an oath before the
body to avenge their Friend.   On that stormy night, amidst
the thunder and lightning that burst from the heavens, and the
shouts and imprecations of a maddened mob, the soul of Marat
passed into the soul of the people.   The Terror may come ; its
men are ready.

[1] 'Marat, l'Ami du Peuple,' by Alfred Bougeart, tome ii., p. 284.

CHAPTER LXXXVI.

THE DEATH OF CHARLOTTE CORDAY.

Saturday, July 20, 1793.

Marat's funeral took place on Tuesday night, and at eight o'clock on Wednesday morning Charlotte Corday appeared before the Revolutionary Tribunal.

She was wearing a white gown spotted with black, and a broad-brimmed hat, from under which her long chestnut hair hung loosely down upon her shoulders.[1] Her youth, her beauty, and her tranquil manner, produced such an impression upon the public that the Maratists, who were in the majority in the

---

[1] In the 'Note on the Trial and Sentence of Charlotte Corday,' written by Chauveau-Lagarde, and published in tome iii. of the Vicomte de Ségur's work entitled 'Les Femmes, leur Condition et leur Influence dans l'Ordre Sociale,' we read 'No painter, to my knowledge, has given us a faithful portrait of this extraordinary woman. It may have been possible to give some idea of her strongly-built though graceful figure, of her long hair hanging loosely down upon her shoulders, of her eyes shaded by their long lashes, and of the oval shape of her face ; but it would have been impossible for any artist to paint the great soul which shone forth from every feature.' Harmand, a member of the Convention, has drawn the following portrait of Charlotte Corday in his 'Anecdotes Relatives à la Révolution' : 'Mdlle. Corday was of middle height, of rather strong build, with an oval face, large and pronounced but beautiful features, and blue, piercing eyes somewhat severe in their expression ; she had a well-shaped nose and mouth, chestnut hair, and hands and arms fit to serve as a model ; her manners and deportment were full of grace.' Next to this portrait let us place that which the editors of the 'Répertoire du Tribunal Révolutionnaire' have left us : 'This woman, who is made out to have been very handsome, was not even good-looking ; she was a robust virago, graceless and awkward, as nearly all strong-minded and philosophical females are. Her face was harsh, insolent, and full-blooded. She was twenty-five years of age, and her masculine bearing made her look much older. She had no idea of shame or modesty.' Charlotte Corday was evidently made out to be either beautiful or ugly, according as the writer was for or against Marat.

court, dared scarcely interrupt her as she quietly replied to
every question; only a few hags occasionally attempted to drown
with shouts the sweet, childlike voice, which in that place had a
strange, tragic sound.

Charlotte Corday denied nothing—neither the deed itself nor
any of the circumstances that accompanied it. She admitted
having premeditated the act for some time, but sought in no
way to justify it. The trial might therefore have been got over
in a few minutes, had it not been for the tactics of Montané, the
presiding Judge, and Fouquier-Tinville, the Public Prosecutor.
In lengthening the proceedings by the examination of a large
number of witnesses, they doubtlessly hoped to drag from the
accused some word or sentence which would have enabled them
to trace the event of July 13 to a vast conspiracy, and so prove
that it was the Girondist deputies now under lock and key who
had not only inspired and prepared the crime, but placed the
knife in the hand that struck the People's Friend.

They were disappointed in their expectations. Charlotte
Corday did not utter a single word which could be used against
her friends.

'What induced you to commit this murder?' 'Marat's
crimes.'

'How can you expect us to believe that you were not advised
to do this, when you tell us that you looked upon one who has
never ceased to unmask traitors and plotters as the cause of all
the ills now devastating France?' 'It is only in Paris that
Marat fascinates the mob; in other departments he is looked
upon as a monster.'[1]

But Montané would not consider himself beaten, and returned
to the charge.

'Who incited you to commit this crime?' 'No one; it was
I alone who conceived the idea.'

For the fourth time Montané put his question.

'This act must have been suggested to you?' 'It is difficult
to carry out the suggestions of others.'[2]

The President then attempted to get from the accused some

---

[1] *Bulletin du Tribunal Révolutionnaire.*
[2] 'Note' by Chauveau-Lagarde, *op. cit.*

information concerning the doings and designs of the members who had fled to Caen.

'What are the runaway deputies doing?'   'They take no part in anything, and are waiting until the reign of Anarchy is over, to resume their posts.'

'How do they occupy their time?'   'By writing songs and proclamations to bring the nation back to unity.'

'Have you not been present at any of the meetings of the runaway deputies?'   'No.'

A letter written by Mlle. Corday to her father a few hours before she appeared in court was then read.   It ran as follows :

'Good-bye, my dear father.   I beg you to forget me, or, rather, to rejoice at my fate ; I shall die a glorious death.   Embrace my dear sister for me, as well as all my relatives.   Do not forget this line from Corneille :

'"'Tis crime that shames, and not the scaffold."'[1]

I am told that Mlle. Corday is the great-grand-daughter of the poet.[2]   Her ancestor would not have disowned some of her replies.

'Who inspired you with so much hatred?'   'I had no need of the hatred of others ; I had enough of my own.'

'What did you hope to gain by killing Marat?'   'I hoped to restore peace to my country.'

'Do you think you have killed all the Marats?'   'This one being dead, the others may perhaps be afraid.'[3]

When some evidence inculpating her was read over, the President asked :

[1] *Bulletin du Tribunal Révolutionnaire.*   The line is from Corneille's 'Comte d'Essex,' Act IV.

[2] According to Louis Blanc (ix. 74) and Michelet (v. 243), Charlotte Corday was only the great-grand-*niece* of Pierre Corneille, but she was in reality the great-grand-*daughter* of the author of 'Cinna' (Lepan edition of the 'Œuvres de P. Corneille,' 1817 ; Prudhomme, 'Femmes Célèbres,' 1826 ; Taschereau, 'Vie de Corneille' ; Ballain, 'Maison et Généalogie de Corneille,' 1833 ; Ch. Vatel, 'Charlotte de Corday et les Girondins,' 1872.

[3] Note' by Chauveau-Lagarde.

'What have you to answer to this?' 'Nothing, except that I have succeeded.'

In addition to these noble, clear replies, there came others betraying compassion and deep feeling.

Simonne Evrard burst into tears whilst giving her evidence, and Charlotte Corday, in order to put an end to this painful scene, hastened to say, 'Yes—yes; it was I who killed him!'

When an usher handed her the knife with which she had killed Marat, she turned from it with a shudder, and said in a broken voice : 'Yes, I recognise it.'

The President pointed out that she had plunged the knife into Marat's breast perpendicularly in order to be quite sure of succeeding, for had she struck her victim horizontally the blow would not have been fatal. Fouquier-Tinville dilated upon this point, and added : 'You must be well acquainted with this kind of work.' 'Oh, the monster!' she cried ; 'he takes me for an assassin !'[1]

With the exception of these two or three expressions of feeling, Mlle. Corday preserved the same serenity of temper and outward appearance throughout the trial. Perceiving that a painter in the body of the court was attempting to delineate her features, she turned her face towards him so that he could better execute his work. In her letter to her father she wrote : 'I have engaged Gustave Doulcet to defend me, but such a crime permits of no defence ; it is only a matter of form.' In Doulcet's absence,[2] it was Chauveau-Lagarde who, at the instance of the President, appeared for her. He did not attempt an impossible and useless defence, and one of which the accused would no doubt have disapproved, but limited himself to a few brief remarks.

---

[1] 'Note' by Chaveau-Lagarde. The *Bulletin du Tribunal Révolutionnaire* only made Charlotte Corday reply, 'Certainly not.'

[2] Doulcet de Ponté-Coulant, a member for Calvados in the Convention, was born at Caen in 1764 ; he was, therefore, only four years older than Charlotte Corday. He was unaware that she had chosen him to undertake her defence. In a letter to the President of the Revolutionary Tribunal dated July 20, he stated that he had only received Charlotte Corday's letter that morning—open. He was a senator under the Empire, and a peer of France under the Restoration and the July Monarchy, and has left some 'Souvenirs Historiques,' published in 1862.

'The accused admits having committed the horrible crime with which she stands charged; she admits that it was long premeditated; she admits all the awful details; in a word, she admits everything, and, glorying in her deed, seeks to justify nothing. And that, in my mind, is her justification. This imperturbability in a young woman of her age, and this sublime self-abnegation in the face of death, are unnatural, and inspired by that political fanaticism which guided her hand. It is your duty, fellow-citizens, to weigh this consideration in the scales of justice.'[1]

A look of satisfaction stole over the face of Charlotte Corday as she listened to her counsel's words. Chauveau-Lagarde had defended her in a manner entirely in accord with her wishes.

The jury were unanimous in their verdict.[2] Neither that verdict nor the sentence of death pronounced by the President seemed to trouble the prisoner. She only asked to be taken by the gendarmes to her counsel, and said to him, with much sweetness and grace: 'Sir, I thank you for having had the courage to defend me in a manner worthy of yourself and of me. These gentlemen,' she said, turning to the Judges, 'confiscate all I have, but I will give you a great proof of my gratitude. I beg that you will pay for me what I owe the prison, and I rely on your generosity.'[3]

The execution took place in the evening. An immense crowd filled the streets, and rent the air with their cries when the condemned woman, clad in the red shirt worn by murderers, mounted the tumbrel at the gate of the Conciergerie. A thunderstorm burst forth just as the procession started on its way. The yells of the crowd were accompanied and often drowned by peal upon peal of thunder, and the flashes of lightning lit up the features

---

[1] 'Note' by Chauveau-Lagarde, *loc. cit.*

[2] The twelve jurymen were Jourdeuil, Fallot, Ganney, Leroy, Brochet, Chrétien, Godin, Thoumin, Brichet, Sion, Duplain and Fualdès. 'Leroy,' says Dix-Août, 'was guillotined with Fouquier-Tinville on the 18th of Floréal, year III.' (May 7, 1795). Fualdès was assassinated at Rodez on March 19, 1817, under conditions which made him nearly as celebrated as Charlotte Corday. See in the *Revue des Questions Historiques* for January, 1867, an excellent article by Léon de la Sicotière on 'Charlotte Corday et Fualdès.'

[3] 'Note' by Chauveau-Lagarde: 'Her debts amounted to only thirty-six francs, which I paid on the morrow to the concierge of the Abbaye.'

of the victim, their pallor enhanced by the red shirt that had
been thrown over her fair shoulders. There she sat upon the
horrible car, answering the insults of the hideous wretches
around her with a calm, contemptuous look—a woman who was
about to die, and in whose face there was no sign of fear ; a
woman who had stained her hands with blood, and whom even
honest folk could not help admiring in spite of her crime. It
was a sublime and terrible scene, which will never be forgotten
by those who beheld it.

So dense was the crowd that it took two hours for the
tumbrel to reach the Place de la Révolution.[1] It has been said
that on reaching the foot of the scaffold Mlle. Corday started
at sight of the instrument of death. It is, however, certain
that when she reached the top of the ladder her face had
resumed its wonted serenity and firmness.[2] When the executioner's assistant bared her shoulders, a blush overspread her
features,[3] and to put an end to the scene she herself placed her
head under the knife, as peacefully as a child lays its head upon
the pillow.[4]

The blade fell amidst cries of ' *Vive la Nation! Vive la
République!*' Some wretch, who is said to have been a
Maratist carpenter, seized the head to show it to the people,
and struck it two or three times.[5]

The crowd slowly dispersed. The storm had long spent itself.

---

[1] ' For two hours from the moment of her departure until she reached
the scaffold she maintained the same calm attitude, the same inexpressible
air of sweetness.'—ADAM LUX, quoted by Chéron de Villiers, in his book
on ' Marie Anne Charlotte de Corday d'Armont,' p. 416. Adam Lux was
guillotined November 4, 1793. This enthusiast of Charlotte Corday ' met
his death with really incredible coolness ; he spoke and smiled, and
seemed to look upon his end quite fearlessly. On reaching the scaffold,
he embraced his executioners before laying himself upon the plank ' (' Le
Glaive Vengeur,' by Du Lac, p. 127).

[2] Cabanis, according to the testimony of a friend of his who was an
eye-witness (' Magazin Encyclopédique,' by Millin, tome v., p. 155).

[3] Beaulieu, ' Biographie Universelle.'

[4] *Chronique de Paris,* July 19, 1793.

[5] *Révolutions de Paris,* tome xvi., p. 684 ; *La Chronique de Paris,*
July 19, 1793. The perpetrator of this infamous deed was ' Citizen
Legros, one of the executioner's assistants ' (letter from Roussillon to
La Chronique de Paris). Roussillon was *not* a juryman in the Revo-
lutionary Tribunal, although Louis Blanc says he was. In Charlotte
Corday's trial he sat as a judge, together with Foucault and Ardouin.
Foucault was guillotined May 7, 1795.

The sun was setting behind the trees in the Champs Élysées, lighting up with its blood-red rays the walls of the Tuileries and the windows of that apartment in which Marat sat but a few days ago, and in which Barère and Danton, Robespierre and Saint-Just, will again sit to-morrow.[1]

Saturday, July 27, 1793.

All conversation continues to turn upon Marat and Mlle. Corday. One of my friends yesterday showed me a card similar to that which the murderess had on July 12 left with Duperret to inform him where she was staying. The card, which is looked upon almost as a relic, bears the following inscription :

MADAME GROLLIER,

Tient l'Hôtel de la Providence,

Rue des Vieux-Augustins, No. 19, près la Place de la Victoire-Nationale.

On y trouve des Appartements Meublés à tous prix.

À PARIS.

This morning my friend took me to the Rue des Vieux-Augustins ; the Hôtel de la Providence forms one of the angles of this street and the Rue Soly.[2] It is a tall house, with iron balconies running round the first story. The room occupied by Mlle. Corday is No. 7, looking out into the street.[3]

This little pilgrimage interested me very much. Although my admiration for Mlle. Corday, for the calmness of her attitude before her judges, and for her sublime courage in the face of death, is very great, I am not one of those who approve of the act which she committed. I deplore Marat's murder as much as I did Lepeletier's. Let us leave the dagger to the outlaws

---

[1] Michelet, who has written some admirable pages upon the death of Charlotte Corday, dates it on July 19 instead of the 17th. Thiers dates it on the 15th ('Histoire de la Révolution,' tome v., p. 90).

[2] All this portion of the street has now disappeared to make room for the new Post-office.

[3] Jules Claretie, 'Maison Historique.'

of the Commune and the Convention, let us leave crime to criminals. If we have courage enough, let us rather imitate those Vendeans who fight for God and their King, those peasants who obey the leaders they have chosen whilst we are cowardly enough to obey Robespierre. To them this insurrection is a sacred duty, since they rebel not against the throne, but against the scaffold in defending their proscribed priests, and in worshipping their outraged God.

I must say that all my friends profess feelings of enthusiasm for Charlotte Corday which admit of no restriction or reserve whatever. In their opinion (and again I must say that I do not share their way of thinking) any means that will deliver Paris and France from a monster like Marat are laudable. They think it would have been wrong to allow Marat to fall by the hand of the headsman, since it is now only honest people who die on the scaffold. Some courageous man was therefore required to sacrifice himself and become the executioner of God. Men failing, a woman came forward to do justice. These are some of the ideas of which André Chénier unburdened himself with his usual eloquence to Beaulieu and myself. I had not seen him since the day when we met at Luciennes in February last. He now lives at Versailles, and only left his retreat to visit the places hallowed in his eyes by the remembrance of Charlotte Corday—the hotel in the Rue des Vieux-Augustins, the Jardin Égalité, the house in the Rue des Cordeliers, the Abbaye prison, the Conciergerie, and the Place de la Révolution.

I must add that André de Chénier is most emphatic concerning Charlotte Corday's direct descent from Corneille. He will not admit that she was only his great-grand-*niece*, and proves conclusively that she was his great-grand-*daughter*.

Pierre Corneille had six children. His eldest daughter, Marie, born on January 10, 1642, married Jacques Adrien de Farcy, President of the Treasurers of France ; by this marriage she had two daughters, one of whom, Françoise, married in October 22, 1701, Adrien de Corday, to whom she bore a son named Jacques Adrien de Corday on April 7, 1704 ; the latter married August 22, 1729, Renée Adelaide de Belleau de la

Motte.   Eight children were issue of this marriage, and the third son, Jacques François de Corday d'Armont, was the father of Marie Anne Charlotte de Corday.[1]

'The wretches!' cried Chénier, after having gone through the above pedigree; 'they have murdered in one week the great-grand-daughter of Corneille and the great-grandson of Malherbe.'[2]

[1] See the genealogical table of the Corneille family at the end of the 'Notice Biographique de Pierre Corneille,' in 'Les Grands Écrivains de la France,' edited by A. Régnier.

[2] Three days after the execution of Mlle. Corday, Louis de Malherbe, twenty years of age, was guillotined on a charge of being a refugee.   In vain did he prove that he had left France only to take the waters at Aix-la-Chapelle by order of his doctor, and that Dampierre had told him he might safely return to France without fear of coming under the law relating to refugees.   In vain did his defender remind the jury that he was the great-grandson of the poet Malherbe, and the last of his name.

CHAPTER LXXXVII.

THE HEART OF MARAT.

Monday, July 29, 1793.

I cannot help admiring the distributive justice of the Revolution. It has produced men—such as Brissot, Guadet, Buzot, Vergniaud, Barbaroux and Roland—who have sacrificed honour itself for the cause ; who have stopped at nothing, not even at crime, and who certainly gave proof of great talent and courage. The Revolution casts them into prison, and prepares to drag them to the scaffold. Marat is a criminal and a cowardly wretch ; he is both ridiculous and contemptible, and if he be not mad he is a monster. Living, his place would be in a lunatic's cell ; he dies, and the Republic raises an altar to his memory.

The first to profess this new cult were women. On July 20 the Club of Republican Revolutionary Women, meeting in the library of the former Jacobin church, demanded the erection of an obelisk to the memory of Marat in the Place de la Réunion, opposite the Palais National. On the 24th a deputation of these citoyennes proceeded to the Commune ; that body applauded their patriotism,[1] and ordered a granite obelisk to be erected at the expense of all true *sans-culottes* in honour of the People's Friend, and bearing a record of his works. Whilst awaiting the erection of this stone monument, a collection made by the Patriots has enabled them to put up a temporary wooden one in the Place de la Réunion.[2]

On July 25 an artist named Beauvallet presented the Convention with a bust of Marat. The Assembly decreed that it

[1] *Moniteur*, July 27, 1793.   [2] *Journal de la Montagne*, August 2, 1793.

should be placed in the Legislative Chamber by the side of the busts of Brutus, Dampierre,[1] and Lepeletier.[2] The Commune has placed his portrait in the hall of the Conseil-Général, next to that of Passavant, the brave grenadier of the National Guards who committed suicide on July 17, 1791, in order, so the Patriots tell us, that he might not survive the massacre in the Champ de Mars.[3] There is not a section nor a political club which is not eager to have the portrait or bust of Marat. It is to be found everywhere—in the manufactory of the Gobelin tapestries and in the Society of Patriots, in the Treasury and in the Club of the Friends of Liberty.[4] The play-houses will not remain behindhand. The Théâtre Molière, now called the Théâtre des Sans-Culottes, has already given the signal.

The Commune, on the demand of the Grey Friars Club, has changed the name of the street in which the hero died to that of Rue Marat, and the Rue de l'Observance is in future to be called the Place de l'Ami du Peuple.[5] The former section of the Théâtre Français, which, after the Tenth of August, became the section of Marseilles, has given up the latter name for that of Marat.

In the Hôtel des Invalides[6] one of the wards is now called by the name of Marat. It runs parallel with that named after Ankastroom, the assassin of the King of Sweden.[7]

Marat in the Invalides! The name of this cowardly sycophant associated with such glorious memories and inscribed on those walls that speak only of honour and courage! The memory of Marat to be interwoven with that of Condé, of Luxembourg and of Turenne! It is impossible to imagine a more odious profanation. Carry Marat's body to the Pantheon if you will, citizens, but do not stain the honour of the Invalides with his name!

---

[1] General Dampierre was mortally wounded during the attack on the woods of Ruism and Saint-Amand on May 8, 1793.

[2] *Moniteur*, July 27, 1793; Beaulieu, 'Les Souvenirs de l'Histoire,' July 25, 1793.

[3] 'Marat, l'Ami du Peuple,' by Alfred Bougeart, tome ii., p. 293.

[4] 'Inventaire des Autographes de la Collection de B. Fillon,' No. 556; 'Inauguration des Bustes de Marat et de Lepeletier,' eighty-six original documents mostly addressed to Palloy, 1793.

[5] *Moniteur*, July 28, 1793.   [6] A home for old soldiers.

[7] Beaulieu, 'Essais Historiques,' tome iii., p. 36.

On July 26 a deputation from the Grey Friars Club appeared before the National Convention—Danton being that day in the Presidential chair—and announced that the Club had decided to erect an altar to the heart of Marat in their place of meeting on the following Sunday. The Convention resolved that a deputation of twenty-four of its members should be present at the ceremony.[1]

The festival was duly celebrated yesterday.[2]   It commenced in the garden of the Luxembourg, where a richly-decorated altar had been erected at the entrance to the principal avenue. Upon this altar was placed a magnificent urn taken from the Crown Jewels, and containing Marat's heart.   The Grey Friars Club had been authorized to select one of the finest vases in the collection 'in order that the remains of the most inveterate enemy of kings might be placed in a vessel that had belonged to the Crown.'[3]

The enormous crowd that filled the garden consisted of deputations from the political clubs, and from every representative body, including the Convention and the Commune ; the vast assembly of Patriots contained a large proportion, too, of women and children.

An orator got upon a chair and read a speech, which began as follows : ' O cor Jesus ! O cor Marat !—Sacred heart of Jesus ! Sacred heart of Marat ! You have the same right to our devotion !' Comparing the acts and teachings of the Son of Mary with those of the Friend of the People, the orator then tried to prove that the Grey Friars and the Jacobins were the Apostles of the new Gospel, in which the shop-keepers were the publicans, and the aristocrats the Pharisees. ' Jesus Christ was a prophet,' he added, ' but Marat is a god.   Nor is that all,' he cried. ' I may say that Marat's helpmeet may be well compared to Mary ; the latter saved the infant Jesus in Egypt, whilst the former saved Marat from the sword of Lafayette, the Herod of the New Era.'[4]

Citizen Brochet, another Grey Friar, was the next to speak.

<hr />

[1] *Moniteur*, July 28.   [2] *Mercure Français*, No. 105, August 3, 1793.
[3] *Nouvelles Politiques Nationales et Étrangères*, No. 212, July 31, 1793.
[4] *Révolutions de Paris*, No. 211, July 20 to August 3, 1793.

After having complimented the previous speaker upon his oratorical powers, he expressed some surprise that anyone should dare to liken Jesus to the divine Marat. He then proceeded to show that Jesus had created superstition and fanaticism—odious monsters which Marat had destroyed. 'Jesus defended Kings,' he said, ' but Marat had the courage to crush them. We have heard enough of this Jesus ; the story is all a silly myth, a wretched tale which has stifled Liberty in its cradle. Philosophy alone should be the guide of Republicans ; their only god is Freedom.'[1]

This speech was received with shouts of applause. The Commandant of the Forces of Paris then came forward and offered to provide at his own expense shrubs and flowers wherewith to adorn Marat's grave.[2]

Night was now approaching, and Marat's heart was taken from the altar on which it had been exhibited like some saintly relic and borne in procession from the Luxembourg garden to the Grey Friars Club to the music of the *Ça ira*, the Hymn of the Marseillais, and the *Carmagnole*. The urn containing the precious burden was then suspended by a long chain from the roof of the hall, and the President, gazing upon the sacred vessel, uttered these words : ' Precious and divine remains ! Shall our souls be perjured ? You demand to be revenged, and your assassins still live ! Arise, Grey Friars ! It is time. Let us avenge Marat and console the heart of weeping France.'[3]

Citizen Brochet, the speaker on July 28, was a juryman in the Revolutionary Tribunal ; he was one of those who on July 17 pronounced Charlotte Corday guilty. In his evidence at Fouquier-Tinville's trial, Depâris, the clerk of the court—the man who after the murder of Lepeletier by one of his namesakes called himself Fabricius—spoke of Brochet as one of the *solid* jurymen, one of those who always voted *feu de file*. The names of the judges and the jurymen should have been drawn by lot, but Depâris informs us ' that they were all carefully selected.' This was especially the case in important trials like those of Hébert, Danton, and others. Holding three different posts—that of an officer in the army, that of a

[1] *Révolutions de Paris*, No. 211, July 20 to August 3, 1793.
[2] *Ibid*.   [3] *Journal de la Montagne*, No. 63.

member of the Revolutionary Committee, and that of a juryman—
Brochet indulged in the three-fold pleasures of arresting, examining,
and condemning (Wallon, 'La Terreur,' tome ii., p. 253). At the
sitting of the Jacobins on October 2, 1793, Brochet, in his efforts to
outdo Hébert, who asked for the immediate execution of Brissot
and his accomplices 'whatever their number might be,' demanded
the suppression of the ordinary forms of justice in the trial of conspirators (*Moniteur*, October 6, 1793). Arrested together with
Fouquier-Tinville and many other officials of the Revolutionary
Tribunal, Brochet was acquitted on the 17th of Florial, year III.
(May 6, 1795). He was again arrested by order of his section, and
again liberated on October 5, 1795. Under the Consulate he was
included in the decree of banishment passed at the end of the year
1800. He was taken to Oléron, and being shipped for transportation in 1804, died at sea at the age of fifty-two.

CHAPTER LXXXVIII.

Sunday, August 4, 1793.

I was very anxious to attend the distribution of prizes at the University, which took place at five o'clock to-day—not at the Sorbonne as formerly, but in the hall of the Jacobin Club in the Rue Saint-Honoré. The invitations are, alas! no longer sent out by the Rector in the name of the University, but by the Procureur-Général-Syndic on behalf of the Departmental Directory.

On the daïs sat Citizen Dufourny,[1] the President of the department, and the officers of the University, with Citizen René Binet, the Rector, at their head.[2] Round these were grouped the administrators of the department, the members of the Court of Appeal, the Commissioners of the sections, and deputations from the National Convention, the Electoral Assembly, and from all the administrative and judicial bodies. The Judges of the Revolutionary Tribunal were present in full force, but their President, Citizen Montané, was conspicuous by his absence, the National Convention having issued an order for his arrest four days ago. In his place we have Fouquier-Tinville, with his pale face and narrow brow, his small round eyes and his black hair.[3] It is an extraordinary piece of luck to have both him

---

[1] Concerning Dufourny de Villiers and his part in the Revolution of May 31, see Chapter LXXVI. After the 9th of Thermidor Dufourny was charged with being a Terrorist.

[2] René Binet (1732—1812), well known for his translations of Horace, Virgil, and Valerius Maximus, author of a 'Histoire de la Décadence des Mœurs chez les Romains.'

[3] 'Le Nouveau Paris,' by Sébastien Mercier, ch. clii.

and his deputy Fleuriot-Lescot here together; the Tribunal does not sit to-day, and the ceremony will therefore not be disturbed by the noise of the tumbrel passing through the Rue Saint-Honoré on its way to the Place de la Révolution, nor by the cries of the crowd insulting the victims.

Citizen Dufourny opened the proceedings with a speech from which I take the following passages:

'*Enfants de la Patrie, le jour de gloire est arrivé!*[1] Children of equality, though you are crowned with laurel on this eventful day, I must ask you to remember that these wreaths are not emblems of pride, like those of tyranny, but rewards for industry, and for the exercise of talents which will glorify and defend the Republic.

'The books which will be distributed among you will teach you your duty as men and citizens; they will be accompanied by a copy of the Constitution. You will study this document in order to defend it, and reflect upon it in order that you may extend it.'

The citizens and their wives, who filled the galleries, frequently interrupted the speaker with their applause, and he often had to repeat sentences which he had not been allowed to complete. 'I invite the spokesman of the deputation from the National Convention,' he said in conclusion, 'to present to you our congratulations, the prizes and the wreaths.'

The oldest member of the deputation from the Convention then took the chair, and Dufourny again rose:

'Young citizens, it seemed to give you pleasure to be called "Children of your country," and your joy proves that you are worthy of the name. The venerable patriarch who is now in the chair is worthy of your respect, not only on account of his age, but also on account of his virtues.'

The Assembly, and the young people especially, having loudly demanded the name of the new chairman, Dufourny explained that this venerable citizen, Boucher Saint-Sauveur, had been one of the first defenders of Liberty in the illustrious district of the Grey Friars, that he was a member for Paris in the Convention, and a stanch supporter of the Mountain.

---

[1] The first line of the Hymn of the Marseillais.

Dufourny—one of the foremost members of the Jacobin Club, and one of the ringleaders of the rising of May 31—and Boucher Saint-Sauveur—a friend of Danton, a regicide deputy and a stanch supporter of the Mountain—these are the men who now preside over our University meetings; these are the models held up before our children; these are the guides which are given them ! '*Enfants de la Patrie, le jour de gloire est arrivé !*' In the reign of the Tyrant we were crowned by Malesherbes, but you are to be crowned by Fouquier-Tinville !

Citizen Crouzet, the Principal of the Collège du Panthéon, then read a poem in French on Liberty. Dufourny once more rose to propose that the Convention be requested to have Crouzet's poem printed at the expense of the nation, and distributed throughout the Republic. Boucher Saint-Sauveur undertook to support the request, and the distribution of the prizes was then proceeded with. Binet called over the names of the successful competitors, and each of the lads, after being embraced by the venerable citizen in the chair, received a crown of oak-leaves and a copy of the Constitution.

On my return home I took out my old prize-lists, all of which are headed with the following inscription :

> *Alma studiorum Parens, primogenita Regum Filia,*
> *Universitas Parisiensis.*

Amplissimo V. D. N . . . Rectore In Scholis Sorbinicis congregata ad solemnem Proemiorum litterariorum distributionem athletas suos hoc ordine coronat et remuneratur.

More than one of these young *athletes* has become celebrated. Under the well-known names of La Harpe and the Abbé Delille I find those of Chauveau-Lagarde, who defended Charlotte Corday, of Andrieux, the author of ' Les Étourdis '; of Collin d'Harleville, the author of ' Le Vieux Célibataire '; of Beffroy de Reigny, the author of ' Nicodème dans la Lune,' and of ' Le Club des Bonnes Gens.' How many then fought for these innocent laurels who were destined soon to meet upon another battle-field, eager for the fray, burning with hatred and fighting in these *plus quam civilia bella,* not for a bloodless victory, but for life !

Here are the names of Robespierre, Gouy d'Arcy, and Boufflers, members of the Constituent Assembly; and of Hérault-Séchelles, Camille Desmoulins, and Gorsas, members of the Convention.

Maximilien Robespierre was one of the most distinguished pupils of the Collège Louis-le-Grand, which he entered at the beginning of the school-year of 1769-70, and which he left in 1776. In the same class we find the future *Cousin Jacques*, the witty and inoffensive Beffroy de Reigny,[1] who frequently competed successfully against him. Young Maximilien, who had received a scholarship from the Abbé de Saint-Waast, is thus described in the examination-lists: '*Ludovicus Franciscus Maximilianus Maria Isidorus De Robespierre Atrebas, c collegio Ludovici Magni.*' In 1772 he obtained the second prize for Latin composition, and a sixth accessit for Latin verse; in 1774 a fourth accessit for Latin verse, and in 1775 the second prize for the same subject, and a third accessit for Greek composition.

Camille Desmoulins was three classes lower than Robespierre. He also carried off numerous distinctions: in 1774, the second prize for Latin composition; in 1775, the second prize for the same subject; in 1778, a ninth accessit for French prose.

A little older than Robespierre and Camille Desmoulins, Joseph Gorsas, who has now been outlawed by them, pursued his studies at the Collège du Plessis-Sorbonne. In 1769 he had to content himself with a third accessit in Latin prose. Like Gorsas, Vergniaud (who had received a scholarship from Turgot), Lafayette, Chaumette, and, if I am not mistaken, Anacharsis Cloots, all attended the Collège du Plessis. Vergniaud's name does not appear among the prize-winners at the general examinations—a fact which is easily explained. His studies at the college were confined to philosophy, and this subject, like mathematics, could not be taken alone in the general competitions.

---

[1] 'I do not think,' wrote Beffroy de Reigny, 'that there are many Frenchmen who have studied Robespierre so attentively as I have done; we were in the same class, and rivals for the first places in rhetoric. Chance willed it that I obtained them, a fact for which he never forgave me.' Concerning Beffroy de Reigny, see 'Les Originaux du Siècle Dernier,' by Charles Monselet.

Of all the students who have distinguished themselves at the University since 1747, when the general competitions were first instituted, the most brilliant and able is undoubtedly my friend, André de Chénier, the author of ' Advice to the French People concerning their Real Enemies,' of some excellent articles in the *Journal de Paris*, and of some poems which, when published, will place him in the front rank of the poets of France.   The same year in which Camille Desmoulins obtained a ninth accessit for French prose André de Chénier was awarded the first prize in that subject, and a first accessit for Latin verse.   He was a pupil of the Collège de Navarre.

Small as my share was in these general examinations, and although I never went farther than two accessits gained in 1777, I cannot help feeling once more the hopes and fears of my youth whenever I attend a prize distribution at one or other of the colleges, but especially when I visit my own—that of Louis-le-Grand.

When I entered the old college in 1764, our Principal was the Abbé Poignard.   He was replaced in 1778 by the Abbé Bérardier, a kind, tolerant, and witty man who, on December 29, 1790, officiated at the marriage of Camille Desmoulins.   A deputy of the clergy of Paris in the States-General, the Abbé Bérardier refused to take the oath after the establishment of the civil constitution of the clergy, and being especially held up to public execration, he nearly lost his life in the September massacres.

The director of our studies was the Abbé Audrein, a preacher of remarkable ability, and a deputy for the Morbihan in the Legislative Assembly and in the Convention.   He did not follow the example set him by the Abbé Bérardier, and he is now the episcopal curate of the Constitutional Bishop of Vannes.[1]

Our professor of philosophy was the Abbé Royou, who has since become so famous, and of whom I have frequently had occasion to speak in these pages.

---

[1] Audrein, who had voted for the death of Louis XVI., was assassinated on November 19, 1800, by a band of Royalists.   At the time of his death he was Bishop of Quimper.

Of those who sat at his feet more than one was destined to make a name in politics or letters, amongst them being Robespierre, Desmoulins, Loustallot, editor of the *Révolutions de Paris*, François Suleau and Stanislas Fréron, a nephew of the Abbé, editor of the *Orateur du Peuple*, and a deputy for Paris in the National Convention. In the years preceding the Revolution the Collège Louis-le-Grand also had within its walls General Dumouriez, Duport-Dutertre, who was Minister of Justice from November 22, 1790, to March, 1792, and impeached after the Tenth of August; Lebrun-Tondu, Minister of Foreign Affairs from the Tenth of August, 1792, to June 21, 1793; Nicolas Lullier, Procureur-Syndic de la Commune, who had the honour of being invited on July 14 last to replace Marat on the benches of the Convention; Noël, *couronné* by the Académie in 1788 for his 'Éloge de Louis XII.,' and in 1790 for his 'Éloge du Maréchal de Vauban,' a founder of the *Chronique de Paris*, and a principal clerk in the Department of Foreign Affairs; Picard, whose 'Visitandines,' 'Conteur' and 'Cousin de Tout le Monde,' give proofs of great humour; Lesur, like Camille Desmoulins, a native of Guise, and author of the 'Apothéose de Beaurepaire,' recently played at the Théâtre Français; Auguste de Piis, formerly secretary to the Comte d'Artois, and the author of many vaudevilles, songs and stories in verse, to say nothing of a poem in four cantos entitled the 'Harmonie Imitative de la Langue Française;' and Luce de Lancival, who, after occupying the chair of rhetoric at the Collège de Navarre at the age of twenty-two, gave up his professorship for an ecclesiastical career, gained for himself a great name in the pulpit, broke his vows after the Revolution, and now seems to be turning his thoughts to the stage.

Yesterday evening Citizen Champagne, the Principal of the Collège Louis-le-Grand, gathered round his table the prize-winners of the year, and a few of the old students. He did his best to animate the proceedings, but without success. Could we forget that if François Suleau was absent it was because he had been massacred on the Tenth of August? Could we forget that his body had been cut to pieces, and his head carried through the streets of Paris on a pike?[1] And where was

---

[1] Auguste Vitu, 'Notice of François Suleau.'

Boufflers, one of our old boys, a member of the Constituent Assembly, and one of the forty immortals of the Académie Française? He has, alas! been obliged to seek refuge abroad in order to save his head. Where was Duport-Dutertre? Arrested soon after the Tenth of August, he is still awaiting his trial before the Revolutionary Tribunal in the prisons of the Republic.[1] Where was Lebrun-Tondu? He has been in a state of arrest at his own house in the Rue d'Enfer since June 2, and is also waiting to be summoned before the terrible Tribunal.[2] Where was the Abbé Royou? Threatened with the loss of both life and property, and obliged to live in concealment, he died of grief on June 21, 1792, on hearing of the invasion of the Tuileries. And were there not others who were as good as dead to us—Robespierre, Fréron, Lullier, and Camille Desmoulins?

At the end of the evening I remained alone with M. Champagne,[3] who spoke to me with tears in his eyes of the old college he loved so passionately, and of which he is forced to witness the decay. After having had as many as three thousand students upon its lists at one time, it now has scarcely a hundred. The endowments which formerly enabled it to maintain a large number of exhibitioners have been seized, and neither the Legislative Assembly nor the Convention has troubled to replace this source of income. M. Champagne still manages to educate and board a few students, but it is almost entirely at his own expense, his constant appeals to the Minister of the Interior, the Commune of Paris, and the Pantheon section, meeting with very little response.

Our poor college has not only lost its students, but also its name. In 1792 the Revolution ordered that the Collège Louis-

---

[1] Duport-Dutertre was guillotined on the 8th of Frimaire, year II. (November 28, 1793), on the same day as Barnave.

[2] Lebrun left his house in the Rue d'Enfer on the 26th of Frimaire, year II. (December 16, 1793), and hid himself in the house of a restaurant-keeper named Desenne, living in the Rue de la Liberté. Arrested on December 23, 1793, on information furnished by Citizen Arthur, a paper-maker, of the Rue des Piques, he was guillotined on December 27, 1793 (7th of Nivôse, year II.).

[3] 'Notice sur M. Champagne,' by M. Dacier. See also the article on Champagne in the Supplement to the 'Biographie Universelle.'

le-Grand should in future be called Collège des Boursiers, and in 1793 it changed the latter name to that of Collège de l'Égalité.

M. Champagne told me that the greater part of the building is to be turned into a prison, and that only one set of apartments looking out upon the Rue Saint-Jacques is to be kept for purposes of study.[1] Much the same is to be done with all the other colleges.   On July 13, Robespierre, acting in the name of the Committee of Public Instruction, laid before the Convention a plan of education drawn up by Michel Lepeletier. 'With the memory of his virtues,' he said, 'Michel Lepeletier has left his country a plan of education which seems to have been drawn up by the genius of humanity. On hearing it, you will feel more keenly the loss we have sustained, and one proof more will be given to the world that the most implacable enemies of Kings are the truest friends of mankind.' It was Lepeletier's idea—and in this Robespierre and the Committee of Public Instruction are with him—that all intellectual work and all literary study should be prohibited in the name of the sacred law of Equality. 'Boys,' we read in Lepeletier's plan, 'should be trained to till the ground, employed in manufactories, or sent out upon the highroads to pick up the stones.'

The colleges suppressed, and the halls in which our pious masters educated us in the love of letters—*humaniores litteræ !* —converted into cells, and serving as ante-rooms to the Revolutionary Tribunal and the scaffold ! This is to what we have come in less than a year after the overthrow of the Monarchy, ten months after the proclamation of the Republic !

Like that of Louis-le-Grand, the Collège du Plessis was turned into a prison. 'Le Plessis,' wrote one of its inmates, 'formerly the

----

[1] 'There, surrounded by eight students and a band of professors, Champagne persisted in keeping up his college, paying for the board of his pupils, whom he called his children, out of his own pocket, and out of the slender resources he could scrape together. He was visited almost daily by some official or other, urging him to give up possession ; but Champagne's brain was more fertile in concocting ruses and stratagems to keep the building confided to his care than were those of the men who wished to destroy it.'—'Notices sur M. Champagne,' by M. Durozoir and by M. Dacier.

abode of learning, was now become that of misery and death. Many
of the captives it contained had passed some years of their youth
within those very walls, and in that courtyard where they had given
vent to their exuberant spirits, they now sat drearily awaiting their
trial. They were only allowed to come down for an hour after each
meal—three hours of fresh air, twenty-one of solitary confinement
in their cells. The discipline in Le Plessis was the most severe in
Paris, the prison being under the immediate supervision of Fouquier-
Tinville, who governed it with the greatest barbarity. As a rule, its
inmates only left it for the scaffold.' In another contemporary
account of this place we read : 'This ancient college had become
the store-house, as it were, of the Conciergerie. During the reign
of the triumvirate a multitude of victims of both sexes, and of all
ages, were sent there from the Conciergerie, which, in spite of the
daily batches carted off to the scaffold, could not contain all upon
whom the law laid its hand. Le Plessis was also the repository for
the prisoners from the provinces, and the house was soon too small
for its guests. Openings were made in the walls that were next to
those of the Collège Louis-le-Grand, and these two buildings soon
formed one and the same Bastille ' ('Suite des Anecdotes sur la
Maison d'Arrêt du Plessis ' ; 'Histoire des Prisons,' by Nougaret).
Fouquier-Tinville spent the period of his captivity in the prison of
Plessis. 'Transferred,' says *La Vedette*, 'to the Collège du Plessis,
he had been advised for the sake of his own safety to keep his door
and window closed. On the 23rd of Frimaire (December 13, 1794)
he begged to be allowed to take the air in the courtyard, but the
threats of the prisoners made him fear for his life. On the morrow
he attempted to open his window, but the curses of those outside
compelled him to close it again at once.'

CHAPTER LXXXIX.

THE VENDÉE.

Thursday, August 8, 1793.

THE Convention has just ordered the garrison of Mayence to proceed to the Vendée.[1]

Great hopes are entertained that these troops, consisting of well-disciplined veterans, and commanded by tried Generals, will put an end to the innumerable defeats which the rebels have inflicted upon the battalions of Parisian volunteers.

It is very difficult, nay, almost impossible, to obtain correct information in Paris concerning this campaign which has now been going on for the past four months so near the capital. The rebels have no newspapers, and their letters, if they wrote any, would not reach Paris. In addition, therefore, to the meagre account of the operations given by Revolutionary journals—the only ones now existing—we have nothing but the incomplete and unreliable stories of the invalided volunteers to fall back upon.

I will give a few of the notes taken by me at different dates, and relating more particularly to the raising of battalions in Paris for service in the Vendée.

Monday, April 29.—Evening sitting of the Conseil-Général de la Commune. At half-past nine the Mayor announces that he has just come from the Committee of Public Safety ; that matters in the Vendée are going from bad to worse ; and that the Committee has entreated him to confer with the sections

---

[1] These troops, having surrendered on July 23, 1793, had been allowed to return to France, on condition that they would not serve against the Allied Powers.

and the Commune of Paris upon the best means of promptly relieving our brethren who are fighting against the rebels. The Committee of Public Safety considers it most advisable to adopt the ideas expressed by the department of the Hérault. Chaumette is the first to speak after the Mayor. 'The fanatical priests,' he cries, 'must be sacrificed! We must do as we did on the Tenth of August. Blood, citizens—blood! We must cut off our arms to save our bodies.' The whole of his speech is in this strain, and he concludes by reading the draft of an address to the people of Paris.

On the motion of the Procureur-Général-Syndic the Conseil-Général decrees that all its members shall be summoned to meet at nine o'clock on the following morning; that Commissioners shall be sent to all the sections to inform them that the Bon-Conseil Section has already given its support to the energetic resolve of the department of the Hérault, and that the Conseil-Général looks to them to put an end to the civil war before another week has elapsed. The Conseil further decrees that Chaumette's speech shall be printed that night, and proclaimed in the principal squares of Paris on the morrow.[1]

The decree of the Commune, as well as Chaumette's speech and manifesto, was received with loud applause. There was, however, not much real enthusiasm, and certainly no desire to take part in the expedition. My neighbour on the right asked me how many miles it was to Vendée. 'About one hundred and fifty,' I replied. 'Oh, well,' he observed, 'the rebels have not reached Paris yet, then.' 'I would willingly go,' said a National Guard sitting on my left, 'it's a very good thing; but if we all go, and the neighbouring departments, taking advantage of our absence, each send five or six thousand men to the capital, Paris will be in a pretty pickle!'[2]

Tuesday, April 30.—At two o'clock to-day, two municipal officers, accompanied by a public crier, published the proclamation of the Commune in the Halles. The crier in a drawling voice read out as follows:

---

[1] 'Histoire Parlementaire de la Révolution Française,' by Buchez and Roux, tome xxvi., p. 207; 'Tableaux de la Révolution Française,' by Adolphe Schmidt, tome i., p. 164.
[2] Adolphe Schmidt, tome i., p. 167.

'*To the People of Paris.—Temporary Enlistment.*

'Citizens, hasten to the assistance of your country. The Republic is in danger in the Vendée; support it with your patriotism and your strength. There must be no mercy and no quarter for the rebels.'[1]

During the reading of the proclamation many of the by-standers turned away and showed no desire to hear the end of the address, or the inducements held out to recruits.

A fish-wife answers the last of the crier's phrases with an oath, and the words: 'The devil take them; I won't let my man go!'

At this the bystanders break out into laughter,[2] and as soon as the municipal officers have gone they speak out a little more boldly. 'They ask for twenty thousand men,' says one; 'a little later they will ask for ten thousand more, and then for another five thousand, so that at last there will be no one left. There are at least two thousand gendarmes in Paris; why don't they send them instead of disturbing peaceful citizens?' 'Numbers of volunteers,' says another, 'return from the frontiers daily; only yesterday more than sixty were arrested at the Bondy barrier. They go out by one barrier and come in by another, after taking the money of the sections, and so robbing the nation; why are not all these people sent off?' Others say, 'What good will a fresh expedition do? We always have been, and we always shall be, betrayed.'[3] The last remark is received with almost unanimous approval by the crowd.

Sunday, May 12.—On May 1 the Commune issued a decree ordering the formation of an army corps of 12,000 men. Each sectional company composed of 126 men was to furnish fourteen recruits. These were to be selected by a Commission composed of six members of the Revolutionary Committee of every section, and of one member of the Conseil-Général de la Commune. The recruits were to be chosen as far as possible from amongst the unmarried men performing clerical duties in Government and other offices.[4]

[1] Buchez and Roux, tome xxvi., p. 207.
[2] Schmidt, tome i., p. 167. [3] Schmidt, *loc. cit.*
[4] Buchez and Roux, tome xxvi., pp. 348, 352, 354, 370.

This decree gave rise to serious disturbances in many of the sections, and more especially in those of Bon-Conseil, the Pont-Neuf, Marseilles, and l'Unité.

On Saturday, May 4, meetings were held in the Champs Élysées and the Luxembourg Garden, at which 500 or 600 young men, after having elected a chairman, protested against the decree of the Commune, and swore not to obey it.[1]

On Sunday there were fresh demonstrations. A procession of about 400 young men set out from the Champs Élysées and proceeded along the Rues Saint-Honoré, des Lombards and de la Verrerie, the Quai Lepeletier, and the Pont Notre Dame, where some arrests were made. Monday witnessed a renewal of these occurrences.[2]

In the last number of the *Révolutions de Paris* Prudhomme refers to the unpopularity of the conscription in the following terms :

‘ The result of the conscription for the Vendée does not redound to the credit of the capital ; one would almost think that there was no patriotism left. Everyone seems to be hanging back. Prompt assistance was required, and several thousand men were asked to send in their names before the end of three days ; we doubt whether a few hundred will have done so at the end of a fortnight.’[3]

Thursday, May 16.—The most absolute form of Anarchy reigns in the forty-eight sections. A few have obeyed the decree of the Commune ; others have demanded that the conscripts shall draw lots, but the majority have pronounced in favour of voluntary service.[4] Unfortunately, there seems to be but little zeal to volunteer. In the Faubourgs the Patriots have declared that their presence in Paris was more necessary than ever ; that it was their duty to stay and prevent the Brissotins and Rolandists from scuttling the Republic.[5] The Faubourg Saint-Antoine demanded that a beginning should be made by sending off the priests and the signatories of the petitions of Eight Thousand and Twenty Thousand.

---

[1] Buchez and Roux, tome xxvi., p. 359.
[2] Robespierre's speech in the National Convention on May 6, 1793.
[3] *Révolutions de Paris*, tome xvi., p. 281.   [4] *Ibid.*, p. 284.
[5] Schmidt, tome i., p. 211.

The sections at last opened their eyes to the fact that, with regard to both men and ammunition, money was the sinews of war, and that if *volunteers* were wanted they would have to be paid. This principle being accepted, the recruitment proceeded in a much more satisfactory manner, and at a rate in exact proportion to the sum offered. In Prudhomme's paper we read:

'Some sections have promised 200 francs to every man enlisting, others 400, and a few have offered as much as 500 francs. This difference in price, which is due to the fact that the funds of every section are not in an equally prosperous condition, naturally causes a great difference in the number of recruits in each district. The poor section which offers 200 francs does not make up the required total of men so quickly as that which gives 500. . . . The object of the present conscription is merely a military outing; in two months' time all these soldiers will have returned to their homes; for this many of them will have received 500 francs, and some of the sections even promise their men a pension.[1] It is, therefore, not entirely heroism which inspires the Parisians to enlist for service in the Vendée, and the so-called volunteers are already being called *heroes at 500 francs apiece.*'[2]

Friday, June 14.—The rebels have taken Saumur and Clisson. They are now threatening Angers, La Flèche, Tours, and Le Mans. People talk of the necessity of raising 30,000 men, but there is a great difference between talking about it and doing it. Many go about saying, 'Let us rise!' but no one rises. In the sections many a speaker gets into the tribune, and, after dilating upon the dangers which threaten the Republic, resumes his seat, satisfied with the applause that his speech has evoked. 'He speaks well,' is heard on all sides; but it goes no farther.[3] The members of the Jacobin Club give most excellent reasons why they should not go and do battle. 'We are the lights and the apostles of the Republic,' they say. 'If we go, we shall not be able to enlighten the people and watch the traitors, therefore it is our duty to remain behind.'

The sentiment which animates the bulk of the population of

---

[1] *Révolutions de Paris*, tome xvi., p. 290.
[2] Concerning the *heroes at 500 francs*, see the 'Volontaires de 1791—1794,' by Camille Rousset.
[3] Schmidt, tome ii., p. 32.

Paris not belonging to any political club, and which includes men of all classes, may be thus summed up : 'If the rebels come to Paris, we are ready for them ; either they will kill us or they will not kill us, but the latter is most probable. If, however, we go and meet them in the provinces we are sure to perish. By staying in Paris we therefore risk being plundered, but certainly save our lives.'[1]

The men who will *rise* are therefore only those who will be paid for doing so. What other volunteers can we hope to find in the ranks of the newly-formed battalions? The supporters of the Girondist party are only too delighted to see the success of the rebels increase the embarrassment of their adversaries in the Convention ; no help is therefore to be expected from them. The supporters of the Mountain, too, are fully determined not to leave Paris, excusing themselves on the ground that their presence here is the only thing that prevents the Brissotin party from once more raising its head. Robespierre has spoken. He has given the Patriots to understand that they must not go. On the evening of the 12th he spoke as follows in the tribune of the Jacobin Club, and his language is sufficiently clear :

'I am in receipt of information concerning the disasters in the Vendée. I notice that whenever we receive news of events of this kind recourse is always had to one and the same measure —that of sending fresh battalions to be butchered. The people are always urged to go, but the people do not seem to understand that this is a trick of their enemies, and that the latter seek to destroy the Republic by civil as well as by foreign war. They are no doubt looking forward to the time when there shall not be a single *sans-culotte* left, and when the field will be free for rogues, aristocrats, and enemies of Liberty. They rely upon treason for getting every one of our Patriots murdered. Paris is the stronghold of Liberty. Paris is the centre of attack, and the loyal citizens must be got out of the capital so that it may be left without defences. I therefore insist that an army capable of intimidating tyrants must be kept in Paris, and that army must be composed of the *people* itself.'[2]

[1] Schmidt, tome ii., p. 33.
[2] Buchez and Roux, tome xxviii., p. 196. A document found amongst Robespierre's papers, and written entirely with his own hand, contains the

Robespierre thus recommends the Patriots not to go and try conclusions with the Vendeans. It is a piece of advice very easy to follow, and there is no doubt that it will be followed.

Sunday, June 16.—At yesterday's sitting of the Conseil-Général Révolutionnaire, Citizen Millier, a Commissioner sent to the districts in revolt, presented a report which is published this morning in the *Affiches* of the Commune. 'The Vendean peasants,' says Millier, 'have received the blessings of their priests and a promise that they shall *rise on the third day*, should they be fortunate enough to die fighting for their God and their King. Fanaticism is their only support.'[1] I am quite willing to accept this statement, but I must be allowed to remark that this fanaticism is of a very disinterested kind, and more praise-worthy than the motive which dictated the departure of the *heroes at 500 francs apiece.*

July 5.—The *Journal de Paris National* publishes a letter written by Citizen Prévost, and dated from La Rochelle June 25, from which I take the following passage : 'The rebels are all dressed as peasants, and many of them are only armed with sticks. They are, however, more hardy and brave than veterans, and when they engage in battle they bellow like oxen, and fall upon our gunners with their sticks.'

The humanity displayed by the Vendeans is equal to their heroism. A large number of volunteers who had been made prisoners by the rebels have been liberated, and are now back in Paris. They report that they met with no ill treatment, the Vendeans contenting themselves with cutting their hair, tearing the facings off their uniforms, and sometimes destroying the coats themselves. All declare that they will not take up arms against the Vendée again.[2]

I have seen one of the passes which were handed to the prisoners ; it reads as follows :

following : 'The internal dangers arise from the middle classes ; to conquer these classes, we must rouse the *people*. The Convention must make use of the people, and the *sans-culottes* must be paid to stay in the towns ; they must be armed, enlightened, and aroused' ('Rapport fait au Nom de la Commission chargée de l'Examen des Papiers de Robespierre et de ses Complices,' by E. B. Courtois, a member of the Convention, at the sitting of January 5, 1795, p. 181).

[1] *Moniteur*, June 18, 1793.   [2] Schmidt, tome ii., p. 89.

' Domaigné, Commander of the cavalry in the Christian army, hereby permits . . . . to pass through the lines in consideration of his having taken an oath to be faithful to religion, to Louis XVII., and to the Royal House of France, and never to bear arms against the Christian Monarchy.'[1]

The moderation of the rebels is the more praiseworthy since from the beginning of the operations the Convention has ordered all Vendean prisoners to be killed without exception. On March 19, after hearing the report of Cambacérès upon the outbreak, the Assembly issued the following Decree :

' Article 1.—All persons who are convicted of having taken part in the rebellion, or in the counter-Revolutionary riots, or of having worn the white cockade, or any other sign of revolt, shall be outlawed.

' Article 2.—If they are taken or arrested armed, they shall be handed over to the executioner and put to death within twenty-four hours after such fact has been attested before a military Commission formed of the officers of each division employed in quelling the disturbances.'

The *Révolutions de Paris* could not refrain from drawing attention to the reprehensible nature of this Decree, and to the deplorable consequences which could not fail to result from it. ' We are perfectly certain,' wrote the editors of that paper, who can surely not be charged with being too lenient towards the rebels in the Vendée, ' that this unfortunate campaign would have been a less bloody one if the law had reserved its anger for the ringleaders, and contented itself with making prisoners of the unfortunate peasants who were taken armed, instead of sending them to the scaffold.'

In an address which he has just published at Caen, and a few copies of which have reached Paris, Barbaroux speaks in almost similar terms concerning the Decree of March 19. ' A few battalions,' he says, ' might have put down the revolt in the Vendée were it not that a decree of death had gone forth, not only against the ringleaders (which was but just), but also against the peasants who had been led astray by them ; this measure made the latter desperate.'

[1] *Journal de Paris National*, No. 103, May 13, 1793. Domaigné, Commander of the Vendean cavalry, was killed at the capture of Saumur, June 10, 1793.

This is very well said ; but why did Barbaroux wait to speak these words until he was proscribed and outlawed himself? It was by him and his friends, who were then in the majority in the Convention, that the Decree of March 19 was passed. If it pleases him to forget that fact, we have a right to remind him of it.

July 27, 1793.—Each day brings fresh and curious revelations concerning the scandalous luxury in which the Generals of the Republic and the representatives of the people indulge.

The volunteers who have returned to Paris relate that General Santerre leads a life of almost Oriental voluptuousness —that he has the finest horses, the best cooks, and the prettiest women.[1]

In the Convention Chasles speaks in the following terms of General Berruyer : ' Never did a General make a more ostentatious display, and he is only to be approached on bended knees.'[2] Now it is the *Général-Ministre* Ronsin who drives about with four of his courtesans in an elegant chariot, escorted by a troop of fifty hussars,[3] whilst again we hear of the representatives of the people travelling in carriages drawn by six horses, and bullying the inn-keepers if there are not at least half a dozen candles on the table.[4]

What discipline can there be in an army when its leaders set such an example ?

The administrators of Mayenne-et-Loire, in a letter read before the Convention on April 24, 1793, complained of the many acts of robbery and violence which the soldiers of the Republic committed. On July 1 the *Moniteur* published an article on the present condition of the Republican armies engaged against the rebels. The writer was Carra, a member

---

[1] Schmidt, tome ii., p. 23.   [2] Sitting of April 24, 1793.
[3] ' Compte rendu à la Convention Nationale,' by Philippeaux (' Bibliothèque Historique de la Révolution, 1802 '), British Museum.
[4] 'Mémoires Manuscrits,' by Mercier du Rocher, p. 187.   See in Savary's work, 'Guerres des Vendéens et des Chouans contre la République,' tome iii., p. 77, a letter from the President of the district of Cholet to General Turreau, dated January 25, 1794 : ' General, your soldiers, who call themselves Republicans, indulge in such debauchery and in such horrible practices as would disgust even a cannibal. The bearer of this letter will give you all the information you require to enable you to punish the guilty and repress this fury.'

of the Convention, and formerly Commissioner to the armies, who, after having bestowed praise upon the line regiments generally, confessed that the behaviour of the Parisian battalions was reprehensible. ' The 500 francs,' he says, ' which were given to each of these volunteers have unfortunately corrupted a good many of them.'

In his report (already mentioned) to the Conseil-Général Révolutionnaire, Citizen Millier expresses himself as follows concerning the German Legion, composed partly of foreign deserters and of Parisian volunteers : ' The battalions which are known as the German Legion indulge in debauchery and in excesses of all kind, and are accompanied by about 400 women.'[1]

August 2, 1793.—This morning there appeared in the *Affiches* of the Commune a letter written to a member of the Conseil-Général by Bruslé and Lachevardière, the Commissioners of the Commune in the Vendée. This letter, dated July 28, contains the following lines : ' It is impossible to give an account of all the outrages committed by the " 500 franc men " in the army. I will simply enumerate one or two which will make you shudder. The daughter of the Mayor of Saumur, a girl of nineteen, was violated in her mother's arms ; two servants in the same house shared a similar fate. These women died of despair in the camp at Chinon.'[2] In the Jacobin Club this evening an officer confirmed this information. ' Your successes in the Vendée,' he said, 'have been few, and your losses constant. There is not one of your Generals who has confidence in his men. The latter are adepts only in treason and debauchery.

[1] *Moniteur* of June 18, 1793. 'With every battalion,' wrote one of the Commissioners with the Republican army in the Vendée to the Committee of Public Safety, 'there is a horde of women, who corrupt the soldiers, and, by inciting them to plunder, disorganize the army ' (' Correspondance inédite du Comité de Salut Public,' tome i., p. 427). Carnot wrote from his post with the Army of the North : 'The bands of women who accompany our army are a terrible plague ; they are almost as numerous as our soldiers. The barracks and the camps are full of them, and the morality of the men cannot well be worse. These women enervate and do ten times more harm to the troops than the fire of the enemy. At Douai, where at one time the garrison was reduced to 350 men, there were nearly 3,000 women in the barracks ' (*op. cit.*, tome ii., p. 10).
[2] Buchez and Roux, 'Histoire Parlementaire,' tome xxviii., p. 404 ; *Mercure Français*, No. 106.

The battalions hailing from Paris are not all, it is true, composed of Parisians, but "500 franc men" are not those from whom we can expect victories. The majority of them have deserted like cowards, and some, sooner than fight, have drowned themselves in the Loire. No crime is too heinous for them. With plunder and outrage they are familiar, and their excesses are committed not only upon rebels, but upon Patriots!' In the course of his speech this officer spoke of the Vendeans as 'men who fight with their scapularies and rosaries in their hands, and who, armed only with staves, rushed upon our guns. These wretched creatures,' he added, 'do not fight for the nobles, whom they detest, but for those whom they call their good priests.'[1]

Thus, on the one hand, we have men who 'have deserted like cowards,' and to whom 'plunder and outrage are familiar,' whilst on the other we have men who fight like demons though 'armed only with staves,' and who are reproached with nothing worse than carrying scapularies and rosaries—which of these, I would ask, are really the 'wretched creatures?'

It was at the Jacobin Club that the evil was pointed out, and at the Grey Friars that the remedy was suggested. 'Let us,' said one of the speakers, 'adopt vigorous measures to exterminate the villains in the Vendée and in other parts of the country. Let us prepare red-hot shot and set fire to some forty or fifty villages in the affected departments. Such rigorous measures would only be an act of justice, for though there may be some innocent men in the midst of these insurgents, they are, nevertheless, cowards whom we ought not to spare. But before we can do this, we must find soldiers, and compel even our enemies to accompany us. The whole of the middle classes and all the shop-keepers ought to be enrolled on the Tenth of August. We want 50,000 men, and when we have them we shall find plenty of work for them to do ; we have might on our side, and we must use it.'[2] This speech was received with loud and prolonged applause.

Meanwhile Barère was employing similar language in the

---

[1] ' Histoire Parlementaire,' tome xxviii., p. 405.
[2] *Journal Historique et Politique*, August 10, 1793.

Convention. 'The extermination of evil is a meritorious action,' he said, at the sitting of August 1. 'Louvois was accused—and justly accused—of having laid waste the Palatinate when acting in the Tyrant's cause. The Palatinate of the Republic is the Vendée; destroy it, and you will save the country. The Committee of Public Safety has prepared measures which aim at the extermination of this rebellious race of Vendeans, and at the destruction of their crops, their home-steads, and their belongings. A surgeon uses the knife where he finds a cancer; at Mortagne, at Cholet, and at Chémille, the political surgeon must employ a similar instrument. Cut out the Vendée, and you will save the country.'[1]

After the reading of Barère's report, the Convention passed a Decree ordering the destruction by fire, not only of forty or fifty villages, but of whole departments. The following are a few of the articles of this Decree

'Article 6.—The Minister of War shall send combustibles of all kinds to be used in the destruction of the woods and forests.

'Article 7.—The dwellings of the rebels shall be destroyed, their crops cut by companies of workmen, and their herds seized.'

'Article 14.—The goods and chattels of the rebels in the Vendée are hereby declared to be the property of the Republic.'[2]

I have only one observation to make concerning this Decree. I desire to point out that it was not those who passed it, but those at whom it is aimed, who are called the *brigands*.

---

[1] *Moniteur*, August 7, 1793.

[2] Decree of August 1, 1793 : *Moniteur*, August 2. This Decree was executed with real barbarism. According to the evidence given by Luminais before the Council of Five Hundred on January 26, 1797, houses, farms, and agricultural implements to the value of not less than a milliard were destroyed (*Moniteur*, January 29, 1797 ; 'Tableau des Pertes causées par la Révolution,' by Sir Francis d'Ivernois, tome i., pp. 111, 112).

CHAPTER XC.

Tuesday, August 13, 1793.

In 1789, France, being called upon to choose men who were to lay its grievances and its wishes at the foot of the throne, elected the most worthy and meritorious representatives that could be found. Never, perhaps, had a political assembly contained so much talent and intelligence combined with courage, eloquence, and generous intentions. It may be urged that all these qualities did not produce the happy results which we had a right to expect, but it must not be forgotten that talents, intelligence, courage, eloquence and disinterestedness are now considered dangerous and mischievous when looked at by the light of those false principles which have induced the members of the Commune to wipe out the past, and to legislate, not for man as he is, the creation of God, but for the abstract being created by Rousseau.[1]

In the same way as the good fairies used to turn buttercups and daisies into diamonds and pearls by simply touching them with their wand, so has the Revolution, the most wicked of witches, turned all the virtues of the National Assembly into vices. Deplorable as the transformation has been, we ought not to forget that the majority of the members of that Assembly had good intentions, and that many of them made good use of their talents. If they have, alas! overthrown the Monarchy—if they have brought about a Revolution when they only wished to institute reforms—they have at least shed incomparable brilliancy upon the last days of *la vieille France.* An assembly

[1] See Taine, ' La Révolution,' tome i., p. 277.

that numbered in its ranks such men as Mirabeau, Maury, Barnave, Cazalès, Malouet, Clermont - Tonnerre, Chapelier, Sieyès, Mounier, Montesquiou, Lally - Tolendal, Thouret, Lafayette, Boisgelin, Merlin de Douai, Talleyrand-Périgord, Bergasse, Bailly, Duport, and Lameth, could not fail to leave a great impression behind it.

From the Constituent to the Legislative Assembly the drop is a considerable one, and yet this second body contained many men of real merit. On the Right sat Jaucourt, Beugnot, Vaublanc, Ramond, Pastoret, Hua, Becquey, Quatremère, Dumas, and Girardin. On the Left were Vergniaud, Guadet, Brissot, Isnard, Lasource, Gensonné, and Condorcet.

Great as the drop was from the Constituent to the Legislative Assembly, the drop from the latter body to the Convention was still greater. Though there are a few members of the Constituent Assembly in the Convention, they are all men of inferior ability. Men like Robespierre, Petion, Buzot and Barère, who were to play the principal parts in the new Legislature, scarcely counted in the National Assembly. Robespierre, with his harsh voice, faulty pronunciation, and disorderly flow of language, could not be expected to shine in a company of trained orators.[1] By the side of Mirabeau, the Torch of Provence, the Candle of Arras threw but a feeble light. Robespierre enjoyed some slight success for the first time on May 30, 1791 ; but his language was more smart than eloquent, and after commencing well he soon relapsed into his usual hash of words.[2] To-day he reigns almost supreme in the Convention. Since the removal of Vergniaud, Guadet, Gensonné, Lasource and Lanjuinais on June 2, that Assembly has but a single orator worthy of the name. Danton's language may be unequal, cynical, and even brutal ; but it is frequently lit up with flashes of eloquence. He may be only the Mirabeau of the pot-house and the street, but, like Mirabeau, he is at times sublime. After him there is nothing. The few men of talent whom we see on the benches of an assembly that has cowered beneath Marat, and applauds

---

[1] 'Mémoires de Meillan'; 'Mémoires de Durand de Maillane'; Lacretelle, 'Dix Années d'Épreuves pendant la Révolution.'
[2] 'Mémoires de Malouet,' tome ii., p. 135.

Robespierre, maintain an obstinate but prudent reserve. Merlin of Douai, the great lawyer whom the Convention has inherited from the Constituent Assembly, only speaks in support of the most cowardly motions. Taken as a whole, the Legislative Body is incurably mediocre. A good example of its capabilities was furnished by the Constitution of June 24, which is the most impracticable and unwieldy scheme that it is possible to imagine.

The National Convention can, however, lay just claim to superiority in one particular. It has understood better than its predecessors that the people are ready to forgive anything in those who amuse them, that they will submit to the worst form of despotism without a murmur, provided that in exchange for their liberty they are given plenty of sights. What sights could be better than the execution of Louis XVI. and that of Charlotte Corday? What shows could be finer than the funeral of Michel Lepeletier and the burial of Marat? What dramatic spectacle has ever equalled that of the festival of the Tenth of August?

The anniversary of the fall of the Monarchy had been chosen as the day on which the French people were to accept the Constitution of June 24.

In accordance with the programme drawn up by David, the festival commenced at daybreak. In the report adopted by the Committee of Public Instruction, and laid before the National Convention on July 11 last, the great painter had expressed himself in the following terms :

' All Frenchmen who wish to celebrate the Festival of Unity and of Indivisibility will rise before the dawn, so that the touching scene of their gathering may be illumined by the sun's first rays ; that beneficent luminary whose light extends over the whole universe will be for them the symbol of truth to which they will address their songs of praise.'[1]

At the appointed hour the National Convention, the delegates of the primary assemblies, the constituted authorities of Paris, the political clubs, and the people, had assembled on the site of the Bastille. The ruins of the old fortress were covered with the following inscriptions :

[1] *Moniteur*, July 15, 1793.

'An old man has shed many bitter tears on this stone.' 'I
have been dying here for the past forty-four years.' 'My virtues
brought me here.' 'The betrayer of my wife cast me into this
cell.' 'Light has never shone upon this stone.' 'My avaricious
children buried me here.' 'Sleep has fled from me for ever.'
'They have covered my face with an iron mask.' 'Sartine smiled
at my misfortunes.' 'I was forgotten.' 'Lasciate ogni speranza,
voi ch'entrate.' 'Oh, my friend!' 'I have been chained to
this stone for forty years.' 'Hell must have vomited kings and
priests.' 'They crushed my faithful spider before my eyes.'
'My children—oh, my children!'

Amid the ruins of the Bastille there rose the fountain of
Regeneration, being a colossal statue of Nature, around the base
of which ran the words : 'We are all Nature's children.' From
the breasts of the statue spurted forth into a vast ornamental
basin two jets of sparkling water, an emblem of Nature's inexhaustible fecundity. Hérault-Séchelles, the President of the
Convention, strode up to the fountain, and apostrophized it as
follows :

'O Nature, Sovereign both of savage man and of civilized
nations! this immense people gathered together before your
image at the first rays of the dawn is worthy of thee—it is free.
O Nature! may the expression of the eternal attachment of
Frenchmen to thy laws be acceptable to thee, and may this
beneficent water which gushes from thy breasts, may this pure
beverage with which our first parents quenched their thirst, con-
secrate in this cup of Fraternity and Equality the oaths which
France will take on this, the fairest day that has ever dawned.'

The President then took a superb agate goblet,[1] and having
filled it with water from the fountain, besprinkled the pedestal
of the statue. He then drank, and the cup was passed to the
eldest member in each of the eighty-seven deputations from the
primary assemblies. Their names were called out in alpha-
betical order, with a flourish of trumpets, and as each delegate

---

[1] At the sitting of August 16, 1793, the Convention, on the motion of
Lakanal, decreed that the cup used at the ceremony of the regeneration
on the Tenth of August was to be placed in the National Museum, with
an inscription recording the sublime use to which it had been put
(*Moniteur*, August 17).

drank, a salvo of artillery announced the consummation of this act of brotherhood.

When this part of the ceremony was concluded, a general discharge of artillery gave the signal for the procession to start. It proceeded along the Boulevards in the following order :

First came the political clubs in a body, and carrying a banner on which the Eye of Vigilance was represented piercing a thick cloud.

Then followed the National Convention. Eight of its members carried an open ark containing the Declaration of the Rights of Man and the Act of Constitution, and every deputy had in his hand a bunch of corn and some fruit. They were surrounded by the delegates of the departments, who were bound to each other by a light tricolour ribbon, thus forming a kind of chain round the Convention.

The delegates of the primary assemblies, to the number of about 8,000, carried a pike in one hand and an olive branch in the other.[1]

After them there was no distinction of persons or functionaries, and no particular order or regularity was observed in the procession. Members of the Executive Council and of the Commune, municipal officers wearing their tricolour sashes, judges clad in black, and wearing their Henri IV. hats adorned with black plumes—all mingled with the vast crowd.

Here and there, however, were to be found a few distinct groups—the pupils of the Institution for the Blind, seated on a rolling platform ; the babes from the Foundling Hospital borne along in white cradles ; an old man and his wife seated on a barrow, and drawn along by their children ; some printers' men carrying a press inscribed with the words : ' There is no liberty without it.' Over a number of representations and attributes of arts, sciences, trades and popular virtues floated a banner with these words in gigantic letters :

' SUCH IS THE SERVICE WHICH INDEFATIGABLE LABOUR RENDERS TO SOCIETY.'

A group of soldiers preceded in triumphal fashion a chariot

[1] Danton's speech in the Convention on August 12, 1793 (*Moniteur*, August 14).

drawn by eight white horses, and containing an urn in which had been deposited the ashes of those heroes who had died for their country. Around this funeral car there were no marks of mourning, no hangings of black, no muffled drums, and no cypress wreaths; on the contrary, the relatives of the heroes who accompanied it bore garlands of bright-coloured flowers, whilst a military band played its most enlivening strains.

A little farther on came a detachment of infantry and cavalry, and in their midst was a tumbrel laden with the attributes of Monarchy and aristocracy—a tumbrel similar to that in which the condemned are taken to the scaffold, and bearing this inscription :

'IT IS THESE WHICH HAVE ALWAYS BROUGHT MISFORTUNE UPON SOCIETY.'

The procession passed in this order along the Boulevard Poissonnière, where a triumphal arch had been erected to commemorate the events of October 5 and 6. On one side of this structure were the words : 'The people rushed in upon them like a torrent—they disappeared.' On the other : 'The tyrants were driven out like beasts of prey.' There were also inscriptions running: 'The people's justice is terrible !' 'But its mercy is great !'

A peculiar feature in this triumphal arch were the paintings representing the heads of those body-guards who had been massacred at Versailles. Under the arch were the heroines of October 5 and 6, seated on their guns, some carrying olive-branches and others bearing trophies. Stopping before them, the President of the Convention cried : 'What a glorious sight is this ! Here we have the weakness of woman allied to heroism ! O Liberty ! these are thy miracles ! When the crimes of the Kings were about to be expiated with blood in the courts of Versailles, it was Liberty which inflamed the hearts of a few women to drive out or kill the satellites of the tyrant ! O women ! Liberty attacked by a host of tyrants has need of a whole nation of heroes—it is your duty to produce them ! Instead of the flowers which adorn beauty, the representatives of the sovereign people offer you these laurels, which are an emblem of courage and victory; you will keep them, and hand them down to your children.' With these words Hérault-Séchelles gave them a fraternal kiss, and placed upon the head of each a wreath of laurel; the procession then resumed its course along the Boulevards amidst renewed enthusiasm.

The Place de la Révolution had been fixed upon for the third halting-place. On the remains of the pedestal of Louis XV.'s statue a plaster figure of Liberty had been set up. It was surrounded by a few young oaks and poplars, the branches of which bent beneath the weight of different tributes offered to the goddess, consisting of red caps, tricolour ribbons, songs, inscriptions and pictures. At the feet of the statue was an immense stake on which lay the attributes of Monarchy, and standing between the stake and the statue Hérault-Séchelles delivered his third speech:

' Here it was that the blade of the law struck down the Tyrant. Let them be also destroyed, these shameful insignia of a slavery which despots have sought to perpetuate in every shape and form! Let the flames devour them! Let justice and vengeance, the tutelary divinities of free nations, bring execration for ever upon the name of the wretch who, seated on a throne supported by generosity, basely betrayed the confidence of a magnanimous people! Let the pike and the cap of Liberty, the plough and the ear of corn, and the emblems of every trade by which society is enriched and embellished, henceforth be the only heraldry of the Republic! Sacred soil! yield in abundance those gifts which may be shared by all men, and be sterile in all that can only serve for the exclusive enjoyment of pride!'

Then, taking a lighted torch, Hérault-Séchelles set fire to the stake; throne, crown and sceptre, lilies, escutcheons and arms— all were destroyed by the crackling flames. As the fire burst their bonds, 3,000 birds flew up like living sparks from the stake, each having round its neck a tricolour ribbon bearing these words : ' We are free—be like us!'

The fourth halt was made in front of the Invalides. On the summit of a rock in the middle of the esplanade stood a colossal statue representing *The French People crushing Federalism.*

The inscription ran : 'Aristocracy has appeared under a hundred different forms, but the almighty people has everywhere crushed it.'

After a fourth speech from Hérault-Séchelles, who heaped curses upon the monster of Federalism, the procession wended its way to the Champ de Mars, where the last halt was to be made. Here stood two figures symbolical of Liberty and Equality, and holding between them a tricolour ribbon from which hung a huge plane—the national plane which was to bring all men to the same level.

The members of the National Convention, and the eighty-seven delegates from the departments, as well as those sent by the primary assemblies, mounted the steps of the national altar, whilst an immense crowd filled the vast extent of the Champ de Mars. Standing on the highest step of the altar, and supported by the oldest delegate present, Hérault-Séchelles proclaimed the result of the votes taken in the primary assemblies, that result being the unanimous acceptance of the Constitution by the eighty-seven departments. 'A year ago,' he cried, 'our territories were occupied by the foe ; we proclaimed the Republic, and we were victorious. Now, whilst we are laying the foundations of a new France, Europe attacks us on all sides ; let us swear to defend the Constitution to the death, for the Republic is eternal !' As the President of the Convention deposited the Act of Constitution and the returns of the national vote in the ark, which was now resting on the altar of the country, the cannon thundered forth a salute, and the spectators redoubled their shouts of joy.

The eighty-seven delegates of the departments, each of whom had carried a pike in the procession, then stepped forward and handed these weapons to Hérault-Séchelles, who bound them up into one great bundle with a tricolour band. Again the cannon rent the air to celebrate an act consecrating the unity and indivisibility of the Republic in the eyes of the people.

Descending the steps of the altar, the members of the Convention proceeded across the Champ de Mars to the temple erected to receive the ashes of the soldiers who fell in the defence of the Republic.

As the funeral urn was deposited in the vestibule of the temple, the members of the Convention, who had taken up their places under the colonnade, uncovered; their example was followed by all the spectators, and a deep silence reigned. Placing one hand upon the sacred vessel, and holding in the other the laurel wreath brought in honour of the dead warriors, the President spoke as follows:

'Let us conclude this glorious day by taking a solemn farewell of our brethren who have fallen in battle. Dear and precious remains of brave and dauntless men! I respectfully salute you, and I embrace this sacred urn in the name of the French people, placing upon it the wreath of laurel with which the country and the National Convention have entrusted me. Your memory does not inspire us with grief, and therefore we do not weep; we would rather honour you with our admiration, and more especially by following your example. Dear citizens! true-hearted warriors! we will be worthy of you; we will earn your praise by avenging you. We will come and tell you that our hands have completed your work; that the weapons you left us were invincible; that we have seen the triumph of that Republic which was strong enough to cope with every tyrant, and to defy a whole combination of vile passions and degraded nations—of that Republic which has embraced the cause of humanity, and whose aim it is to save the world!'

The festival concluded with a fraternal banquet, followed by singing and dancing, and at ten o'clock there was a performance of a military tableau entitled 'The Bombardment of the Town of Lille.'

I am not one of those who are enthusiastic about this festival, but it would be childish not to admit that as a whole it was grand and imposing, and that its dramatic pomp was not without a beauty of its own. The last part, consecrated to the memory of the soldiers who died for their country, affected me deeply. Hérault-Séchelles did full justice to his part; at times he was really eloquent, and surpassed even Robespierre himself. The Republic, however, is still a hateful thing to me, and the water which flows from the breasts of the statue of Nature will not wash out the blood with which it is stained.

Wednesday, August 14, 1793.

I have just learnt that on Friday last, on the eve of the festival, Petion's wife and child—the latter a boy of ten years old—were taken to the prison of Saint-Pélagie. On the occasion of the festival of the Federation of 1792, a year ago, the delegates of the departments fraternized with the people of Paris, and crowded, as they did but a few days since, around the altar of the country in the Champ de Mars. The performance then given was much the same, and so were the actors, with a few exceptions; the enthusiasm, too, was quite as great. A year ago, however, the people were shouting 'Vive Petion! Vive le Roi Petion!' A few days before that—on the Tenth of August, 1792—*King* Petion, the Mayor of Paris, though entrusted with the maintenance of public order, had become the accomplice of the lawless conspirators, and delivered Louis XVI. into their hands. Where is Petion to-day? In 1792 the people were enthusiastically shouting 'Petion or Death!' On Saturday last they were furiously shouting 'Death to Petion!' Impeached and outlawed, he is hiding that head now claimed by the guillotine, and the eve of the festival of the Tenth of August is chosen as a fitting day on which to drag his wife and child to the prison cells. When Mme. Petion arrived at Saint-Pélagie, Mme. Roland, who has been detained there since June 24, met her with these words: 'When I kept you company in the Mairie on the last Tenth of August, and shared your anxiety, I little thought that we should spend the first anniversary of that day in Saint-Pélagie, and that the fall of the throne would lead to your own disgrace.'[1]

As Petion had been the hero of the *fête* of the Federation of 1792, so was Hérault-Séchelles the hero of the *fête* of the Constitution of 1793. Where will Hérault-Séchelles be in a year's time?[2]

[1] 'Mémoires de Mme. Roland,' p. 302. Mme. Petion and her son were liberated on December 9, 1794. Mme. Lefebvre, Petion's mother-in-law, who had come to Paris to plead with the Convention on behalf of her daughter and grandson, was awarded the honours of the sitting on September 8, 1793, arrested the next day and condemned to death, and executed on the 24th of the same month for alleged unpatriotic utterances' (Vatel, 'Charlotte Corday et les Girondins,' tome ii., p. 259; H. Wallon, tome ii., p. 191).

[2] Hérault-Séchelles was guillotined on April 5, 1794.

Thursday, August 15, 1793.

BEAULIEU came to see me this morning, and I could not help telling him how deeply I had been impressed by the *fête* of the Tenth of August. 'Are you mad?' he cried, 'and are you also beginning to admire David's grand ballets? To what have we come if such displays inspire honest men like you with any other sentiment than that of indignation and contempt? These buffoons, after having proscribed their priests, have taken it into their heads to hold their religious festivals all the same, and some of them seriously propose that we shall adore the sun, whilst others suggest that we should worship Nature. David wishes us to address our songs of praise to the beneficent luminary which sheds its light over the whole earth and which should be to us a symbol of truth.

'Hérault-Séchelles invites us to bow down before Nature, " the sovereign of savage man and of civilized nations," to take oaths of fidelity, and to swear eternal attachment to that power !

'And what of the triumphal arch in the Boulevard Poissonnière? I will pass over this glorification of the horrible deeds of October, and will say nothing of the honour paid to women for the part they took in the massacre, but I cannot forgive David his monstrous idea of decorating his triumphal arch with paintings in which we see the heads of the body-guards who were murdered at Versailles.[1] The idea is no doubt worthy of

---

[1] Beaulieu, 'Essais Historiques sur les Causes et les Effets de la Révolution,' tome v., p. 468 'This trophy, worthy of the ogres of whom we read in fairy tales, was left standing for more than a year after its erection. The Parisians were so accustomed to all these sights that they paid them no attention.'

the bosom-friend of Marat, but in my eyes it is sufficient to
tarnish the brilliancy of the *fête* which arouses your enthusiasm !
Was it not also a monstrous idea to have chosen for the site of
one of the *altars* the spot on which the scaffold was erected on
January 21, on which so many innocent victims have been
despatched, and on which but a few days before the blood of a
poor gendarme had been spilt ?[1] I know what you are going to
say . . . .'

As a matter of fact, I was not going to say anything at all,
but he was wound up, and went on without waiting to see
whether I wished to speak or not :

'It may have appeared to you that the fourth halting-place,
that of the Invalides, was the most inoffensive of all. The
colossal plaster statue that stood there holding in one hand the
fasces of the departments, and aiming a deadly blow at the
monster of Federalism with the other, formed a very ugly
group, the significance of which, however, was not to be mistaken. The people took it in at a glance, and when Hérault-
Séchelles uttered these words, " Citizens, you must treat those
who wish to divide you in the same way as those who seek to
crush you," they were not content to applaud, but clamoured
furiously for the death of the Twenty-two members—of Brissot,
Vergniaud, and their imprisoned colleagues.

'I grant you that the fifth act was less offensive ; it was set
in a magnificent frame, and with befitting scenery. The first of
the two tableaux of which this act was composed was a marvel
of stage management. The proclamation of the new law from
the summit of the national altar as from another Sinai ; the
sacred ark receiving the records of the nation's votes ; the
delegates of the primary assemblies mounting the steps of the
altar to testify to the people's will ; Hérault-Séchelles' utterance : " Never has a greater Republic proclaimed its will more
unanimously "—all this was thoroughly dramatic, and that you
know as well as I do.

'Whether the scene with which the proceedings terminated,

---

[1] The gendarme Jonas was guillotined August 7, 1793. He had been
condemned for having spoken disrespectfully of the Convention in a *café*
a few months before (*Bulletin du Tribunal Révolutionnaire*, No. 80).

and which moved you to tears, was more seriously meant than the farce of the people's will and its unanimity is open to doubt. In this David certainly surpassed himself. The sepulchral temple, the sacred urn, the *dear remains*, the classic colonnade under which the members of the National Convention stood like so many poets in Elysium, the enormous crowd with upturned faces come to honour their dead, was, I must confess, a scene well calculated to appeal to the imagination, excite enthusiasm, and move all hearts. Your emotion was pardonable, but you must not think badly of me for not having shared it. When I saw Hérault-Séchelles—that fine gentleman who now belongs to the Mountain, this Sybarite playing the Spartan —when I saw him embrace the urn of the martyred founders of Liberty, and water it with his tears, I could not repress my indignation.

' Our brethren and friends, our best and bravest, are dying on the frontiers for France ; and here mountebanks like Hérault-Séchelles and Collot-d'Herbois, cowards like Barère and Merlin, beggars like Amar and Bourdon, and sharpers like Delaunay and Fabre, trade upon their heroism, parade in the spoils that others have won, and cry : "Admire us, O ye people ! Love and bless that Republic which we have established for you, for which our soldiers have bled, and for which heroes and martyrs have given their lives !" They deck themselves with the shrouds of the brave men who have fallen on the field of battle, and they speak familiarly of victory who are only acquainted with fear ! They tell us that they founded and organized armies, when we know that it is their greatest pleasure to denounce our Generals, to cast them into prison, and to send them to the scaffold. Already in the month of May they guillotined General Miaczinski and Adjutant-General Devaux. Generals Dillon and Lamorlière are under lock and key, whilst General Beysser has just been summoned before the Committee of General Security, which is equal to being arrested.[1] General Lescuyer was guillotined yesterday,[2] and to-day the trial of General Custine will begin before the Revolutionary Tribunal !

---

[1] Beysser and Dillon were both guillotined April 13, 1794.
[2] *Bulletin du Tribunal Révolutionnaire*, No. 81.

'Such has been, and is, the work of the men who dared to speak of courage, patriotism, and freedom. On August 1 they decreed that all kinds of combustibles were to be sent to the Vendée in order to lay waste the woods and forests; that the crops were to be cut, the cattle seized, and the homes of the rebels destroyed. Incendiarism was the order of the day; whole departments were devastated by legislative measures, and amongst those deputies who dishonour our soldiers with their admiration not a single one rose to protest. The decree was passed without debate, and by a unanimous vote.[1]

'On the same day the Convention decreed that the property of all outlaws was to be confiscated by the Republic.

'On the same day it decreed that Marie Antoinette was to be taken to the Conciergerie, and brought before the Revolutionary Tribunal.

'On the same day it further decreed that the tombs of the Kings in the Church of Saint-Denis and in other places throughout the Republic were to be destroyed on the following Tenth of August.

'All these decrees were passed without debate, and by a unanimous vote,[2] at a sitting presided over by Danton, who on the preceding day had given utterance to the following theory of wholesale murder and massacre amidst the applause of the Assembly: "Be like Nature, which aims at the preservation of the species without considering individuals."[3]

'The sitting of August 1 had been the prologue of the festival of the Tenth, which again had its epilogue in the sitting of the 12th. On that day the delegates of the departments appeared at the bar of the Convention, and their spokesman declared that the moment had come to make the enemies of the people bite the dust; he therefore demanded the immediate arrest of all suspects. Hérault-Séchelles supported this demand in a few harmonious and well-turned phrases, similar to those

---

[1] *Moniteur*, August 2, 1793.

[2] *Mercure Français*, No. 106. In his 'Diurnal de la Révolution de France,' Beaulieu speaks of the sitting of August 1 in the following terms: 'The details of this sitting remind one of the deeds of a horde of maddened savages destroying the last remains of a costly temple.'

[3] *Moniteur*, August 1, 1793 : sitting of July 31.

which he had uttered two days before when presenting these same delegates with the holy cup of equality and fraternity as they stood grouped around the statue of Nature. Danton, too, congratulated the delegates of the primary assemblies upon having taken the initiative in turning the *Terror* against the internal foe in the National Assembly. " We will do as they wish," he cried ; " there shall be no amnesty for any traitor. The just man shows no mercy to the wicked. Let the blade of the law fall in vengeance upon the enemy within the camp." He concluded by supporting the demand for the arrest of all true suspects.

' Robespierre went one better than Danton. He deplored the indulgence extended to conspirators, and complained of the tardiness of the Revolutionary Tribunal. This austere citizen absolutely thirsts for justice. " We must stimulate the zeal of the Revolutionary Tribunal," he said ; " its verdicts should be returned within twenty-four hours after the proofs have been laid before it."[1] And then, without any shouts or furious gesticulations like Danton, but in a calm manner and a mincing voice, this kind man asked that much more active measures should be taken to unearth the plots woven at the instigation of the English Government ; that when once a man had been arrested and charged with conspiracy he should not be liberated on cowardly pretexts and frivolous considerations ; that when one committee had issued a warrant no other authority should be allowed to set it aside ; that France, its government, its administration, and its armies, should be purged of traitors ; that the Revolutionary Tribunal should be directed to try Custine within twenty-four hours ; that the Tribunal should likewise proceed to try without delay all the conspirators who had been impeached, and that all rogues and villains should be sacrificed to the shades of their innocent victims.[2]

' Having said so much, this paragon of humanity naïvely added that he had nothing to say concerning the other measures.[3]

' After Robespierre and Danton had spoken, the Convention

---

[1] *Moniteur*, August 14, 1793. [2] *Ibid*. [3] *Ibid*.

decreed that "all suspected persons were to be immediately arrested." '

Hereupon Beaulieu drew from his pocket and handed me the *Moniteur* of August 14, containing a full report of these proceedings, which were quite as execrable as those of August 1. After some time the worthy man continued : ' And yet there are some brave folk left in this France of ours, after all ! If there be nothing to equal the cowardice of these wretched deputies, what heroism do we find displayed by our Generals and soldiers on the frontiers ! What heroes these Vendean peasants are, dying for God and their King ! I do not know whether you have read the report drawn up by Gossuin in the name of the Commission charged with the collection of the returns relating to the acceptance of the Act of Constitution. It is there recorded as the most convincing proof of the wishes of the French people for a Republican form of government, that, out of the 44,000 communes of the Republic, the commune of Saint-Donan, in the department of the Côtes-du-Nord, was the only one which asked that the son of Capet should be placed upon the throne, and that the clergy should be reinstated.[1] That is true courage, *mon ami !* To face the bullets and to scale a redoubt is grand and heroic, but I am not sure whether it is not a proof of still greater heroism to remain faithful to one's faith and one's King when a whole nation bows to the tempest of error and crime.'

[1] Report laid before the Convention August 9, 1793 (*Moniteur*, August 12).

CHAPTER XCII.

THE SALON.

Thursday, August 22, 1793.

On August 8 David, the Academician, read to the Convention his impeachment of the academies—'the last stronghold of the aristocracy.' His attack was directed more particularly against his colleagues in the Academy of Painting—'a crowd of old men whose chronic state of lethargy has worn out all the seats in the institution, from the humblest stool to the presidential chair—enemies of progress, who prevent the rise of talent, and who present in all its ugliness a fair specimen of the animal called *Academician*.' Already in a weak and tottering state since 1779, the Academy of Painting and Sculpture could not resist this supreme attack. Its suppression was decreed.[1] Until 1789 the Salon of the Louvre was restricted to members of the Academy of Painting, Sculpture, and Architecture. The artists who were not Academicians could only exhibit for two hours on the morning of the eighth day after the festival of Corpus Christi in the open air in the Place Dauphine.[2] This privilege was abolished by the Constituent Assembly, which established the principal of free exhibition (an excellent thing when not abused). According to the wording of the decree passed in 1791, ' All native or foreign artists, whether they be members or not of the Academy of Painting and Sculpture, shall be permitted to exhibit their works in the exhibition held in the Louvre.'

[1] See 'L'Institut de France et les Anciennes Académies,' by M. Léon Aucoc. *Le Moniteur*, in its account of the sitting of August 8, 1793, does not mention David's speech or the suppression of the academies.

[2] ' Histoire de la Société Française pendant la Révolution,' by Edmond and Jules de Goncourt, p. 347.

The catalogue for this year contains 832 exhibits : 627 paintings and drawings, 181 pieces of sculpture, and 24 architectural subjects.   The number of exhibitors is 348.

David has sent nothing.   He has, indeed, promised to paint the death of Marat in the same way as he delineated that of Michel Lepeletier, but as yet he has only been able to make a sketch of his picture.   Those who have seen this sketch in his studio agree in saying that it promises to be a masterpiece.[1]

Failing David, who is more often in the Convention than in his studio at the Louvre, failing also Mme. Lebrun, Doyen and many other Academicians who have left the country, I find in the list of exhibitors the names of Vien, Suvée, Lethière, Bonvoisin, Taunay, Houdon, Monsiau, Boilly, Drolling, Roland, Chaudet, Duplessis, Isabey, Lagrenée the younger, Pajou junior, Taillasson, Bosio, Carle Vernet, Charpentier, Demarne, Robert, Chancourtois, Demachy, and Lespinasse.

Amongst the most noteworthy pictures were the ' Portrait of a Man ' and ' Portrait of a Woman,' by Prud'hon ; portraits by Drolling and Gautherot ; ' Jesus amongst the Learned Men,' by Taunay ; ' Orpheus ' and ' Eurydice,' by Lethière ; ' The Interior of a Palace at Rome,' by Robert ; ' Hunting in English Fashion,' by Carle Vernet ; ' The Death of Seneca,' by Lefevre ; ' Amor and Psyche,' by Lagrenée the younger ; ' Helen,' by J. B. Vien ; and ' Endymion,' by Girodet.   Vien's picture represents ' Helen pursued by Æneas in the Temple of Vesta,' where she has taken refuge, and is saved by Venus, who holds back the arm of her son.   This picture would have been the success of the Salon if Girodet, a young débutant, had not carried all before him with his painting of ' Endymion.'   His canvas only contains a single figure—that of the hunter sleeping in the woods.   The moonlight shining through the branches of the trees falls full upon him, and its rays are so soft and caressing that they seem to be

---

[1] It was not until November 14, 1793, that David presented the Convention with his painting of ' The Assassination of Marat.'   The Convention decreed that the honours of the Pantheon were to be awarded to the Friend of the People, and that the pictures of Lepeletier and Marat, painted by David, and presented by him to the nation, were to be placed in the Legislative Chamber (*Moniteur*, November 16, 1793).

the very breath of Diana, the goddess of the forests, who is in love with the young Nimrod.

Girodet, a pupil of David's, is only twenty-six years old.[1] He was awarded the grand prize of Rome in 1789 for his picture of 'Joseph making himself known to his Brothers.' His 'Endymion' is the painted figure-study which every pupil of the Villa Médicis is obliged to send to Paris. Another pupil of David's, François Gérard,[2] only twenty-three years of age, has also exhibited a canvas full of promise; it is Daniel's judgment on the chaste Suzannah, and is remarkable for the delicacy of its drawing and the freshness of its colouring.

The subjects borrowed from the Old and the New Testament are less numerous than in preceding years. I have, however, found about a score, amongst which are three good pictures by Taunay: 'Abraham and the Three Angels,' 'Ruth and Boaz,' and 'Jesus amongst the Learned Men.' I will also mention 'Moses taken from the Water,' by Lagrenée the younger; 'The Annunciation,' by Bosio; 'The Death of Joseph,' by Bonvoisin; 'Jesus Christ in the House of Martha and Mary,' by Lélu; 'The Burial of Jesus,' by the same painter; and the 'Mission of the Apostles,' by Lemonnier.

The scarcity of religious subjects is compensated for by the abundance of mythological ones. Never have I seen so many Amors and Psyches. We have 'The School of Love,' by Dupuis-Pepin; 'The Nest of Love,' by Frédéric Shall; 'Love and Folly,' by Monsiau; Désoria's 'Nymphs bathing surprised by Cupid'; 'Love and Psyche,' by Lagrenée the younger;

[1] Girodet de Coussy, better known as Girodet-Trioson, was born at Montargis, January 5, 1767, and died in Paris, December 9, 1824. His principal pictures are the 'Endymion,' 'Hippocrates refusing the Presents of the Ambassadors of the King of Persia,' the 'Scene of the Deluge,' the 'Burial of Atala,' and 'Pygmalion and Galatea.'

[2] François Gérard was born at Rome in 1770, and died in Paris in 1807. Influenced by David, his master, whose behaviour during the Revolution was that of the vilest of Maratists—'the stupid David whom I formerly celebrated,' wrote André Chenier—Gérard was unfortunate enough to allow himself to be enrolled as a juryman of the Revolutionary Tribunal, and his name is to be found on the 'Liste des Juges et Jurés' drawn up on September 28, 1793. This, however, did not prevent him from becoming under the Restoration Painter-in-Ordinary to the King, a Baron, an officer of the Légion d'Honneur, and a Knight of Saint-Michel.

Fougeat's 'Psyche sleeping abducted by Zephyr'; 'Psyche taken to the Rock,' by Chevreux; Vallain's 'Ceyx and Halcyon'; 'Hercules overcoming the Lion,' by Lejeune; Neveu's 'Ariadne Abandoned'; Bonvoisin's 'Eurydice given up to Orpheus'; 'Œdipus liberated from the Tree by a Shepherd'—the figures in which are by Lethière, and the landscape by Bidault.

The 'Iliad' and the 'Æneid' have inspired numerous paintings: 'Achilles recognised by Ulysses' and 'Achilles restoring Briseis to Agamemnon's Envoys,' by Désoria; 'Hector on his Death-bed, with Andromache and Astyanax his Son bewailing his Fate,' by Bosio; 'Venus wounded by Diomedes,' 'Polymenes sacrificed by Pyrrhus,' 'Ajax struck by the Lightning,' and 'The Death of Dido,' all by Lélu; and Bonvoisin's 'Æneas held back by Creusa his Wife.'

It was Mascarille's idea to write the whole of Roman history in madrigals. Since David painted his 'Socrates about to drink the Hemlock,' his 'Brutus,' and his 'Oath of the Horatii,' we are in a fair way to see the whole of Roman and Greek history put on canvas. In the Salon of 1793 we can see 'Tarquin and Lucrece,' by Tardieu; 'The Death of Virginia' and 'Cæsar crossing the Bosphorus,' by Lélu; 'Cornelia, the Mother of the Gracchi,' by Bosio; 'The Brave Deed of Hasdrubal's Wife killing her Children on seeing her Husband's cowardly surrender to the Conqueror of Carthage,' by Bonvoisin; the 'Death of Seneca,' by Lefevre; and an immense canvas by Taillasson bearing the following superscription: 'Pauline, the wife of Seneca, not wishing to survive her husband, cuts open her veins. Nero, hearing of her resolve, issues an order for her to be saved. She is already unconscious, but the blood is stopped, and she is restored to life.' There are two Lacedemonian pictures, one by Perrin, the other by Naigeon, the catalogue indicating the subject of the first in the following words: 'A Spartan assembly is discussing the question whether the women and children should be sent out of the town before it is attacked by Pyrrhus. A woman enters the assembly, and, speaking on behalf of her companions, offers to fight for the Republic.' The following is the subject of Naigeon's picture: 'A Lacedemonian woman, seeing her son killed at her feet at the siege of a town, cries, "Call his brother to replace him!"' The picture shows the brother appearing on the scene.

These two pictures by Naigeon and Perrin attract a good deal of attention, as does also 'Archimedes occupied in solving a Problem during the Siege of Syracuse,' by Chaudet, one of our greatest sculptors, who has for once deserted the clay for the pallet.

But the crowd is thickest—and this is but natural—around the patriotic scenes, amongst which are 'The Taking of the Bastille,' by Thévenin; 'The Festival of the Sans-Culottes amidst the Ruins of the Bastille,' by Pourcelli; 'The Federation of the French on the Fourteenth of July, 1790,' by Demachy; 'The Siege of the Tuileries by the Brave Sans-Culottes,' by Desfonts; 'The Tenth of August, 1792,' by Berthaud; 'The Sacrifice to the Country, or the Departure of a Volunteer,' by Malet; 'Setting out for the Front,' by Petit-Coupray; 'The Death of Beaurepaire,' by Desfonts; 'The Attack on a Village,' by Berthaud; and two canvases by Duplessis representing 'The Halt of an Army.' For these two small pictures I would give nearly all the immense canvases that fill the Salon.

There is fighting on our frontiers, and wholesale slaughter in many parts of the country. On leaving the Louvre, whether we go by the quays or by the Rue Saint-Honoré, we are liable to meet the tumbrel carrying the victims of the Revolutionary Tribunal to the scaffold, and yet there are many tender hearts that are moved by the sentimental works of Trinquesse and Garnier, entitled 'The Good Mother' and 'Maternal Cares,' and by similar pictures. There is also a 'Paul and Virginia,' and it would be interesting to know whether Bernardin de Saint-Pierre has visited the Salon and seen the painting whose subject is borrowed from his novel. Louis XVI. had appointed him Director of the Jardin des Plantes and of the Cabinet d'Histoire Naturelle, but, thanks to the Republic, he is no longer anything, not even an Academician, and is preparing to leave Paris for Essonne. The other day he said to one of his friends:

' In giving up my post I hope that I may be allowed to end my days in a cottage.'[1]

Neither 'Paul weeping for Virginia' nor 'The Lesson for Young Mothers' can make us forget for long the horrible realities that surround us, for here and there we come across the portraits of some of our principal Revolutionaries like hideous reminders.   Here is Sainte-Huruge, by Ducreux ; here, painted by the same artist, Laveaux, President of the Criminal Tribunal of August 17.   Here are the members of the Convention, Dubois-Crancé, Quinette, Hérault-Séchelles, Lacroix, the elder Delaunay and Jean Debry—all painted by Laneuville, whilst Maure has sat to Gautherot, Mallarmé to Bonville, and Couthon to Ducreux.   The last-named artist has also had the honour of painting Robespierre.   The portrait of the deputy for Paris is slightly flattered, but it is a very fair one on the whole.   The eyes are deep and clear, the forehead high and somewhat protruding, the nose a little tipped, the mouth well drawn, and the chin boldly accentuated.   In the matter of dress, Robespierre has made no concessions to the new principles ; his hair is powdered, and he wears lace frills and cuffs like a member of the old aristocracy.[2]   We have already had two portraits of him in the Salon of 1791—one by Mme. Guyard, an Academician, and the other by Boze.   The first bore the inscription 'The Incorruptible,'[3] and underneath the second had been written some verses on a sheet of paper which had gradually become longer as each patriotic poet added his quota.[4]   In 1793 the Muse of Poetry is silent ; the hour is not fitted for pretty rhymes.   If there be any still made, they are reserved for the divine Marat.

Hauer, the artist who painted Charlotte Corday's portrait during the trial, exhibits 'The Death of Marat.'   Amongst the

---

[1] 'Essais sur la Vie et les Ouvrages de Bernardin de Saint-Pierre,' by L. Aimé-Martin, p. 230.

[2] There is rather a large number of portraits of Robespierre, the most remarkable being those painted by Boze, Mme. Guyard, Ducreux, David, and Gérard.   The Department of Prints of the Bibliothèque Nationale possesses about forty engraved portraits.   See Ernest Harmel, 'Histoire de Robespierre,' tome iii., p. 295.

[3] *Révolutions de Paris*, tome x., p. 127.

[4] *Feuille du Jour*, October, 1791 ; 'Histoire de la Société Française pendant la Révolution,' by Edmond and Jules de Goncourt, p. 337.

sculptures I find two busts of the People's Friend, one by Beauvallet, the other by Feneau.

Michel Lepeletier is even better represented than Marat himself. Of that martyr the Salon contains a portrait bust by Deseine, a deaf-mute, another by Fessier, and a third by Florion ; a recumbent figure representing 'Michel Lepeletier on his Death-bed writing his Last Words '(!), by Citoyenne Desfonds ; and a Saint-Fargeau, a small allegorical model in terra-cotta by Citoyenne Charpentier.

The honours of the Salon, however, are carried off by Jean Jacques Rousseau. Whilst Voltaire has only a single statue, executed by the deaf-mute Deseine, Jean Jacques has five or six in marble, in plaster, and in terra-cotta. One by Ricourt shows him holding in his hand the *Contrat Social* as the basis of the Constitution. A group by Racarit represents 'Time and Philosophy erecting a Statue to Rousseau crowned by the Genius of Liberty.' Amongst the pictures there are at least three which are devoted to him. Voltaire was the hero of the Constituent Assembly, where he sat amongst the Blacks.[1] Rousseau is the hero of the Convention, and would have had a seat on the Mountain.

In spite of the example set by David, the painters are decidedly less Republican than the sculptors. The reason of this may be that outside the Government there is no one left to buy busts and statues ; hence all these patriotic masses of plaster—'Liberty and Equality,' by Berthélemy ; the bust of

---

[1] When the Constituent Assembly established itself in the Riding-School of the Tuileries, the former use to which the place had been put suggested fresh appellations for the members of the Assembly. On the Right sat many ecclesiastics, and all on that side were therefore baptized ' Blacks ' (black horses). The Blacks retorted by calling their adversaries ' Greys,' and afterwards ' Bays.' As neither of the latter names seemed to find favour, the deputies of the Right hit upon the idea of calling the members of the Left the ' Rabids '—this was the name given to the hired horses which were generally used for short journeys, in order to avoid the expense of the Royal post. The name soon came into popular use. In *L'Ami du Peuple* Marat never ceased to shower invectives upon the Blacks and the arch-Blacks. Camille Desmoulins followed his example in the *Révolutions de France et de Brabant*. It is from the latter that I take the following lines, which appeared in No. 23, April, 1790 · ' We warn Messieurs the Blacks, the Aristocrats, the Impartials, the *ci-devant* Nobles, the members of the Clergy and of the Right, the Capucines, the Rabid Robinaucrats, and all other enemies of the Revolution.'

General Dampierre, by Collomar ; 'The Tenth of August,' in terra-cotta, by Morgan ; 'The Mountain,' in terra-cotta, by Beauvoillé ; a model for a triumphal column to be erected on the site of the Bastille, by Citoyenne Desfonds ; a full-length figure of Franklin, in terra-cotta, by Suzanne ; 'Liberty accompanied by Unity and Equality,' by the same artist ; 'A Republican upholding Unity and Equality,' a model in plaster, by Boisot ; 'Brutus taking an Oath to kill Cæsar,' by Dardel ; 'The Tenth of August represented by the Genius of France destroying the Crown and Sceptre,' by Van-Wayenberghe, who died on July 3 last, at the age of thirty-seven ; a model of a monument to be erected in gratitude to the Supreme Being and Liberty, by Jacob ; 'The Sovereign People,' a statue by Milot ; 'The Invincible Virtue of the Revolution,' by the same sculptor, who also exhibits a plaster statue of a priestess of Liberty crowning a wedded couple.

Danton is conspicuous by his absence ; he has made way for Robespierre and Marat. There is, however, a portrait-bust of his wife, the cast for which was taken a week after her death.

It is worthy of note that, of all the Republican works just mentioned, not a single one was created by an artist of any renown. Three sculptors of the first rank have exhibited this year, but all three have carefully eschewed politics. Chaudet, as I said before, painted 'Archimedes at Syracuse.' Roland sent a marble statue of Paris, whilst Houdon[1] exhibited no less than five works—a bust of a woman in bronze, a bust of a child in plaster, a Vestal, a statue of General Washington, and a masterly figure called 'La Petite Fileuse.'[2]

---

[1] Houdon (1741—1828) was denounced in 1794, being accused of the heinous crime of having the statue of a saint in his studio. His wife was alone when the Patriots of the quarter came to verify the accusation. Without betraying the slightest agitation, Mme. Houdon hastened to unveil the so-called seditious statue, and, taking advantage of the fact that it did not bear any particularly significant attribute, she boldly described it as a figure of Philosophy, as might be imagined by its gravity of expression and majestic attitude. The Patriots swallowed this explanation, and a few days later the saint left the studio of the artist for the place of honour in the vestibule of one of the public buildings ('Académie des Beaux Arts,' by Henri Delaborde).

[2] Houdon's 'Fileuse' is now in the possession of M. Ernest Legouvé, of the Académie Française.

Briefly, the Exhibition of 1793, in spite of a certain number of good pictures and noteworthy statues, is much inferior to that of 1791, and far below that of 1789. The first Salon of the Republic has opened its doors to all comers, it is true, but on the whole it smacks of mediocrity.[1]

---

[1] 'The Exhibition of 1791 was a very remarkable one.' 'Mediocrity is always numerous, *teste* the Exhibition of 1793' ('Essai sur les Moyens d'encourager la Peinture, la Sculpture, l'Architecture et la Gravure,' by J. B. P. Lebrun, pp. 6, 7).

CHAPTER XCIII.

THE LAST DAYS OF THE ACADÉMIE FRANÇAISE.

Saturday, August 24, 1793.

Poor Marat died too soon. He who hated Academicians as cordially as he did Kings and Queens did not live to see the destruction of the academies. Already in 1790 he wrote in the *Ami du Peuple:* 'The Académie des Belles-lettres and the Académie Française are pure luxuries—why should they be a charge upon the nation? I will go further, and add that the Académie Française is perfectly useless. Ought we, then, to allow a thousand poor labourers to die of hunger in order to maintain forty idlers, whose only function it is to chatter and to amuse themselves? For the well-being of arts and sciences it behoves us to get rid of academical bodies in France.' In his number of March 16, 1791, he wrote: 'In the eyes of the philosopher the academies are only institutions of luxury, monuments erected to the glory of Princes, a sort of menagerie in which are collected at great expense, like so many curious animals, the most famous quacks and pedants.'

The Friend of the People would therefore have hailed with applause the decree passed by the Convention on August 8 'suppressing all academies and literary societies hitherto licensed by the nation,' and thus abolishing by one stroke of the pen the Académie Française, the Académie des Belles-lettres, the Académie des Sciences, the Académie de Peinture et de Sculpture, the Académie d'Architecture, la Société d'Agriculture, the Académie de Chirurgie, and the Société de Médecine. It was the Abbé Grégoire who suggested this suppression in the name of the Committee of Public Instruction — the same

Grégoire who, in the course of a debate on the academies in the Constituent Assembly in August, 1790, declared that the usefulness of these institutions was manifest. And it was David, the painter, who, in 1785, was proud to be admitted to the Royal Academy of Painting, that now worked most zealously in bringing about its destruction.

Of all these institutions the most illustrious was the Académie Française, and from information furnished me by one of its members, I am enabled to write the last chapter of its history.

For some time past the number of the Academicians had greatly diminished; the Forty had become scarcely more than a dozen. The seats of the Abbé Radonvilliers and the Duc de Duras, who died in 1789; of M. de Guybert, who died in 1790; of M. de Rulhière, who died in 1791; of M. Séguier and of M. de Chabanon, who died in 1792; of the Maréchal de Beauveau, and of M. Lemierre, both of whom died in 1793, had not been filled. Cardinal de Bernis, the King's Minister at Rome, and Comte de Choiseul-Gouffier, the Ambassador to the Porte, have been kept out of France by the Revolution. The Duc d'Harcourt, the tutor of the Dauphin, has been compelled to take refuge in England with that branch of his family which has dwelt in Great Britain since the days of William the Conqueror. The Prince de Rohan has retired to that part of his principality situated on the right bank of the Rhine. The Abbé Maury, M. de Boisgelin, the Archbishop of Aix, and the Chevalier de Boufflers, members of the Constituent Assembly, emigrated at the end of 1791. M. d'Aguesseau was denounced as a Royalist in 1792, and since then we have been without news of him; M. de Montesquiou - Fezenzac fled to Switzerland after his impeachment; M. de Condorcet, impeached on July 8 of this year, has also left the capital. Another fugitive is Sylvain Bailly, a member of the Académie Française, of the Académie des Sciences, and of that of Inscriptions and Belles-lettres. M. de Nicolaï, President of the Chambre des Comptes, and M. de Roquelaure, Bishop of Senlis, and the King's chief Almoner, are in prison. M. de Malesherbes, the defender of Louis XVI.; M. de Loménie de Brienne, Archbishop of Sens; the Duc de Nivernais, M. de Florian, Comte de Bissy, M. de Saint-Lambert, and M. Marmontel, Permanent Secretary to the Academy, have all left Paris for different parts of the country.

There are, therefore, certainly not more than a dozen Academicians left in the capital, and these are La Harpe, Chamfort, Sedaine, Target, Gaillard, De Bréquigny, the Abbé Delille, Barthélemy, Vicq-d'Azyr, Ducis, Suard, and Morellet.

Until August 5 last the weekly meetings continued to take place with almost unfailing regularity, but it must be understood that these assemblies were very different from those held before 1789. Politics had banished all conversation ; there was no longer any talking—it was all quarrelling. The Revolutionaries were in a minority, and this was undoubtedly the only assembly in Paris in which such a state of things could be found to exist. On the side of the Revolution were Chamfort, La Harpe, Sedaine, Ducis, and Target ; opposed to them were Gaillard, the Abbé Delille, De Bréquigny, Suard, Morellet, Vicq-d'Azyr, and Barthélemy—seven against five.[1]

At their meeting of August 5 they unanimously agreed to suspend their sittings. On June 24 last Morellet had been elected Rector, and Vicq-d'Azyr Chancellor. Morellet will therefore have had the honour of being the last Rector of the Academy—an honour which he fully merited both by his courage and his presence of mind under trying circumstances.

In conformity with the decree ordering the abolition of all tokens of royalty and nobility, such as crowns, lilies, and coats-of-arms, some workmen were sent to the Louvre at the end of July to make a clean sweep of all these vestiges of feudalism and aristocracy.[2] They mutilated the panels of the doors and the apartments, destroyed the pictures by Rigaud and Lebrun which adorned the grand hall of the Académie des Inscriptions, effaced the portrait and name of Louis XIV., and tore down the tapestries that were studded with the royal lilies of France.[3]

---

[1] 'Mémoires sur le XVIII. Siècle et sur la Révolution Française,' by l'Abbé Morellet, tome ii., p. 52.

[2] After the death of the Chancellor Séguier, in 1672, Louis XIV. became the patron of the Académie Française, and since then it had held its sittings in the Louvre ('Histoire de l'Académie Française,' by Paul Mesnard, p. 26).

[3] 'Mémoires de Morellet,' tome ii., p. 55.

The hall of the Académie Française was evidently about to be
subjected to similar outrages. Morellet thought it better not
to wait for the Revolutionary workmen, but to forestall them
by saving as much as possible. He was the Rector, and in the
absence of M. Marmontel, who had been gone for more than a
year, he was also discharging the duties of the Secretary. He
therefore considered himself fully entitled and obliged to use
every effort for the preservation of the objects entrusted to his
care.

The property of the Académie included about eighty portraits
of Academicians; full-length portraits of Richelieu and of
Chancellor Séguier; about twenty busts and medallions; a
library of 500 or 600 volumes, consisting of dictionaries,
grammars, and other works by members of the Académie;
finally the papers of the Institution, the Act relating to its
establishment in 1635, and a full and continuous report of its
transactions, as well as of all its immediate relations with our
Kings.[1]

Morellet commenced by taking down all the portraits and
piling them up in one of the galleries of the hall in which the
public assemblies were held.[2] Having accomplished this, he did
not hesitate to carry to his own house the whole of the Archives
of the Académie and the manuscript of the Dictionary.

A few days later, soon after the decree of August 8 had been
passed, the doors of the apartments in the Louvre, occupied by
the academies, were sealed up. It is unnecessary to add that
none of the officers of the institutions whose property was thus
seized were invited to witness this act, but one evening Morellet
received a visit from the Suisse of the Académie, who had been
ordered to tell him that the Commissioners were coming to
break the seals the next morning. On proceeding to the
Louvre at the appointed time, he found himself in the presence

---

[1] 'Récit fait à la Seconde Classe de l'Institut, sur la Manière dont les
Titres et les Registres de l'Académie Française ont été conservés dans la
Révolution, par M. l'Abbé Morellet, pour être replacés dans la Bibliothèque de l'Institut,' read in public assembly on March 6, 1805, on the
occasion of M. Lacretelle's reception.

[2] These portraits were found in 1804, and replaced by the care of two
members of the Institut, MM. Lacuée and Raymond ('Mémoires de
Morellet,' tome ii., p. 56).

of Dorat-Cubières, Secretary and Registrar of the Commune,
and of the grammarian Domergue,[1] both equally hostile to the
Académie Française. The two Commissioners treated the unhappy Rector in the most democratic manner possible, telling
him that the Dictionary of the Academy was absolutely worthless, that its plan was a rotten one, that it had been badly constructed, and that whatever it contained that was anti-Republican
would have to come out. They concluded by demanding the
copy which the Académie was preparing for a new edition. 'I
have a few sheets at home,' replied Morellet; 'the rest are
distributed amongst my former colleagues. I will collect them
and give them up as soon as I receive an order to that effect
from the Committee of Public Instruction.' Dorat-Cubières
was satisfied with his reply, and he was allowed to withdraw.
A few days later he received an order from Citizen Romme, the
President of the Committee of Public Instruction, to send him
the manuscript of the Dictionary, which he thereupon hastened
to do.[2] The reports of the proceedings and the other manuscripts were never asked for.[3]

The Académie Française perished together with the Monarchy.
Their resurrection will be simultaneous. Pellisson was not
wrong when he wrote at the end of his ' Histoire de l'Académie
Française jusqu'en 1652,' ' The fortunes of the Académie will
probably follow those of the State.'

———————

The Revolution suppressed the Académie Française and proscribed the Academicians, who, with a few exceptions, were all
exiled, imprisoned, or executed. The refugees and proscribed were :
the Cardinal de Bernis, the Comte de Choiseul-Gouffier, the Duc

---

[1] Urbain - Domergue (1745—1810) was elected a member of the
grammar section of the Institut as soon as it was established, and sat
upon the Commission charged with the revision of the 'Dictionnaire de
l'Académie.' He was afterwards Professor of General Grammar at the
École Centrale des Quatre-Nations, and Professor of Classics at the
Lycée Charlemagne. His principal works are the 'Grammaire Française
simplifiée' (1778—1792) and the 'Grammaire Générale Analytique'
(1798).

[2] 'This manuscript was almost lost, and it was Garat who saved it
from a heap of worthless papers, where it had lain forgotten for three or
four years.'—MORELLET, tome ii., p. 60.

[3] 'Mémoires de Morellet,' tome ii., p. 59.

d'Harcourt, the Cardinal de Rohan, the Abbé Maury, M. de Boisgelin, the Chevalier de Boufflers, M. d'Aguesseau, M. de Montesquiou-Fezenzac, the Abbé Delille, and M. Suard. Those sent to prison were : MM. de Roquefaure, La Harpe, the Abbé Barthélemy, Chamfort, Loménie de Brienne, Florian, and the Duc de Nivernais. To the guillotine went Bailly, Malesherbes, and Nicolaï. Condorcet committed suicide to escape the scaffold, and his example was followed by Loménie de Brienne, the Archbishop of Sens. Speaking of the latter in his 'Mémoires' (tome ii., p. 113), the Abbé Morellet says :

'At first cast into the prison at Sens, he was in February, 1794, sent home in charge of custodians, who had been directed not to lose sight of him. His brother, coming from Brienne to see him, was arrested, together with several other male and female relatives. The Archbishop was then summoned to Paris by an order of the Committee of General Security, and roughly treated by his custodians. One morning, his brother, before leaving for Brienne with the Commissioners to see the seals placed on his property there, entered the Archbishop's room and found him dead. He is said to have poisoned himself during the night with a mixture of stramonium. The men who were to have brought him to the capital wished to revenge themselves upon his nephew, the Abbé Loménie, by alleging that he must have known of his uncle's intentions, and by a refinement of cruelty they obliged the Abbé to be present at the opening of the Archbishop's body, and to sign the *procès-verbal*.' The Comte de Loménie de Brienne, ex-Minister of War, and brother of the Archbishop of Sens ; his three nephews, the Abbé Martial de Loménie, François de Loménie, a Colonel of Chasseurs, and Charles de Loménie, a Knight of Saint-Louis and of Cincinnatus ; and his niece, Mme. de Canisy, were all guillotined May 10, 1794.

In danger of being arrested for the second time, Chamfort attempted to kill himself in his room in the Bibliothèque Nationale. He first used a pistol, which only mutilated his nose and put out his right eye ; he then seized a razor, and slashing his throat without being able to sever it, he next stabbed himself in the region of the heart, finally cutting his legs to open the veins. He lingered on for a few months, and died April 13, 1794.

Florian, imprisoned in the gaol of Porte Libre, left it after the fall of Robespierre, and died a few weeks later, on September 13, 1794. La Harpe speaks of Florian's death in the following terms : 'Though he escaped the scaffold in Thermidor, he only passed from his prison to his death-bed, being carried off in a few days by a fever contracted amidst the horrors of his situation. During his state of delirium, his sensitive imagination, that had received an irremediable shock, constantly conjured up all the monsters of the Revolution.   He will ever be accounted amongst the number of its victims, for in the eyes of God and man it killed him as surely as if it had sent him to the scaffold.'

La Harpe's remarks concerning Florian may be applied with equal justice to Vicq-d'Azyr, another Academician.   Having formerly been physician to Marie Antoinette, he expected every moment to be arrested, taken before the Revolutionary Tribunal, and sent to the scaffold.   He could get neither rest nor sleep— the guillotine was ever present to his terrified imagination.   He died on June 20, 1794, at the age of forty-six.   In the delirium of fever he never ceased speaking of the Revolutionary Tribunal, and his friends, Bailly, Malesherbes, and Lavoisier, who had been executed, were always before him calling him to the scaffold. 'The dreams of this dying man,' said Lémontey, 'show us of what kind was the sleep of all honest folk in those dread times.'

CHAPTER XCIV.

ROBESPIERRE PRESIDENT.

Monday, August 26, 1793.

ROBESPIERRE the elder was on Thursday last elected President of the Convention ; this is the first time that he has been called upon to occupy the chair.[1] He has been a member of the Committee of Public Safety since July 27, and is also President of the Jacobin Club.[2] To-day he is the most important personage in the Republic, and its most powerful representative. It is therefore interesting to know what are his ideas and his programme, and whoever has heard his last speeches in the Convention and at the Jacobin Club is sufficiently enlightened on these points.

According to Robespierre, all our misfortunes are due to one and the same cause—treason ; and the only remedy for them is the guillotine. I take the following passages from his speech at the Jacobin Club on August 11 :

' Peculiar circumstances have brought to my knowledge some terrible truths. . . . The reverses of our armies and the insolence of our enemies are due to one cause—villainous treason. . . . The external foe would never have set foot on French soil—nay, I will go so far as to say that he would never have been bold enough even to attempt it—if he had not been able to rely on the traitors we support. The success of our foes is neither due to their courage nor to their talents ; it has always been treason which has gained it for them. It is treason which has caused our towns to capitulate, and every fortress that we have lost has been deliberately given up. . . .

---

[1] *Moniteur*, August 24, 1793.
[2] Hamel, ' Histoire de Robespierre,' tome iii., p. 107.

'Dumouriez disappeared, and the people thought that treason was scotched. But Dumouriez had successors. . . .

'Custine accumulated cannon and ammunition of every kind in Mayence, and all was given up to the Austrians. Dumouriez and Custine are both agents of the English party, and they have a number of accomplices in our midst.

'The camp of Cæsar has just surrendered almost without striking a blow. It has been treacherously handed over by General Kilmaine. . . .[1]

'Dumouriez, though a fugitive, is still practically in command of our armies. Custine, an Englishman, like his chief, followed his plans and his advice as closely as possible, and to him was due the capitulation of Mayence. Kilmaine, another Englishman, followed the same course at Palliancourt, and soon we shall have a similar occurrence at Cambrai. . . .

'Kilmaine is now replaced by General Houchard,[2] whom I believe to be an honest man ; but we have so many reasons to mistrust everyone about us, that I prefer to reserve my opinion until events have justified it. . . .

'The cause of so many of our misfortunes is undoubtedly the impunity of crime. . . . Who is there that is not filled with indignation at the thought that Custine, the assassin of so many of our brethren, of so many women and children, and of so many thousands of patriots, still lives ? What knave is there who, seeing his impunity, will not make a bid for the honour of serving the Monarchy against the poor *sans-culottes* who cannot afford to pay assassins and cut-throats ? And who is there amongst you that does not wonder at the inaction of a Tribunal in which the people once had implicit confidence, and which, though possessing a heap of proofs against Custine, hesitates to use them ? The culprit still lives, and his head is more safe upon his shoulders than mine or that of any patriot ! . . .

'The procedure of the Revolutionary Tribunal is now as slow as that of the old courts ; it clings to the insidious forms of

---

[1] General Kilmaine was deprived of his command and thrown into prison ; he did not recover his liberty until the 9th of Thermidor.

[2] General Houchard was guillotined November 15, 1793.

chicanery which have ever distinguished our Bar. But even a
court under the old *régime* would try a man charged with
murder in four days, and yet this man, who during the past four
years has murdered 300,000 Frenchmen, laughs at the proofs
that would condemn him. He is innocent, the assassin of our
brethren ! He will kill off nearly the whole human race, and
soon there will be only tyrants and slaves left !

' All the ringleaders of the conspiracy, Stengel, Miranda,[1] and
several others—all except Miaczinski, the least guilty of the lot,
and the one to whom pardon might perhaps be extended when
the others have been handed over to the avenging blade of the
law—all have escaped.'[2]

After having sent the Generals to the guillotine, Robespierre
wishes to give the journalists their turn—not because they
refute his ideas, the liberty of the press being long dead, but
because some of them are impertinent enough to pass over his
genius and his virtues in silence.

' Neither must we leave unpunished,' he says, ' those journalists
whose connections with London and Berlin are so evident—those
men who, subsidized by our enemies, inspire the people with
terror and consternation whilst pretending to be most zealous
for their interests. These men, I say, must be punished.'

The man who spoke these words is the same who always professed that the liberty of the press was an inviolable and sacred
right ; that it should be unlimited and absolute ; and that the
right of publishing one's opinions, either through that channel
or in any other way, was so evident a consequence of the
liberty of the citizen that the necessity for dwelling upon it
pointed to the present or recent existence of despotism.[3]

After the Generals and the journalists come the aristocrats,
and in Robespierre's eyes the poorest beggar that walks the
streets is an aristocrat if he be suspected of feeling no more than
a moderate amount of admiration for the *Incorruptible*.

' We must also punish those conspirators who take a fiendish
delight in seeing the people obliged to march to the defence of

[1] Generals Miranda and Stengel had been brought before the Revolutionary Tribunal and acquitted in May, 1793.
[2] Buchez and Roux, ' Histoire Parlementaire,' tome xxviii., p. 453, etc.
[3] *Journal du Club des Jacobins*, No. 399.

their country, and to leave the ground clear for fresh plots. Not one of them must be allowed to escape, and if all our patriots are obliged to go to the front, the aristocrats should first be placed in chains.

'There is another class of men quite as dangerous, appealing as they do to pity. We must clear our streets of those people who go about with poverty, starvation and aristocracy written on their faces; these men are paid to trade upon the credulity and compassion of the people.'

Treason is everywhere, says Robespierre. It is to be found in the mess-room and in the editorial office; the whole world is plotting, from the aristocrats down to the beggars. But that is not all; plots are hatched even in the Convention itself, and there are traitors in the Committee of Public Safety. This revelation Robespierre kept for the end of his speech:

'I was about to forget the most important discovery of all. Elected against my will to be a member of the Committee of Public Safety, I have seen many things which I should never have dared to suspect. I have seen on the one hand patriotic members straining every nerve to save their country, and on the other traitors weaving their plots in the heart of the Committee itself, and doing so the more boldly since they were certain of going unpunished. Since examining the government more closely, I have been able to see all the crimes which are daily committed in its name. The people will save itself. . . . We must keep up a continuous fire upon our foes without, but we must crush all those within.'[1]

On August 12 Robespierre repeats his utterances of the previous day in the tribune of the Convention, demanding that France, its administration, its government, and its army, be purged of traitors. On August 14, we again find him speaking at the Jacobin Club. A universal conscription has been suggested, but he declares that such a measure is unnecessary. 'We are not in want of men,' he says; 'what we require is

---

[1] 'Histoire Parlementaire,' tome xxviii., p. 458. Buchez and Roux have taken this speech of Robespierre's from the *Républicain Français* (No. 271) and from the *Journal de la Montagne* (No. 272).

virtue and patriotism in our generals.' And he adds : ' There is a class of men against whom we must be on our guard, and to whom we must attribute the greater part of the evils that surround us . . . .'

' Tell us what you propose !' shouts a member.

At these words Robespierre, who had pushed his spectacles back upon his forehead, turned towards the side from which the interruption came ; his cheeks were livid, and a tremor of agitation ran through his limbs. Readjusting his spectacles upon his nose, he continued in his harshest accents :[1]

' What I propose ! Who is the man that is bold enough to say that I have not brought forward sufficient proposals ? The spies of the English are to be found even in the most patriotic assemblies. The new system upon which they work consists in disparaging every proposition that is made, of discouraging the people, and of persuading it that its ruin is inevitable. I accuse them of ridiculing every honest proposal brought forward by the friends of Liberty in the interests of the country, and of materially aiding by such behaviour the criminal designs of kings upon our freedom.

' It is not sufficient to make war upon George and upon all those men called potentates ; if we do not include their accomplices, if we do not lay our hands upon the men whom they pay to further their ends, the Republic will never be safe.

' Such are the journalists, men whose sole aim it is to calumniate the people and the patriots, and to envenom the public mind, and whose mercenary and murderous pens distil the most dangerous of poisons daily.

' These are the men whom we must punish, and whose criminal attempts we must crush. I will therefore once more sum up my proposals.

---

[1] 'Souvenirs Personnels,' serving as an introduction to J. Fiévée's 'Correspondance avec Bonaparte.' 'He was a little below the medium height. The movements of his arms and shoulders were almost convulsive, whilst his face and eyes lacked expression. The harsh accents of his voice were very disagreeable to his hearers ; he shouted out his words, instead of speaking them. Residence in the capital had not improved the elegance of his language, and from his pronunciation one could easily detect that he was a provincial' ('Histoire de la Conjuration de Maximilien Robespierre,' by Montjoie).

' The removal of the generals from their posts, and the exercise of great care in replacing them by reliable men.

' The substitution of men possessing both administrative talent and patriotism for all those now holding government appointments.

' The arrest of all these hateful journalists, whose pens write naught but sedition, and whose existence is an ever-growing menace to society.'[1]

At the Jacobin Club yesterday evening Robespierre returned to his proposals respecting the safety of the country.

' We must wage eternal war,' he said, ' upon the agents of Pitt and Coburg, who infect our towns and our departments. On the summit of the Mountain I will give the signal to the people, and I will say: " These are your enemies—strike them down!"

' I have been examining the judicial forms in which it pleases the Revolutionary Tribunal to clothe its proceedings. It takes this court whole months to try Custine, the assassin of the French nation. If Tyranny could regain its power for twenty-four hours, every one of its antagonists would be crushed. Then, say I, Liberty should adopt similar methods; it holds the avenging blade which should rid the people of its most inveterate enemies—they who would let it remain idle are guilty.

' A tribunal which was established to aid the march of the Revolution must not be allowed to become a drag upon our progress; it should be quite as active as crime, and it should never get into arrears. It should be composed of ten persons, whose sole occupation is the discovery and punishment of crime; it is unnecessary to have more than one judge and jury, since the Tribunal only deals with one sort of crime—that of treason—and only metes out one punishment—that of death. It is ridiculous for men to deliberate upon the form which the punishment shall take when there can be only one, and when it is applicable *ipso facto*.'[2]

Robespierre's whole system and his whole policy may therefore be summed up in the following words—to bring before the

---

[1] *Le Républicain Français*, No. 274.   [2] *Ibid.*, No. 285.

Revolutionary Tribunal the generals, aristocrats, and suspects ; to free the Tribunal from all judicial forms, and to impress upon it the expediency of condemning the guilty within a limited time.[1] It is Robespierre rather than the unhappy Custine who deserves to be called the assassin of the French nation. His real place is a cell in a criminal lunatic asylum, but the National Convention confers upon him the honour of electing him to the Presidential chair.

[1] Robespierre's speech on August 25, 1793 : Buchez and Roux, tome xxviii., p. 478.

CHAPTER XCV.

Thursday, August 29, 1793.

GENERAL CUSTINE's trial, which commenced on August 15, lasted thirteen days, terminating at nine o'clock on the evening of the 27th.

Adam Philippe Custine, formerly Commander-in-Chief of the armies of the Rhine and of the Moselle, and afterwards commanding those of the North and of the Ardennes, has been found guilty of having entered into criminal relations with the enemies of the Republic with a view either to ensure them a free passage into French territory or to deliver up to them towns and fortresses belonging to France—relations which have more particularly resulted in the surrender of the towns of Frankfort, Mayence, Condé, and Valenciennes.

No one believes that General Custine is a traitor, except, of course, those rabid Jacobins and fanatical Patriots who will not admit that our reverses can be due to anything but treason. All who have a grain of common-sense left know well enough that Custine, formerly a representative of the nobility of Mayence in the States-General, would never dream of betraying the Republic, being one of those who, though formerly stanch supporters of the Monarchy, have since gone over to the other side, and have burnt their boats.

In spite of the length of the trial, and the large number of witnesses called, not a single proof of the alleged treason could be brought forward.

One document only was produced in support of the charge. Maribon-Montaut, a representative of the people with the armies of the Rhine and the Moselle, deposed that an officer named Boze had been sent by Custine during the siege of Mayence to demand an interview with General Doyré, who was in command of that place, and that he handed the General a letter from Custine containing an invitation to deliver up the city to the Prussians.[1]

This letter, dated April 9 last, was in the possession of Fouquier-Tinville, who submitted it to the inspection of the jury.

Custine replied that he had neither written, dictated, nor signed the letter — that, in fact, he knew nothing at all about it.[2]

In addition to the improbability of a man of Custine's standing writing such a letter—which would have been rather the act of a madman than of a traitor—Harger and Blin, two experts in handwriting, declared that the signature in the letter was a close imitation of that of the General, but that it was at the same time an evident forgery.[3]

Among the other counts in the indictment, three only were at all of a serious nature. Custine was charged with having deprived Strasburg of a large portion of its artillery—of having committed the same crime at Lille—and of having, it is true, dragged all the cannon to Mayence, but of having let that town run short of provisions.

Concerning Strasburg, one of the witnesses—and by no means a doubtful one, for it was the deputy Merlin (of Thionville)—unexpectedly vindicated the General's conduct. ' It is wrong,' he said, ' to charge Custine with having taken the guns from the ramparts of Strasburg to send them to Mayence.   The truth is : (1) that he took them from the artillery park, and not from the ramparts of the city ; (2) that there were by no means too many guns in Mayence ; and (3) that more than half of them are at the present moment disabled on account of the constant use to which they have been put.'

With regard to Lille, Custine replied that he had called upon General Favart, the Commander of the place, to give up only

---

[1] Buchez and Roux, ' Histoire Parlementaire,' tome xxix., p. 263.
[2] *Op. cit.*, tome xxix., p. 328.   [3] *Ibid.*

forty-one cannon, and not seventy-six, as stated in the charge; that more than enough had been left for the defence of the city; and that it was not until after he had taken the opinion of an authority on the subject that he had given orders for these guns to be removed to the Camp de la Madeleine. The explanations given by the accused were not refuted.[1]

With regard to Mayence, several witnesses declared that the charge brought against Custine—that of having starved the town—was without foundation.

Nicolas Haussmann, a member of the Convention, deposed that in January last he had an interview with the accused in Mayence concerning the food-supply of that city; that in March the stock of flour consisted of 30,000 sacks; and that it was only due to Beurnonville's ill-will that Mayence had not received fuller supplies before the blockade.

Simon Lepaux, an officer in the 29th Regiment of Infantry, declared that until the day of the surrender every soldier in Mayence had received a daily allowance of two pounds of bread and a bottle of wine.[2]

Another officer, Daniel Schramm, after having exonerated Custine from all blame concerning the fall of Frankfort, added: 'In Mayence it was the supply of meat alone that failed; if there was a want of forage, it was due to the presence of about 1,500 horses that were not required. There was abundance of bread and wine until the moment of the capitulation; the mills were at work during the whole time, and only three of them were destroyed.'

After having gained brilliant victories, Custine has suffered some defeats; it may be that he has committed technical blunders, but they cannot efface his services, his talents, or his bravery. He was undoubtedly in the right when he replied as follows to a witness who criticised his operations: 'If it were as easy to carry on war as it is to talk about it, there would be no battles lost: they would all be won.'

During these thirteen long days Custine defended his position inch by inch, replying to everything and to all with rare

---

[1] 'Histoire Parlementaire,' tome xxix., p. 325.
[2] Ibid., p. 332.

lucidity, ability, and presence of mind.   At the end of the case he spoke for an hour and a half, and even Tronson-Ducoudray, who defended him on those points having no relation to military matters, did not make a better show of talent or of eloquence.

Whilst the jury deliberated, Custine had been removed from the court, and when he re-entered it he could read his sentence in the ominous silence that reigned amongst the audience. Coffinhal, the President, then acquainted him with the finding of the jury, their verdict declaring him guilty on all three charges.   There had, however, been one dissentient voice on the first question, two on the second, and three on the third.[1]

After Fouquier-Tinville had invoked the full penalty of the law, Coffinhal informed the prisoner that he might, either personally, or through his defenders, say anything he wished in reply to the demand of the Public Prosecutor.

Custine, seeing neither Tronson-Ducoudray nor his other counsel, who had both left the court after the announcement of the verdict, replied: 'I have no defenders; they have disappeared.   My conscience is clear — I die innocent and in peace.'

He heard his sentence bravely, and seemed quite indifferent to the applause with which it was hailed, as well as to the cries of vengeance and of death that came from the mob in the courtyard below.[2]

It was then nine o'clock, and the condemned man was taken to the Registrar's room.   After having written a letter to his son,[3] and asked for a priest,[4] he lay down upon the bed.   The

---

[1] 'Histoire Parlementaire,' tome xxix., p. 336.

[2] The members of the jury who had not voted for death narrowly escaped being torn to pieces by the crowd ('Le Tribunal Révolutionnaire de Paris,' by Émile Campardon, tome i., p. 91 ; 'Biographie Universelle,' article 'Fualdès').

[3] M. A. Bardoux gives the text of this letter in 'Mme. de Custine' (p. 63), but dates it 10 p.m., August 28.   Its real date is August 27, for Custine was executed on the morning of the 28th.

[4] The following is the text of the letter written to the Bishop of Paris by the Registrar of the Revolutionary Tribunal, not on August 28, but on August 27, a few moments after the sentence · 'Citizen, you are desired to send a minister of religion to Citizen Custine, who has just been condemned to death, and who is to be executed at half-past nine to-morrow morning.   I am informed that he wishes to see the minister at once.—WOLF, Registrar.'

Abbé Lothringer, sent by the Bishop of the department of Paris, arrived almost immediately, and remained with the General until nearly eleven o'clock. On leaving he was asked by Custine to return at six in the morning.[1]

At the appointed hour the priest returned to his post, and the condemned man resumed his confession, which was not concluded until half-past seven. After praying in silence for a few moments, he sat down to breakfast, and requested the Abbé to go and recite the mass for the dying. As the priest was about to leave, the General asked whether he could not be allowed to receive the last Sacrament. The Abbé expressed his regret that he had no power to administer it, but added that, since God took the will for the deed, the desire to receive it was sufficient.

When the priest returned after celebrating his mass, he recited the seven penitential Psalms and a portion of the Litany with Custine, concluding his offices with a prayer for the dying. The concierge then entered with an unsealed letter written to Custine by his daughter-in-law. Custine would not read it, saying that it would only increase his grief, and handed it to his confessor with a request that the latter would console the writer.

At nine o'clock Custine mounted the tumbrel. The Abbé Lothringer was by his side, and during the journey from the Conciergerie to the Place de la Révolution the priest continued to read passages from a book of prayers, and several times gave the condemned man his crucifix to kiss. The General wore his military cloak, and kept his eyes raised heavenwards. On reaching the foot of the scaffold, he knelt and recited the words : ' O crux, ave, spes unica !' His eyes then wandered from the crucifix to the guillotine, and from that instrument to heaven ; embracing his confessor, he then asked for his blessing. At this, shouts of laughter burst from the crowd, and cries of 'The coward !' were heard.

A moment after, the head of the *coward* who had taken

---

[1] ' Interrogatoire de l'Abbé Lotbringer ' (' Archives Nationales,' carton W 285, dossier 131).

Worms, Spires, Koenigstein, and Frankfort, rolled into the basket.

The Abbé Lothringer has been arrested and taken to the Abbaye ; seals have been placed on his papers.[1]

Custine's daughter-in-law has been sent to Saint-Pélagie.[2]

---

[1] *Moniteur*, September 4, 1793.

[2] *Ibid.* See the interesting work written by M. Bardoux on 'Mme. de Custine' (Delphine de Sabran), who was born in Paris, March 18, 1770, and died at Bex, in Switzerland, July 25, 1826. In July, 1787, she had married Armand Louis Philippe François de Custine, son of the General. Brought before the Revolutionary Tribunal January 3, 1794, François de Custine was condemned to death ; he was only twenty-five years of age. Henri Wallon has published in his 'Histoire du Tribunal Révolutionnaire de Paris' (tome ii., p. 322) the letter which he wrote to his wife whilst the tumbrel and the executioner were waiting for him.

Thursday, September 12, 1793.

Tuesday, September 3.—The police authorities place before the Convention a report upon the number of prisoners now lodged in the prisons of Paris, and which amounts to 1,607.

On Barère's motion, the Convention confirms the decree of the Committee of Public Safety, ordering the Théâtre de la Nation to be closed, and all the actors and actresses to be arrested.[1]

After hearing a report from Lecointe-Puyraveau, a member of the Committee of Food Supply, the Convention decrees that there shall be a maximum price of wheat uniform throughout the Republic; that from to-day until October 1, 1794, a hundredweight of wheat of good quality shall not cost more than fourteen francs. Another decree is passed forbidding all traffic in that commodity.

In demanding the immediate execution of the decree relating to the maximum, Danton expressed himself in the following terms :

' The Convention must decide to-day between the interests of the monopolizers and those of the people. . . . Nature has not abandoned us, therefore let us not abandon the people. They would only be doing themselves justice if they fell upon the aristocrats and took from them by force what the law should have granted them. Let us pass our decree to-day, and put it into practice to-morrow.'

Wednesday, September 4.—At daybreak crowds of workmen assemble on the Boulevards and in the adjacent streets com-

---

[1] This was on account of the performance of a piece named ' Paméla.'

plaining of the difficulty of procuring bread, and demanding an increase of wages.[1]

At one o'clock the Town Hall is invaded by a vast mob numbering several thousand workmen. Secretaries are appointed, and a petition is drawn up and submitted to the meeting, which thereupon appoints a deputation to present it to the municipal body. On being admitted to the sitting of the Commune, the spokesman of the deputation gives vent to the grievances of his fellow-artisans in the following words: 'Citizens, the difficulty of procuring bread increases daily. We ask you to take into consideration such measures as the commonweal demands—to conceive some means by which those who have been at work the whole day, and who have need of their night's rest, may be able to obtain the handful of bread they receive without having to rise before the dawn and to lose half their day in waiting for it.'

A lively discussion is opened between the Mayor and the workmen, the deputation meanwhile gradually increasing until the hall is full. On all sides is heard the cry of ' Bread—give us bread !'

Chaumette, the Procureur de la Commune, proceeds to the Convention to inform that body of what is going on.

In the meantime the municipal officers adjourn to the larger hall, generally occupied by the Conseil-Général, and soon this is also filled to overflowing. The discussion is resumed, and arguments and proposals follow one upon another amidst the incessant cry of ' Bread ! bread !'

Chaumette returns from the Convention and reads the decree ordering a maximum price to be fixed upon all articles of prime necessity. ' It is not promises we want,' is the answer he gets, ' but bread, and that immediately !'

The Procureur de la Commune then gets upon the table and thunders forth the following words :

' I, too, have been poor, and therefore I know what the poor suffer. This is an open war of the rich against the poor · the former wish to crush us ; we must forestall them—that is all. We must crush them ourselves ; we have the power in our hands. Wretches that they are ! They have devoured the

---

[1] Report laid before the Convention by Chaumette, September 4, 1793 (*Moniteur*, September 7, 1793).

fruit of our labour ; they have eaten the very rags from off our backs ; and they would like to quench their thirst in our blood ! I demand that sufficient flour be sent to the Halles each day to provide the bread required for the morrow ; that the National Convention be asked to pass a decree authorizing the immediate organization of a Revolutionary army, and that this army be sent into different parts of the country to superintend the collection of wheat, and to stop the tactics of the rich dealers by handing them over to the arm of the law.'

Citizen Hébert, Chaumette's deputy, has no desire to be out-done by his chief, and makes the following suggestion :

' Let the people proceed to the Convention in a body ; let it surround the Assembly as it did on the Tenth of August, on the Second of September, and on the Thirty-first of May ; and let it not desert its post until the representatives of the nation have adopted such measures as will save the country. . . . Let the Revolutionary army set out the moment that the decree authorizing its departure is passed, but let us take care that a guillotine be included in the baggage of each battalion !'

These proposals are loudly acclaimed, and a meeting is appointed to be held at eleven o'clock on the morrow, at the doors of the Convention. Night fell, and the crowd gradually dispersed.[1]

Thursday, September 5. — The sitting of the Convention opened at nine o'clock, Thuriot being in the chair. Merlin, of Douai, a lawyer whose talents are only equalled by his cowardice, declares that the Revolutionary Tribunal is unable to cope with the amount of work now upon its hands ; that it is most im-portant that traitors and conspirators should be punished for their crimes with as little delay as possible, since any such delay in meting out justice to the guilty only emboldens those who are still weaving plots. He therefore proposes in the name of the Committee of Legislation a Decree of which the following are the first four articles :

' Article 1.—The Extraordinary Criminal Tribunal established by the law of March 10 last shall in future be divided into four sections.

---

[1] *Le Républicain Français*, No. 294 ; *Le Journal de la Montagne*, No. 96.

'Article 2.—The powers of each of these sections shall be equal to those of the other three, and they shall all sit simultaneously.

'Article 3.—The number of the judges shall accordingly be increased to sixteen, including the President and the Vice-President.

'Article 4.—The number of the jurymen shall be increased to sixty, and the Public Prosecutor shall have five deputies. There shall also be an increased number of registrars and clerks.'

This Decree, which aims at increasing the number of victims, does not meet with the slightest opposition in the Assembly; it is passed unanimously and without debate.[1]

At one o'clock the President announces that a large number of citizens of Paris demand permission to present a petition to the Assembly. This having been accorded them, a deputation enters, headed by the Mayor and several municipal officers.

After a few words from Pache, Chaumette reads a petition drawn up by the Conseil-Général de la Commune, and of which the following are the principal passages:

'Mountain for ever celebrated in the pages of history! be the Sinai of the French—thunder forth the eternal decrees of justice and of the people's will! Long enough have the flames of patriotic passion burned within you; let them burst forth in violent eruption! Holy Mountain! become a volcano whose burning lava may for ever destroy the hopes of the wicked, and turn to ashes those hearts in which any love of tyranny is left.

'Let there be no quarter and no mercy for traitors! If we do not outstrip them, they will outstrip us. Rear up the barrier of Eternity between us and them.

'The Patriots throughout the country, and the people of Paris in particular, have exercised enough patience. They have been long played with, but the day of justice and righteous anger has come.

'We are deputed to ask you to raise the Revolutionary army, the formation of which you have already decreed. Let the nucleus of that army be immediately formed in Paris, and let it be increased in all the departments through which it passes by such men only as desire a Republic one and indivisible; let this army be continually followed by an incorruptible and formidable tribunal, and by the dread instrument which by a single blow puts an end to plots and to the lives of the plotters! Hercules is ready; you have only to arm him with his club, and soon the soil of Liberty will be rid of all

---

[1] *Moniteur*, September 6, 1793.

the brigands that infect it. The cause of the people has been long enough delayed; it is time for its enemies to be struck down.'

Loud and prolonged applause breaks from all parts of the hall, and Thuriot invites the deputation to the honours of the sitting.

Chaumette asks for permission to make a few additional remarks. In the name of the Conseil-Général de la Commune he demands that all the parks and gardens which are now laid out for ornament should be cultivated, and dwells particularly upon the garden of the Tuileries. 'Republicans,' he says, 'will take a special delight in gazing upon what was formerly a piece of Crown land when it produces those commodities of which we are most in need.'

The citizens who accompanied the deputation are then admitted to the bar, and take their seats on the floor of the hall and on the benches of the Right amidst cries of '*Vive la République!*' Some of the men carry banners bearing the words: '*Death to tyrants!*' '*Death to aristocrats!*' '*Death to monopolizers!*'

Moïse-Bayle, a deputy for the Bouches-du-Rhône, puts the demands of the petitioners in the form of a motion which is supported by the speeches of Raffron, Billaud-Varennes, Léonard Bourdon, Gaston, Drouet and Danton. When the latter appeared in the tribune, he was hailed with such shouts of applause that for some moments he found it impossible to speak. At last he gained a hearing, and delivered a speech celebrating the sublime greatness of the people—of that people which clamours for the guillotine to be perambulated throughout the whole of France.

'We must,' he cried, 'turn to account the sublime impulse which animates this people that now crowds around us. When a people declares its own wants, when it offers to march against its enemies, no other measures should be adopted than those which that people itself suggests, for it is the national genius that inspires it.

'There is no reason why we should not organize this Revolutionary army at once. Let us develop, if possible, the measures laid before us.

' The vast body of true patriots and of *sans-culottes* who have
a hundred times laid low their enemies still exists ; it is ready
to move ; it only requires to be carefully led to upset all the
plans of the country's foes.   It is not enough to have a
Revolutionary army—we must all be Revolutionaries ourselves.

' We have to punish not only the enemies whom we have
caught, but those who are still at large.   The Revolutionary
Tribunal must be divided into such a number of sections [cries
of ' It is already done !'] as will enable us to send an aristocrat
to his account each day.

' I move for a report upon the best means of increasing the
activity of the Revolutionary Tribunal.   Let the people see its
enemies fall !   The people is great—all honour to the people !'

Danton concluded by inviting the Convention to agree to the
following measures :

' 1. There shall be a Revolutionary army, and the Minister of
War shall immediately draw up a plan of its organization.

' 2. The sections of Paris shall assemble in extraordinary meeting
every Thursday and Friday, and every citizen who claims an indemnity for loss of time in attending such meetings shall receive
forty sous per day.

' 3. The Convention places 100,000,000 francs at the disposal of
the Minister of War for the manufacture of rifles, the manufacture
of these weapons not to be stopped until France has placed a gun in
the hands of every good citizen.'

Danton's three proposals are adopted.

It is afterwards resolved, on Billaud-Varenne's motion, that
the members of the Revolutionary Committees who devote their
time to the public service shall receive an indemnity equal to
that given the electors.

On Bazire's motion, it is further unanimously resolved

' 1. That the Conseil-Général de la Commune shall draw up a
list of the members of all the Revolutionary Committees, and shall
be empowered to remove from office any member or members whose
patriotism it suspects.

' 2. That these committees, when thus reorganized, shall immediately proceed to arrest and disarm all suspects.

' 3. That they be consequently given full powers to act accordingly without invoking the aid of any other authority.'

All these motions, and many others equally violent and sanguinary, are adopted without debate or remark.

Merlin, of Douai, reappears in the tribune, and proposes that death shall be the punishment for the following offences : For selling or buying assignats ; for asking different prices when the payment is to be made in cash or assignats ; for having spoken disparagingly of assignats ; for having refused to receive them in payment, or for having given or received them at anything below their face value.

Meanwhile Robespierre has taken the chair vacated by Thuriot.[1] The Committee of Public Safety is again represented in the tribune by Barère, the cowardly orator who hides the blade of the guillotine beneath the flowers of rhetoric. The following is an extract from his *Carmagnole* of September 5 :

'The Royalists have taken it into their heads to organize a movement. This last movement they shall have, but it will cost them a Revolutionary army which will carry into effect that grand idea we owe to the Commune of Paris : "Let terror be the order of the day !"

'The Royalists wish for blood—well, they shall have that of the conspirators, of Brissot, and of Marie Antoinette.

'The Royalists wish to disturb the work of the Convention, but they will find that the Convention will disturb their own. They wish to overthrow the Mountain, but the Mountain will crush them first !'

---

[1] Michelet, who is very glad to sacrifice Robespierre to Danton and the Dantonists whenever an opportunity presents itself, speaks of him as not having dared to appear in the Convention on September 5 : 'Robespierre,' he says (tome vi., p. 271), 'was President of the Assembly from August 26 to September 5 inclusive, and it was his duty to be in the chair until the evening of the 5th. He had sufficient grounds for fear, the enemies of the Mountain having loudly declared that it was Robespierre whom Charlotte Corday ought to have murdered. He knew perfectly well that Hébert was a rogue who would have welcomed another Royalist outrage, and that he would have been delighted to be rid of his masters, Robespierre and Danton. These legitimate fears had probably presented themselves to the minds of Robespierre's friends, who are even said to have placed their hero under lock and key, in order to keep him out of danger. However that may be, he was certainly not seen on the 5th, and the Dantonists alone had to receive the attack led by their enemies.' This is one of Michelet's innumerable blunders ; both the *Journal des Débats* and the *Moniteur* for September 6, 7, and 8 testify to Robespierre's occupation of the Presidential chair during the sitting of the 5th.

On Barère's proposal the Convention decrees that Paris shall have an armed force composed of 6,000 men and 1,200 gunners, paid for by the Treasury, with which to crush the counter-Revolutionaries, and to execute wherever it shall be necessary the Revolutionary laws and the measures of Public Safety passed by the National Convention. This force shall be publicly recruited, and its pay shall be the same as that of the Gendarmerie Nationale of Paris. On the motion of Billaud-Varenne, the Convention repeals and annuls the decree forbidding house-to-house searches to be made at night—a decree which had been passed on Gensonné's motion at the beginning of the session. The final motion is also proposed by Billaud-Varenne, and is to the effect that the ex-Ministers Clavière and Lebrun shall be immediately brought before the Revolutionary Tribunal.

The Assembly adjourns at five o'clock.

The sitting is resumed at eight o'clock for the purpose of re-electing officers. Billaud-Varenne receives 149 out of 217 votes, and is consequently proclaimed President.

This election is fully in keeping with the abominable proceedings of the rest of the day, the heroes of which are Danton and Billaud-Varenne, both of whom had already won their laurels in September, 1792.

On the morning of September 3, when the massacres were at their very height, Billaud-Varenne, the deputy of the Procureur de la Commune, proceeded to the Abbaye prison. A heated discussion was going on concerning the victims' spoils between the Committee of the Section, which was presiding over the butchery, and the wretches who were performing the work. Settling the question in their own way, the cut-throats robbed the prisoners after having killed them. Billaud-Varenne then mounted a platform, and spoke as follows to his *workmen:*

'My friends—my good friends, the Commune sends me to beg you not to bring dishonour upon this glorious day. The Commune has been told that you robbed these rascally aristocrats after having meted out justice to them. I shall take care that you are paid the wages that were agreed upon. Be as noble, as great, and as generous as the profession which you follow ; let all things on this great day be worthy of the people whose sovereignty is committed to your care.'

Who shall say which are the greater wretches—the *workmen* who on September 2, 3, 4, 5, and 6, 1792, *toiled* in the prisons at a wage of twenty-four francs per day, or the deputies who, receiving a similar wage, chose on September 5, 1793, Billaud-Varenne to be their President and the chief representative of the people of France ?

CHAPTER XCVII.

FOURTH FORTNIGHTLY REVIEW (*conclusion*).

Thursday, September 19, 1793.

At the sitting of September 5 'terror' was made the order of the day. I was therefore compelled to dwell upon the proceedings of that sitting, and will consequently have to somewhat compress my review of those days which followed.

Sunday, September 6.—Garnier (of Saintes) in the name of the Committee of General Security lays before the Convention the draft of a law concerning aliens.

All aliens born in countries with which the Republic is at war are to be arrested. Artists and workmen are excepted, but shall be compelled to find as sureties for their good behaviour two citizens of their Commune of undoubted patriotism; a further exception will be made in the case of those who have given proofs of loyalty to the Republic, and of attachment to the French Revolution. Strangers found wearing any disguise whatever, or who shall pretend to belong to a nation other than their own, shall be liable to capital punishment. Sentence of death shall also be passed upon all foreigners born in countries with which the Republic is at war who shall enter France after the passing of this law.[1]

The draft is passed without debate, and by a unanimous vote, as has now been the rule for some time past in the case of all laws of proscription and all decrees of death.

One of the Secretaries reads a letter, dated September 2, from the representatives of the people with the army of Brest.[2] In

---

[1] *Moniteur*, September 8, 1793.
[2] Turreau, Ruelle, Méaulle, and Cavaignac.

this communication Turreau and his colleagues give the following account of the execution of the decree of August 1, ordering the destruction of the places in which the rebels have taken refuge :[1]

'We are executing your decree to the letter. This great act of national justice is inspiring the rebels with salutary terror ; famine, death, and desolation, are to be seen on all sides.'[2]

Three fresh members have been added to the Committee of Public Safety, which is gradually becoming more of an executive power ; the new men are Billaud-Varenne, Collot-d'Herbois, and Granet. The Committee is now composed of twelve members, the others being Robespierre, Barère, Couthon, Prieur (of the Marne), Hérault-Séchelles, Robert Lindet, Saint-Just, Thuriot, and Jean-Bon Saint-André.

The rumours that have been circulated during the past two or three days concerning Toulon are officially confirmed. On August 28 the sections of Toulon accepted the offer made to them by Admiral Hood, commanding the English squadron, to protect them, to re-establish the Constitution of 1791, and to place Louis XVII. on the throne. The acceptance was accompanied by a general display of the white cockade. In the name of the Committee of Public Safety Barère lays before the Convention and gets that Assembly to pass an ' *Address from the National Convention to the Frenchmen of the South.*' This document concludes as follows : ' Let vengeance be inexorable ! Let the cowardly inhabitants of Toulon, the horror and shame of the earth, disappear from the soil of free men !'

In moving that this address be printed, Gaston, a member for the Ariège, complains that the Government has been somewhat tardy in laying information before the Assembly, and in taking its measures. ' We remedy the evil when it is done ; we call in the physician when the patient is dead. It is easy to see that Lyons is not so well warmed as it should be. It is more than a week now since we heard of the burning of any houses. We are not told what Lavalette is doing before Lyons ; we have, indeed, but very meagre accounts of this town,

---

[1] See above, Chapter LXXXIX   [2] *Moniteur*, September 8, 1793.

which ought to be in ashes. Shall we allow ourselves to be again lulled into false security ?[1]

During the night between September 5 and 6 the Revolutionary Tribunal had passed sentence of death upon nine inhabitants of Rouen, accused of having in January last, during the King's trial, drawn up and signed an address in his favour, and further of having displayed the white cockade and destroyed the Tree of Liberty. The following is the list of names : Jacques Leclerc, editor of the *Chronique Nationale et Étrangère* ; Georges Michel Aumont, a lawyer ; Aubin Mérimé, a coachman ; Jacques Eudeline, a servant ; Delalonde, a servant, aged twenty-two ; Bottais, a miller, aged twenty-one ; Henry, a tailor, aged eighteen ; Maubert, a servant, aged eighteen ; and Mme. Drieux, a dressmaker. The eight men were guillotined at one o'clock on the 6th, whilst a short respite was granted the woman.[2]

The theatres continue to be well frequented, and several fresh pieces have been produced. On September 5 the first performance of ' La Moisson,' an opera in two acts, took place at the Opéra Comique National in the Rue Favart. The first performance of ' Roméo et Juliette,' an opera in three acts, is announced to take place in the theatre in the Rue Feydeau on the 7th. On the 6th, on the evening after the execution of the eight inhabitants of Rouen, the Théâtre du Palais-Variétés produced ' L'Ami du Peuple ; ou, Les Intrigants dévoilés ' (The Friend of the People ; or, The Plotters Unmasked).

The greatest amusement in Paris at the present moment is, however, to be found neither in the theatres nor in the Revolutionary Tribunal. The new craze is a game of chance known by the name of *lotto*. In nearly all the cafés *lotto* is played with absolute frenzy. Young and old, rich and poor, lose whatever they possess. The Café Français in particular, at the corner of the Rue de Notre-Dame-de-Recouvrance and the Boulevard Poissonnière, is daily filled with players who hold

---

[1] *Moniteur*, September 8, 1793.
[2] Wallon, ' Le Tribunal Révolutionnaire de Paris,' tome i., p. 258.

their sittings there from two o'clock in the afternoon until eleven o'clock at night, and even later.[1]

Saturday, September 7.—A good day for the Convention; it received two pieces of news one after another which caused it great joy. The sitting was just about to terminate, when Billaud - Varenne, the President, rose and said: 'I beg to announce that Petion is arrested;[2] the hour of traitors has come.' Almost immediately afterwards Barère announced that Brunet was in the Abbaye.[3] But yesterday Brunet was Commander-in-Chief of the Army of Italy; to arrest a General, to send him to the Abbaye, thence to the Revolutionary Tribunal and to the scaffold, is quite a common performance nowadays. The Parisians no longer excite themselves about such a trifling matter. September 7 happened to be the *fête* of Saint-Cloud, and the good citizens betook themselves thither in crowds,[4] and danced, it appears, according to their wont. No doubt it was on account of this suburban *fête* that the Palais-Égalité seemed so calm and the *cafés* so empty. The Place de la Révolution, on the contrary, was full of people who had come to witness the execution of a refugee, Tunduti de la Balmondière, formerly a Lieutenant in the regiment of Monsieur. On reaching the foot of the guillotine he smiled, and, shrugging his shoulders, said: 'So this is the instrument about which so much fuss is made! I do not fear its action!' A few moments before, as the tumbrel was passing a baker's shop, at the door of which a large crowd had gathered, he cried: 'Cowardly fools! You want a Republic, and you have no bread to eat! I give you my word

---

[1] Adolphe Schmidt, tome ii., pp. 114 and 116; Dauban, 'La Démagogie en 1793 à Paris,' p. 391.

[2] This news was false. Petion had not been arrested. After the failure of the insurrection in Normandy, he left Caen, and took refuge in Brittany, whence he made his way to the Gironde. He committed suicide on the same day as Buzot, June 18, 1794, in a field of barley, where his body was found eight days later, eaten by worms and dogs.

[3] Brunet was guillotined November 14, 1793.

[4] Police report of the local observer, Rousseville: Schmidt, tome ii., p. 115. The preceding year the *Fête* of Saint-Cloud had come immediately after the massacres in the prisons. Even that fact had not stopped the flow of people. In the *Révolutions de Paris*, tome xiv., p. 444 (September 8, 1792), we read: 'On Friday last the people of Paris proceeded to the *Fête* of Saint-Cloud with as much tranquillity and in as large numbers as in time of absolute peace.'

that before six weeks are over you will have a King—and you want one badly!'[1]

Sunday, September 8.—The Convention decrees that the section formerly known as that of the Pont Neuf shall henceforth bear the name of Section Révolutionnaire.

The woman Drieux, condemned three days ago with the eight other inhabitants of Rouen, who were executed on the 6th, has been sent to the scaffold, the doctors having declared her pregnancy to be feigned. The unhappy woman pleaded in vain for mercy on account of her two children, whom her death will leave destitute.[2]

At the Jacobin Club in the evening Robespierre denounces General Kellermann, who is in command of the troops outside Lyons. 'Kellermann,' he said, 'is, if not the author, at least the principal cause of the length of the siege. It is he who has been at the bottom of all the plots that have defeated the objects of this campaign, and under such a man no patriotic efforts can ever have any success. It is he who is the author of the treason of which we have heard so much in the course of the operations.[3]

Monday, September 9.—The police authorities lay before the Convention the statistics of prisoners at present detained in the gaols of Paris. Their number amounts to 1,794.[4]

On Lakanal's motion the military schools are suppressed. A member demands that an exception be made in favour of the

---

[1] 'Le Glaive Vengeur,' p. 106 ; Schmidt, tome ii., p. 113.

[2] Wallon, 'Le Tribunal Révolutionnaire de Paris,' tome i., p. 358. A poor chimney-sweeper named Soyer, included in the charges made against Leclerc, Aumont, and the other inhabitants of Rouen, was arrested a few days later, and condemned to death September 21, 1793. Concerning this man we read in the 'Compte Rendu fait aux Sans-culottes par Dame Guillotine,' p. 211 : 'Here the *sans-culottes* tremble with rage. Can it be that the lowest ranks of the populace contain a traitor and a slave sold to exiled nobles ? Soyer, the poor but honest man, should have restricted himself to sweeping chimneys : when he allows himself to be the instrument of crime, his guilt is all the greater, and the levelling blade of the law mows him down like so many others.'

[3] *Moniteur,* September 11, 1793. Kellermann was dismissed from his post three days after his denunciation by Robespierre. Arrested and sent to the Abbaye, he was not brought before the Revolutionary Tribunal until after the 9th of Thermidor, and was then acquitted (November 8, 1794).

[4] *Moniteur,* September 10, 1793.

establishments of La Flèche and of Vendôme, but his demand is not granted. The military school of Auxerre is the only institution of the kind which is to be provisionally kept open.

A letter was read from André Dumont, who has been sent out on a mission as a representative of the people to the department of the Somme. It runs as follows :

'CITIZEN COLLEAGUES,

'I have scarcely time to write to you; I believe that all the Dukes, Counts, and Marquises we ever had have taken refuge in this part of the country. By letting arrest follow upon arrest I will cut out the cancer, and the department, once properly healed, will only require a little nursing in future. Sixty-four refractory priests were living together in a splendid national building in the centre of this city. As soon as I heard of this, I at once had them all taken through the streets to the gaol. This kind of show, which was a novelty to the inhabitants, produced a good effect ; shouts of *"Vive la République !"* were heard on all sides as this herd of black cattle passed through the town. You must tell me what I am to do with these three-score of animals whom I have thus exposed to public ridicule.'[1]

Tuesday, September 10.—The Army of the North has just gained an important victory. On the 6th and the 8th of this month, General Houchard beat the enemy and captured the town of Hondschoote, which ensures the deliverance of Dunkirk and Bergen.

This brilliant success has left our Jacobins in Paris very cool. Not a word of it was mentioned at the club in the Rue Saint-Honoré, and it was equally ignored by the Conseil-Général de la Commune.[2] These excellent Patriots would rather have a thumping defeat which enables them to prefer charges of treason than a victory which might bring popularity to the Generals, who are their *bêtes noires*.[3]

---

[1] *Moniteur*, September 10, 1793.

[2] Buchez and Roux, 'Histoire Parlementaire,' tome xxix., p. 94.

[3] General Houchard was brought before the Revolutionary Tribunal on October 24, six weeks after his victory. He was guillotined November 15. Beugnot, who saw him at the Conciergerie, has left the following description of him 'Houchard was six feet high ; there was a wild and terrible look in his eyes ; a shot had disfigured his mouth, and had sent it round towards his left ear ; his upper lip had been split by a sabre-cut,

Wednesday, September 11.—The term for which the Committee of Public Safety was originally established having expired, the Convention unanimously confirms and prorogues its powers for another month.

Another General has been arrested. This time it is not an aristocrat like Custine or Dillon, but a good *sans-culotte*, General Tuncq, who has allowed himself to be defeated near Chantonnay by the Vendeans. The following is a brief sketch of this mushroom General; it is taken from the minutes of the sitting of the Jacobin Club on September 11 :

' A citizen gives a sketch of Tuncq's life in order that the public may have some data upon which to form their opinion. Tuncq was a bailiff of Bordeaux, and had to flee from that city and several others on account of his crimes. In order to procure money, he married all the women in the surrounding districts. He has wives and children in every corner of the Republic. He is so little of a Republican that he has worn all the crosses of Malta, of Saint Louis, and of other orders, and has successively assumed the titles of Duke, Marquis, and Count, in his marriage certificates, although he was fortunate enough to be born one of the people.'[1]

Bailly, the former Mayor of Paris, has just been arrested at Melun.[2] This piece of news excited great enthusiasm in the Conseil-Général de la Commune.[3] It was the same at the Jacobins, where Maure, the deputy for the Yonne, cried : ' The Commune of Melun has written to know what is to be done with Bailly. We shall go to that town to-morrow, citizens, and I will tell you what we shall do with him—we will send him to you alive.'[4]

Thursday, September 12.—Four days ago the number of prisoners was 1,794. To-day it amounts to 1,877, and is made up as follows : Conciergerie, 249 ; Grande-Force, 38, five of

---

which had also damaged his nose, and two other scars adorned his right cheek in two parallel lines. The rest of his body had suffered no less than his head. His breast was one mass of scars. It seemed as if victory had taken a delight in mutilating him ' ('Mémoires du Comte Beugnot,' tome i., p. 191).

[1] Buchez and Roux, 'Histoire Parlementaire,' tome xxix., p. 103.
[2] Bailly was arrested on September 8, three days after his arrival at Melun, where he had hired a house.
[3] *Moniteur*, September 4, 1793.
[4] Buchez and Roux, tome xxix., p. 100.

whom are soldiers; Petite-Force, 143; Saint-Pélagie, 131; Madelonnettes, 195; the Abbaye, 97, amongst whom are twelve soldiers and five hostages; Bicêtre, 851; Salpétrière, 108; in the cells at the Town Hall, 62; and 3 at the Luxembourg.[1] The three prisoners at the Luxembourg are the deputies Duprat, Mainvielle and Lehardy.

Palissot, the author of ' Le Cercle,' of ' Les Philosophes,' and of the ' Dunciade,' will probably go and join them there before long. On his demanding a certificate of citizenship, Chaumette inveighed against him in the following terms :

' Palissot, a man of letters, whose works have made a sensation, has allowed his pen to rust rather than use it in favour of Liberty. How could he indeed write in its favour, he who was a counter-Revolutionary even before the Revolution; he whose sacrilegious efforts have incessantly tended to stifle human reason in France, and who, in league with the authors of despotism, has not ceased to persecute the men of genius who sought to enlighten their century ? It was Palissot who, like some destructive worm, tried to blight the laurels of the celebrated Rousseau, and he did not blush to insult this sublime though unhappy man in his infamous comedy ' Les Philosophes.' He even dared to represent Rousseau on all fours eating a lettuce. Thrice cursed be the monsters who have plunged the venomous steel of calumny into the sensitive heart of Rousseau ! It is the duty of Patriots to avenge the sincerest friend humanity ever had, the Angel of Light who taught men what liberty was and knew how to make them desire it. It is the duty of practical philosophers to punish in an exemplary manner the enemy of all philosophy. I therefore oppose Palissot's demand for a certificate of citizenship, and may this act of justice serve as an expiatory sacrifice to the shades of the good and famous Rousseau, whose memory will be ever dear to all good, feeling, and virtuous hearts !'[2]

Friday, September 13.—At the sitting of the Commune the Corn Market Section complains that portraits of Charlotte

---

[1] *Moniteur*, September 13, 1793.

[2] Conseil-Général de la Commune de Paris, sitting of September 12, 1793; *Moniteur*, September 15.

Corday are being sold in the streets. The Conseil charges the police authorities to seize all such prints, as well as those in which Custine is represented in a favourable light.

The Luxembourg Section denounces the behaviour of those *citoyennes* who daily insult the tricolour cockades worn by respectable Republican females. Upon its demand the Conseil decrees that no women shall be admitted to public buildings and gardens who do not wear that honourable sign of liberty. This Decree will be printed and circulated.[1]

On the same evening a deputation from the Fraternal Club of Unity visits the Jacobin Club to likewise protest against the insults to which the national cockade is exposed when worn by female patriots, and demands that a decree be passed ordering all women to wear that decoration.[2]

Saturday, September 14.—At the sitting of September 9 Maure and Drouet had denounced the Committee of General Security, which appeared to them to be no longer quite up to the mark, and had asked that this Committee should be entirely renewed, and composed, not of twenty-four members, but of only nine safe and solid men perfectly inaccessible to corruption, and especially indifferent to dinners.[3] A decree embodying this proposal was passed. At its sitting of the 14th, the Convention decided that the reorganized Committee should be composed of twelve members, whose names are as follows: Vadier, Panis, Lebas, Boucher Saint-Sauveur, David Guffroy, Lavicomterie, Amar, Ruhl, Lebon, Voulland, Moïse, and Bayle.

Sunday, September 15.—The number of prisoners has risen to 2,020.[4] The Patriots regard this as of no importance, and on the very day when these figures were laid before the Commune the Fraternity Section invited the Conseil-Général to adopt more severe measures against the enemies of the Republic, and especially to order a house-to-house visitation in Paris, to be carried out on the same day and hour, and in the most rigorous

---

[1] Conseil-Général de la Commune de Paris, sitting of September 13, 1793; *Moniteur*, September 16.

[2] Jacobin Club, sitting of September 13, 1793, Leonard Bourdon in the chair.

[3] Buchez and Roux, tome xxix., p. 58.

[4] *Moniteur* of September 18, 1793.

manner. The Conseil promised the petitioners that it would neglect no opportunity of bringing all aristocrats and evil-minded persons under the blade of the law.[1]

After the Fraternity Section came that of Unity; its complaint was that the police authorities are too amenable to the wiles of the pretty women who come to demand the liberation of imprisoned suspects.

The Political Club of Melun complains of the action of the conductors of the water-coaches in carrying passengers who are not provided with passports. The Conseil thereupon decrees that the conductors of the public stages shall inscribe upon a register the names of all the passengers, and shall call upon them to produce their passports in order to see whether the names on the passports and those on the register agree. This decree is to be inserted in the *Affiches*, and sent to the sections.

Whilst the Conseil-Général de la Commune is engaged in these deliberations, the Jacobin Club is reminded by Desfieux that it had promised to leave no stone unturned to bring Marie Antoinette, as well as Brissot, Vergniaud, Guadet, and their accomplices to trial. The crimes of the latter are well known. What need, then, to find fresh ones of which they might have been guilty? There is only one question, the solution of which will necessarily lead to their condemnation and death: Was or was there not a plot in existence for restoring in France the former provincial divisions, and had or had not Brissot, Petion, and the rest, had a hand in that plot? 'More than this,' says Desfieux, 'is immaterial; that crime alone calls for death.'

Desfieux is succeeded by Terrasson. 'With regard to Marie Antoinette,' he says, 'it is not necessary for the Convention to pass a decree authorizing and ordering her trial; she is simply a private person, notorious only on account of her crimes. Her roguery should, however, not entitle her to privileges; she must be tried before the ordinary courts.'

Monday, September 16.—The Conseil-Général is informed that the ex-Mayor Bailly has been taken to the prison of La

---

[1] *Moniteur, loc. cit.*

Force, whereupon the hall re-echoes for several minutes with frenzied applause.

On Hébert's proposal the Commune passes the following Decree :

'The Conseil-Général, after having heard a deputation from the artistes of the Opera,

'And having taken into consideration the fact that the theatre would acquire fresh lustre and prosperity if advantage were taken of the solemn promise made by the artistes to purge the lyric stage of all works that might wound the principles of Liberty and Equality which the Constitution has made sacred, and to substitute patriotic works in their place ;

'And having further taken into consideration the fact that the present managers have declared their intention of closing this theatre and discontinuing their payments ;

'Authorizes the artistes of the Opera to administer the affairs of that establishment provisionally ;

'And moreover decrees, as a measure of general security, that Cellerier and Francœur, the managers of the Opera, shall be arrested as suspects, and that seals shall be placed on their papers, and on those of the present managing committee of the Opera.

'The police authorities are entrusted with the immediate execution of the preceding article.'[1]

Tuesday, September 17.—At its sitting of the 17th the Convention had before it two proposals, one by Collot-d'Herbois, and the other by Barère. The Committee of Public Safety had suggested that all Royalists, all anti-Republicans, should be transported to Guiana, but Collot rose and spoke against the measure in the following terms : 'I do not approve of the transportation to Guiana proposed by the Committee ; this measure is desired by the counter-Revolutionaries themselves— this punishment, far from intimidating them, inspires them with fresh hopes. We must transport no one, we must destroy all conspirators and bury them in the soil of Liberty ; we must arrest them all, and the places in which they are confined must be undermined, whilst a burning match is always kept ready to blow them up in case the prisoners or their partisans should

---

[1] Conseil-Général de la Commune, sitting of September 16, 1793 ; *Moniteur*, September 19.

make any fresh attempts against the Republic. They have really arrested the march of the Revolution, and you would scruple to arrest them in turn! I demand that this measure be adopted throughout the Republic.'

Barère, who succeeds Collot-d'Herbois in the tribune, is careful not to fall foul of the abominable sentiments uttered by the bloodthirsty actor, and contents himself with saying in his most unctuous accents: 'Like Collot-d'Herbois, I am fully of opinion that we must not spare conspirators, and that the blade of the law must strike them; but I must point out that there is a large number of suspects who, though they have not yet conspired, entertain aristocratic or Monarchical sentiments which might become very dangerous. I therefore think that a nation which adopts a fresh form of government has the right to send away all such individuals as are known to be opposed to it. I propose as a Revolutionary measure that all who since the Tenth of August, 1792, have not shown themselves friendly to the Republican Government shall be transported far from that society which they hate.'

All these proposals were referred to the Committee of Public Safety.

But the honours of the sitting of September 17 belonged neither to Barère nor to Collot-d'Herbois; the man who had most right to them was Merlin, of Douai, who, on behalf of the Committee of Legislation, presented to the Convention a law relating to suspects. This law, which was immediately passed, consists of ten articles, the first of which runs as follows:

'Article 1.—Immediately after the publication of the present decree all suspects found at liberty on Republican soil shall be arrested.

'Suspects are:

'1. Those who by their behaviour, their intercourse, their speeches or their writings, have shown themselves to be partisans of tyranny, and of Federalism, and enemies of Liberty.

'2. Those who cannot bring proofs, in the manner prescribed by the law of March 21 last, of their means of existence or of the discharge of their civic duties.

'3. Those to whom certificates of citizenship have been refused.

'4. Public officials suspended from the discharge of their duties by the National Convention, or by its Commissioners, and especially those who have been, or should have been, discharged from their posts by virtue of the law of August 12 last.

' 5. Such of the former nobles (including the husbands, wives, fathers, mothers, sons or daughters, brothers or sisters, and agents of refugees) who have not constantly manifested their attachment to the Revolution.

' 6. Those who have emigrated in the interval between July 1, 1789, and the publication of the law of April 8, 1792, whether they returned to France within the time prescribed by that law or before it.'[1]

At the sitting of April 3 last Marat had said : ' I demand the formation of a Committee of General Security which shall have the power to arrest every person whom it shall believe to be a suspect.' The Committee of General Security demanded by the Friend of the People has been formed, and even he could not possibly have found any fault with its composition. Has it not amongst its members Panis, who on September 3, 1792, signed the circular of the Vigilance Committee recommending the departments to cut the throats of all conspirators and traitors ?[2]

The Friend of the People had asked that all suspects in Paris only should be arrested. The Decree of September 17 orders the arrest of all suspects found, not only in Paris, but throughout the whole of the Republican territory.

One word more : This law relating to suspects will cause the arrest of thousands upon thousands of Frenchmen—perhaps of several hundreds of thousands.[3] Not a single deputy rose in the Convention to oppose it, and it was passed without a word of debate.[4]

---

[1] *Moniteur*, September 19, 1793.

[2] Concerning the circular of September 3, 1792, see Mortimer-Ternaux, ' Histoire de la Terreur,' tome iii., p. 308.

[3] In No. 4 of his *Vieux Cordelier*, dated December 20, 1793, Camille Desmoulins places the number of prisoners at 200,000. ' Open the prison doors,' he wrote, ' of these 200,000 citizens whom you call suspects, for in the Declaration of Rights there are no prisons for suspects, but only for those charged with crimes.'

[4] *Moniteur* of September 19, 1793.

CHAPTER XCVIII.

THE 'SUSPECT' LAW.

Thursday, September 26, 1793.

THE law relating to suspects is perhaps the most abominable of all those which the Convention has passed. There are a few people, however, who try to find excuses for its authors. 'It is undoubtedly,' they say, 'a sad thing—a terrible one, if you wish—but it is absolutely necessary for the Republic to defend itself. Attacked on all sides, on the Rhine and on the Scheldt, on the Alps and on the Pyrenees, in the Vendée, at Lyons and at Marseilles, it has, after all, only replied to the blows which have been dealt it.'

This excuse is wrong in one particular only, and this is that it comes somewhat late.

The Republic is attacked, but whose fault is that?

It was the Legislative Assembly, under the influence of Brissot and of the Girondist deputies, which on April 20, 1791, declared war against the Emperor of Germany.[1]

It was the Convention which on February 1, 1793, declared war against England and the United Provinces.[2]

It was the Convention which on March 7, 1793, declared war against Spain.[3]

Internally, the Republic, which at the outset had met with no resistance, did itself, by its long course of tyranny and crime, compel even the most patient subjects to rebel, and shake off the yoke of blood and iron that weighed so heavily upon them.

---

[1] *Moniteur* of 1792, No. 113. [2] *Moniteur* of 1793, No. 34.
[3] *Ibid.*, No. 68.

And here at least, as far as regards Lyons and the Vendée, the words of Montesquieu are strictly true: 'The real author of a war is not the side that declares it, but the side that renders it inevitable.'

But in any case, it is urged, the Republic was attacked, and had a right to defend itself. Be it so. But how is it that the moment chosen for having recourse to the most odious measures, and for promulgating the most outrageous laws, is the very moment when the Republic is everywhere victorious, and when its enemies both within and without have been crippled?

Toulon fell into the hands of the English on August 28, but everywhere else success has crowned the efforts of the Republican Government, and there has not been a day during the last month that has not brought the news of some check imposed upon its adversaries or of some triumph gained by its arms.

Let me commence with the rebellion in the South. On August 25 General Carteaux, after having relieved Avignon and the department of Vaucluse, driven the Marseillais across the Durance and taken possession of the town of Aix, made his entry into Marseilles, accompanied by Albitte, Salicetti, Escudier, Nioche, and Gasparin, the representatives of the people.[1]

On August 28 Bentabole and Levasseur, the representatives of the people with the Army of the North, announced that our troops had driven the enemy from Roncq, Turcoing, and Lannoy.[2]

On the same day, August 28, Dagobert, who is in command of the Army of the Eastern Pyrenees,[3] wrote, from the centre of the enemy's camp before Mont-Libre, that he had routed the Spanish, and captured their camp just as it stood, with eight pieces of artillery, all their ammunition, and a large quantity of baggage.

---

[1] Report laid before the Convention by Jean-Bon Saint-André on September 9, 1793 (*Moniteur* of September 11).

[2] *Moniteur* of September 2, 1793.

[3] Dagobert de Fonteville, one of the most popular Generals of the wars of the Revolution, was 'an ardent Royalist who took no pains to conceal his antipathy to the cause he served, except in his official despatches' (Fervel, 'Campagnes de la Révolution dans les Pyrénées-Orientales,' tome ii., p. 29, etc. See also the unpublished memoirs of Cassanges, quoted by M. Vidal in his 'Histoire de la Révolution dans les Pyrénées-Orientales,' tome iii., p. 55).

On August 30 another despatch was received from General Dagobert, this time dated from Puycerda. He had taken Belver and Puycerda, and had advanced through the gorge of the Ségre to within three leagues of Urgel without having overtaken the enemy, who, struck with terror, were retreating in hot haste. In twenty-four hours he won back for the tricolour flag the Valley of Carol and French Cerdagne, and captured the whole of Spanish Cerdagne for the Republic.

On August 30 good news also came from the Vendée to the effect that General Rey had beaten the rebels at Airvault, near Parthenay.[1]

On September 4 General Dagobert gained a fresh victory over the Spanish, taking 300 prisoners, thirty of whom were officers —amongst them being the commander of the artillery and three Colonels—and capturing fourteen pieces of artillery and a large quantity of ammunition.[2]

On the same day, September 4, Robespierre spoke as follows at the Jacobin Club: 'We shall be victorious without Toulon, and our successes elsewhere are safe guarantees of this. Marseilles is already in the hands of the Patriots; Bordeaux has returned to its senses, and Lyons will soon fall before the efforts of the Republican troops. The armies of the North, of the Rhine, and of the Moselle are doing famously.'[3]

On September 5 letters were read in the Convention from Garreau, the representative of the people, and from General Desprez-Crassier, announcing a brilliant victory gained by the Army of the Western Pyrenees over the Spanish. As on the eastern side of this frontier, the enemy has been entirely driven from French territory, and their entrenchments captured and destroyed.[4]

News of success also came from the Vendée, where matters seemed to take a fresh turn consequent on the arrival of the Army of Mayence. General Lecomte, commanding the division of Luçon, did indeed receive a check at Chantonnay on September 5, but on the very next day Gillet, the representative of

---

[1] *Moniteur*, September 5, 1793.　　[2] *Ibid.*, September 15, 1793.
[3] Buchez and Roux, 'Histoire Parlementaire,' tome xxix., p. 25.
[4] *Moniteur*, September 6, 1793.

the people with the Army of Brest, wrote from Nantes: 'We fought yesterday from seven in the morning until four o'clock in the afternoon, and the rebels were entirely defeated. They attacked us on three sides at once, but they were everywhere repulsed and beaten.[1]

On September 7 the representative Turreau wrote from the Ponts-de-Cé, near Angers: 'I have the honour to report to the Convention a fresh victory gained by our troops. For some time past communications with Ponts-de-Cé, a very important post, were interrupted, but they are now re-established. The heights of Erigné, which cover the bridges on the left bank of the Loire, have been gallantly captured.'[2]

It is, however, the Army of the North that has gained the most considerable and important successes. On September 5 the villages of Oudezeele, Hezeele, and Bambeck were captured at the point of the bayonet.

On the 6th Marshal Freytag attacked our troops encamped at Roexpoède; forced to retreat, he and Prince Adolphus of England were made prisoners for a few moments.

On September 8 these preliminary successes were crowned by the brilliant victory of Hondschoote, General Houchard capturing from the enemy three or four standards, five pieces of artillery, with ammunition and baggage, and a large number of prisoners, many of whom were men of distinction, amongst them being a Hanoverian General.

The effect produced by this victory was very great. Already on the 9th the Duke of York, fearing to be cut off, raised the siege of Dunkirk, and abandoned fifty-two pieces of artillery and all his baggage.[3]

On September 13 the Republican troops, under the command of Generals Béru and Hédouville, took Menin, Wervick, and various passages of the Lis, which were defended by the Dutch army and by extensive entrenchments. About forty pieces of artillery were abandoned by the enemy, who fled in disorder towards Bruges and Courtrai.[4]

[1] *Moniteur*, September 10, 1793.   [2] *Ibid.*, September 12, 1793.
[3] 'Histoire Parlementaire,' tome xxix., p. 93.
[4] *Moniteur*, September 17, 1793.

Whilst these fortunate events were taking place in the North, the Army of Mayence, which had entered Nantes on September 6, was commencing its operations. On the 9th a column of 6,000 men, under the orders of General Beysser, swept the whole of the left bank of the Loire from Nantes to the sea.[1]

On the 11th the advance guard of the Mayence army, commanded by General Kléber, seized Port Saint - Père. The capture of this post opened the road to the Vendée, and re-established communications between Nantes and La Rochelle.[2]

Three days later, on September 14, the same troops took possession of Legé, thus effecting a junction with those under the command of Beysser, which have successively captured Pornic, Bourgneuf, and Machecoul.[3]

At the sitting of September 15 the Convention received news from Toulon and from Lyons. Gasparin, Salicetti, and Albitte, the representatives of the people, wrote from Beausset that General Carteaux had driven the enemy from the defiles of Ollioules, that our troops had advanced to within half a league of Toulon, and that they had taken the heights which command the city, and had established their batteries there.[4]

Dubois-Crancé, Gauthier, and Laporte, the representatives of the people with the Army of the Alps, also wrote under date of September 11: 'You may rely upon it that before the week is out sixty or a hundred thousand men will have drawn such a circle around Lyons as will effectually prevent anything from entering that city, and thus enable us to take it by assault in three days. Saint-Étienne is in our hands. The rebels made a sally on the Bourbonnais road, and attacked the redoubt of Salvigny; but they were repulsed, and obliged to retreat with twelve cartloads of dead, and a much larger number of wounded. Meanwhile Kellerman is driving back the Piedmontese, and a column which was sent by way of Roanne has captured Montbrisson, whence all the rebels have fled to Lyons. In the Vendée there is therefore nothing more to fear, and Lyons will soon be completely surrounded.'[5]

---

[1] *Moniteur*, September 15. 1793.   [2] *Ibid.*
[3] Savary, 'Guerres des Vendéens et des Chouans,' tome ii., p. 140.
[4] *Moniteur*, September 17, 1793.   [5] *Ibid.*

The sitting of the 16th had also its batch of good news. The representatives Milhan and Ruamps wrote from Wissembourg: 'Our army attacked the enemy yesterday at several different points, and was everywhere victorious. At Lauterbourg the enemy lost 1,500 men, and if our forces had been greater the Austrians would have been completely exterminated.[1]

The provisional commander of the Army of the Moselle announced that he, too, had attacked the enemy, and that, having captured their advance posts, he had obliged them to take refuge in their entrenchments.

On September 17 the Republic was therefore victorious all along the line. This is so true that on September 16 Barère, speaking in the name of the Committee of Public Safety, was able to say: 'Things are going very well in the South; in the Vendée they are also much better.'

On the 18th Jean-Bon Saint-André announced the entry of the Republican troops into Furnes, and many advantages gained over the Piedmontese and the rebels of the Vendée, Lyons, and Toulon.[2] The hour of danger was therefore past, and true statesmen would have understood that the moment was come for measures of clemency and generosity. This view of the case, however, seems to have entirely escaped the men of the Convention. It is a characteristic of the vile and vulgar soul to preserve its rancour even after victory, and to regard the latter rather as an encouragement to indulge in fresh and intensified cruelty.

---

[1] *Moniteur*, September 18, 1793.   [2] *Ibid.*, September 19, 1793.

Sunday, October 5, 1793.

YET another *day*, and one that will mark an epoch in the history of the ' Terror.'

The day before yesterday the Convention was holding a sitting, with Cambon in the chair. The galleries were crowded, for it was known that André Amar was to read a report against the Girondists in the name of the Committee of General Security. The sitting had commenced at two o'clock. A letter had been read from the representatives of the people with the Army of the Alps, and another from the Commissioners of the National Treasury. On Merlin's report, Article 10 of Clause VIII. in the second part of the Law of September 29, 1791—an article providing for the adoption of the milder form of opinion in cases of dissension in the Legislature—had been revoked, and, on the proposal of Mailhe, it had been decreed that the Sisters of Mercy who still discharge the duties of nurses in some of the hospitals were to be replaced by more patriotic women. Suddenly applause burst forth from all parts of the hall : André Amar had made his appearance in the tribune.

Amar[1] shares with Hérault-Séchelles the honour of being the

---

[1] André Amar, deputy for the Isère, was one of the most pitiless members of the Committee of General Security. The two following notes concerning him are to be found in the unpublished papers of Courtois : ' Amar was the Grand Inquisitor of the Committee of General Security. Being himself an ignoramus, he held the knife ready to strike all men of letters. . . . He was a very great epicure, and his *gourmandise* was second only to his brutality. One day he was told of the unhappy wretches whom Carrier was throwing into the waters of the

most elegantly-dressed man in the Convention. The former Treasurer of the King, now one of the Mountain, has not thought it necessary to sacrifice his old habits of a Society beau to his new opinions ; at most has he consented to lay aside the large diamond which formerly glittered on one of the fingers of his left hand. He still wears the finest and the whitest linen, elegantly embroidered cuffs, and well-dressed frills. This dainty fop, with his fair hair, blue eyes, and pale face, who is so extremely careful in the choice of his words, had ascended the tribune to ask the Convention to send a hundred of its members to prison and the scaffold.

His opening phrases were full of promise. ' Before commencing to read the report,' he said, ' I am directed to ask you to make an order that no member of the Assembly shall be allowed to leave before the report is concluded, and the Convention has arrived at its decision.' This was agreed to. It was also decreed that no citizen in the galleries would be allowed to leave before the end of the sitting. The President thereupon gave the necessary orders to the officer on duty, who hastened to put them into execution. Several of the deputies, however, still managed to effect their escape.[1]

The doors then being locked, Amar commenced his report by reading the list of the members impeached. Whilst this long roll of more than a hundred names was being gone through, a dead silence reigned in the hall. The members of the Mountain, certain that their names were not included, regarded with ferocious curiosity the faces of the members of the Plain and of the Gironde. The latter affected to assume a bold front, but the majority of them could ill conceal their anxiety and the terrible agitation that had seized them. Some of them wandered through the corridors that were still left open, going in and out of the hall a hundred times as they passed from fear to

Loire. " So much the better," he is reported to have said ; " the salmon we get from the Loire will be all the fatter." ' (Charles Vatel, ' Charlotte de Corday et les Girondins,' tome i., p. 31. See some curious pages on Amar by Philarète Chasles in his ' Mémoires.' tome i., p. 52, etc.)

[1] ' Mémoires ' of Dulaure, edited by Taschereau in the *Revue Rétrospective*, tome xx.

hope, and from hope to fear.[1] When André Amar stopped, after having read the last name, the Assembly presented a never-to-be-forgotten spectacle. All the members of the Mountain were on their feet, shouting and waving their hats. Some, however, thought the list too short, and flung at Amar the names of forgotten conspirators, and of traitors who had been passed over. In the Centre and on the Right there was a great rushing to and fro of impeached members, who took counsel amongst themselves and drew up a short document—a letter which was to be read to the Convention, and in which they declared that they had never conspired against the Republic. Like their chiefs on June 2, the last soldiers of the Gironde answered this blow with a declaration. Those of their colleagues whose names had not been mentioned had great difficulty in concealing their satisfaction. Many even betrayed in cowardly fashion the joy with which their souls were filled ; it escaped them in every one of their looks, and in their whole demeanour—an imprudent display which was carefully watched by their enemies, and which insulted the sorrow of their neighbours and friends whose names were on the fatal lists.

Perhaps I am wrong in being so severe. Am I quite certain that in their place I should not have done as they did, and that I should have thought less of myself than they ?

---

[1] Dulaure, whose name did not appear in the list of impeached members, but who was mentioned in Amar's report, has related his impressions, and shown us at the same time the feelings that must have animated his colleagues. 'I perceived,' he says, 'the depth of the abyss by which I was to be swallowed up. My wife, my father, my family, and my friends presented themselves before me ; they were the dearest ties which bound me to life, and which made me regret it. . . . This last idea agitated me most. I looked about me on all sides. Seated in a part of the hall where everyone could see me, I noticed that each time my name was mentioned many eyes were fixed upon me, whilst some seemed to rejoice at my position. . . . Amidst the fear that tortured me, I felt one ray of hope. . . . Placed thus between fear and hope, or, rather, between life and death, I was in a terrible state of torture. The more I hoped, the more terrible seemed the object of my fear ; the more I feared, the dearer seemed to become the object of my hope. It is impossible to fully describe this state of anguish ; one must have felt it to know what it means. My agitation did not allow me to remain in my place, and I rose to mix with the crowd which thronged the approaches and the centre of the hall. . . . The sitting seemed to be of interminable length, and wandering through the corridors, which were still free, I went in and out of the hall a hundred times.'

Silence having meanwhile been re-established in the hall and galleries, Amar read his indictment, which took him more than two hours to get through, and in which Brissot, Gensonné, Vergniaud, and more than a hundred of their colleagues, are represented as the authors and the accomplices of a plot against the unity and indivisibility of the Republic, and against the liberty and safety of the French nation. Amar and the members of the Committee of General Security have not taken the trouble to draw very much upon their imagination, having merely given a bald reproduction of Camille Desmoulins' 'Histoire des Brissotins.' In concluding his pamphlet, Camille had proposed that the Brissotins should be *vomited forth* from the Convention, and that the Revolutionary Tribunal should be amputated.[1] This is exactly what Amar proposed. The draft of a Decree with which his report concluded contained four articles. The two first ordered forty deputies to be brought before the Revolutionary Tribunal ; the third confirmed the decree of July 28 last, declaring twenty deputies traitors to their country, and making them outlaws, whilst the fourth ordered that those who had signed the protest of June 6, and who had not yet been brought before the Revolutionary Tribunal, should be immediately arrested. The number of deputies coming under this head amounted to sixty-six.[2]

To ask an assembly to proscribe 126 of its members *en bloc*

[1] 'The History of the Brissotins ; or, Fragments of the Secret History of the Revolution and of the First Six Months of the Republic,' had appeared in May, 1793. In this odious pamphlet, Camille Desmoulins proposed to send to the scaffold the deputies of the Gironde, and Brissot, Petion, and Sillery in particular, all of whom had acted as witnesses at his marriage. In asking the Jacobin Club to undertake the expense of printing the work, he himself said that all who read it would immediately ask, 'Where is the scaffold ?' ('Tableaux de la Révolution Française,' by Adolphe Schmidt, tome i., p. 245). The pamphlet having been printed at the expense of the Jacobin Club, Camille asked Prudhomme to speak of it in the *Révolutions de Paris*. 'This work,' he added, 'will send the Brissotins straight to the scaffold—I will answer for that' (Prudhomme, 'Histoire Général et Impartiale des Erreurs, des Fautes et des Crimes commis pendant la Révolution Française,' tome v., p. 129).

[2] The protest of June 2 against the events of May 31 bore seventy-five names, but as nine of the signatories figured amongst the deputies brought before the Revolutionary Tribunal, or amongst those who were declared traitors to their country and outlawed, there remained sixty-six to be arrested. The protest of the seventy-five is exhibited in the Musée des Archives, case 212, No. 1,361.

is an unheard-of act. In my opinion, however, what took place in the Convention of October 3 was still more prodigious, when this impeachment of 126 duly-elected representatives of the nation was agreed to without debate.[1] Not a single deputy rose to oppose this odious and abominable measure, to ward off that monstrous thing called outlawry, or to remind the Assembly at the very least that this protest against the events of May 31, signed on June 6 by seventy-five deputies, had received no publicity whatever, and that it had been condemned to oblivion by its authors themselves.[2]

The Decree having been passed, the manner of its execution still remained to be determined. 'There is a very simple way,' said Thuriot ; ' the names of the accused will be called out and they will appear at the bar in reply.'[3] This proposal was adopted.

A few moments later we saw the impeached deputies rise in their places as they heard their names called over, and proceed to the space before the Bar, like sheep destined for slaughter.[4] Not more than twenty-five appeared ;[5] the rest had either not been in the Convention or had managed to escape before the doors were closed. The twenty-five members were marched from the bar into one of the rooms adjoining the lavatories, where they were left till nightfall. At eight o'clock they were transferred to the guard-house of the Palais National, and during that short journey they were subjected to every kind of insult on the part of the mob.[6]

At two in the morning an armed force came to take them to the houses of detention. It was composed of citizens and of a strong detachment of mounted gendarmes. With this escort the deputies crossed the Place du Carrousel, and proceeding

---

[1] Dulaure's 'Mémoires.'

[2] See the very rare and curious pamphlet entitled 'Les Représentants du Peuple détenus à la Maison d'Arrêt des Écossais, en Exécution du Décret de la Convention Nationale du 3 Octobre, 1793 (vieux style), à leurs Collègues les Représentants du Peuple siégeant à la Convention Nationale et au Peuple Français.' This pamphlet is dated as follows : ' Written at the House of Detention called Des Écossais on the last day of the Sans-Culottides of the 2nd year of the French Republic one and indivisible.'

[3] *Moniteur*, October 5, 1793.

[4] ' Historique des Traitements essuyés par les Députés Détenus et les Dangers qu'ils ont courus,' by D. Blanqui, in tome i. of ' L'Histoire des Prisons de Paris et des Départements.'

[5] Dulaure's 'Mémoires.'   [6] D. Blanqui, *op. cit.*

along the Quai du Louvre, the Pont Neuf, and the Quai des Orfèvres, reached the Mairie. The room into which they were taken, and which is capable of holding about forty persons, was already crowded with over fifty prisoners. Many of the deputies were obliged to pass the rest of the night standing up, in an atmosphere so foul that it was almost impossible to breathe.[1]

In the morning—this was yesterday—the prisoners were taken back to their homes, in order to see the seals placed on their papers, and this having been done, they were sent to a wing of the Maison de la Force called the New Building. There they have been placed on the sixth floor, in a room which they share with thirty other prisoners. The air filters into the apartment through tiny apertures, and there are no beds; but along the walls are some shelves covered with sacks of straw, these apologies for mattresses being infested with vermin. These details have been furnished me by one of Mercier's friends who is amongst the twenty-five members.[2]

It is exactly four years ago to-day that the mob of Paris, headed by Théroigne de Mericourt,[3] Maillard, and Jourdan Coupe-tête, invaded the palace at Versailles, butchered the bodyguard, heaped insults upon the King and Queen, and brought them back captives to the capital. As Louis XVI. was dragged from Versailles, so have the Brissots, the Merciers, the Carras, and the Gorsas, been dragged in turn from the Tuileries. As the royal inviolability was disregarded and trodden under foot four years ago, so has the inviolability of the representatives of the people been now treated. They wish us to protest against the outrage of October 3, 1793, forgetting that they themselves applauded the outrage of October 6, 1789.[4]

---

[1] Blanqui, *op. cit.*

[2] Sebastien Mercier, the author of the 'Tableau de Paris' and joint-editor with Carra of the *Annales Patriotiques*, was a member for Seine-et-Oise. Arrested on October 3, he was successively sent to different prisons, and did not recover his liberty until October, 1794.

[3] Her real name was Terwagne, and she had been born at Marcourt, a village situated on the Ourthe, close to the little town of Laroche ('Portraits Intimes du XVIII. Siècle,' by E. and J. de Goncourt, p. 365).

[4] Brissot in particular had written two articles to defend the establishment of a Committee of Inquiry, of which he had been appointed a member, and which was the forerunner of the Committee of General Security. In one of these articles, speaking of the massacre of the bodyguard, he wrote: 'But this crime, if it be one. . . .' (Charles Vatel 'Charlotte de Corday et les Girondins,' tome ii., p. 237).

CHAPTER C.

Monday, October 7, 1793.

THE ex-Capucine Chabot is to be married, and, since his bride is said to be young and good-looking, it would be interesting to know why the bridegroom has for some time past worn such a mournful and preoccupied look. It is not, I take it, that he cares much for the thunderbolts of the Church, nor for the contempt of honest men, for he has long been accustomed to degradations of every kind. Can it be that he is afraid of his friends 'n the Mountain, or of his comrades in the Jacobin Club, who would scarcely forgive him for marrying a rich woman? A dowry is spoken of amounting to not less than two or three hundred thousand francs. As a Capucine monk, the Jacobins and the Grey Friars were delighted to see him treading under foot with great ostentation his vows of obedience and chastity, but it is a different matter altogether with regard to the vow of poverty, and to break it in such a flagrant manner might cost him dear. Those who are jealous would have all the more scope for revenge, since the future Citoyenne Chabot is not only rich, but a foreigner and an aristocrat into the bargain. She is the sister of one Baron Frey, who calls himself Citizen Junius Frey, and who makes a boast of the most advanced form of Republicanism, but who is none the less held in suspicion by a great many on account of the considerable sums at his disposal and his interference in the affairs of the Republic.[1]

Although the love of riches is as blind as any other love,

---

[1] 'Mémoires de René Lavasseur,' tome ii., p. 165.

Chabot has, nevertheless, apprehended the danger before him.
Whether he will succeed in warding it off is another matter.
Yesterday evening he appeared in the Jacobin Club with a
dirty handkerchief tied round his head, his throat, chest, and
legs uncovered, and wearing a jacket and breeches of coarse
material, and clogs stuffed with straw[1]—a strange costume, truly,
for a man about to marry a rich heiress. It almost seemed as
if he had put on an extra coat of dirt for the occasion, relying
no doubt upon his squalid appearance to banish thoughts of
the dowry of 200,000 francs. The *fiancé* of Citoyenne Frey
mounted the tribune, and, after having spoken briefly in favour
of the Club printing at its expense a pamphlet by Anacharsis
Cloots—another German Baron who works for the Republic,
which is, perhaps, another way of working for the King of
Prussia—he came to the subject that he has most at heart.

'I take this opportunity,' said Chabot, 'of informing the
Club that I am about to marry. Everyone knows that I have
been a priest, and even a Capucine; I must therefore give you
the motives that led to my resolve. As a legislator, I deemed
it my duty to set an example of every virtue. I am reproached
with being too fond of women. In allying myself to one in
accordance with the law, a step which I have long desired to
take, am I not doing my best to silence that calumny? Three
weeks ago I was unacquainted with the woman I am about to
marry. Brought up, according to the custom of her country,
in absolute retirement, she had never come into contact with
strangers. I was therefore not in love with her, and even
now I am in love only with her virtue, her talents, and the
purity of her Republicanism; in the same way she herself feels
attracted towards me only by the repute of my patriotism. I
had not the slightest intention of proposing to her, but went
to one of her brothers, Junius Frey—an estimable man of
letters, and well known by two very patriotic works, the "Anti-
fédéraliste" and "La Philosophie Sociale"—to ask her hand
for one of my relations. "To you, citizen, and to you alone,
will I give her," said Junius Frey. I told him that the whole
of my income amounted to 700 francs, and that I gave

---

[1] Beaulieu, 'Biographie Universelle.'

even that up to my father and mother, the one eighty and the other eighty-five years old, who were more patriotic and energetic than myself, and who had ruined themselves to educate me. " No matter," he replied ; " we give her to you for your own sake, and not for your fortune." I have been much calumniated in this matter, citizens ; it has been said that I had money, since I married so well. I will read you my marriage contract, and from this you will learn that the whole of my fortune consists of **6,000** francs.'

After perusing that document, Citizen Chabot concluded with the following words :

' I now invite the Club to appoint a deputation to be present at my wedding, and at the civic banquet that will follow it. I am happy to say that no priest will darken this function with his presence, and that we shall employ only civil officers. The deputation will be good enough to attend at eight in the morning, for I desire that all may be over before nine o'clock, in order that I may not have to be absent from the National Convention. My wife has told me that I would cease to have her love if it should make me neglect even for once the Convention or the Jacobin Club.'[1]

Chabot's matrimonial statement was received with prolonged applause. He had, however, no sooner left the tribune than a marjoy asked for permission to speak, and this marjoy was no other than Citizen Dufourny, formerly President of the Conseil-Général de la Commune. Dufourny did not fail to dwell at length upon the clauses of the famous marriage contract, and to bring into relief both the dowry of Citoyenne Frey and her nationality. He concluded by declaring that the Club could not appoint a deputation to attend the marriage of one of its members, and still less the banquet.[2]

Upon this a very lively discussion took place. In spite of the authority which Citizen Dufourny so justly enjoys, a majority was found to decide that a deputation should attend

---

[1] *Journal des Débats et de la Correspondance de la Société des Jacobins ;* sitting of the 14th of the first month of the year II. of the French Republic.

[2] *Moniteur* for 1793, No. 19.

both the marriage and the banquet.   Spartans though they be, our Jacobins could not resist the desire of sampling the products of the German Baron's kitchen.

For all that, were I in the place of the ex-Capucine priest, I should not feel quite at my ease.   It is not safe to marry a woman who has a dowry of 200,000 francs.   In spite of the eccentricities of costume and his exaggerated language, in spite of his sanguinary proposals and his outrageous speeches, of his dirty jacket and his greasy breeches, Chabot is now known by all the world to be a rich man, and from being rich to being suspected is but a step—an easy step even for one whose clogs are lined with straw.[1]

---

[1] Chabot was brought before the Revolutionary Tribunal together with his two brothers-in-law, Junius and Emmanuel Frey.   He tried to escape his sentence by taking poison.   After having written his political will in the form of a 'Lettre aux Français,' he swallowed the contents of a phial containing a mixture for external use (March 17, 1794).   Having survived his attempt at suicide, he stood his trial, together with Danton, Camille Desmoulins, Fabre d'Églantine, Delaunay, D'Angers, Basire, Hérault-Séchelles, and others, and was guillotined with them April 5, 1794.

CHAPTER CI.

Sunday, October 13, 1793.

The great lawyer, Merlin of Douai, or, as he is already called, Merlin-Suspect, has found a commentator worthy of him in Chaumette. The day before yesterday the Procureur de la Commune explained to the Conseil-Général who were suspects, and by what signs they might be known. This little treatise of Chaumette's is well worth being preserved, and I therefore reproduce it in its entirety.

'The following are suspects, and should therefore be arrested as such :

'1. Those who in public assemblies attempt to stem the people's will by cunning speeches, seditious cries, or murmurs.

'2. Those who in a more prudent manner speak mysteriously of the misfortunes of the Republic, lament the fate of the people, and are always ready to spread bad news with an affectation of grief.

'3. Those who change their behaviour and their language according to events; who, though dumb concerning the crimes of the Royalists and Federalists, loudly inveigh against the least faults of the Patriots, and, in order to appear Republican, affect a studied austerity and severity quite out of keeping in Moderates or aristocrats.

'4. Those who pity the avaricious farmers and merchants against whom the law is obliged to take measures.

'5. Those who, though always having the words " Liberty " and " Republic " on their lips, frequent the society and interest themselves in the fate of the former nobles, counter-Revolutionary priests, aristocrats, Feuillants, and Moderates.

'6. Those who have taken no active part in the Revolution, and who excuse themselves from so doing by the payment of contributions, by patriotic gifts, and by serving in the National Guard either personally or by substitute.

'7. Those who have received the Republican Constitution with indifference, and have given utterance to false fears concerning its acceptation and duration.

'8. Those who, though having done nothing against Liberty, have done nothing for it.

'9. Those who do not attend the sectional assemblies, and who excuse themselves on the ground that they cannot speak, and that their business keeps them back.

'10. Those who speak with contempt of the constituted authorities, of the emblems of the law, of the political clubs, and of the defenders of liberty.

'11. Those who have signed counter-Revolutionary petitions or frequented anti-patriotic societies or clubs.

'12. The followers of Lafayette and the assassins who proceeded to the Champs de Mars.'

The Conseil-Général, after hearing the Procureur-Syndic's treatise, ordered the same to be printed.[1]

It must not, however, be supposed that the list drawn up by Chaumette is a complete one. At the sitting of September 5, Basire, the friend of Danton, informed us that there were two classes of suspects—the first composed of the former nobles and priests ; the second comprising 'shopkeepers, merchants, stock-jobbers, notaries, attorneys, stewards and managers, and the independent gentlemen who were swindlers by profession and education.'[2]

For the rest Basire only echoed the words of Danton. Had not the latter said but a few days before : 'We must aim a blow at the business men who hastened on the fall of the nobles and priests in the hope of enriching themselves, and who now, with

---

[1] *Moniteur*, October 12, 1793.
[2] *Ibid.*, September 7, 1793.

still more sinister aims, desire a counter-Revolution; we must be as relentless towards these as towards the aristocrats'?[1]

It is not, however, only the big merchants and the *aristocratic shopkeepers*[2] who are suspects. The meanest artisan, and even the water-carriers, are included in that denomination. Did not Chaumette's deputy, Citizen Hébert, tell the Conseil-Général on September 23 'that there were refugees even amongst the water-carriers,' and as a result of that denunciation were not instructions sent to the police authorities to keep a watchful eye on 'those gentlemen'?[3]

Not only the water-carriers, but even the chimney-sweepers, are suspects. On September 21 a poor devil named Soyer, a chimney-sweeper of Rouen, was condemned and guillotined as a Royalist.

Suspects also are the *Muscadins*, those who have clean hands, neatly-kempt hair, and well-shod feet.[4]

Suspects are the women who wear no tricolour cockade in their caps.[5]

Suspects, too, are those who have not reversed their chimney-plates adorned with the lilies of France, and those who have retained any piece of furniture or plate bearing this proscribed emblem.[6]

---

[1] Sitting of August 21, 1793 (*Moniteur* of September 2). In this speech Danton denounced the commercial aristocracy. On December 25, 1793, Basire in his turn declared that the commercial aristocracy was the vilest of all.

[2] 'Neither must I forget to tell you that the *aristocratic shopkeepers*, especially in these cantons, have not yet been taken in hand' (letter from Brune to the members of the Committee of Public Safety, dated September 24, 1793, *Revue Rétrospective*, 1834, tome ii., p. 292). Brune—the future Marshal of the Empire—was then on a mission in the south.

[3] Sitting of the Commune of September 23 (*Moniteur*, September 25).

[4] Sitting of the Convention of September 13, 1793 (*Moniteur* of September 15).

[5] Decree of September 21, 1793 (*Moniteur* of September 23).

[6] Decree of October 12, 1793. 'Duquesnoy, a member for the Pas-de-Calais, whilst on one of his missions, had the driver of a military waggon shot because he found a lily engraved on his sword' ('Biographie Universelle,' article on Duquesnoy, by C. F. Beaulieu) Citizen Duplessis, the father-in-law of Camille Desmoulins, was arrested as a suspect because there was found in his house a clock with hands that were shaped something like a lily, a trunk on which was the maker's name surrounded with lilies, and an old portfolio bearing the faded imprint of the same

'It amuses me to think,' said Beaulieu to me but a few days ago, 'that Robespierre himself comes under the law of suspects—he who has in his room the books that he gained as prizes at the Collège de Louis-le-Grand, and which are all decorated with splendid lilies! As for myself, I believe that, although I have not "changed my behaviour and my language according to events," and although I have never figured amongst "the followers of Lafayette," nor amongst "the assassins of the Champ de Mars," I am one of those to whom all the other characteristics mentioned by Chaumette would properly apply.[1] After that,' he added, with a laugh, 'who can hope to escape the law of suspects if Robespierre himself comes within its action? I thought that I had really come across someone who had nought to fear in this respect. It was a brave fellow who took an active part in the deeds of the Twentieth of June, of the Tenth of August, and of the Thirty-first of May, and who *worked* at the Abbaye on September 2. "Here is one," I said to myself, "who cannot possibly be a suspect," but I have since learnt that he has a lily tattooed on his shoulder.'

'Really,' said I to Beaulieu, 'it can only be infants in arms. . . .'

'Take care, my friend,' he replied; 'don't go too fast. Chaumette, it is true, has forgotten them in his list, but their turn will come.'[2]

<hr>

flower. In No. 6 of his *Vieux Cordelier* Camille Desmoulins is very indignant concerning this arrest, but it must not be forgotten that he was one of the first to vote for the law of suspects.

[1] Beaulieu was arrested as a suspect October 29, 1793, and imprisoned in the Conciergerie. 'I was kept,' he says, 'for four or five months in the Conciergerie, and six at the Luxembourg.' He did not recover his liberty until after the 9th of Thermidor. See his 'Essais sur les Causes et les Effets de la Révolution de France,' tome v., p. 287.

[2] In the 'Anecdotes relatives à quelques Personnes et à Plusieurs Événements Remarquables de la Révolution,' by J. B. Harmand, a member of the Convention, we read: 'Some time after the death of Robespierre it was decreed that all the Revolutionary Committees should lay before the Committee of General Security the charges upon which prisoners then under detention had been arrested. When I reached the committee, I asked for what reasons Mdlle. de Chabannes, then thirteen years old, was detained. These reasons were thus set forth: "*Chabannes, aged eleven years and a half, arrested for having drunk the aristocratic milk of her mother.*"

CHAPTER CII.

Friday, October 18, 1793.

It was on August 2, at two o'clock in the morning, that the Queen was transferred to the Conciergerie. On leaving the Temple prison, where her two children and Madame Elisabeth were still detained, she forgot to stoop, and struck her head against the top of the wicket-gate. On being asked whether she had hurt herself, she replied : ' Oh no ; nothing can hurt me now.'[1]

On the day before the Convention had decreed that she was to be brought before the Revolutionary Tribunal.[2]

On October 3 it was decreed that the Tribunal in question should proceed without further delay to try the widow Capet.[3]

On October 6, Pache, the Mayor of Paris, Chaumette, the Procureur de la Commune, and Hébert, his deputy, together with Friry, Laurent, and Séguy, Commissioners of the Conseil-Général, and Heussée, the Administrator of Police, drew up a *procès-verbal*, at the foot of which, next to their signatures, are to be found those of the cobbler Simon and of the Dauphin. The wretched authors of this infamous document have put into the mouth of the royal child the most abominable accusations against his mother and his aunt. On October 6, 1789, some of the mob tried to assassinate the Queen at Versailles, and massacred the guards who were placed as sentinels at her door ; but what is this crime compared with that of Pache, Hébert,

---

[1] ' Récit des Événements arrivés au Temple depuis le 13 Août, 1792, jusqu'à la Mort du Dauphin, Louis XVII.,' by Mme. Royale ; ' Collection des Mémoires relatifs à la Révolution Française,' tome xix., p. 223.

[2] Decree of August 1, 1793, article 6 (*Moniteur* of August 2).

[3] *Moniteur*, October 5, 1793.

Chaumette, and their satellites—the crime of October 6, 1793 ? 'Crime has its degrees,' said Corneille. On that day, then, the Revolution must have reached the highest point, the limit beyond which it was impossible for crime to go.

On the morrow Pache, Chaumette, Laurent, Séguy, and Heussée, returned to the Temple accompanied by the municipal officer Daujon, and by David, the painter, who is now as intimate with Chaumette as he was once with Marat. This time they had Mme. Elisabeth and the daughter of Marie Antoinette brought before them, and confronted with the little Dauphin, subjecting them to a cross-examination that would recall the *Actes* of the early martyrs, were it not a slander upon pagan executioners to compare them with those of the Revolution.[1]

On Saturday last, October 12, at six o'clock in the evening, the Queen was examined by Herman in the presence of Fouquier-Tinville. On the 13th the indictment was read over to her, and on the 14th, at eight in the morning, she appeared before the Tribunal.

Herman presided, supported by four judges — Coffinhal, Maire, Donzé-Verteuil, and Deliège. The jurymen were Antonelle, formerly member for the Bouches-du-Rhône in the Legislative Assembly ; Renandin, a lute-maker ; Souberbielle, a surgeon ; Ganney, a wig-maker ; Besnard ; Fievé, a member of the Revolutionary Committee of the Museum section ; Lumière, a member of the same committee ; Thoumin ; Chrétien ; Nicolas, a printer to the Revolutionary Tribunal ; Sambat, a painter ; Desboisseaux ; Baron, a hat-maker ; Devèze, a carpenter ; and Trinchard, a joiner.[2]

---

[1] History itself stands helpless before such infamies as will scarcely bear mention. We must restrict ourselves to reproducing this passage from the narrative of Mme. Royale. 'Chaumette,' she says, 'questioned me concerning a number of wicked things of which my mother and my aunt were accused. I was so horror-struck and so indignant that, in spite of the fear in which I was, I could not help saying that it was an infamous lie. In spite of my tears, they insisted upon my replying. There were some things that I did not understand, but what I understood was so horrible that I wept with indignation' ('Récit des Événements arrivés aux Temple,' p. 233).

[2] In a letter quoted by M. Campardon (tome i., p. 120), and preserved in the Archives, W 500, Trinchard boasts in the following terms of having tried the Queen : 'I inform you, my brother, that I was one of the jury that tried the savage beast that devoured a large part of the Republic, the one who is known as the former Queen.'

The Queen was pale and looked ill ; her hair, now entirely white, made her appear twenty years older than she really was;[1] her black widow's dress was threadbare, like that of some poor working woman, but the proud stateliness of her bearing and the dignity of her movements betrayed the daughter of Maria Theresa. She made her way to the iron armchair as if she were about to take her place on a throne. To all those present—to the *sans-culottes* and the *tricoteuses* who thronged the hall, to the judges and jurymen who were about to send her to the scaffold—she was still Marie Antoinette of Lorraine, and even more of a Queen than she had been at Trianon or Versailles.

The trial lasted for two days and two nights, during which the Tribunal sat continuously. It was only at rare intervals that the Queen was able to take a little food, and yet she bore up bravely through it all, allowing not a single word to pass her lips which might compromise those who had had the honour of serving her. I will reproduce here only a single incident of this never-to-be-forgotten trial.

The cowardly Hébert had reiterated the infamous accusation contained in the declaration which, together with Pache and Chaumette, he had given young Capet to sign. To this Marie Antoinette had made no reply. A juryman having insisted upon an answer, the President again questioned her concerning the matter of which Citizen Hébert had spoken. 'If I have not replied,' she said, 'it is because Nature refuses to reply to such an accusation made against a mother. I appeal to every mother here.'[2]

In the night between the 15th and 16th Chauveau-Lagarde and Tronson-Ducoudray, appointed by the Tribunal to defend the prisoner, acquitted themselves of their task with courageous eloquence. When Chauveau sat down after having spoken for two hours, the Queen said in accents of emotion : 'How tired you must be, M. Chauveau-Lagarde! I am deeply grateful to you for all your trouble.'[3]

---

[1] She was only thirty-eight years of age, having been born November 2, 1755.

[2] *Bulletin du Tribunal Révolutionnaire ;* Buchez and Roux, 'Histoire Parlementaire,' tome xxix., p. 358.

[3] 'Notice Historique sur les Procès de Marie-Antoinette et de Mme. Élisabeth,' by Chauveau-Lagarde.

The accused was then led out of the court, and the President summed up in a long and fiery speech that was a fitting sequel to Fouquier-Tinville's indictment. He then put to the jury the four questions which they would have to solve, and which reduced themselves to two points—whether Marie Antoinette had been guilty of complicity with foreign Powers and with the conspirators at home.

After an hour's deliberation, the jury returned and declared that their finding had been in the affirmative. Brought back to the court, the Queen heard her sentence with perfect calm, descending the steps and traversing the hall without uttering a single word or making the slightest gesture ; on reaching the barrier that kept back the crowd, she raised her head majestically.[1]

It was then half-past four in the morning.[2]

Less than half an hour afterwards the call to arms was beaten in every section of Paris. At seven o'clock the armed forces were afoot ; at ten numerous patrols were parading the streets ; from the Palace of Justice to the Place de la Révolution cannon were drawn up at all the approaches to the bridges, squares and open spaces.

At seven o'clock Citizen Sanson, the executioner, presented himself at the Queen's door. 'You are very early, sir,' she said ; 'can you not postpone it a little while ?' 'No, madame ; I have had orders to come.'[3] She was ready to follow him. On returning to her prison a few hours before, she had written a long letter to Mme. Elisabeth ;[4] then, after having rested for a while on a truckle-bed placed near the window, she had pro-

---

[1] Chauveau-Lagarde, 'Notice Historique,' etc., p. 45.
[2] *Bulletin du Tribunal Révolutionnaire*, No. 32, p. 138.
[3] Prudhomme, *Révolutions de Paris*, tome vii., p. 96.
[4] This letter is dated as follows : '*This 16th of October, at half-past four in the morning.*' The original is exhibited in the Musée des Archives, by the side of Louis XVI.'s will. Mme. Elisabeth never received this letter, which, handed by Fouquier-Tinville to Robespierre, was found among the papers of the latter after the 9th of Thermidor, preserved by Courtois, and finally handed to Louis XVIII. Chateaubriand, in his speech to the Chamber of Peers on February 22, 1816, said of this letter : 'The hand that wrote it was as firm as the heart that dictated it ; the writing is not changed in the least. Marie Antoinette wrote to Mme. Elisabeth from her prison-cell with the same tranquillity as amid the pomp of Versailles' ('Œuvres Complètes,' tome xxiii., p. 109).

ceeded to make her last toilet. She herself cut off her hair.
She had only two dresses, the one black and the other white,
and chose the latter, no doubt in memory of her husband, who
on January 21 had clad himself all in white. The Abbé
Girard, Constitutional Vicar of Saint-Landry, sent by Bishop
Gobel, presented himself at that moment. 'Do you wish me to
accompany you, madame?' 'As you wish, sir,' replied the
Queen; but she refused to accept him as a confessor.[1]

At twelve or fifteen minutes past eleven[2] she left the Conciergerie. The crowd thronged the approaches to the prison,
and every window, balcony, or roof that afforded a view of the
entrance was occupied. I was stationed only a few paces from
the tumbrel, which was drawn by a strong white horse led by a
man with an evil-looking face;[3] a wooden plank served for a
seat, and there was neither straw nor hay on the floor. The
Queen got into the cart, looking pale but dignified; the priest,
in civilian dress, seated himself beside her, while the headsman's
assistant found room at the bottom of the vehicle. Sanson,
who was closer to the Queen, held the ends of a stout rope with
which the arms of the illustrious victim were bound behind her;
he remained standing, and held his three-cornered hat in his
hand. Marie Antoinette wore a white skirt with a black
petticoat under it, a white bodice, the sleeves of which were
trimmed with black ribbon at the wrists, a white muslin fichu,
and an entirely plain lawn cap.[4]

A large body of gendarmes, both mounted and on foot,

---

[1] The letter from the Queen to Mme. Elisabeth concluded with these
words: 'Good-bye! I am now going to devote myself to my spiritual
duties. As I am not free to do as I like, they will probably bring me a
priest; but I protest that I will not say a word to him, and that I will
treat him as an absolute stranger.'

[2] 'Récit du Supplice de Marie-Antoinette,' by Citizen Rouy, an eye-
witness, reproduced by M. Daubau in 'La Démagogie en 1793 à Paris,'
p. 465.

[3] Narrative of the Vicomte Charles Desfossez, an eye-witness, given by
M. A. de Beauchesne in his work on 'Louis XVII.,' tome ii., p. 145.

[4] 'Déclaration de Rosalie Lamorlière,' a servant at the Conciergerie
during the Queen's captivity, reproduced by Émile Campardon in 'Marie-
Antoinette à la Conciergerie,' p. 141, etc. 'On her way to the scaffold
she wore only a plain lawn cap without lappets or any signs of mourning,
and wore also her black stockings and stuff shoes, the only pair of each
that she had, and which she had not spoilt during the seventy-three days
she was with us.'

surrounded the tumbrel, which followed the usual route. All along the way the Queen gazed with indifference upon the armed force which, to the number of more than 30,000, formed a double line in the streets through which she passed, and also upon the immense crowd that rent the air with cries of ' *Vive la République !*'[1] As the procession passed the Church of Saint-Roche, the steps of which were thronged with spectators, there was loud applause, which Marie Antoinette seemed not to hear, and during the whole of the route her face betrayed neither anger nor despair.[2] In the Rues du Roule and Saint-Honoré she gazed attentively at the tricolour flags which hung out before the houses. On passing the Jacobin Club, over the door of which was the following inscription in gigantic letters, ' *Manufactory of Republican Weapons to crush the Tyrants,*' she turned and put a question to the priest, who thereupon held up the small ivory crucifix he had in his hand. Grammont, the actor,[3] who was escorting the tumbrel on horseback, at that moment rose in his stirrups, and, flourishing his sword, shouted at the top of his voice, ' This is the infamous Antoinette !' concluding his exclamation with a foul oath.

The tumbrel reached the Place de la Révolution a few minutes after noon. Although her hands were tied behind her, Marie Antoinette did not require any help in getting out of the cart. For a moment her eyes fell upon the Palace of the Tuileries ; she then lifted them heavenwards and bravely ascended the steps of the scaffold.[4] Having accidentally trodden on Sanson's foot, she turned to the executioner, who had uttered a slight cry of pain, and said : ' I beg your pardon, monsieur ; it was quite unintentional.[5]

---

[1] 'Le Glaive Vengeur,' pp. 116, 117.   [2] *Ibid.*

[3] Nourry, also called Grammont, an actor at the Théâtre de la Montansier, had taken part in the massacre of the prisoners of Orleans at Versailles, September 9, 1792. He became an Adjutant-General in the Revolutionary army, and served in the Vendée. Included in the trial of Chaumette, Gobel, Dillon, and others, he was condemned to death, together with his son, April 13, 1794. It is related that, desiring to embrace his son before ascending the scaffold, the latter repulsed him with the words : ' It is you who brought me here !' (Dauban, ' Les Prisons de Paris sous la Révolution,' p. 238).

[4] 'Le Glaive Vengeur,' pp. 116, 117.

[5] *Révolutions de Paris,* tome xvii., p. 96 ; Mercier, ' Le Nouveau Paris,' ch. xcvii.

The execution, with its horrible preliminaries, occupied about four minutes, Marie Antoinette behaving all the time with admirable courage and resignation. It was she herself who with a movement of her head threw off her cap. At a quarter past twelve all was over. The executioner held up the Queen's head to the people amidst the cries of ' *Vive la République !* ' that fell from thousands of lips.[1]

At that moment a young man forced his way through the line of soldiers that surrounded the scaffold, and, rushing to the place where the blood was trickling down, dipped his handkerchief in it. He was immediately arrested.[2]

[1] ' Le Glaive Vengeur,' p. 117.
[2] This young man was named Antoine Maingot. For particulars of his trial, see ' Marie-Antoinette à la Conciergerie,' by Émile Campardon, p. 161.

CHAPTER CIII.

THE RESTAURANTS.

Tuesday, October 22, 1793.

' *Universus mundus exercet histrionam!* Was this sentence of Petronius ever more true than it is to-day? Paris, especially the Paris of 1793, is one huge theatre. For those who are certain, on seeking their beds at night, that they will not be dragged off to prison before the morn; for those who are not in hourly dread concerning the fate of some relative or friend; for those, in a word, who live only out of curiosity, what a constant variety of grotesque and sanguinary scenes are placed in endless succession upon the stage of the capital! How many tragedies and comedies in a hundred acts are played both in the clubs and in the sections, in the Revolutionary Tribunal and in the National Convention, in the theatres, in the prisons, and in the streets! What strange and curious things are seen! How the laughter mingles with the tears, and what wondrous contrasts do we not find!

Famine has now reached a terrible stage. There is an almost entire absence of certain commodities, such as sugar and soap,[1] and the difficulty of procuring any bread at all is daily increasing. The crowds now begin to gather before the bakers' shops at four in the morning, and the people often have to wait six or seven hours to be served.[2] Sometimes mothers, with large families awaiting their return, are sent away without a morsel after having wasted a deal of their time.[3] Two ounces

---

[1] Police report of October 19, 1793 (Adolphe Schmidt, tome ii., p. 133).
[2] Schmidt, tome ii., p. 104.   [3] *Ibid.*, tome ii., p. 128.

of bread for each person per day[1] is the maximum allowance now made to the poor.

Whilst famine is on the increase, and bread is daily getting scarcer, the fashionable restaurants are replete with delicacies, with fine wines and costly liqueurs. The cellars of the nobles have been sold by auction, and all that has not been drunk by the Patriots has been eagerly snapped up by the keepers of eating-houses and *cafés*. Thrown out of employment by the ruin of their masters, the *chefs de cuisine* of the former aristocracy have passed from the service of princes, nobles, and financiers into that of the public.[2] The net gain resulting from the Revolution might, after all, prove to be the abolition of the monopoly of tit-bits; up to the present it seems to have brought no profit to anyone except gourmands.

Before the Tenth of August I used to go and dine at Méot's with Beaulieu once a week. The worthy Méot, whose customers have changed, but whose sentiments have, I believe, remained the same, said to me a few days ago: 'We see nothing of you now, sir; why is it? I still consider it an honour to receive gentle-folk, I do assure you, and we can serve you just as well as we used to—or,' he continued, with some show of pride, 'we can serve you even better than before the Revolution. I can offer you a choice of twenty-two kinds of red wine and of twenty-seven white; of a very large number of dessert wines, and of sixteen different kinds of liqueurs.'[3]

After Méot,[4] the best *restaurateur* in Paris is Beauvilliers, the

---

[1] 'As a child of twelve I used to go and wait for these two ounces at four in the morning in the crowd stationed in the Rue de l'Ancienne-Comédie, receiving them at the hands of M. Loquin, the baker, whose shop still exists, but is now filled with excellent rolls. If I had got there later, M. Loquin's stock might have been exhausted. There were four in our family, and I brought home eight ounces of bread for the day.' —A letter written by M. Audot, and reproduced by A. Granier de Cassagnac in his ' Histoire des Girondins et des Massacres de Septembre,' tome i., p. 72.

[2] 'The cooks of the princes, cardinals, canons and other dignitaries did not remain long idle after the emigration of the imitators of Apicius, but became *restaurateurs*, and announced that they were about to profess and practise the *science of the jaws*, as Montaigne says, for everyone that was willing to pay.'—MERCIER, ' Le Nouveau Paris,' ch. clix.

[3] 'Souvenirs de Paris,' by Kotzebue, tome i., p. 226.

[4] The Abbé de Lille has sung the praises of Méot in Canto III. of his ' L'Homme des Champs':

'Their appetite insults the noble art of Méot.'

former *chef* of the Prince de Condé; both have their salons in the Palais Égalité.[1]

After these come:

Rose, the caterer of the Hôtel Grange-Batelière.[2]

Venua's Restaurant, in the Rue Saint-Honoré.[3]

Léda's, at the corner of the Rue Sainte-Anne and of the Rue Neuve-des-Petits-Champs.[4]

The restaurant in the Hôtel Vauban, in the Rue de la Loi, formerly Rue de Richelieu.

The Restaurant Gervais, in the courtyard of the Riding-School, with its salons opening out upon the Terrasse des Feuillants.

The Restaurant Masse and the Restaurant Véry in the Palais Égalité.[5]

[1] In 1790 Beauvilliers had become the owner of three arcades in the Palais Royal for the price of 157,500 francs. In 1814 he published 'L'Art du Cuisinier,' a real masterpiece in the opinion of Colnet, the witty author of 'L'Art de Diner en Ville.'

[2] 'One day a carriage arrives at Sucy (where the family of Sainte-Amaranthe were living in 1793) containing the Comte de Morand, little Monsieur Poirson, the French Consul at Stockholm, and M. de Pressac, a brilliant conversationist, formerly an officer in the Guards, and a son-in-law of M. de Marbœuf. During dinner M. de Fenouil proposes to take the ladies to Paris, where each of the guests will entertain them in a fashionable restaurant. M. de Fenouil himself chooses Méot, MM. de Pressac and Poirson vote for Beauvilliers, and M. de Morand for the famous Rose, the caterer of the Hôtel Grange-Batelière' ('La Famille Sainte-Amaranthe,' by Mme. A. R., the daughter of an Adminstrator of Finance under Louis XVI.). M. Jules Claretie has given some very curious extracts from this pamphlet in his work on 'Camille Desmoulins.'

[3] The *Petites Affiches* for April, 1793, contains the following: 'Citizen Venua, restaurant-keeper at No. 75, close to the Riding-School, having also an entrance in the house called the Hôtel des Tuileries, opposite the Jacobins, in the Rue Sainte-Honoré, announces that on and after April 18 there will be dancing on Sundays and holidays in his salon, where good beer and all kinds of iced drinks will be found. There are separate rooms for club-dinners. He contracts for all kinds of entertainments, including weddings and other festivities.'

[4] 'Léda is already a rival of the famous Méot. Guzzling is the fundamental basis of present society.'—MERCIER, 'Le Nouveau Paris,' ch. ccxxxv.

[5] In his 'Mémoires,' where he speaks of the restaurants of Paris as an authority on the subject, Dr. Véron gives 1805 as the date of the establishment of the Restaurant Véry. This is a mistake. In Gorsas' paper, *Le Courrier de Paris*, tome xxi., p. 35 (February 3, 1791), there is a petition from the section of the Palais Royal to the Conseil de la Commune, in which the following occurs: 'Last week the waiters at Véry's restaurant in the Palais Royal, No. 83. . . .' The brothers Véry had in 1790 become the owners of three arcades for the price of 196,275 francs.

The restaurant kept by Barthélemy, Maneille, and Simon in the Rue Helvetius, opposite that of Louvois.

We have already had the 'History of the Revolution' by two Friends of Liberty. We shall no doubt some day have the 'History of the Revolution' by two gastronomists. Meanwhile I will give a few notes that may possibly assist them.

Mirabeau the elder would after an evening sitting often go and sup at Velloni's, the Italian *restaurateur* in the Place des Victoires. One night he came in accompanied by Talleyrand-Périgord, the Bishop of Autun, and at one o'clock in the morning General Lafayette, in civilian costume, came and joined them. This little entertainment got bruited about, and did not fail to call forth many comments.[1]

Mirabeau the younger—Mirabeau-Tonneau—did not frequent the same restaurants as his senior, but held his court at Masse's, in the Palais Royal, where he was supported by the Comte de Montlosier, the Marquis de Belbœuf, and a few of their friends, all men of wit and imbued with ardent Royalism. These meetings resulted in the publication of weekly pamphlets sparkling with wit—'Le Déjeuner' or 'La Vérité à Bon Marché,' 'Le Dîner' or 'La Vérité en Riant,' 'La Moutarde après le Dîner,' 'La Tasse de Café sans Sucre,' etc. Whilst the Royalists were amusing themselves with the production of these smartly-written pamphlets, the Revolution went on its way. This was no bees' battle, where a few grains of dust are sufficient to damp the ardour of the combatants :

> ' Hi motus animorum, atque hæc certamina tanta
> Pulveris exigui jactu compressa quiescent.'

It was also at the Palais Royal, in the Restaurant Beauvilliers, that Rivarol, assisted by Peltier, Champcenetz, and the Marquis de Bonnay, prepared the 'Actes des Apôtres' during dinner.[2]

The aristocrats who did not edit papers after their wine, and who did not bespatter their tablecloth with ink, had chosen the salons of Méot for their meeting-place[3]—the worthy Méot

---

[1] 'Œuvres' of Camille Desmoulins, tome ii., p. 108.

[2] Beaulieu, 'Essais,' tome ii., p. 42.

[3] 'Mémoires sur Divers Événements de la Révolution et de l'Émigration,' by A. H. Dampmartin, tome i., p. 424. 'The Jacobins showed

whose succulent dinners made Camille Desmoulins' mouth water. 'I am perfectly willing,' he cried, 'to celebrate the Republic provided the banquets are held at Méot's.'[1] We know, of course, that the Republican Camille is anything but a Spartan. Did we not already in 1790 read in the *Petit Dictionnaire des Grands Hommes:* 'The journalists have bread, whilst honest folk are without it. Desmoulins, who formerly slept in a truckle-bed, now lies on a couch of blue damask. At one time he was reduced to the diet of Strabo's valet Thaler—fruit, onions, and a bottle of water; now he dines at Masse's for nine francs'?

Mirabeau the elder and Mirabeau the younger, Talleyrand and Lafayette, Rivarol and Champcenetz, aristocrats and *constitutionnels,* have all made way for the Girondists. The latter frequently met at Venua's, whose salons open out upon the Rue Saint-Honoré, and whose gardens extend as far as the Terrasse des Feuillants.[2] The Jacobin Club was not far off, and one evening—it was December 7, 1792—a member of the Club got into the tribune, and denounced the Girondists in the following terms: 'It is my custom to go and dine at Venua's. There are two dining-rooms in this restaurant. In one of them I perceived a well-set-out table which induced me to enter. I found myself in the company of eighty deputies, and I could not refrain from asking my neighbour whether the dinner had been arranged. It seems that he had taken me for one of the guests. Barbaroux was in the chair, and Buzot kept the whole table in a roar by his witty speeches. At the end of the meal each one present paid his six francs.'[3]

great activity in digging mines that made some of the more enlightened of their enemies fear for the consequences of their explosion. The *Constitutionnels* amused themselves, so to say, with the toys of power; frivolous circumstances transformed themselves in their eyes into grave events. They regarded as so many victories the couplets sung at the Vaudeville, the speeches made at the Café de Valois, and the jokes perpetrated at Méot's, the fashionable *restaurateur.* These three places were unanimously regarded as the rendezvous of pure Royalists.'

[1] 'Histoire Politique et Littéraire de la Presse en France,' by Eugène Hatin, tome v., p. 308.

[2] The Hôtel Meurice stands on a portion of the site of Venua's restaurant, and partly on that of the restaurant kept by Léda ('Mémoires Secrets,' by the Comte d'Allonville, tome iii., p. 402).

[3] Buchez and Roux, tome xxi., p. 249.

One party drives out another. The Mountain has replaced the Gironde, not only in the committees and in the Ministerial offices, but even in the salons of Venua.[1] On October 17 last, on the morrow of Marie Antoinette's execution, the habitués of that restaurant saw Robespierre, Saint-Just, Barère, and Vilate enter a private room. Joachim Vilate, formerly a priest and a professor at Guéret and at Limoges, is, as is well known, on the most intimate terms with Robespierre and Barère. Discretion is not one of his strong points, and, proud of the favour he enjoys with the masters of the day, he does not hesitate to repeat all that they say in his presence. If he is to be believed the following is a part of the conversation that took place that day at Venua's tables.

Requested to give some account of the Queen's trial, at which he had been present, Vilate spoke of Hébert's charge, and of the sublime cry of the accused woman—'*I appeal to every mother here!*'—and did not conceal the profound impression made upon the audience by these words. Robespierre was seized with a violent fit of anger, and, dashing his plate upon the ground, he cried: 'This fool of a Hébert! is it not enough that she is really a Messalina? Must he make her an Agrippina into the bargain, and so clothe her with interest in the eyes of the people during her last moments?' This outburst was followed by a long silence, broken at last by Saint-Just, who remarked: 'Morality will be a gainer by this act of justice.' Hereupon Barère added: 'The guillotine has cut the Gordian knot of European diplomacy.'

The conversation went on for some time, whilst the exquisite cheer and the costly wines exercised their usual influence upon the guests. Barère, more verbose even than usual, declared that in his opinion all nobles, priests, lawyers, and doctors were the sworn enemies of the Revolution, and should be treated as such.

---

[1] After the 9th of Thermidor, one of Mallet du Pan's correspondents wrote to him from Paris: 'I am obliged to leave you. I am going to dine in the house in which the Raynevals, the Mirabeaus, and the Garats once dined—which has since then also accommodated the Gundets, the Gensonnés, the Rolands, the Barères, and the Prieurs de la Marne, and in which the Talliens, the Frérons, and the Carlettis now regale themselves' ('Mémoires et Correspondance' of Mallet du Pan, collected and edited by M. A. Sayons, tome i., p. 413).

Summing up his reflections in one of those metaphors he so dearly loves, he observed: 'The vessel of the Revolution can only reach port on waves of blood.' 'That is so,' replied Saint-Just; 'it is only from heaps of the dead that a nation can be regenerated.'

Following Barère's metaphor, Robespierre pointed out the two dangers which the vessel of the Republic should avoid with equal care: on the one hand, too great a number of executions, and an amount of bloodshed that would disgust humanity; on the other hand, a cowardly moderation and a false sensibility, which would sacrifice the commonweal to save a few heads. It was Barère who concluded the discussion with the following words: 'We must commence with the Constituents and the most conspicuous members of the Legislature; that rubbish must be cleared away to give us room.'[1]

Being a friend of luxury and of good cheer, and having neither the language nor the habits of a Spartan, Barère prefers the kitchen of Venua to that of Méot, and it is in the *red room* of the latter that he likes best to hold his select parties. Here, again, we owe to Vilate the record of Barère's memorable sayings in this *red room*. One day Barère was dining together with Vilate and Hérault-Séchelles—the elegant Séchelles, who is also an adept at reconciling the severest principles with the most lax observance of morality. 'Nature,' said Hérault, 'will be the goddess of the French, and the universe will be her temple.' The conversation then turned upon the Revolutionary Government which there was some talk of establishing. Said Hérault-Séchelles, with a sigh: 'Was Raynal right, after all, in declaring that a nation can only be regenerated in a bath of blood?' To this Barère replied: 'What is the present generation compared with the immensity of the centuries to come?'[2] And with these words they each poured themselves out a glass of that marvellous *eau-de-vie* which comes from the cellars of Chantilly, and which is sold at

---

[1] 'Causes Secrètes de la Révolution du 9 au 10 Thermidor,' by Vilate, formerly a juryman of the Revolutionary Tribunal of Paris, p. 2. During the 'Terror' Vilate had changed his name to that of Sempronius Gracchus. 'I had the Revolutionary madness,' he says, 'to hide the obscurity of the name of my fathers under that of a name illustrious in Roman history.'

[2] 'Continuation des Causes Secrètes de la Révolution du 9 au 10 Thermidor,' by Vilate.

sixty francs per bottle.[1] On another occasion the following
words fell from Barère : ' We will burn all the libraries. The
only literature we require is the history of the Revolution and
its laws. If it were not for the immense conflagrations which
repeatedly ravage the earth, this would soon be naught but a
world of paper.'[2]

Février, who in 1791 bought a large portion of the Galerie
Montpensier, has no *red room* like Méot. On the contrary, he
makes a show of most Republican simplicity. Here there are
no salons with rich hangings, but low-vaulted cellars, to which
access is gained by a flight of steps, and where the tables are
illumined by a few feeble lights fixed here and there along the
walls. It is easy to understand that this is not attractive to
Barère, any more than the remembrance of the blow received
here by Michel Lepeletier.

Though Robespierre has been known to dine once or twice
with Barère at Venua's and at Méot's,[3] such an event is entirely
out of keeping with his habits, for he always takes his meals at
home. Sometimes, however, after his daily walk in the Champs
Élysées he dines at one of the restaurants near the Pont Tournant,[4] in a room looking out upon the Place de la Révolution.[5]

Amongst the habitués of the Restaurant Gervais on the
Terrasse des Feuillants are Carnot the elder and Collot-
d'Herbois.[6] The restaurants which are good enough for

---

[1] *Petites Affiches*, Thermidor, year III.   [2] Vilate, *op. cit.*

[3] ' Mémoires de Barère,' tome ii., p. 20.

[4] The Pont Tournant spanned the moat which then separated the
Tuileries from the Place Louis XV.

[5] ' Histoire Générale et Impartiale des Erreurs, des Fautes et des Crimes
commis pendant la Révolution Française,' by Prudhomme, 1796-97,
tome v., p. 151.

[6] At the sitting of the Convention of March 26, 1795, Carnot, after
having admitted that he had inadvertently signed a warrant for the
arrest of two of his own clerks, whom he, however, believed to be
good, honest men, added : ' I did not even give myself time to go and
dine at home, although I lived in the Rue Florentin, but went to dine
every day at a restaurant in the Terrasse des Feuillants, kept by a man
named Gervais. Robespierre got to hear of this, and made out a warrant
against him, although he did not know his name, but merely described
him as " the keeper of the first restaurant on the right past the door of
the Riding-School." I myself, as well as Collot, signed this warrant
unwittingly, and when we went to dine there we were shown our
signatures ; we immediately hastened back to the Committee, and had
the warrant cancelled ' (*Moniteur*, March 30, 1795).

Robespierre, Carnot, and Collot-d'Herbois are, it seems, too common for the members of the Commune, and particularly for Hassenfratz, Hébert, and Chaumette, who, at the end of a sitting in which they had bewailed the misery of the people, and thundered forth against the aristocrats and the monopolizers, proceeded to the Palais de l'Égalité, where, in the salons of Méot and Beauvilliers, they ordered the finest dishes and the most costly wines.[1]

For some time past *le Grand Premier de l'Hôtel Vauban* is very much in favour with the gourmands. It is there that Citizen Antonelle, one of the jurymen who tried Marie Antoinette, and one of those appointed to try Brissot, comes almost every evening to recruit his strength after the fatigue and worry of the day.[2]

The Providence, however, of the first-class restaurants are the Dantonists, for whom nothing is good enough or dear enough. This band of voluptuaries comprises Lacroix, Hérault-Séchelles, Fabre d'Églantine, and last, but not least, Danton himself, their worthy chief. Was it not he who, at the end of a repast at which Cavaignac and several other members of the Convention

---

[1] Prudhomme, 'Histoire Générale,' tome v., p. 133.

[2] 'Antonelle, too dissipated, too gluttonous, and too devoted to the worst orgies of the Palais Royal, to think of anything else' (Louvet, 'Mémoires Inédits,' p. 39—MS. in the Bibliothèque Nationale). M. Vatel, in his work on 'Vergniaud,' tome ii., p. 322, has given some of Antonelle's *menus* found by him amongst the papers relating to Babœuf's trial (Archives Nationales, W, 567). The following is a specimen:

MEALS SERVED AT THE HÔTEL VAUBAN TO CITIZEN ANTONELLE.

October 18, 1793 (old style).

	Francs.	Sous.
Béchamelle d'aillerons et foie gras - -	5	0
October 31.		
Poularde fine rôtie - - - - -	6	0
November 3.		
Dinner for three - - - - -	30	0
Champagne - - - - - -	6	10
November 4.		
2 cailles au gratin - - - - -	5	0
Ris de veau - - - - - -	4	0
12 mauviettes - - - - -	3	0
Bread - - - - - -	0	6
Sauterne - - - - -	10	0

were present, used the following words?—'At last our turn has
come to enjoy life. Sumptuous homes, delicate fare, exquisite
wines, silks and satins to wear, beautiful women—all these are
the reward of power. Since we are the stronger, let us therefore
appropriate them. After all, what is the Revolution? A
battle. And, as in every battle, should not the leaders share
among themselves the *spolia opima?*[1]

[1] Louis Blanc, 'Histoire de la Révolution,' tome vii., p. 96. Louis
Blanc relates this anecdote upon the authority of Godefroy Cavaignac,
to whom it was told by his mother.

CHAPTER CIV.

FEAR.

Thursday, October 24, 1793.

'THE whole of the Revolution may be conjugated as follows: I am afraid, thou art afraid, he is afraid, we are afraid, you are afraid, they are afraid.'[1] These words by Joseph Michaud are as true as they are witty. Courage, it is true, is not yet dead in France—a fact of which our armies give good proofs. It shines with equal brilliancy in the camp and in the prison, on the field of battle and on the scaffold. When we are about to die, we are indeed the sons of the Frenchmen of yore, but far above this courage in the face of death there is another form of courage, higher, more noble, and more worthy of a loyal heart— the courage which resists the prejudices and the passions of the mob in the public squares; the courage which, in an assembly of patriots, dares to oppose a misled majority, an unjust law, or a criminal measure. This is the courage that is of most use in revolutionary times; of most use and least found. It is absolutely wanting in the Convention itself, where each day the most iniquitous and barbarous decrees are unanimously adopted without debate. The Committee of Public Safety or the Committee of General Security sends one of its members into the tribune. He reads a long report, concluding with the draft of a Decree, and the matter is ended. Whatever it may be, the Decree is accepted in advance; not one voice will be heard to oppose it, nor will any hand be raised in dissent.

On the 12th of this month, three days after the entry of the

---

[1] 'Esquisses Historiques, Politiques, Morales et Dramatiques au Gouvernement Révolutionnaire de France,' by Ducancel, p. 51.

Republican troops into Lyons, Barère submitted the following Decree in the name of the Committee of Public Safety :

'The National Convention will appoint a Commission of five members to punish, according to martial law and without delay, the counter-Revolutionaries of Lyons.

'All the inhabitants of Lyons shall be deprived of their arms, which shall immediately be distributed amongst the defenders of the Republic. A portion will be handed over to the patriots of Lyons who have been oppressed by the rich and the counter-Revolutionaries.

'The city of Lyons shall be destroyed ; all that was inhabited by the rich shall be demolished. There shall remain only the houses of the poor, the habitations of the murdered or proscribed patriots, and the buildings specially devoted to industry, charity, or public instruction.

'The name of Lyons shall be effaced from the list of the cities of the Republic.

'The agglomeration of houses left will in future be known by the name of Ville Affranchie.[1]

'A column shall be erected on the ruins of Lyons, and the following inscription shall inform posterity of the crimes committed by that city, and of the punishment meted out to the evil-doers : *Lyons waged war against Liberty ; Lyons is no more !*'[2]

Nothing resembling this Decree has ever yet figured in history, and yet it was adopted unanimously.[3]

Whoever wishes to make a study of the innumerable forms that human cowardice can assume, has only to take his place each day in the Legislative Chamber at the Tuileries and watch from the gallery the physiognomy, the gestures, the words, and the silence of the members of the Convention. In one who was formerly noted for the elegance and care with which he dressed, fear betrays itself in the negligence of his attire ; in another by the disorder of his speech ; in one who was an Academician by his professed hatred for the Academy, and in another who was a priest by his hatred of the Church. Of these two deputies seated side by side, the one never utters a word, whilst the other speaks

---

[1] This name was changed to that of Commune Affranchie, the Republic recognising all agglomerations of inhabitants as communes only.

[2] Decree of October 12, 1793 (*Moniteur*, October 13).

[3] *Mercure Français*, No. 116.

incessantly. What is it that prevents the first from opening his mouth? Fear. What is it that causes the other to speak so glibly? Fear again. Then we have men who have sat in couples for years; one suddenly rises to the summit of the Mountain, whilst the other hides in the depths of the Swamp; it is fear that makes the one seek concealment and the other prominence. Some, again, are continually changing their places. Yesterday you left them on one of the benches of the Right, whilst to-day you will find them in the Centre; to-morrow they will be on the Left—they are afraid. Some, it is true, stoutly stick to the same seats; they are as much afraid as the others, but they have grasped the fact that to avoid attracting attention it is best to stay where they are. These are the men whom I look upon as the smartest, and who will certainly be the last left upon the field of battle; far from imitating the poor devils who absent themselves from the sittings as much as possible in order to escape notice, they, on the contrary, never miss a single one,[1] and Robespierre himself is not more exact and regular in his attendance.

It would be a curious task, well worthy the attention of a political naturalist, to classify our Conventionals, taking for a basis of classification not the names of the parties to which each of them belongs, but the different sorts of fear that characterize them. Each would thus be arranged according to genus and family, and in every family what a number of varieties there would be! M. Lacépede, who was a deputy for Paris in the Legislative Assembly, and who has been lucky enough to escape being returned to the Convention, is well capable of drawing up such a list as I have mentioned, since he has already given us a 'Natural History of Snakes' and one of 'Reptiles.'

In his place I will attempt to describe, not a genus, nor even a variety (for that would be beyond my powers), but an individual belonging to the variety named the Silent.

Sieyès was returned to the Convention by three departments: the Gironde, the Orne and the Sarthe. He came to the Assembly preceded by an immense reputation. Had he not written the

[1] 'Mémoires de Meillan,' member for the Basses-Pyrénées in the National Convention.

famous pamphlet 'What is the Third Estate ?'[1] And on the
morrow of the Royal Sitting had he not uttered these words, big
with revolution: 'We are to-day what we were yesterday—let
us deliberate'? His speeches on the royal veto, on the liberty
of the press and of religion, and on the new division of France
into departments and districts, of which idea he had been the
promoter; his plan for the institution of juries both in civil and
criminal matters—so many circumstances, in fact, in which he
had been permitted to play a foremost part, and which had
brought his great talents into prominence, left no doubt that
he would become one of the most influential members of the
National Convention and one of its leading orators. The Convention has now sat for more than a year, and Sieyès has appeared
in the tribune only once; this was on January 25, 1793, when
he read a report on the organization of the Ministry of War.
In vain has the Assembly successively appointed him to be a
secretary, a member of the Committees of Constitution and of
Public Safety—he obstinately persists in refusing to open his
lips. On the occasion of the King's trial, when nearly all the
members gave reasons for their manner of voting, only four
monosyllables escaped him. On the question of guilt: 'Yes.'
On the question of the punishment to be awarded the King:
'Death.' On the question whether there should be an appeal to
the people: 'No.' And on the question of respite also 'No.' As
remarkable, however, for the regularity of his attendance as for
his silence, he has never missed a single sitting.[2] He is always
there, approving of everything and voting with the majority on
every question. Whether he be in the corridors or in his seat,
he is rarely seen without a copy of *Père Duchesne* in his hand.
He delights in the filthy prose of the low-minded Hébert; his
face is wreathed in smiles, and he cannot help betraying his
satisfaction when he reads that influential sheet.[3]

[1] January, 1789. The exact title of the pamphlet runs: 'Qu'est-ce
que le Tiers-État? Tout. Qu'a-t-il? Rien.'
[2] Notice on his life, written by himself (year III).
[3] Paganel, 'Essai Historique et Critique sur la Révolution,' tome iii.,
p. 95. In this, however, Sieyès merely imitated the Girondists. Paganel,
who was himself a member of the Convention, and who speaks of what
he has seen, further tells us: 'Two-thirds of France were terror-stricken

In September, 1789, M. de Montlosier, on making his first appearance in the Constituent Assembly, where he had been sent to replace M. de la Rousière, who had resigned his seat, met the Abbé Sieyès at the door of the Assembly, and after a brief exchange of compliments asked him what he thought of the body then sitting. Sieyès hesitated for a moment, and then replied, with downcast eyes: 'It is an abyss; to throw one's self into it is to stop there.'[1] This was most probably what he said to himself on the day when he threw himself into the Convention —a real abyss if ever there was one. To be quite certain of staying there to the end, he chose a seat almost next to that of Robespierre.[2] My eyes have frequently wandered from one to the other—from the somewhat expressionless face of Robespierre to the proud features of Sieyès—to his noble brow, indicating deep thought and power, to his eagle eye and his thin, pursed-up lips.[3] Frequently, too, have I surprised in myself feelings of hatred for Robespierre side by side with feelings of contempt for Sieyès.

As he is on the benches of the Assembly, supporting the vilest decrees with his silence and his vote, so is he in the committees. He attends them regularly, takes a prominent seat near the table, and at the end of a quarter of an hour rises to pace up and down the room. However grave the question may be, and however terrible the measures under discussion, he says nothing. Should any member turn to him and press him to give his opinion, he never fails to fall in with the others. And this man, who now allows himself to be led by Collot-d'Herbois, by Billaud-Varenne, or by Vadier, is the man who in our enthusiasm we hailed four years ago as the prophet and the legislator of the Revolution, the man whom Mirabeau called his master, and who wrung this

---

by the mere name of *Père Duchesne*, and yet those who most execrated Hébert's doctrines, and those who were most disgusted by his style, were equally eager to read his obscene journal. . . . The Girondists and the Moderates came to their seats in the Convention with a copy of *Père Duchesne* in their hands, and smiling at its matter.'

[1] 'Mémoires sur la Révolution Française, le Consulat, l'Empire, la Restauration et les Principaux Événements qui l'ont suivie,' by the Comte de Montlosier, tome i., p. 255.

[2] 'Mémoires, Correspondance et Manuscrits du General Lafayette.'

[3] 'Mes Récapitulations,' by N. Bouilly, tome i., p. 221.

cry from him : 'There is at least one man in France—and a man
destined to be our leader in that National Assembly which is to
decide our fate !'[1] I will give yet another trait of his, and then
leave him. A few days ago he was informed that one of the
men with whom he came most into contact had been arrested.
'This devilish fellow,' he said, ' is always trying to compromise
me.' And he then proceeded to support with all his weight the
charges that hung over the unhappy man.[2]

Will France, now trembling before the deeds of the National
Convention, ever awaken to the fact that the cowardice of these
men, with the exception of a very small number, is even greater
than their cruelty? Never were the words of Tacitus more
applicable than in this instance : ' *Pavebant terrebantque.*'

Roland, the Minister of the Convention (quoted by Barrière in
his edition of the 'Mémoires de Mme. Roland,' p. 322), speaks of
the deputies of the Girondist party in the following terms: 'Some
were afraid of the daggers with which I myself was threatened ;
others, believing they possessed some popularity, were afraid of compromising it, whilst a frequent plea was the necessity of preserving
one's influence for more important matters. Sometimes, too, one
could hear the following words, used either in good faith or otherwise : " What does it matter? We must let them say what they
like, and not irritate them. They will get to know each other, and
there will be an end of them." There is no human weakness or
folly of which I have not been a patient witness. Though I am
ashamed to say so, I am unable to point out a single man who acted
with manly courage. All deplored the fate that urged them on, and
gazing in abject terror at the future by the light of the present,
they found no resources to remedy the evil—their pallor was that
of fear, and their abandonment that of despair.'

Mme. Roland, whose faults should not make us forget her
tremendous courage, has expressed an opinion upon the Conventionals which will be endorsed by history. In the work which she
calls 'Mes Dernières Pensées,' she speaks in the following terms of
the members of the Plain and of those of the Girondist party, who,
after having tolerated the events of May 31, were in turn impeached
on October 3, 1793: ' Would that they had had my courage, these

---

[1] Sainte-Beuve, ' Causeries du Lundi,' tome v., p. 167.
[2] Benjamin Constant, ' Portraits. Le Livre des Cent et un,' tome vii.

pusillanimous creatures, these men unworthy of the name, whose weakness concealed itself beneath the veil of prudence! They would then have atoned for their first mistakes; they would on June 2 have strenuously opposed and rescinded the decrees which they had allowed to pass. The cowards! They temporized with crime, and they were bound to fall in their turn. But their fall is one of shame; they are pitied by none, and posterity cannot do otherwise than regard them with the utmost contempt.'

Let us close with two lines more of Mme. Roland, taken from her brief notice on Buzot: 'The French have been ungrateful to their defenders, and those whom they should have cherished and honoured were proscribed by an assembly of cowards governed by rogues.'

CHAPTER CV.

October 24 to 30, 1793.

THE trial of Brissot and the twenty deputies summoned to appear with him before the Revolutionary Tribunal commenced on October 24. In spite of the enormous crowd that throngs the palace each day to watch the proceedings, or at least to see the accused, I managed to gain admission to some of the sittings. These are held in the Salle de l'Égalité,[1] and last from nine in the morning until five in the afternoon.

The tribunal is presided over by Herman, assisted by Foucault, Scellier, Denizot, and Ramey ; Fouquier-Tinville discharges the duties of Public Prosecutor, whilst the clerical ones are undertaken by Paris, who, since the assassination of Michel Lepeletier by one of his namesakes, has changed his patronymic for that of Fabricius. There are fifteen jurymen : Antonelle, Nicolas, Thoumin, Devèze, Souberbielle, Renaudin, Lumière, Fiévé, Baron, Ganney, Trinchard, Sambat, Brochet, Aigoin, and Laporte.[2] With the exception of the last three, all served on the jury that tried the Queen.

The accused, twenty-one in number, and all members of the Convention, are : Brissot, Gensonné, Vergniaud, Lauze-Duperret, Carra, Gardien, Dufriche-Valazé, Sillery, Fauchet, Duprat, Lasource, Boyer-Fonfrède, Ducos, Lacaze, Mainvielle, Duchastel, Le Hardy, Boilleau, Lesterp-Beauvais, Antiboul, and Viger.

Brissot has taken the iron armchair reserved for the leader of

---

[1] The other section of the Revolutionary Tribunal sat in the Salle Saint-Louis, then called Salle de la Liberté. Both the halls in which the Tribunal held its sittings were destroyed by the Commune in 1871.

[2] Campardon, 'Le Tribunal Révolutionnaire de Paris,' tome i., p. 154.

the batch,[1] and is described in the indictment as the organizer and principal member of the 'plot against the unity and indivisibility of the Republic.' This plot has never existed in point of fact, but the enemies of the Girondist party are not far wrong in regarding Brissot as their most formidable opponent. He possessed energy, courage, and ability, but what could he do with men who refused to obey their leader, and with lieutenants who put so much vigour into their speeches that they had none left for action, the most eminent among them—Vergniaud—being not less remarkable for his careless and idle habits than for his eloquence ?

In reply to the questions respecting their names, age, profession, and place of birth, Brissot declared that he was thirty-nine, and a native of Chartres. The majority of the prisoners are, like him, below the age of forty. Lasource is thirty-nine, Viger thirty-six, Gensonné and Le Hardy thirty-five, and Duprat thirty-three. Several are under thirty, Mainvielle and Ducos being twenty-eight, and Boyer-Fonfrède and Duchastel twenty-seven.[2] Vergniaud has just completed his fortieth year, having been born at Limoges May 31, 1753, and I have shown in what manner the Commune, the sections, and the National Convention celebrated the anniversary of his birthday.[3]

Only one of the accused has passed his fiftieth year; this is the Marquis de Sillery, the husband of Mdlle. de Saint-Aubin, Comtesse de Genlis, who is fifty-seven.

Seven counsel appeared for the prisoners: Chauveau-Lagarde, Tronson-Ducoudray, Julienne,[4] Lafleutrie, Guyot, Lasalle, and

---

[1] See the engraving representing the Revolutionnary Tribunal during the trial of the twenty-one members in the *Récolutions de Paris*, tome xvii., p. 147.

[2] Revolutionary Tribunal, sitting of October 24, 1793.

[3] The certificate of his birth was given by C. Vatel in 'Vergniaud,' tome i., p. 174.

[4] Julienne, a young man of very good address, but of extraordinary petulance, both in his words and gestures, depriving himself by the rapid flow of his language of a deal of its effect. His concise style sometimes left much to be desired in the way of development which in his own mind he deemed superfluous. Appointed an advocate to the Prefecture de Police under the Empire, Julienne's whole time was taken up by petty matters. Had he been less worried and occupied, his marvellous abilities would have gained him a place in the foremost ranks' ('Souvenirs' of Berryer the elder, tome i., p. 319).

Guinier. Chauveau-Lagarde is entrusted more particularly with the defence of Brissot and Vergniaud.

It is impossible to follow the trial without being disgusted with the impudence of the accusers, the infamy of the witnesses, and the want of dignity displayed by the judges and the jury. But at the same time it is difficult to forget that the accused men were nearly all without any pity for Louis XVI. The indictment drawn up against them by Amar, and laid before the Convention by him on the third of this month in the name of the Committee of General Security, is a tissue of calumnies and lies. But what else than a similar tissue of calumnies and lies was the indictment drawn up against Louis XVI. by Dufriche-Valazé, and laid before the Convention on November 6 last in the name of the Special Commission of Twenty-four? People are naturally indignant on reading in Amar's report : ' Pitt wished to assassinate the faithful representatives of the people ; Brissot and his accomplices have more than once attempted to get some of their colleagues murdered, and they themselves assassinated Marat and Lepeletier.' Such accusations are abominable, but were not those more abominable still which Dufriche-Valazé incorporated in his report, and to which he referred when he cried : ' Of what was this monster not capable ? I will show him to you waging war upon the whole human race !'[1] Only a few days ago Marie Antoinette was seated on those benches now occupied by the deputies of the Gironde, and Dufriche-Valazé was called to give evidence together with Bailly and Manuel ; but whilst the ex-Mayor of Paris, as well as the former Procureur de la Commune, showed some respect for the terrible misfortunes of the Queen, and were careful to say nothing that might further the plans of Herman and Fouquier-Tinville, Dufriche-Valazé, on the contrary, permitted himself to support the charges. When Herman and Fouquier had already marked him out for their victim, he became their accomplice. Though Dufriche-Valazé is the only one guilty of the double crime of exerting all his strength to condemn Louis XVI., and of supporting the charges against Marie Antoinette, several of those now being tried with him—Brissot,

---

[1] ' Rapport sur les Crimes du Ci-devant Roi,' by Dufriche-Valazé.

Vergniaud, Gensonné, Carra, Ducos, Lesterp-Beauvais, Boyer-Fonfrède, Lasource, Boilleau, and Duprat—voted with him for the death of the King.[1]

Persecuted in their turn, and brought before a bloody tribunal, Brissot and his colleagues might have expiated their crime by a full repentance, and after so much weakness have at least gained themselves some honour in the face of their enemies by the firmness of their attitude. But far from doing this, they adduced their behaviour in the trial of Louis XVI. as a claim upon the indulgence of their judges, and sought in this way to efface the remembrance of their opposition to the Commune and Marat. The facts with which they were reproached they shifted upon the shoulders of their absent friends, and denounced even their own relatives. Instead of bravely laying down their lives, they defended themselves as if they had some hope of escape, and acted, not like warriors who fall nobly in the arena, but like cunning lawyers, who plead extenuating circumstances. In the history of the Revolutionary Tribunal, as in that of the Convention, the names of the Girondist deputies will always be associated with chicanery.[2]

The Revolution of May 31 was expressly directed against them; it is to that movement that they owe the honour of appearing before the Tribunal to-day; yet, incredible to relate, they applauded that very Revolution, and sang the praises of the Commune that overthrew them.

'I have,' said Fonfrède, 'pleaded many a time on behalf of the municipality of Paris.'[3]

'France has given its opinion on this Revolution,' said Duprat, 'and I fully approve of what was done on May 31.'[4]

When Fouquier produced a letter written by Vergniaud to the Club of the Récollets of Bordeaux, inviting the men of the

<hr>

[1] Vergniaud, Gensonné, Carra, Ducos, Boyer-Fonfrède, Lasource, Boilleau, and Duprat voted for death and against the respite, Brissot, Lesterp-Beauvais, and Dufriche-Valazé voting for death and in favour of the respite. Mainvielle and Viger had not been able to take part in the King's trial, the former not having taken his seat in the Convention until January 25, 1793, and the latter until April 27.

[2] For proofs and details of this see 'La Légende des Girondins,' by Edmond Biré, ch. xi.

[3] *Bulletin du Tribunal Révolutionnaire*, part ii., No. 47.   [4] *Ibid*, No. 62.

Gironde to hold themselves in readiness, the great orator replied
' Had I had any intention of realizing what I wrote, the moment
was come; but, on the contrary, in the sitting of May 31 I got
a Decree passed, informing the armies of what had taken place
in Paris. Filled with admiration at the behaviour of the
inhabitants of this city on that day, I brought forward a
motion recognising that they had deserved well of their
country.'[1]

Vergniaud has probably never been more eloquent than in
the speeches made by him since the beginning of the trial. He
has uttered some magnificent phrases whilst enumerating the
services he has rendered the Revolutionary cause, and it is
perfectly true that neither Danton nor Robespierre has
rendered greater ones. He has laid a claim to glory for the
part he played on the Tenth of August, but in doing so he
betrayed a singular want of dignity and courage. When on
that eventful day he ascended the tribune to propose the provisional suspension of the chief of the executive power in the
name of the Commission of Twenty-four, he uttered the following words in accents full of emotion:[2] 'I am come in the name
of the Special Commission to lay before you a very rigorous
measure, but the grief with which you are yourselves filled will
enable you to judge how important it is for the country that
you should adopt it at once.'[3]

Chaumette bore witness to the emotion betrayed by Vergniaud
on the overthrow of the most illustrious throne in the world as
to a criminal fact. 'I charge Vergniaud,' he said before the
Tribunal, 'with an affectation of most profound grief at the
downfall of a throne which was undermined by crime, and for
the destruction of which he himself presented the decree.' And
Vergniaud, far from treating this contemptible accusation as it
deserved, and taking credit for the tears he had shed—noble
tears which might have washed away his faults in the eyes of
posterity—Vergniaud took a most solemn oath that he had
looked upon the misfortunes of the Tyrant with indifference,

[1] *Bulletin du Tribunal Révolutionnaire*, No. 43.
[2] 'Histoire de la Terreur,' by Mortimer-Ternaux, tome ii., p. 341.
[3] *Moniteur*, August 12, 1792.

and that the grief which had filled him was due to no other cause than the misfortunes of the people and the massacres of which that unhappy people were the victims.[1] That it was the people who were massacred on the Tenth of August is, of course, taken as an accepted fact.

More miserable still was the reply made by Vergniaud to another charge brought forward by Chaumette, in which he was reproached with having got himself nominated at the sitting of the Tenth of August for the post of Governor to the Prince Royal. He was not afraid to confess in justification that in proposing this measure he had had some ulterior object in view, and that it had been his aim to place the son of Louis XVI. in the hands of the people as a hostage. 'When I drafted that resolution,' he said, 'the battle was not yet won, and victory might have favoured despotism; in that case the Tyrant would not have failed to bring the Patriots to trial. It was amidst these uncertainties that I proposed to give the son of Capet a Governor, in order to place in the hands of the people a hostage who might be very useful to them in case they were conquered by tyranny.'[2]

'The motive alleged by the accused,' replied Fouquier, 'does not appear to be the true one, for if the Tyrant had been victorious he would have cared very little whether his son had a Governor or not; that would not have prevented him from avenging himself upon the Patriots.' And to this simple and sensible observation Vergniaud could make no reply.[3]

The orator did not, it is true, imitate certain of his confederates, who cast all the blame upon the shoulders of their absent friends—upon those friends who, though in hiding to-day, will probably be discovered to-morrow, and whom these terrible denunciations will infallibly send to the scaffold.[4]

Dufriche-Valazé denounced his colleague Valady in the following manner. In his deposition Chaumette had said: 'A red placard appeared in Paris at a moment when the city was in

---

[1] 'Procès de Brissot et de ses Complices,' p. 29. [2] *Ibid.* [3] *Ibid.*
[4] The *Bulletin du Tribunal Révolutionnaire*, which was accused of having shown itself very favourable to the prisoners, says in its No. 40 : 'They all agree in throwing most of the blame upon their contumacious accomplices, such as Guadet, Barbaroux, etc.'

some difficulty with regard to its food-supply. An invitation was held out in this placard to massacre the Jacobins and the Grey Friars in order to get bread. The author of this placard, which was addressed "To Honest Men," was for a long time unknown. At last an officer of the law suspected that it must be either Valazé or Valady, his accomplice, but I cannot say for certain which of the two it really was.' Valazé hastened to declare that he had had no hand in the publication of that placard, and that Valady was the author.[1]

Lasource denounced Isnard. 'Chabot,' he said, 'has just charged me with having demanded the impeachment of Robespierre and Anthoine in the meeting which took place in the Rue d'Argenteuil. He is mistaken; I do not remember whether I supported that proposal, but it was certainly made by Isnard.'[2]

Lauze-Duperret charged Barbaroux with having raised a revolt against the National Convention at Caen.[3]

The President also read a letter addressed to Lesterp-Beauvais and directed against Marat—a communication which was therefore very compromising for its author. It was not signed, but simply subscribed with an 'A' and an 'F,' and Lesterp-Beauvais was kind enough to tell the Tribunal that these initials meant 'Amable Frichon.'[4]

Nothing is more painful than the task I have set myself here, and I am constantly asking myself whether it does not denote a want of pity to dilate upon the weaknesses of those who, persecuted by implacable enemies, are condemned to the scaffold before they are tried. More than once since I commenced these pages describing the trial of Brissot and his friends has the pen fallen from my fingers, but I feel I must go on to the end. Every day innocent men and women are brought before the Revolutionary Tribunal. Even the oldest and the weakest give proofs of the most indomitable courage; none show signs of cowardice, and none seem to defend themselves by lies or by reticence. Public attention, distracted by other sights, scarcely

---

[1] *Bulletin*, No. 49. Outlawed July 28, 1793, Izarn de Valady, member for the Aveyron, took refuge with a relative in the district of Périgueux, but he was arrested, condemned by the Tribunal of the Dordogne, and executed December 5, 1793.

[2] *Bulletin*, No. 56.   [3] *Ibid.*, No. 62.   [4] *Ibid.*

deigns to dwell for a moment upon their innocence and heroism. In that same hall are now seated the men who overthrew the Monarchy, assassinated the King, and passed, or helped to pass, innumerable decrees of death; and these men, though steeped in crime, have not even the courage which has never failed any of those whom they sent to the bar of Fouquier-Tinville's tribunal. But they are young and eloquent; their phrases are well turned and their delivery perfect; that is why the public takes an interest in them, and why, not content with giving them its pity, it is even beginning to bestow upon them its admiration. I will go as far as pity, but I cannot say I admire them. I maintain, on the contrary, that it is a duty to lay bare their weaknesses. The history of men whose fall is ignominious because their lives were without virtue furnishes a lesson which should not be lost.

There is one, however, amongst the Twenty-one to whom the sympathy, respect, and homage of honest men may go. This is Duchastel, the deputy for the Deux-Sèvres, the youngest of all the accused; he did not belong to the Legislative Assembly, and therefore did not take part in the criminal plots woven by the Brissot faction in that shameful period between the separation of the Constituent Assembly and the meeting of the National Convention. In the Convention his courage never failed for a moment, and his conduct to-day is no other than it was during the trial of the King.

The President asked him: 'Who were the other passengers on board the vessel on which you were arrested?' 'They all had different names,' replied Duchastel, not without a faint smile. Herman could get no more out of him except a reply to this one other question. 'Was it not you,' he asked, 'who came and voted against the death of the Tyrant in your night-cap?' And Duchastel replied in tones of assurance: 'As I have not to blush for any of my actions, I admit that it was I.'[1]

These proud words will set the public conscience at rest. Thanks to Duchastel—thanks to his firm and loyal attitude— justice and honour, violated by shameless judges and betrayed by weak-minded prisoners, will at least have been avenged!

[1] 'Procès de Brissot et de ses Complices,' p. 68.

CHAPTER CVI.

October 30, 1793.

HAVING drawn attention to the weaknesses of the Twenty-one, it is but just that I should dwell for a moment upon their accusers and judges.

Amongst the witnesses for the prosecution, five were members of the Convention, and voted for the impeachment at the sitting of October 3. These are Citizens Chabot, Fabre d'Églantine, Maribon-Montant, Léonard Bourdon, and Duhem. Was it not a violation of the most elementary rules of justice to hear as witnesses those who ordered the prosecution? Was there not a danger of their testimony being transformed into an absolute charge? And was that not precisely what happened, especially in the case of Chabot, whose so-called examination occupied two sittings?[1]

On September 23 last Citizen Brochet, a member of the Jacobin Club, complained that the indictment against Brissot and his accomplices had not yet been read to the Convention, and expressed his indignation at the delay in the punishment of those culprits. Brochet sat on the jury which was to decide their fate, and the idea that it was his duty to keep an open mind on the subject probably never occurred to him.

These things, which would have appeared monstrous at any other time, attract no notice at all to-day, and had there been no more serious blots in this trial, I should not have stopped to dwell upon them. They were, however, followed by the most

---

[1] Chabot's examination fills eighteen columns of the *Moniteur*.

outrageous measure and by the most iniquitous proceeding of which the Convention has yet been guilty.

On the rising of the court on October 27, Hébert, who had given evidence in the trial, rushed to the Jacobin Club and laid bare a pretended plot to save the prisoners from the blade of the law—a plot concocted by the majority of the newspapers and by the *Bulletin du Tribunal Révolutionnaire* in particular. 'The men now on their trial,' he said, 'are the most cunning and scheming wretches one can imagine, and they have great advantages over their accusers, who are only the defenders of the rights of the people. The accused may write in their justification, but their accusers, on the contrary, bound down by their duty and by the discharge of the manifold functions which such duty entails, have not the time to do so in an efficient manner. A plot is certainly in existence to save these villains from the blade of the law, and you will be astonished to hear what means are being employed to make it succeed. The craft and imposture displayed by the editor of the *Bulletin du Tribunal Révolutionnaire* in editing his paper is almost incredible. There is no sheet that is more dangerous to public opinion . . . Chabot delivered a speech before the Tribunal yesterday in which he described with both genius and sincerity the misfortunes caused by the men who wished to federalize France.' Hébert concluded his speech by demanding (1) That the *Journal de la Montagne* should report the sittings of the Revolutionary Tribunal during the trial of Brissot ; (2) that Chabot should be invited to repeat his speech in the Club and that it should then be printed and reproduced in the papers.

A citizen, who had been summoned to appear as a witness before the Tribunal, then expressed his indignation at the delay in the course of justice in a matter in which guilt was so evident.

Another citizen demanded that a Commission should be appointed to denounce the editor of the *Bulletin du Tribunal Révolutionnaire* to the Committee of General Security. This proposal was immediately adopted, but the honours of the sitting were carried off by the spokesman of a deputation from 400 political clubs of the South. This worthy expressed the wonder that had filled him when, on his arrival in Paris, he had found the Revolutionary Tribunal to be nothing but an ordinary court, and had seen that evidence and other forms of justice were required to try Brissot, a villain that ought to have been shot offhand.[1]

On the morrow, the 28th, the Jacobin Club again had the pleasure of hearing Hébert, who had written in his paper:

'Why are the brave judges of the Tribunal fooling about? Are so many ceremonies required to cut short the villains whom the people have already tried?'[2]

Hébert commented upon his article in the following terms at the Club:

'The grand jury has already given its verdict; public opinion has sat upon the crimes of this atrocious faction, and before the Tribunal was formed that opinion had condemned them.

'We know that Brissot and Gensonné, that Duchastel, the incendiary of Calvados, that Fauchet, a priest who preached republicanism and martial law—we know that these men cannot make good their escape, but there is one phœnix among them whom the people would like to see rising from his ashes, and that is Vergniaud.

'There is another in whom the women of the Republic interest themselves because he is—and I must admit it—a handsome man; it is he whom Marat called the ferret of the Gironde, and everyone will allow that in a matter so complicated and requiring so much cunning the *rôle* of ferret was not an unimportant one. His relationship with Mme. Condorcet gained him the favour of all the women of her clique. Ducos is the man whom the women have taken under their protection.'[3]

Hébert concluded by moving that a deputation be sent to the National Convention to demand the condemnation of Brissot and his accomplices within twenty-four hours. Chaumette, who was also a witness at the trial, attempted to prove the criminality of the men who accepted the mission of defending the conspirators. 'The form of trial,' cried the Procureur de la Commune, 'should be the same here as it was in Rome, where the culprit passed from the Capitol to the Tarpeian Rock. I move that the men who defend the assassins of the people be held up to public contempt and execration, and that this

---

[1] *Moniteur*, October 30, 1793.   [2] *Le Père Duchesne*, No. 304.
[3] *Moniteur*, October 31, 1793.

resolution be sent to the criminal courts, to the forty-eight sections, and to the political clubs.'

Chaumette's motion was passed, as well as the proposal made by Hébert to go and demand Brissot's condemnation within twenty-four hours. The Jacobin Club, moreover, decided that it would go in a body, and invited the galleries to join the deputation.[1]

There is little doubt that Hébert had come to some arrangement with Herman and Fouquier-Tinville before proceeding to the Jacobin Club, for on that same evening of October 28 the President of the Tribunal and the Public Prosecutor addressed a letter to the Convention, asking that body to set aside all the formalities that hindered the work of the court.[2]

Immediately after hearing this letter read on the 29th, the Convention admitted the deputation from the Jacobin Club to the bar, when Citizen Audouin, the spokesman, a son-in-law of Pache, expressed himself as follows :

'Citizen Representatives,—You have established a Revolutionary Tribunal charged with the punishment of conspirators. We believed that we should see this Tribunal laying bare crime with one hand and crushing it with the other, but the court is still fettered with forms that compromise its liberty. You have public opinion on your side, therefore strike. We propose to rid the Revolutionary Tribunal of those forms which stifle conscience, and to pass a law giving jurymen the right to declare that they have heard enough evidence ; then, and then only, will traitors be unmasked and Terror be the order of the day.'[3]

The demands of the deputation from the Jacobins were immediately complied with, and the following Decree, drawn up by Robespierre, was adopted at the same sitting :

1. When a trial before the Revolutionary Tribunal has lasted for more than three days, the President of the Tribunal shall be bound at the opening of the following sitting to ask the jury whether they have heard sufficient evidence.

2. If the jury reply in the negative, the trial will proceed until the jury have made a contrary declaration.

3. If the jury reply that they have heard sufficient evidence, judgment can immediately be pronounced.

---

[1] *Moniteur*, October 31, 1793.   [2] *Ibid.*, October 30, 1793.   [3] *Ibid.*

4. The President shall allow no appeal to be made against the provisions of this law.

5. The Convention refers to its Committee of Legislation that part of the petition relating to the abrogation of the forms that hinder the operations of the special criminal tribunals, and requests it to present its report thereupon to-morrow.

6. The Convention decrees that this decision shall be immediately forwarded to the President of the Extraordinary Criminal Tribunal.[1]

Not a single member of the Convention spoke against this abominable Decree, nor did a single one raise his hand against its adoption.

On the morrow, at the opening of the court, Fouquier-Tinville demanded the application of the new law, whereupon Herman asked the jury whether they had heard sufficient evidence. They retired, and on their return Antonelle declared in their name that they had not yet arrived at any conclusion. The trial was then continued, but no fresh witnesses were called, the proceedings being entirely confined to a series of questions addressed to Duprat, Mainvielle, Lesterp-Beauvais, Le Hardy, Fauchet, Lacaze, Antiboul and Sillery—that is to say, to those of the accused who held a secondary place in the trial, and whose replies were not calculated to make any impression on the audience. Neither Vergniaud nor Gensonné, neither Brissot nor Lasource, was examined at this decisive hour, and Herman was therefore enabled to go on without a hitch for half the day. At three o'clock he adjourned the court, which did not meet again until five. This interval of two hours was no doubt turned to account by Fouquier-Tinville and Herman, for as soon as the sitting was resumed, Antonelle rose and declared that he and his colleagues had heard sufficient evidence, although in reality no fresh matter of any kind had been placed before the court, and no witness of importance had been heard since

---

[1] 'Procès Verbal de la Convention du 8 Brumaire' (October 29, 1793) Amongst the papers of Robespierre was found a rough draft of this Decree written by his own hand; he had recommenced it no less than four times. This draft, with its corrections, was reproduced in the second volume of Robespierre's 'Papiers Inédits.' On the part played by Robespierre in the condemnation of the Girondists, see Vatel, 'Vergniaud,' tome ii., p. 437, etc.

the morning. Hereupon the jury immediately retired to the
Council Chamber, before the Public Prosecutor had made his
usual demand for a verdict, before the accused or their defenders
had been able to proffer a word of reply, and before the President
had even summed up the evidence. At half-past ten they sent
word into court that they were ready to give their verdict, and
were immediately admitted. Each of them then replied sepa-
rately to the questions that were put by the President. Many
of them gave the reasons upon which they based their opinions,
but all agreed upon the guilt of the accused. The latter were
then brought into court, and Fouquier, in the name of the
Republic, demanded that Brissot and his accomplices should be
condemned to death in conformity with the law of December 16
last, which provided that ' all who shall attempt to destroy the
unity and indivisibility of the Republic shall be punished with
death, and their property confiscated for the good of the State.'

This created a profound sensation in court. Whilst the
majority of the public applauded with all its might, the few
honest men scattered here and there throughout the hall felt
keenly for these unfortunate victims, nearly all endowed with
remarkable talents, who were guilty, no doubt, of many faults,
but innocent at least of the crimes for which they were condemned.

On hearing Fouquier-Tinville demand their condemnation in
the name of the Republic, and in conformity with the law of
December 16 last, I, for my part, could not help thinking that
no one had contributed more to the establishment of the
Republic than Brissot, Vergniaud, and Gensonné, and that the
law of December 16, 1792, is mainly their work, since it was
passed—and unanimously passed—at a time when the Girondists
were in a majority in the Convention.

Some of the prisoners heard Fouquier's demand in a kind of
dull stupor, whilst others gave way to rage and despair. Brissot
hung his head, and seemed to resign himself to his fate. The
Abbé Fauchet lifted his eyes to heaven, and his trembling lips
were probably asking of God that pardon refused him by men.
Lasource appeared overwhelmed, whilst Duprat, on the contrary,
seemed to defy his judges. Boilleau, lifting his hat on high,

cried, 'I am innocent!' and harangued the court at some length.

Boyer-Fonfrède threw himself into the arms of Ducos, and said to him, ' *Mon ami*, it is I who have brought this upon you.' Ducos replied, ' Console yourself, *mon ami ;* we will die together.' Gensonné asked for permission to speak on a point of law, but his words were lost in the uproar.[1] Suddenly, amidst the cries, the supplications, and the yells of indignation that filled the court, the words, ' I am dying!' were heard by one or two of the prisoners, but the tumult was so great that they remained unnoticed.

Meanwhile the President ordered the gendarmes to lead the prisoners away. The attitude of Sillery at that moment was sublime ; though a sufferer from gout, and scarcely able to stand, he threw the crutch that supported him into the centre of the hall, crying in loud and sonorous tones, ' My sentence gives me back all my strength.'[2] On leaving the court, many of the accused who had prepared their defence in writing tore up the documents, and scattered the pieces broadcast. Some of the crowd believed, or pretended to believe, that these papers were assignats, trampling upon them, and tearing them into shreds amidst cries of ' *Vive la République !*[3]

All the prisoners had now left the hall except the one who had uttered the words ' I am dying!' and whose lifeless body lay on the benches bathed in blood. Herman, however, who seemed to be entirely indifferent to this horrible sight, proceeded to pass sentence of death and confiscation of property upon Brissot and his colleagues.

This formality being concluded, the Tribunal, on receiving an intimation that one of the condemned had stabbed himself, decided that the individual in question should be examined and attended to by the sworn officers of health, who would thereupon immediately present their report. After a rapid examination, the surgeons declared that the condemned man now lying in the

---

[1] 'Les Mystères de la Mère de Dieu dévoilés,' by Vilate, an ex-juryman of the Tribunal of Paris, ch. xiii.

[2] *Les Révolutions de Paris,* tome xvii., p. 149.

[3] *Bulletin du Tribunal Révolutionnaire.*

court had expired, whereupon the Tribunal ordered two of its ushers to identify the corpse, and to draw up and hand in their *procès-verbal* at once.

Nappier and Deguainier, the two ushers charged with this duty, reported to the Tribunal that the body was that of Charles Éléonore Dufriche-Valazé.

Fouquier-Tinville then rose, and demanded that the body of Valazé should be guillotined in the Place de la Révolution together with Brissot and the other prisoners. Even Herman recoiled before this nameless deed which Fouquier had proposed as the most simple and natural thing in the world,[1] and the Tribunal merely ordered Valazé's body to be taken to the place of execution in a tumbrel accompanying those of his accomplices, and to be buried together with the latter.[2]

The court rose, and the crowd that filled the hall rushed out to impart the *good news* to the numbers who, in spite of the lateness of the hour, were patiently waiting in the vestibule and corridors of the Palace of Justice,[3] and by whom it was received with loud and prolonged cries of ' *Vive la République !*'

[1] 'Procès de Fouquier-Tinville.' Evidence of the Registrar Wolff, No. 23, p. 2; replies of Fouquier, No. 24, p. 3.
[2] *Bulletin du Tribunal Révolutionnaire*, No. 64.
[3] Letter from Pache, Mayor of Paris, to Henriot.

CHAPTER CVII.

Friday, November 1, 1793.

At noon yesterday[1] the condemned men left the Conciergerie to be taken to the scaffold in three tumbrils. They were in their shirt-sleeves, and bareheaded, and their hands being already tied, their coats had been loosely thrown about their shoulders. A smaller tumbril that followed the others contained the body of Valazé, lying on its back, with its face uncovered. In spite of the rain that fell in torrents, a larger crowd than had ever been seen at any execution[2] thronged the streets, squares, and bridges, and every window that commanded a view of the procession was eagerly besieged. The tumbrels followed the usual route, which lay along the quay as far as the Pont Neuf, across the Place des Trois-Maries, and along the Rue de la Monnaie, the Rue du Roule, and the Rue Saint-Honoré; then, turning down the Rue Nationale, they reached the scaffold, erected between the Garde-Meuble and the pedestal of Louis XV.'s statue, replaced since the Tenth of August by the statue of Liberty. All along the route thousands of voices rent the air with shouts of ' *Vive la République!* ' *Down with traitors!*

The attitude of nearly all the condemned was dignified and firm. Though Boilleau cried to the people, ' Do not confound me with the Brissotins: I do not share their opinions; I am a

---

[1] The execution of the Girondists took place on Thursday, October 31, and not on October 30, as twice erroneously stated by Michelet (tome v., pp. 386 and 397).

[2] *Bulletin du Tribunal Révolutionnaire*, No. 64 ; *Révolutions de Paris*, tome xvii., p. 148.

stanch Mountaineer "[1]—though Carra seemed struck with stupor,[2] and Brissot and Fauchet were pensive and sad,[3] many of the victims gazed upon the crowd with looks that spoke of courage, contempt, and indignation. To the wretches who shouted, ' *Vive la République !*' they replied, ' *Vive la République ! but you will never get it.*'[4] Duchastel, whose young and manly features were aglow with intrepidity and enthusiasm, flung the following words at his insulters with pitying contempt, ' Poor Parisians ! we leave you in the hands of those who will make you pay dearly for your folly of to-day.'

The dismal procession took an hour to perform the journey, and as soon as it reached the Place de la Révolution, the condemned men were drawn up in line along the foot of the scaffold. Boyer-Fonfrède and Ducos were in the last tumbrel, and as they got out their lips met in a brotherly kiss. The others followed their example, and this touching scene, instead of appealing to the hearts of the spectators, seemed, on the contrary, only to increase their rage, for the cries of ' *Down with the traitors !*' became more furious than ever. Meanwhile one of the victims had mounted the scaffold ; it was the Marquis de Sillery, who, being the eldest, no doubt owed to this circumstance the privilege accorded him of dying first. His demeanour in the Place de la Révolution before the executioner was no other than it had been before Fouquier-Tinville's Tribunal on the preceding day. He even bowed to the spectators on his right and left with the same easy grace as if he had been in a drawing-room.[5]

The whole execution occupied thirty-eight minutes. Whilst awaiting their turn, the condemned men at the foot of the guillotine sang the refrain :

> ' Plutôt la mort que l'esclavage
> C'est la devise des Français !'[6]

Most of them, on reaching the top of the scaffold, addressed the crowd, but their words were immediately drowned amidst

---

[1] 'Histoire Secrète du Tribunal Révolutionnaire,' tome i., p. 176, by Roussel.

[2] 'Le Spectateur Nocturne,' by Restif de la Bretonne, tome viii., p. 564.

[3] *Bulletin*, No. 64.

[4] *Révolutions de Paris*, tome xvii., p. 148.   [5] *Bulletin*, No. 64.

[6] 'Procès de Brisset et des Vingt-et-un Députés ses Complices,' p. 80.

shouts and yells of execration. I am informed on good authority
that Ducos, who remained in his usual excellent spirits and
jovial mood to the end, said to the executioners as they seized
him : 'It is high time for the Convention to proclaim the
indivisibility of the body.'[1] Fauchet, on the contrary, was in a
state of such prostration that he had to be carried to the
guillotine.[2] Vergniaud made his way up the steps with the
calm, disdainful air that was habitual to him. When he
appeared on the platform, gazing down upon the crowd from
the top of this novel tribune, there was a roll of the drums.[3]
Were the authorities afraid that he was about to speak, and
did they wish to drown his voice ? Perhaps. I myself do not
think that he had any such intention, but it is impossible for him
to have heard the roll of the drums without remembering the
Twenty-first of January and the last moments of Louis XVI.

Viger was the last to be executed ;[4] why he was kept till then
is not known. He could certainly not have been looked upon
as the most guilty, having entered the Convention but a few
weeks before May 31, and having played only a secondary part
throughout.

As Viger's head fell into the basket, the spectators waved
their hats, and the square re-echoed with wild shouts of ' Vive la
République !' for more than ten minutes.[5]

For the past twenty-four hours my mind has been continually
filled with thoughts of the Twenty-one—of these men, almost
all in the prime of life and endowed with brilliant talents,
who were sacrificed before the eyes of a hostile mob, and who,
as they mounted the steps of the scaffold, mutely saluted the

---

[1] Beaulieu, 'Le Diurnal de la Révolution,' October 31.
[2] 'Mémoires Secrets,' by the Comte d'Allonville, tome iii., p. 375.
[3] 'Le Spectateur Nocturne,' by Restif de la Bretonne, tome viii.,
p. 564.
[4] According to certain historians, Vergniaud was executed last. 'The
ranks at the foot of the scaffold were rapidly thinning,' says Lamartine ;
'one voice alone continued singing the Marseillaise—it was that of
Vergniaud, who was executed last.' 'When Vergniaud's grave and
solemn voice sang last,' says Michelet. This is an error. Le Bulletin du
Tribunal Révolutionnaire plainly says : 'Viger was executed last.'
[5] Bulletin, No. 64.

tumbrel in which lay the dead body of the colleague and friend who had gone before them.

Never, perhaps, had condemned men gone to execution accompanied by a fiercer hatred or persecuted by a more horrible clamour. In one section a certain Jilliard had been appointed member of a Commission charged with the presentation of a petition to the National Convention on October 31. He was, however, not at his post, and this evening he excused himself in the following terms: 'The pleasure of seeing the heads of our traitorous deputies fall was the only thing that could make me forget my duty.'[1]

Whilst the ultra-Revolutionaries are shrieking for joy at the death of the Brissotins, many of the Royalists are applauding the punishment meted out to them. An old man worn out by age boasted yesterday that he had performed a journey of four leagues on foot in order to witness the death of 'the wretches who sent their King to the scaffold.'[2]

I must conclude with the admission that Brissot, Vergniaud, and their friends contributed more than anyone to the overthrow of the Monarchy, and history offers few examples of an ingratitude comparable with that of the Parisians whose yells of execration drowned the dying words of the men who organized the Twentieth of June, who completed the work of the *heroes* of the Tenth of August, who amnestied the cut-throats of Avignon, who allowed the massacres of September to go on under their very eyes without raising a finger or uttering a word of disapproval, who passed multitudinous decrees of proscription and death against priests, refugees, and suspects, who erected the scaffold of the Twenty-first of January, and who voted for all those measures of which the Revolutionary Government and the Terror are the outcome.

---

[1] This declaration was placed on the register of the section, p. 46, sitting of November 1, 1793. 'Vergniaud,' by C. Vatel, tome ii., p. 335.

[2] Bailleul, 'Almanach des Bizarreries Humaines,' p. 27.

Amongst the twenty-one members who laid down their lives on October 31, there were several who must not be confounded with the Girondists. More than half of them—thirteen out of the twenty-one—did not sit in the Legislative Assembly, and should therefore not share the responsibility of the leaders of the Brissot party during that disastrous period from October 1, 1791, to September 20, 1792—from the end of the Constituent Assembly to the opening of the Convention. These thirteen were: Antiboul, Boilleau, Carra, Duchastel, Duprat, Gardien, Lacaze, Le Hardy, Lesterp-Beauvais, Mainvielle, Sillery, Valazé, and Viger. There were some, no doubt, who, like Carra, the editor of the *Annales Patriotiques*, or like Mainvielle, a leader of the cut-throats of Avignon, vied in revolutionary ardour outside the Legislative Assembly not only with Brissot, but with Marat himself. Others there were who, without having played so guilty a part before their entry into the Convention, distinguished themselves during the trial of Louis XVI. by a line of conduct which made them in that instance outdo even the most violent Mountaineers. Such were Dufriche-Valazé and Jacques Boilleau, the latter during his own trial giving proofs of the most deplorable weakness, and declaring that he was now a frank Mountaineer. It is but just to recall the fact that Viger sat in the Convention for one month only, and that he displayed great courage whilst in that Assembly; that Duchastel, though seriously ill, was carried on a stretcher to the Riding-School on January 16 in order that he might record his vote in favour of Louis XVI. amidst the fierce yells of the Mountain; that Le Hardy gave such loud expression to his sentiments of humanity and justice during the King's trial, during the debates on the attempt to impeach Marat, and on several other occasions, that he was taunted as a Royalist by the rabble in the galleries, at whom he flung this proud reply: 'You have prostituted the names of *Royalists* and of *counter-Revolutionaries* to such an extent that they have become synonyms for those of *friends of law and order.*'

It is the duty of honest men to accord Le Hardy, Viger, Duchastel, and some of their companions, the sympathy which should never be withheld from courage and the respect that we owe to death. If they committed mistakes (and who in those troublous times was exempt from these?), their blood and their repentance has obliterated them. It is a well-known fact, and one that should be stated here, that the Abbé Lothringer, the confessor of Custine, was permitted to see the condemned men on the night between October 30 and 31, and that six of them—Fauchet, Le Hardy, Viger, Lesterp-Beauvais, Gardien, and Lauze-Duperret—received absolution. In a letter written by the Abbé Lothringer, and published in the *Annales Catholiques* (tome ii., p. 322) and in the *Républican Français* (August 23, 1797), he says: 'Amongst the twenty-one deputies there were seven who sought spiritual consolation.' He then proceeds to give the names just mentioned, but states that he has forgotten the seventh. There is little doubt that it was Duchastel, alone among the rest worthy of receiving in his last hour this reward for his noble and generous conduct, and who, belonging to one of the most religious provinces of France, was not likely to refuse the consolations of religion as was done by Brissot and Carra, by Vergniaud and Ducos, and by Antiboul and Boilleau, the journalists and lawyers of the Girondist party. We have it on the authority of the Abbé Lothringer that Fauchet, after having received absolution, heard Sillery's confession. It is certain, therefore, that eight out of the twenty-one confessed their sins and abjured their crimes before mounting the scaffold.

The Abbé Lambert, who was on terms of great intimacy with Brissot, accompanied the Abbé Lothringer to the Conciergerie on the night between October 30 and 31, and M. Poujoulat has incorporated his narrative in his ' Histoire de la Révolution Française ' (tome ii., p. 94), from which we learn that Gensonné also confessed himself, and that, cutting off a lock of his hair after his confession, he said to the priest: 'My father, you have done me a great service; I ask you for one favour more, and that is to take this lock of hair to my wife. You will get her address from Mme. Brissot, who is at Versailles, and you will try and console her as well as you can.' The Abbé Lambert also states that Brissot having refused his services, Lasource turned to him with the words : 'Since you believe in God and immortality of the soul, why do you not confess your sins? Soon to appear before your Maker, have you none with which to reproach yourself? Ought you not to be happy that you may cleanse your soul at the approach of your last moments? I am a Protestant minister myself, but I think that the Catholic priest is clothed in incomparable grandeur when he approaches a death-bed with his consolation.'

Brissot, Vergniaud, Gensonné, Carra, Ducos, Boyer-Fonfrède, and Lasource—and I am reluctantly compelled to add Valazé—must therefore go down to posterity as having been not only condemned by their fellow-men, but unpardoned by their God. Those who boast that they never allow themselves to be blinded by cowardly sophisms will judge them severely, but let us at least admit that they laid down their lives on the scaffold with dignity and courage. Who knows whether a cry of repentance did not escape Brissot as he stood at the foot of the guillotine and saw the heads of his friends roll into that awful basket? Who can say whether Vergniaud, on hearing the roll of the drums—an echo of January 21—did not recognise in that terrible coincidence, and in the blow that was about to strike him, a well-deserved punishment; whether he did not send up one cry for forgiveness; and whether his tongue, then about to be silenced for ever, did not utter one of those prayers which as a child he had learnt from his mother's lips, and which, even when grown up, he had repeated in the halls of the Sorbonne seminary?

INDEX

'ADMINISTRATION MILITAIRE,' i. 140

Aimé-Martin (Louis), 'Essais sur la Vie et les Ouvrages de Bernardin de Saint-Pierre,' ii. 259

Aïssé (Charlotte Élisabeth), 'Lettres,' i. 384

Alissan de Chazet (André René Polydore), 'Mémoires, Souvenirs, et Portraits,' i. 321

Allonville (Alexandre Louis d'), Count, 'Mémoires Secrets de 1770 à 1830,' i. 11, 238, 295, 301, 360, 361 ; ii. 336, 367

Alluaud (François), 'Notice sur Vergniaud,' i. 10

Almanach des Muses, 1793, ii. 47

Almanach National de France, ii. 62, 70

'Almanach Royal' for 1792, i. 112

Ambigu (L'), i. 85

Ami du Peuple, i. 10 ; ii. 51, 260

Ami du Roi (L'), i. 8, 9, 56, 82, 213, 326, 345 ; ii. 84

Annales Catholiques, ii. 370

Annales Patriotiques, i. 219, 225, 311 (edited by Carra and Seb. Mercier)

Archives de Rennes, ii. 66

Archives Nationales, i. 1, 103, 131, 278, 280 ; ii. 28, 42, 56, 165, 186

Archives Parlementaires (1787-1860), i. 37, 38, 59, 143, 297

Arnault (Antoine Vincent), 'Souvenirs d'un Sexagénaire,' i. 85

Aucoc (Léon), 'L'Institut de France et les Anciennes Académies,' ii. 254

Avertisseur, i. 215

Babeau (Albert), 'Histoire de Troyes pendant la Révolution,' i. 167

Bachaumont (Louis Petit de). See Petit de Bachaumont (L.)

Bailleul (Jacques Charles), 'Almanach des Bizarreries Humaines,' ii. 368

Bailly (Jean Sylvain), 'Mémoires d'un Témoin Oculaire de la Révolution,' ii. 77-79

Ballain, 'Maison et Généalogie de Corneille,' ii. 205

Bandot, 'Mémoires inédits,' i. 262

Barante (Amable G. P. Brugière de), Baron. See Brugière de Barante (A. G. P.), Baron

Barbaroux (Charles Jean Marie), 'Mémoires de Buzot et de Barbaroux,' i. 44, 51

Barbier (Antoine Alexandre), 'Observations sur les " Recueils de Lettres " publiés en 1803 et 1817 sous le Nom de Louis XVI.,' i. 212

Bardoux (Agénor), 'Mme. de Custine,' ii. 280-282

Barère de Vieuzac (Bertrand), 'Adresse aux Français,' i. 308 ; 'Éloges de Montesquieu, de J. J. Rousseau,' etc., i. 54 ; 'Mémoires,' i. 56, 131, 225 ; ii. 339

Barré (Pierre Yon), Radet (Jean Baptiste), and Desfontaines (F. G.), *pseud.* (*i.e.*, F. G. Fouques), 'La Chaste Suzanne,' i. 322

Beauchamp (Alphonse de), Caubrière, and Giraud (Joseph), 'Table Alphabétique et Chronologique du *Moniteur* de 1789 jusqu'à l'an VIII. de la République,' i. 190

Beaulieu (Claude François de), 'Essais Historiques sur les Causes et les Effets de la Révolution,' i. 54, 68, 82, 158, 181, 189, 194, 195, 261, 292, 294, 301, 307, 340, 353 ; ii. 15, 16, 20, 78, 213, 248, 324, 335 ; 'Souvenirs de l'Histoire ou Diurnal de la Révolution de France,' i. 269, 295, 338 ; ii. 7, 102, 140, 213, 251, 367

Beaumarchais (Pierre Augustin Caron de). See Caron de Beaumarchais (P. A.)

Becq de Fouquières (Louis), Introduc-

THE END.

www.ingramcontent.com/pod-product-compliance
Lightning Source LLC
Chambersburg PA
CBHW051509100726
47898CB00005B/1387